ICE FISHING FOR
ALLIGATORS

EDITED BY PEYTON BURGESS
AND CHRISTOPHER CHAMBERS

**CALUMET
EDITIONS**

Minneapolis

SECOND EDITION DECEMBER 2022

10 9 8 7 6 5 4 3 2
ISBN: 978-1-960250-03-2

Cover art & design: Stanley Sallay
Book layout & design: Christopher Chambers and Gary Lindberg
Editorial assistants: Rose Dicks, Nelle Edge
Typefaces: Dante, Helvetica Neu

Fiction doesn't tell us something we don't know, it tells us something we know but don't know that we know. —Walker Percy

Leaving New Orleans also frightened me considerably. Outside of the city limits the heart of darkness, the true wasteland begins.—John Kennedy Toole

Contents

Introduction

This is not just another anthology of fiction from New Orleans. Only a few of these stories are set in the city, and even in those few you will find no streetcars or magnolias, voodoo queens or beignets. That is to say none of the usual clichés. You might say though that New Orleans haunts these stories, that what lurks in these pages is a carnival of original short fiction to delight and disturb, a gallery that runs the gamut from dirty realism to fabulist tales. These stories, wherever they occur, all found their way to New Orleans, rose up through the slush pile to appear for the first time in the pages of the old *New Orleans Review.*

In a recent essay in the *New York Times Book Review,* Cynthia Ozick cites Edmund Wilson on the lifespan of literary magazines, describing how, like us, "they rise to their prime and gradually decline, until in their undeniable irrelevance they give up the ghost—after which they fade from discourse altogether." The stories collected here were first published in the *New Orleans Review* when the magazine was still publishing biannual print issues that featured new work by thirty to forty contemporary writers in each issue. These stories are steeped in the uptown funk in which they were first read, and each in its own way jolted the editors and readers out of their everyday malaise. Only to then sink back beneath the surface to that place where old literary magazines turn to pulp.

The *New Orleans Review,* founded in 1968 by the poet Miller Williams, is perhaps best known for first publishing in an early issue an excerpt of *Confederacy of Dunces* by John Kennedy Toole, a novel which would eventually receive the Pulitzer Prize. Walker Percy, a contributing editor to the magazine at the time, recounts the story of the discovery of Toole's manuscript in his introduction to the novel, now in its thirty-fifth edition from LSU Press. Like nearly all of the stories collected here, *Confederacy of Dunces* arrived at the *New Orleans Review* offices unsolicited.

In its early years, the magazine was a large format regional quarterly, a journal of art and culture that included new fiction and poetry as well as scholarly writing. By the time the magazine began its fourth decade, it had undergone several iterations, been revived in the 1990s by the New Orleans editor and poet Ralph Adamo, and was a nationally-distributed book-sized biannual with a focus on contemporary fiction, poetry, and nonfiction. The magazine gained a reputation for publishing unknown writers and for working closely with writers on their manuscripts, and during those years, work from the magazine was selected for reprint in many of the prestigious annual anthologies: *The Best American* series, *New Stories from the South,* The Pushcart Prize anthology, and The O. Henry Prize anthology, as well as *The Utne Reader* and *Sudden Fiction International.*

It's an undeniable fact that the readers of literary magazines are few, far fewer even than the readers of short fiction in general, who Barry Hannah once likened to the early Christians, a small but passionate cult. Fewer still read old literary magazines, even though the best of the writing found there can be as rewarding as anything appearing in current periodicals or books.

Despite the brief lifespan of literary magazines, good writing has always been and remains relevant. We have, for the benefit of those few passionate, discerning readers of contemporary short fiction, selected and assembled here the best short fiction from a literary magazine in its prime. These stories are indeed haunted by New Orleans, the place in which they were first read, first discussed, edited, and published. Here they are, unexpectedly brought back to the surface, provocative, disturbing, and once again, part of the discourse. Enjoy!

Peyton Burgess and Christopher Chambers
New Orleans

Chris Haven

The Girl With One Arm

The boy was with the girl with one arm. They had been together long enough to know things about each other. He knew the name of the boy that had hurt her most, in third grade, and he knew that was the last time she'd let herself be hurt. He had revealed all the movies and books and bands that he loved, even the most embarrassing ones. But they had been together a short enough amount of time that afterwards, when he was alone, he had to rub his jaw from all the smiling he'd done. They had been together the perfect amount of time.

This was the night.

They sat on his sofa, the one covered with a thin blanket to hide the rips underneath, drinking root beer floats that he had made. He could not believe his luck. He looked at her face and it swam before his eyes and he was thinking how much he might love her, if he could only bring her into focus.

"So," the boy said, deciding he had waited long enough. "What's up with the one arm?" This boy was not one to mess around with too many words. It had taken him far too long, in his opinion, to come to this question. It was the question that popped into his head the very first time he saw her. This question meant everything.

He continued, "One of my friends thinks combine. Another thinks you must be some sort of fugitive."

"Birth affect." The girl always spoke very clearly, but sometimes the boy looked at her lips and his mind was somewhere else.

"You mean defect?"

"Nope."

The arm was gone up to the elbow. The boy was not shy of looking at it, or touching it for that matter, and neither was the girl shy of showing it. Her tops were almost always short-sleeved and often, like tonight, sleeveless.

The boy said, "Well, that's boring. I waited all this time for that? You sure there wasn't anything more?"

"That's it. All the genetic testing came back fine. No explanation." She sipped from the straw in her frosty mug. The boy liked to see her cheeks sink towards her open teeth. "My mom says my right arm is still in her, holding a death grip on her spinal cord."

The boy pictured a dark mother, foreign. He convinced himself that he could see the darkness that had come through to her. He realized that he wanted the girl to speak to him in a language he didn't understand. "You didn't want to come out?"

"Let's say I was conflicted." Her words slurred a bit, chilled by the ice cream drink. He wanted her tongue to shape the faint trace of an accent.

"Are you still conflicted?" The boy was not stupid. He realized that most questions that boys asked of girls were rephrasings of the question of all questions: Do you like me? and too, How much do you like me?

The girl, who was not stupid either, paused. The kind of pause that helps one maintain balance, by keeping the other off-balance. This was one of her best skills.

"That's the lovely part," she said, after enough pausing. "Part of me wanted to stay, part of me wanted to live here." She slurped the last of her drink loudly from the bottom of the mug. "And look who won."

"That was a fantastic root beer float," the boy said.

"You sure know how to make them," she said, as if sincere. This ability of hers to sound sincere when he knew she was being sarcastic was one of the things he loved about her. He felt this quality of hers was one of her purest elements, a square in her periodic table that had accompanied her from her beginning, and would stay with her until the last of her days.

He started to say something to her about elements and tables and atomic numbers, but he did not. He wanted to say impressive things to her, but he was afraid. Still, something of his disquiet must have come through to her because she said, "Maybe you shouldn't have used the caffeinated root beer."

The boy's heart raced. He spoke quickly.

"My friends say I'm only dating you because I think you're vulnerable. They tell me that I've never dated a girl who is as pretty as you, which is true. Without question." He pushed her hair back from her face and looked her in the eye. "They tell me I only had the nerve to talk to you because of the arm."

"Those friends of yours are something else. Are they real sweet talkers like yourself?"

"They call you Lefty."

The girl winced. "And you defend me. I can count on this?"

"I would, but it's not you they're attacking."

"Then what do you say?"

"What can I say? The only other girl I've dated seriously had pneumonia when we met. It was walking pneumonia—nothing she had to be hospitalized for—but still I can't figure out how to prove them wrong."

"You could tell them…" and the girl filled in the blank with an animated gesture, that of punching the friends in their imaginary faces. "I would show you the old one-two," she said, "but I don't think you're ready for that."

"Can you feel your arm?" the boy asked. He was becoming aware that this was the night that he wanted to learn about her body. That night always came with boys, especially young ones. The night they would try to lay bare those parts they could not see.

"Sure," she said, and she squeezed it with her hand.

"I'm being serious here."

"Oh really? Is that what's going on?"

"Yes, it is." He did his best to look injured, then he gave his report. "I just read something about what you can do with a mirror. If you're in pain, you can put a mirror up to one half of your body. You see your body whole, and it teaches your brain that nothing's wrong, and you shouldn't feel the pain." He believed that she had pain, pain that neither of them could see.

"Why would I want to do that?"

"I just thought you might want…" He waited for her to save him, but she would not. He would have to keep talking. "If it was hurting, that maybe you would want to stop it from hurting."

The girl was quiet for a minute and the boy believed she was processing how concerned he was, how caring. Then the girl looked at the boy's face and was instantly pleased. "You don't know what to call it."

Embarrassed, the boy quickly tried to change his tone. "My friends call it the stump."

She scrunched her nose.

"What?"

"I expect that from them. Not you."

"Okay, I admit it. I don't know what to call it. But it is important to me. As a matter of reference."

"What to call it?"

"I can't think of a good thing."

"How about right arm?"

The boy raised his finger. "I see where you're going there. You're going with literal. But that doesn't really capture it, does it? I mean, I can't think of a good enough thing. What about a word that cuts to the heart of things?"

"Why does it have to just be one word? Why must things be reduced?"

"I'm looking for essence. Plus, one word is efficient. It helps us understand."

The girl took a breath, as if she were going to respond at length. Then she turned away and said, "Nah."

"Nah? You give me Nah? Is that all you have?" His voice was rising, and he began to sweat. The muscles in his shoulders were tightening. He felt this was going very well.

"I thought you were in favor of one-word descriptions." She blinked at him slowly.

"I knew there was a reason I liked you."

He tried to pull her close to him, but she lightly pushed him away.

"The reason is this," she said, and she held it up. "The Arm Of Your Dreams."

He looked at her arm and he looked at the form it implied. "The arm of my dreams?"

"No," she said with contempt. "The Arm Of Your Dreams. It's a title, not a random pronoun. It's the same no matter who is speaking of it.

"So if anyone asks, I'm supposed to say, 'I fell in love with her because I saw The Arm of Your Dreams'?"

The boy looked at the girl and he could tell that she heard what he said, that it really registered with her, the part about fell in love because her voice softened a bit as she said, "That's right. Because it's whatever a person dreams it to be."

The boy could not have foreseen any of this, but it had been a surprisingly easy thing to say. He felt a part of himself let go, and he listened to himself say other easily said things.

"Whatever I dream?" The boy moved closer. "Long, creamy, lovely?"

"Mmm."

"Bewitching?" He bent his head to her shoulder.

"Mmm."

"Tender, warm?" He closed his eyes.

"Shriveled," she said, loudly. "Knobby. Cancerous."

He stiffened a bit. "I see."

"Bloody. Burned."

He sat up. "Yes, I get it."

"Leprous…"

"Enough!" He raised his hands in the air, his body tense. He would not look at her.

"Come here," she said, but he could not tell if she was sincere. "Let me rub your back. Let me rub it with The Arm of Your Dreams."

He felt her hand tug on his shirt, but he pulled away. "How do I know it's not a hook?"

"Only you can know your dreams," she said. "Take off your shirt."

He complied. This was not how he'd imagined things going, but he complied.

"Now lay down. That's it. No," she said, without touching him. "No looking back. Close your eyes."

He waited. This moment felt close to what he had wanted, but he was not sure. He sensed movement above him.

The girl asked, "Do you feel anything?"

"No," said the boy, and he felt her disappointment cool the air.

"You need to relax," she said. "There. How about now?"

"Yes," he lied, because he thought it was still possible to lie to her. "I can feel something. Can you?"

"Not yet," she said, "But I'm trying. Are your eyes closed? You have to promise to keep your eyes closed."

The words came to him very easily. "I promise." He could say them again if she asked, he was sure. He loved her for trying to touch him with her missing hand, no matter what happened. The evening was darkening, and he could feel the air from an open window across his body. He was about to tell her this was all he wanted. He was about to tell her how much he loved her in this moment when he felt a finger of warmth on his right shoulder. A knot of breath issued from his lips.

"There."

One, two more fingers. A hand. Rubbing. The invisible hairs on his skin tingled. He did not have to tell her he felt it. It was clear and distinct, unmistakable. Then it was gone. So quickly that he wasn't sure it had happened. He waited, but the feeling did not return.

"I want to see it," he said. "Please, I want to see it."

"Oh baby, you know better."

He relaxed his body back into the sofa, and there it was again. A hand, touching him on his skin, reaching deep beneath the surface. Eyes still closed, in his mind he saw her hand at the end of The Arm Of Your Dreams, and it looked the same as her other hand, a mirror image of it, with no defect, every knuckle, every bone in it whole. It occurred to him, of course it did, that she could just be rubbing his back with her left hand.

"I can touch you like this, with The Arm Of Your Dreams, as often as you like."

This is what it must feel like to be a god, he thought. Nothing to him before had felt so good. His skin hummed. Oh, things were moving fast, as things can. He was the happiest boy on earth. That is, he should have been. Inside, some other thing worked on him. He felt another hand on his throat, squeezing. It made him tense. It made him say other things.

"Is this something we'll always have, you and I?"

"Yes," she said, her voice assuring. "As long as you keep your eyes closed."

Her hand moved to more sensitive areas of his body. He felt as if he were being kissed thoroughly, inside and out. A thought occurred to him and his body tensed. "Have you felt this before?"

"Never." This time, there was no pause.

Immediately, he relaxed again. Never. One word. The essence of the thing. But that other hand inside him squeezed his throat so hard he gave a little jerk and without knowing what he was doing, he almost opened his eyes.

"Oh baby, don't. Don't you want everything? Don't you want what you can see and what you can't? Don't give away what you can't see. Let's not give it away."

"I didn't know," he said. What was it they had?

"All of it is ours."

He felt her hand on his ear, or was it inside? It was like listening to the sea. It was almost too much for him. I'll drown he thought, and even though he didn't speak she seemed to hear him anyway.

"Shh. Don't look. I'll turn to salt. Just like they say. Don't look."

He felt a shiver rise in his back. "Just let me turn over. I want to feel you everywhere."

"You can't. It will be too difficult for you." She waited, and he thought she was relenting, but she said again, firmly, "No."

He felt an ending coming, a relief, but then the hand on his throat squeezed out these words. "How do I know you're not lying?" It was only as he said this that he understood the challenge. He whispered, "Put your other hand on me."

Silence. The hand, whichever hand was on his back, seemed to throb.

"Maybe we should just watch a movie. Weren't we going to watch movies tonight?"

"Do this for me," he said. "Prove it to me."

"To you? You, who has proven nothing to me?"

He wouldn't let her provoke him. He knew he was winning. "Give me a chance. Just give me the chance and I will."

He could feel his sincerity beginning to crack the distance above him.

"But that one is cold. It's the hand I used to hold the drink."

"I don't care."

"Lay down," she said. "Keep your eyes closed."

"I'll keep them closed. I won't look."

"I can't promise anything."

"I understand."

He felt the hand of The Arm Of Your Dreams once again. His muscles melted beneath the touch and he forgot what else it was he wanted. Wasn't there something else? How could there be? And then a circle hit him on his left side, cold and damp, that nearly shocked his eyes open, but he held true. A circle?

"The mug!" He giggled. His world, which had been in a shuffle, suddenly sorted itself out.

"No, it's not," she said.

She sounded serious, but she couldn't be.

"You put the mug on my back," he said, but immediately doubted it. He twisted a bit, but the cold pressure remained. "You're a witch!" He teased, but anything was possible.

"I'm doing what you asked," she said. "I'm giving you everything."

The circle began to warm into the shape of a palm, and above it, five fingers pressing into his flesh. Two arms. Two hands. "I have to turn over," he said. " I feel like my body will fly apart. You have to let me turn over."

"No. That's not how this works."

He expected her hands to push on his back and keep him down. But the pressure stayed the same, maybe even lightened.

"I'll keep my eyes closed," he said desperately. He thought he felt his back rise, to meet the full pressure of her hands again.

"You say that, but what if you open them? Even an accident will be too much."

"But…I want all of you."

"You have all of me. You have it now."

She kept rubbing his back. He still felt both hands on him, and it still felt wonderful, and he did not want her to stop, but a little of the surprise was gone. He could feel it leaking away.

"You have to make your choice now, with your eyes closed," she said. "Is this what you want of me? What you have now, is this what you want? Is this enough for you?"

"Yes, yes, it's enough," the boy said, not knowing what he meant.

"But I have to turn over now." He knew if he opened his eyes, she would be gone to him forever. He began to weep. "Come closer," he said, turning his body.

"Do not do this," she said, but still she came closer.

"Even closer," he said. He was being very deliberate. He felt a tear drop from her eye onto his cheek. He felt two hands grab him, he knew there were two of them, one on each arm. He lost track of which touch was The Arm Of Your Dreams and which was the arm he'd always known, and soon he lost track of his own body.

"I know how you think this is going to end," he told her. "The boy will open his eyes, and the girl will disappear. Isn't that right?"

"Forever," she said.

"Come closer," he said. He felt her lips next to his. "My eyes are closed," he said, and this time he hoped she could see he was not lying. She kissed him, and he felt her mouth wet and warm, and her hands loosened their grip on him, and he could not see, in spite of himself, anything.

Dylan Landis

Barracuda

I let Zola take me dancing. Not for pay. She climbs into a jumpsuit with a brass-ring zipper, positions it low but not lascivious. The clothes she stepped out of she abandons on my floor, leaving me curiously bifurcated—left brain wanting to iron and fold, right brain envying her messy ease.

She hails a cab on my corner, me objecting that it will cost too much and Zola saying I won't have to pay a dime. Barrow Street, she tells the driver, and while I am thinking how much cheaper the subway would be, the driver beams his gaze into the rearview mirror and says, "So, what do you girls do for a living?"

"Carve up rats," I mutter.

"We're models," says Zola. "We model lingerie. For a catalog," she adds sweetly.

I hiss at her.

"Indeed?" says the driver. His eyes lock onto the mirror.

"Could you please watch the road?" I say, though not so he can hear.

His license, near the meter, says Stanislav Mirovsky. The picture shows red-apple cheeks, but sullen eyes. Same eyes I catch in the rearview when I lean to the right. They don't look sullen now.

"Leah, darlin'," says Zola, very low, "I need a favor." She's been gone six days, a week.

"You look like model," says Stan. "I think you hear this all the time, yes?"

"Mmhmm," says Zola, hitting at least five notes. "Do you like models, Stan?" And to me: "I need to borrow your apartment for one night."

Absolutely not, says my brain.

"So," says Stan. "Where you are going? Party?"

It's a reasonable question. I'm wearing a vintage top with a whiff of corset to it, short black skirt. Zola's jumpsuit is satin. It steals a bit of light every time we drive under a streetlamp. She toys with the zipper. A taxi honks; Stan's drifting left.

"My ex-husband wants to see me," says Zola. "For one night. But not at his suite."

"What suite?"

"The one he lives in," says Zola, "at the Regency."

"He lives in a hotel?"

Zola looks up and says, "Sta-an? How much do you think this ride will cost?"

Stan sobers right up: business. "Twelve dollars, I am thinking," he says. "With traffic, maybe fifteen." He's watching the road now. "Fifty cents at night for extra passenger," he says, avoiding any unpleasant surprises. That's me, the unpleasant surprise.

"Robbie believes that I am a better person than I am," says Zola. She stares out the window, lets that percolate. "He believes a lot of things," she says. "He thinks I finally have a real apartment."

She wants your keys, says the brain. She'll never leave. Never. She'll borrow your Citicard—

"Sta-an?" says Zola, leaning forward, reeling him back in. "Is it okay if we call you Stan?"

"I prefer it," he says.

I punch her on the knee. I've grown nervy. But the punch is a lie. I want to feel that brake slip again, want Zola to show me more from her car-crash life. Want to see things that won't let me look away.

Want to drop this apartment business even more.

"Tell us why you like models, Stan," she says.

"You are kidding, yes?" says Stan. "Look in the mirror, you will see why I like models."

"Could we get this apartment thing out of the way?" I say.

Through the long, narrow gaze she turns on me, I see something shift behind her eyes. "Out of the way?" she says, coolly. "I don't think so, no." Then she resolutely looks away, renews her attentions to the front seat. "We looked in the mirror today, Stan," she sings. "Guess what we saw."

"Why don't you show me," says Stan.

"You're crazy," I say, only I whisper it. The thought of her ex-husband, of anyone's ex-husband, reclining on my bed, breathing my air, tossing my keys in his palm, is almost enough to cause a panic.

"I am not crazy," says Zola. "I am incompetent, according to the court. How much money do you have?" Breathe, Leah.

"What court?"

"The court in which I was disinherited," says Zola. "The court that makes it necessary for me to be sweet to my ex-husband. How much money do you have?"

Sixteen dollars, crumpled, I tell her. Plus quarters.

"Is that all?" she says. "What a pity. I have ten or twelve million. I just can't get to it right now." She rests her elbows and chin on the top of the front seat and sings, "Sta-an? If we show you what we saw in the mirror, will you drive us downtown for free?"

My jaw drops. A reflex, enhancing oxygen intake, maybe, or signaling fight-or-flight—regardless, my dental work is on full view.

The eyes in the rearview contract. Maybe he thinks we are taxi inspectors. Maybe he thinks we are worse than that.

"I cannot decide," says Stan, "unless I know what it is that you saw."

"Mmhmm," says Zola. "Should I tell him, Angelica? Do you think he deserves to know?"

"Angelica?" I say.

"Are you listening, baby?" she says, and slides her voice down into the smoke-and-espresso range. "We saw our titties, Stan," she says, and giggles.

Zola never giggles.

I am so shocked I get actual goose bumps, and not merely because of her oblique offer—to bare her breasts; mine are not even remotely under discussion—but because of that word. It feels like a cross between a slap and a pinch. This word is everything I distrust about the world. It pokes like a sharp stick, this word.

"See them," says Stan, "or feel them?"

Zola sits back and says nothing.

"Miss?" says Stan, swiveling his head around.

Zola says nothing, just looks out the window.

"I offend you," says Stan. "I am sorry." Silence from Zola. "Miss?"

"No touching," says Zola, "and no meter."

Ripples of worry while he considers this.

"I can get a fine," says Stan.

"You're already fine," says Zola. And now I hear it, the two-inch purr of a traveling brass zipper.

Stan hits a pothole.

"I turn into sidestreet, for seeing you better," he says. "Okay?"

"No, baby, not okay," says Zola. "You can see just fine in the mirror."

"I can see her," says Stan. He glances at me, the unpleasant surprise. "You I cannot see. You are too short."

"What an interesting thing to tell a woman," says Zola. But she kneels, tucking both heels beneath her. "Can you see me now, baby?" The zipper migrates navelward. I can measure the angle between his eyes, the mirror, and Zola's chest as precisely as if I were setting up a pool shot. Also, I know what will happen now. Every passing driver will stare into our cab. The police will pull up; they'll bring us in. I won't make bail, the lab people will wonder where I am for a few days and fire me, and I am just in the process of losing my apartment for unpaid rent when I notice Zola is checking street signs the way I might check my watch, and I have a revelation: this is just a performance—and she's timing it.

She shrugs the top of her jumpsuit down. I lapse into a kind of prayer: thank you, God, for making Zola wear a tube top underneath.

"Sta-an?" she sings. "Are you ready?"

The light ahead turns yellow, then red. Stan plows through it. Zola is slowly rolling down the top of the tube and Stan is lost, enslaved, distracted within an inch of madness. This I can feel. I stop breathing. He brakes for the next red, twists around to watch the progress of Zola's top. We're waiting, Stan and I, for that next exquisite inch. I am also waiting for the light to turn green, though I seem to be alone in this. But Zola delays. She holds up a manicured forefinger and sticks it in her mouth. Stan and me, we're not stupid. We get the idea.

Forty-eighth Street. I notice Zola noticing where we are. She dips the left side of her top down for a second, pulls it back up while Stan's pupils are still dilating. Women do this to truckers, I think crazily. I've read about it. Truckers call it flashing, just like bar managers. No wonder they keep jackknifing off the road. We pay for all these studies to prove it's lack of sleep, but it's titty, pure and simple.

"You'll get us killed," I say.

"You're in a New York taxi," says Zola. "You could get killed anyway."

We lurch forward. Zola watches the signs.

"Intermission," I observe.

"Smart girl," she says. "Oh, Stan-ley?" We're at Thirty-ninth. Stan locks his gaze into that mirror-breast hypotenuse, and at Thirty-seventh Zola pulls the tube down to her rib cage.

She lifts one breast, then the other, as if introducing them separately. Then, as if the tube has merely slipped, she pulls it up. Leans back. Relaxes.

Stan turns left onto a dark side street, pulls over. Turns the headlights off and swivels to face us. Says heavily: "Again."

"You're supposed to keep driving, darlin'," says Zola, zipping up. "That's part of our deal."

"I am a man," says Stan. "You are torturing me."

"Am I?" says Zola. "I'm sorry, baby. How about you get on the highway to Fourteenth and then I show you my titties again?"

"Now," says Stan. "Hers too." Our eyes meet, his and mine, for the second time.

"Angelica, baby," says Zola, "be a sweetheart and lift your shirt."

I freeze, partly because a man and an Airedale are walking past the cab.

She does it for me. And it's not terrible. It's not even that strange. It's how I imagine a mammogram. Whatever line we've just crossed, it's barely visible to me. I am sure Stan is disappointed. And I am almost relieved to discover how un-erotic this is turning out to be when Zola says, "Are you watching, Stanley, baby?" Then she moves a finger across my skin until we are both lost, me and Stan, and I'm thinking how incredibly good it feels to be bad, to be slumming, the way I always hoped it would feel, and my brain starts talking to God.

"Oh yes," says Stan, and again I hear the sound of a zipper.

Not Zola's.

"Stan, stop that," says Zola. "Be a good boy."

"More," says Stan.

"If you don't drive," says Zola, "we'll walk."

There's a brief struggle in the front seat. Zip. Headlights. Cab starts moving east. Stan looks hopefully in the mirror several times, but Zola is fixing her lipstick, sweeping hair out of her face, telling me she hasn't gone dancing for fun in months.

"Not right to play with a man this way," says Stan, merging onto the FDR.

"But I like playing with men this way, baby," says Zola. "It's what I'm good at."

We turn right on Fourteenth and left on Seventh and we are on some narrow street deep in the Village when the cab stops, throwing us forward.

"Are we here?" I whisper.

"Give me five minutes," says Stan. He sounds like a man who urgently has to pee.

"Noooo," says Zola. "We're models, not working girls."

"One touch," says Stan.

"No," I say loudly.

Stan lets out a kind of roar.

I whisper, "What if he follows us?"

She looks at me in surprise. "Didn't I tell you where we're going?" she says. "No? Silly me. They won't let him in."

I don't see any dance club. We're outside some dead tavern—dark glass, no neon, no music or patrons spilling out. The half-moon awning bears no name. A young man leans by the front door, as if waiting for his date. A bouncer. He's built like a fireplug. I wonder how Stan is built, how mad Stan gets.

"You pay me something," he tells us.

Zola says, "Have you ever seen two women kiss, Stan?"

"Yes," says Stan heavily. "In movie."

He has me beat there.

And it is in the slashed, unhallowed backseat of a yellow cab that Zola kisses me—for what is only the second time—in the coffee-scented fog of Stanislav Mirovsky's breath, and he is whispering Mother of God, which is similar to what I am thinking myself, and the meter clicks and percussion pours into my veins again and I am wondering: is this love? or is this something much more dangerous and exciting? and kiss her back, wondering where to put my tongue, and then knowing, and then not knowing again, and Zola is pulling my hair back, not a caress, no, but so Stan can see better, get his meter's worth, and the muscles in my neck collapse and all the other muscles too and Stan struggles with himself and says yes, it is beautiful, yes, and I am thinking, isn't it, Stan? isn't it the most beautiful thing you have ever seen? And then I worry about my tongue again and should I exclusively nose-breathe in case my breath is not okay, when I am released.

"Thank you, Stan," says Zola, and opens her door. Then she is outside and it is just me sliding by Stan's darkening face.

"Now," says Zola, and puts her hand around my upper arm and steers me toward the blank-faced bar.

"We are not finish," Stan shouts.

Zola nods slightly at the bouncer. He straightens, moves toward the cab. It must mean something to Stan, because the taxi shoots forward as we slip into the bar.

"I don't believe you," I say, following her to a booth.

Zola glances at a waitress, which brings her right over. Me, I could wave my arm in the air for five minutes, and still not get served.

"What don't you believe?" she says. "I could pay Stan, or I could buy you a drink. I chose you."

"Oh, well, in that case," I say. "It was kind of fun."

Zola's mouth opens as if she's about to laugh. "Fun?" she says. "Leading him on like that? Showing him my body to save fifteen dollars? I don't do that for fun, Leah."

"I thought it was a game," I say.

"I know," says Zola. "You thought dancing was a game, too."

I look down until the bourbons come, until finally I am able to ask: "Why can't you see your husband at his suite?"

Zola peers into the amber glow of her drink. "I can," she says. "I just wanted to show him something nice." She tilts her head and smiles, very slightly and a little ruefully, which makes me look down again. "Something I could tell him was mine," she says.

And shrugs. Releasing us both.

I close my eyes and taste the bourbon, feeling selfish, guilty, cold in the heart. Am on my second sip when Zola explains how it works here. How, if the lights flash, it means the police are nearby, and everybody slips into their seats. The bar is not licensed for dancing. It is not licensed to exclude men. "Dance with me," she says. Heart's singing ooh, barracuda, hard and sweet, and under that sweetness, geologically deep, I detect some deeper sound, rich and mellow, and under that, I think, is something molten, something I want to touch.

"Are you listening, Leah?"

"I see men here," I say.

"Those are women," Zola says. "Remember the flashing lights." She half-rises from the banquette. "Be ready," she says, laying a delicate hand, the nails flaring with chipped red polish, on my arm.

I am ready.

Eva Talmadge

Northern

Her name was Nina. Nina Lee. She weighed 108 pounds from the time we started hanging out, but she never looked like the highs had made her lose weight. Big eyes and the god's teeth. Only black girl in the entire scene. And she wasn't one of those hollowed-out soulies you see eyeing you when they want to buy somethingand you know they don't have any money. She walked right up and asked.

"Five is five," I said. "No negotiating on price." We were in the parking lot behind the Kasbar, at the start of the night, up against the fence with the vines on it, out of sight from the street. She started touching my arms, telling me how she liked my hair, me still blond at seventeen, and months without a haircut. She took a clump of it around one finger and put her other hand on my side. "Your shoes are dirty," she said. Shit Converse. I said it was five for a green-and-clear no matter what, and she said all right, and smiled at me, and flashed those teeth.

"Look," she said. "Maybe I could pay you back?" Her hand on my side again, hooking a finger into one of my belt loops. Me looking at my feet. I'd been afraid of her, this neighborhood, across a clear wide street from mine, and black girls who would scratch my eyes and punch me in the face with rings on, soulies or not. Then I said yes, all right, for you, and gave her two. She smiled and said thank you. Thanks. She walked back around the corner in her little flat shoes and her white A-line dress that lit up her skin and I wanted to pull her back by a hemline, and kiss her on the back of her neck, on the tight curls under her hair.

This was Philadelphia, 2001. The Northern scene as I knew it was white kids obsessed with Britain thirty years back, a time when everyone in there had been obsessed with black people, black music, the United States in 1960. The Kasbar was low on customers, on the wrong side of Girard, and hired a DJ to bring in any crowd they could get. I don't know where all those kids came from, not my neighborhood, and certainly not hers, only that they needed speed to stay up, and I had a pharmacy connection, plenty of that: pinks and reds and green-and-clears and even straight-up chalk, which was almost unbearable—Sudafed and sulfur—and made everyone sick. I didn't take much on my own. I always stayed in the parking lot, underage, and sold what I could. I didn't know or care about the music, or what these kids were all about, soulies, who mostly looked to me like skinheads, staying up all night, dancing to this music they called Northern. I didn't dance. But that night I waited for the doorman to cross the street for the store—it was still early enough, still light—and I followed Nina in.

The Kasbar was dark inside, up a long narrow staircase above a restaurant called Hot Stop. There was a bar in the front and a passageway at the back that led through a series of small rooms before it opened on a large space at the end. Nina was there, talking to the DJ. I found a spot in one of the small rooms, one dark except for a strand of red lights tacked up into the molding. The ceiling was covered with old 45s glued over each other like scales. It felt like a hallway cut to join two buildings together, the way it twisted around. I leaned back on the wall, waiting, watching the club fill up.

The soulies wanted to know why I wasn't in the parking lot when they found me inside. I said cops outside, and cash only, you pillheads. "Is this the best you have?" They were crowding around me, making a scene. Nina came over and said, "Well, look who it is."

"Hi, Nina," I said.

"You come in to dance?"

"Just keeping an eye on you." She looked even prettier in the red light.

Soulies from the front room were filing past us, balancing drinks, trying to get to the back, and kids who'd already been to the back were crowding the other way, trying to get to the bar. Nina had to press close to me as we talked, and someone bumped into her, saying, "Sorry, Neen," and for a second she pushed her small, hard breasts against me.

Somewhere around midnight everything jumped. If I'd been outside I would have left for the Level Bar, the Chinese place, or one of the clubs that was always changing names. Wherever there were sales. But here I was, still in the passageway, watching everyone chatter, watching out for Neen, feeling like a last cigarette in a forgotten pack, when a certain song came on and all the kids were on the dance floor at once like a gun had gone off, start of a race. Everyone at the front bar jammed into the hallway, and somewhere in the crowd Nina found me, grabbed my hand, and said, "Come on, try this out," pulling me toward her. I followed her to the dance floor, copying her steps a beat behind, wondering where her boyfriend, the big guy, went, then not wondering so much. It didn't look right, me in my jeans and my old shoes, her in that short dress like the rest of the girls, but soon I got her rhythm down, and Northern makes it easy—vintage soul—you barely need to know how to dance. The kids on the floor made a circle around us, clapping on the half beats, giving Nina space to show off, and the DJ shouted "Frog stomp!" and everyone started stomping. Kids took turns in the middle and I watched them dance as I tried to move right, watching them watch Nina, every kid on her with his eyes. "Just follow me," she said over the sound. And "keep going, you gettin' it," again and again. I chewed my last green-and-clear and felt the old scum in my lungs shift. We danced until four, until the bouncers came in and cut the power off and threw everyone out.

She lived in a split-level apartment just down the block. Half the crowd went back with her, DJ and everyone, and I followed, too. I thought it was funny, this whole pack of white kids marching down the street, kicking cans and asking for cigarettes, loud, who would never come out here during the day. At her house they picked up where they'd left off, music playing, some of them dancing but most of them laying themselves out on the couches, coming down off what I'd sold them, passing out on the floor, under tables, one throwing up in the kitchen. I drank from the sink. The boyfriend was asleep on the biggest couch and Nina, I could tell, was tired. I said she had to pay me and she took me upstairs. Smiling. Those teeth. She said, "You know I don't have any money," and I said, "Is that so?" I tried to fake like I was tough but as she came toward me I stepped back, heel hitting the wall. I didn't know if she wanted to rob me or kiss me or ask to see what else I had, and I thought there could be people up here, I could get jumped. I couldn't help thoughts like that, making her out to be something, and she always knew.

I said, "You're something Nina, you know that?" My voice broke.

She curled a finger over my waistband, into the top of my underwear. She pulled up the elastic and saw the blue and yellow lines. "Yep," she said. Nothing else, just nodding, kind of laughing at me. I looked her in the eye and focused on the shade of difference between the iris and the pupil, then I put my eyes back on her hands to see what she would do. You have the power when you're not the first. She held on, not saying anything, then looked down at my dirty shoes. "Your feet dirty, too?" I laughed and kept on looking at her. "Why you seem nervous?" she said. "You never done it with a girl before?"

"Got me," I said. "Schoolboys only."

"Really?"

"No."

I smelled the dry sweat on her skin, the salt in my limp hair, down my tired legs and rank under my arms, and we both looked up at the same time, then down, and I pulled her toward me, into the wall. She touched my cheek with her chin and I couldn't move, and she tugged me by the elastic again, knee between my legs, jammed her chin into my cheekbone, and found my mouth. I searched her lips for how she tasted, sour, and licked the edges of her teeth. I put my hands on the curve of her back and felt her skin through her dress. Her hipbones jutted out.

She looked at my shirt when she took it off like she thought everything I owned could use a wash. I felt for the button at the back of her dress. "Wait," she said. She closed the door. The room was suddenly dark, save for a long arrow of light coming in around the doorframe, drawing a line to the bed. I stepped on the backs of my shoes to get out of them, then took off my jeans and met her in the middle, coming toward me, and finally did the usual male thing, backing the girl into the bed, but we ended up standing on our knees on the bedspread. I kissed her neck near the hairline and again she said wait. I pulled the dress off. It fell over the end of the bed like a cloud landing, then collapsed out of her shape.

If I was decent I'd shut up here. The music downstairs went up and a surge of Al Wilson came up through the floor. The one about the snake. Nina was touching my shoulders, looking at me like she was waiting to say something. She wasn't wearing a bra, just thin cotton underwear, white, with the outline of an apple sewn on. I backed her into the wall where a headboard would have been and started kissing her breasts. She made a throat-clearing sound that I think meant she liked it, then she said, "So, you into Northern?" I looked up at her and kissed her neck again and said something stupid: "No. Just you."

The long night, dancing, all the sweat that had pooled at the bases of our backs, made her shy about taking her underwear off, and I wasn't sure if all her power over me before had been a play to make me take my turn, take power over her, or if I should be the one asking her how old she really was, if she'd ever done this before. I'd never had a girlfriend. I did it with shy girls who needed a bottle of wine to tell me how bored they were with life, their boyfriends, meaning please make the first move. I pushed the white fabric aside and felt. Every girl is different. She hovered at my fingers. I made my mind up—skip words—and made her come with my hands.

When the sun woke us up she went to her dresser and opened her purse and looked at her pile of coins. She said, "Looks like I'm going to have to owe you for this, too." I thought I could smile like that forever. Me and Nina, happy. The room was filled with light. She looked like a real person, without all the music playing, without the funny 60s dress on. "That one was a free one," I said. Then I had to get out of there before the boyfriend came around.

The air outside was cooler than it'd been the night before, and quieter, the sky hazy with dawn. My ears rang and my shoes were loose. I noticed, walking back toward the wide street, that the last of the trash had been swept from the road.

We didn't talk to each other the next weekend at the Kasbar, not at first, but I told the doorman I was with her and he let me in. I went back to the room with the records on the ceiling and stood there in the red light, looking up, trying to make out names on the labels, but someone had scratched them all off. The DJ was playing a little reggae between rounds of soul. I rolled my eyes at myself. What did I care about records? The dancing had been fun last week and Nina was cute but I'm not a soulie, I said, I'm not into this, or into any idiot subculture scene. But I kept thinking I could recognize some of the songs.

Two skinny guys came over and asked if I had any green-and-clears as loud as they could. I did, but I was saving them already. I had my stock lines: These ones are new. Listen. Have you up for days. "Is this the best you have?" they wanted to know. And, "Will you be at Nina's later?" "Cash first," I said. They started pulling wadded singles out and counting quarters, then a soul song came on.

"Okay," the one said, hurrying. "Give us chalksticks. Do we have enough for that?" I said sure, all right, that works, but I'm going hit you in the ears with all these quarters. They took their Sudafed and went to the dance floor and I hung back on the wall and listened, trying to make out the words. I—wanna testify, it went.

I shook my head. I wasn't dying to know what the song was, or hoping for Nina to come over and ask me to dance. Just business. But I shifted around and I looked for her, waiting for midnight, then I went out to the dance floor and found her like I had just run into her, like I wasn't led like a bug to her, to how her skin shone.

And I lie, I always lie, when I'm in love. It was with the music. Not with her. Northern got into me through the holes in my skin.

Oh, what bullshit. It was for Nina. The image of her. I wanted her and

I wanted to smell like her, the oil in her hair, and I wanted to get to know this music, be a better dancer, belong to something like the soul kids did. I started coming inside every night. And following her home. The boyfriend stopped showing up. We were hanging out all the time. You couldn't do amphetamines like we were—I started doing my own stuff then, a lot of it, nearer my God to thee—and not get hooked on the confidence, or hear that sound, acts that never got famous, and not need to know what it was, try to read the names of the songs on the labels, but the names remained erased. All I saw was Stax and Motown, Okeh, Atlantic, Chess. I didn't care about the money. I gave Nina whatever she wanted. She stopped having to ask.

And one morning I thought I would confess. I love you. I said, "Tell me more about this music," and she laughed at me and told me to come downstairs. "I'll show you my records." We took two pinks and she played me the old 45s that had been her dad's, cue "Frog Stomp," the Velvelettes, Dobie Grey, Wayne Gibson, "Under My Thumb"—that one's a Stones cover, that one I recognized—cue Young Holt, Sam Cooke, Booker T and the MGs, Archie Bell and the Drells—every track a floor stomper, my life, I never thought music could do this person. We didn't talk a whole lot, Nina and me. She put on the Temptations, "Cloud Nine," and we danced all day with the speakers going loud and the lights all off until we collapsed, laughing, over and over, drinking sodas to come down, kissing on the carpet, miming all the lyrics, me trying to give it to her with my drug-tired dick. She said I needed to dress right if I wanted to be seen out with her and pulled a bunch of old men's clothes from a cedar chest, flooding pants and shirts so awful they'd be cool in another five years, a nice belt and shoes so old the leather had turned hard and cracked. Her father's stuff. I said, "I can't do this, everyone will laugh," and she said, "I just want to see how you look." "Don't you boss me," I said, talking back. But she had a way. "All right," I said. "For you. This one time. And only in here."

The pants were busted gray denim and were too big. I held my breath. I was losing weight. She put on "Israelites" and took me for a spin. Desmond Dekker crooned like a woman: After a storm there must be a calm—they catch me in the farm, you sound the alarm—and the beat was so gummy it took me a while to get it. Then Nina kissed me on the side of my face, tilting my head back, and my legs got caught under hers and I fell, taking her with me, and we knocked the record shelf down. She pulled herself on top of me and said, "Damn, you're a fool," and I laughed and said, "Yeah, who made me wear this stupid stuff?" "You," she said, "you the one." And I said, "Lemme show you, I'd feel less naked without any clothes on at all."

She started to get more courage with me, more sure of what she wanted, us taking turns. Lee Perry sang "Give Me Power." When I went down on her she pushed into my mouth like she wanted to get inside me, saying wait, and no, and wait.

I changed my mind the clothes. Dark oxford shirts and loose gray cords, loafers to wear instead of Converse, and I felt ten years older, new hollows in my face. The doorman knew my name. He said I could hang out on his bench if I wanted to sit down between sets, but by then I'd long stopped sitting, only on the bus at the start of the night, because once you get into music and you start on uppers you don't have to sit, even when your legs hurt. When she told me she didn't like my shaggy hair so much I cut it off, ended up looking like my own old man, then I cut it some more, too short, giving the soulies the wrong idea—a little trouble there. They really had been skins. But the bruises made me look even sweeter, Nina said. She never asked me about other fights, the rhinestone-sized dents in my face, or where every mark on me had come from, or when, or how I got here. My dad was off at Willow Grove, a naval captain, hit and yell. My mother was a nurse. I said, "Do you want to see our house?"

She said she didn't want to meet my mom. She wanted to talk about records. I wanted to know where she was born, and how she'd come here, and what it was like to be the center of attention, if she thought the rest of us were fakes, reaching for a past for reassurance, imagining community, teenagers in blackface, taking fashion for a culture, making a costume of it all. She gave me a history of the labels, why again they called it Northern, about Stax and Tamla Motown, the Blackpool and the Wigan. She said her dad had come from London and her mother drove a city bus. She couldn't get over my light hair, how I had girl's hair on a boy's head, and how I'd become so thin. "What's in your pockets?" she said. "Do you love me still?" She said whenever you hear someone telling you a story, you know they're making an excuse. How I got this way. I told her I was home now, this was music I could taste, like salt. I will always be a soulie. I will never be anything else. I said, "Do you think scars show up better on white kids? Do you think we're wrong, the two of us, like this?" She laughed and made me get her change purse, out of the dresser in the dust-covered room, then opened it to show me the ID inside. Her age. She said soul songs are all love songs. There aren't any lyrics about that.

Glen Pourciau

Shake

I was having a discussion with the woman I'd been seeing. Not exactly a discussion. We were on the floor in her den. I was on top of her. We did say a thing or two. We were well along the way but not about to finish. I was unaware of my surroundings. To my surprise, she was not unaware. She saw something. Her head popped up over my shoulder, pushing my head back. She pointed at the window over her kitchen table and chairs. I looked where she pointed. A boy's face. He'd been watching. He saw us see him and he took off toward the alley.
I reacted. I started to get up. She pulled me back down.
"Let him go," she said.
"I'm not letting him go. This is none of his business."
I pulled away from her. I grabbed my pants and shirt and started putting them on.
"He's already gone," she said. "What will you do if you find him?"
"He's in trouble. Let's just say that."
"Don't hurt him. He didn't do anything."
"I call it doing something."
I jammed my feet in my shoes.
"Don't hurt that boy," she shouted at me as I left.
I ran out the back door and around the corner to where my car was parked. I stuck the key in and started it up. I drove slowly around the neighborhood and looked between the houses for him, thinking he might be perched in front of another window. I planned to get out and chase him. He couldn't outrun me. He was too little and wasn't strong enough. I'd grab him and lift him up, look in his face, tell him a few things he'd take with him. He wouldn't forget what I told him or the look on my face. I'd make sure he remembered.
I'd done the same thing when I was little. Not at someone else's place but where I lived with my father. My mother was away. I heard the noise inside the bedroom and wondered. I quietly pushed the door open. My father's pants and shirt were on the floor and he was on top of a woman who wasn't my mother. I didn't know what they were doing, but it made me feel sick to watch.

She saw me and pointed. I saw him pull the plug out. He came after me, sticking out, bouncing. I ran but couldn't get away from him.

"Don't tell your mother," he said when he grabbed me and lifted me.

He stank. The wet hair on his chest stank and his armpits stank. His face was damp. He could feel me shaking.

"You got me?" he asked in my face.

Since he was telling me not to tell her, I knew she'd want to know.

"She's no different than I am. Believe me."

He put me down then. It was right in my face, pointing at me. My face was burning.

"Deal?" he asked but didn't offer his hand. To him, it was a deal whether we shook on it or not.

He went back in the room with the woman. He closed the door. I heard him prop something against it. He said something and I heard the woman laugh.

I turned a corner and saw him walking down the street, left side. His back was to me. He wore a dirty gray T-shirt. Hair cut down to his scalp, like a grown man who's balding. Like me. He walked with his head down, not looking ahead or around. He didn't hear me behind him and it gave him a jolt when I rolled up next to him and ran the window down. He stopped and looked at me. I stayed in the car. It wasn't the way I planned. I saw him shaking, but he didn't run this time. Maybe he figured he couldn't get away or maybe he was waiting to see if I got out of my car before he ran.

"You saw us," I said.

He nodded.

"How long?"

He shrugged.

"Five minutes?"

He shook his head.

"Less?"

He didn't answer.

"You go around looking in people's windows?"

He didn't answer.

"You won't tell anybody what you saw?"

He shook his head.

"You know what you were looking at?"

He nodded.

"It would embarrass her. You understand that?"

He nodded.

"I never told," I said. "Never."

He looked at me and waited, his face red.

"I'm telling you. I saw them. I never told her. I couldn't. What would have happened if I had? To me and to them. Think about that. What would happen? Would it help you? Would it help anything? Keep it to yourself. That's what I'm saying."

He nodded, still shaking.

"Inside your head. That's where you should keep it. Keep it there. You'll learn to do that. You have to."

He waited.

"Don't go back there. Don't look in her window. What's inside people's windows is not your business. You never know who or what you'll be looking at. You follow me?"

He nodded.

"Do you?"

He nodded again.

I saw a couple on foot turn the corner ahead and come toward us. I ran my window up.

I waved at the boy. He didn't wave. I waved again. He waved.

I left him there. As I drove away I watched him in my rearview mirror. The couple walked past him.

I went back to her. She'd dressed. We sat on the sofa in her den.

"You found him?"

She could tell by looking at me.

"Did you hurt him?"

"I didn't get out of the car. We had a discussion."

"Did you scare him?"

"I talked to him. He won't come back."

"I don't want him talking to the neighbors."

"You told me not to go after him."

"I was afraid you'd hurt him."

"He won't talk."

"You're sure? What did you say?"

"I told him a story."

"What story? Was it true?"

I nodded.

"What was it?"

"Between him and me."

"You know this kid?"

"Not before."
She leaned against me. She stopped talking.
    The silence was between us.
We were there in it.

Samuel Ligon

Something Awful

"Can you light this, Jack?" Sally says, bending with a cigarette in her mouth and handing me a book of matches. "I can't make these things work." The matches are soaked. I don't know if she's looking for trouble or not. Both Joe and Elaine must be watching from the other couch as I hold my lighter to her cigarette and try not to look down her sweater. "Thanks, sweetie," she says over the roar of the Pistons game. As she walks away, Joe and Mark resume their discussion—small caps, large caps, this fund versus that fund. "No-load," and other words. I don't know what any of it means.

Joe and Sally live down the street from us, Mark and Beth farther away. They're nice enough, but most of the time they'll bore you to tears. We've only been in Michigan six months, and for some reason, they invite us to their barbecues and drinking parties. And for some reason, we attend. Everybody has kids, except us, which sets us apart and makes us suspect: how lucky we are, yet how unfortunate. Selfish maybe.

Elaine returns to my couch and puts her glass in front of my face, meaning, Make me another drink, so I do.

"Thanks, honey," she says when I hand her the glass.

She passes me a joint.

Sally sits on the couch arm beside me. "What about me?" she says.

I give her the joint.

"What about you?" Joe says, turning off the tv.

She takes a big hit and shrugs. "I don't know," she says.

Joe puts on some awful old music, Genesis or Journey, and Sally starts dancing. She knows her body, seems comfortable with the way it will move. "Come on, Sally," Joe says. He rubs her shoulders. "We'll play a game."

She's wearing a black cotton sweater with little pearl buttons, the top ones undone, and when she throws her arms back, it rides halfway up her perfect stomach so you can see the beginning of her ribs.

"Come on and sit down," Joe tells her.

But Sally keeps dancing, twisting to the music, demonstrating that she's still a viable candidate, even after a baby.

Joe takes her arm and pulls her toward the other couch. "We'll play a game," he says. "Okay, mama?" He places her on the couch and puts on some different awful music, some kind of fusion nightmare, then stands above us, rubbing his hands together, and says, "Trivials or Pictionary?"

Mark shrugs. Beth takes her glass into the kitchen. Sally's sweater hikes up her belly again as she slouches into the couch. Between the buttons, I catch glimpses of her bra, black, with a purple flower between the cups. Joe pulls her up, straightening her. "Up we go," he says. She takes it all very well.

"Trivials or Pictionary?" Joe says again.

Elaine digs her fingernails into my palm. She hates these kinds of games, but I don't know what to do. I can't keep my mind off Sally.

Beth returns with a fresh drink.

"What'll it be, Beth?" Joe says, and she says, "You decide."

"Trivials, then," Joe says, and he walks into the back room.

"I like Pictionarys better," Mark says.

"I need a drink," Sally says.

Joe returns with the game and starts setting it up on the enormous glass coffee table.

"Can't we just talk?" Beth says.

"Don't you want to play?" Joe says.

Sally returns with her drink.

"I hate this game," she says, and I say, "Everyone does."

Elaine gives me a look.

Joe seems hurt, sitting on his knees setting up the game. "Well, we don't have to play," he says. "I don't want to force anyone."

Elaine says, "Maybe, we could play a different game."

"Maybe Pictionarys," Mark says.

"No," I say. "They're all awful."

Elaine gives me another look. I'm stoned and in trouble, and, for some reason, I don't care.

"We've got to play something," Joe says. He's putting the plastic pieces back in the box.

"What about, Something Awful?" I say.

They all look at me.

"He's making this up," Elaine says. "To be cute."

"No," I say, "it's a game I know," wondering when Elaine dropped out of our conspiracy—a month ago, two months ago, tonight?

Sally's eyes are shiny from the booze. "Let's play that," she says.

"How do you play?" Joe asks.

Elaine watches me.

"You tell a story," I say, "something you did—no, the worst thing you ever did. You can cover up certain facts or make them different, but the idea has to be the same."

They're quiet for a second, and then Joe says, "What's the object?"

Sally slaps his shoulder. "All Joe cares about is winning."

"The object is to have done the worst thing," I say. "We'll vote at the end."

Beth says, "That's kind of gross," and Mark squints at me.

"Maybe," I say, "it can be whoever feels the worst about what they did."

"See?" Elaine says, "he's making it up."

"But how would we measure that?" Joe says.

"Oh, who cares," Sally says. "Let's just play."

Joe says, "I'd better check on the kids first," and Elaine leans toward me and whispers, "Don't be around people if you're just going to mock them," and I say, "What?" and she shakes her head, pissed, then hands me her glass for another drink.

When I come back from the kitchen, Sally is on the little expensive couch perpendicular to the big expensive couch where Elaine and I sit. Beth and Mark are on the floor across the table from us. Joe turns down the music and joins Sally, then rubs his hands together again. "Who's going to start?" he says.

Mark pulls a joint from his pocket and it circulates. Elaine passes it to me without taking a hit.

I'm actively ignoring Elaine when Beth says, "I think I've got one. I mean it may not be exactly right—"

"Sure it is," I say.

She sits up and smooths her skirt, everybody watching her, waiting. "I mean, this didn't go on that long. Longer than it should have, I guess, and I never got caught. That was the thing."

"What was it?" Sally says.

Beth takes a long drink, bringing up the tension. "It wasn't much," she says, finally, and Mark says, "Well, what?"

"I stole things," Beth says.

"Shoplifting?" I say.

"It started when I was twelve," she says. "Just gum and little stuff. Combs, barrettes."

Sally and Elaine lean toward her.

"Teenage girls do these things," Beth says, and Elaine says, "Yep," meaning she's back in the room, that I might be forgiven.

"On a dare," Sally says.

"Then it got to be expensive stuff," Beth says, "and it wasn't a group thing anymore. I mean, I didn't tell anybody I was stealing these things."

Joe says, "Like what?" and Beth takes another long drink.

"It became a private thing," she say. "Jewelry, clothes. You know, expensive underwear."

"I did that," Sally says.

"But not for this long." Beth says. "A lot of times I just threw the stuff away and felt kind of guilty and embarrassed."

"How long?" Mark asks her.

"Not that long," she says.

"Did I know you?" he says.

"It stopped in college. I stole a pair of expensive sunglasses. That's not easy. They keep them locked up, and I had to have about twelve pairs on the case and sneak one in my purse when the guy wasn't looking."

"Why was that the last time?" Elaine says. "What made you stop?"

"I don't know," Beth says. "It wasn't—"

"Are we supposed to vote on this?" Joe says.

"Is this awful?" I ask Beth, teaming up with Elaine on the inquisition. "Do you feel awful?"

"Guilty maybe," she says. "It's just that I never got caught."

"Rebellion thing," Sally says. "Not awful."

"It did go on a long time," Joe says.

"A little klepto," Mark says.

"So, do we vote on this?" Joe says.

"It's just a wrong thing I did," Beth says.

Joe stands and rubs his hands together. "Who needs a drink?" he says, but no one responds.

"I have to think of one," Mark says.

"I want one," Sally calls to Joe in the kitchen.

I feel let down by Beth's crime. I look at Elaine. She half-smiles. I never used to worry about her approval. I half-smile back.

Mark extends his legs under the coffee table, squinting and scratching his head.

"What about me?" Sally says, when Joe returns with one drink.

"We can share this one, Mama," he says, sitting on the floor at her feet.

"I've got one," Mark says, and everybody looks at him, waiting.

"It was in college," he says. "In the house."

"Your frat house?" Joe says.

"It seemed bad then," Mark says. "But not—" He runs a hand through his hair. "It would probably be a rape today, but not—"

"What?" Beth says.

"That's why frats should be illegal," Elaine says, and both Mark and Joe stare at her. "What rape?" Sally says, repositioning herself behind Joe.

I look at Sally and she's staring at me, her mouth open a little. Her sweater has pink yarn flowers on it I would like to bite off. She smiles, doesn't disengage eye contact, so I'm relieved when Beth says, "Are you telling me you took part in a rape?"

"I didn't take part," he says, "but, whatever it was—not rape then—whatever it was, I walked in near the end."

"And you didn't do anything?"

Sweat's popping on his forehead.

"I'm not sure what happened exactly."

"I'm gonna be sick," Beth says.

"Fine," Mark says. "I shouldn't have brought it up."

"You finish it now you've started," she tells him.

I look at Sally and she looks right back, smiles again. It sends a shiver through me.

"It was near the end of junior year," Mark says. "Pledge night, everybody's drunk—"

"I can't listen to this," Elaine says, starting to rise.

I take her hand and bring her back down to the couch. "Let him finish."

Beth says, "All right, then, finish."

Elaine digs her fingernails into my palm.

"We'd run out of beer," Mark says, "but there were two reserve kegs for when everybody left. I was looking for a cup."

He takes a drink. "Give me one of those cigarettes," he says to Sally, and she throws him the pack.

"Finish," Beth says.

"I will if you'll let me."

"Go ahead."

"There's this storage room down a long hall in the basement," he says, lighting the cigarette and blowing smoke over our heads.

Beth says, "Will you—" and Mark says, "I am. Just. So I open the door and she's there on the floor, but, I mean, fucked up, like her eyes rolling back in her head. And somebody—you know—and two brothers smoking and watching, making jokes, or whatever, and it's horrible, but she's not screaming or fighting or anything, but, you know, seems to be enjoying it—"

"Right," Elaine says. "Kind of like surgery."

"Who were the brothers?" Joe says.

"Let him finish," Beth says.

"The chick doesn't even know I'm there" Mark says. "That's how bad it is. And Rick's the one that's—"

"Rick Altman?" Joe says.

"But I don't do anything, don't say anything—"

"Until you run upstairs and call the police," Sally says.

"I'm like paralyzed," Mark say. "Mitch closes the door and puts his arm around me."

"Mitch O'Connor?" Joe says, and Mark rolls his eyes and says, "It doesn't matter."

"Mitch O'Connor?" Beth says. "I cannot believe this."

"So you did her too," Sally says.

Elaine digs her fingernails into my palm. Mark shakes his head widely.

"This is before anybody talked about date rape," he says, and Beth says, "You did it, too?"

"Let me finish," Mark says. "Mitch kept talking with his arm around me. 'She's loving it,' he says, and she's making all the right sounds, like she is loving it. But just by the way he's talking, I know how wrong it is, and there are supplies everywhere on steel shelves, paper towels and silverware and stuff."

"But, finally, you do her, too," Sally says.

I look at her and she's grinning, playing with a piece of her hair, twirling it around her finger, scaring the hell out of me.

Mark says, "I'm sick about it. I'm like, 'I'm just getting these cups.' And I have to step right over her to get to the shelf."

"Oh my God," Beth says.

"And then I'm gone, out of there, freaking out in shock—"

"What happened to the woman?" Elaine says, and Mark says, "I don't know."

"Did you talk about this?" Beth says. "Did you confront them?"

"I never said a word."

"Don't you think that's cowardly?" Elaine says.

"That's what I'm saying," Mark says. "I should have done something."

"You could still do something," Elaine says.

"That was fifteen years ago."

"Yeah," Beth says, "but Mitch still comes by when he's in town."

Elaine sighs—or grunts—disgusted, and Beth says, "He's never coming over again. You see to that. We have a child. What about me? You let a rapist in the house?"

"I didn't know what it was exactly."

"That's definitely worse than Beth's," Joe says.

"I'm getting a drink," Mark says, and he walks to the kitchen.

Elaine says, "Sick."

"At least he told the whole story," I say.

Sally looks at me, and says, "How do you know?"

"Knock it off," Beth says. "I can not believe this."

"What about you, Joe?" Sally says. "Did you rape any drunk chick at the house?"

Joe shakes his head. "You heard about it, though," he says.

When Mark comes back from the kitchen, he says, "I know it was horrible. I'm not saying it wasn't horrible." He tries to take Beth's hand, but she swats him away.

Elaine hands me her glass.

"Are you sure?" I ask, and she nods, not looking at me.

"Maybe this isn't such a good idea," I say.

"Just make it," Elaine says.

"It's getting late," Mark says, and Sally says, "But we haven't finished."

I walk into the kitchen feeling as if I've taken part in something that should be reported to the authorities. The ice bucket is empty, so I take some trays from the freezer and while I'm twisting them over the sink, I feel her press up against me and grind.

I drop the tray and spin. Sally's there, smiling. I take her by the shoulders and push her back. She keeps smiling as she squirms out of my hold and rubs herself against me, cupping my crotch with her right hand.

"Hi there," she says.

"Come on," I say in a strangled whisper, "I can't do this. Someone will come in." I've never cheated on my wife, never wanted to be the kind of guy that cheats on his wife.

"Well, when, then?" she says, and I say, "I don't know. I'm making this drink."

She moves her face toward me, keeps the smile on, like she's amused by my childish antics. When she brushes her face against mine and licks around my ear, she smells like shampoo and cigarettes and perfume and garlic and baby powder, and I can hardly breathe.

"Okay," I say, "all right." I push her away again, thinking, I'm not going to make it.

She grabs me one more time and squeezes as she turns to walk out of the kitchen, shaking her ass like a little girl imitating a woman imitating a hooker.

Only Beth and Elaine are in the living room when I return, both silent and staring.

"Where is everybody?" I say, and then Sally and Joe walk in from the back rooms. "Joe tried to rape me in the baby's room," Sally says, laughing, and Joe rolls his eyes.

I try to hide in the couch.

"That's not funny, Sally," Elaine says. "There's nothing funny about rape."

"It was just a joke," Sally says.

"But it's not funny."

"It's okay, Elaine," Beth says, and Elaine says, "I wasn't defending you, Beth. I just don't think it's something to joke about."

I wish she'd let it die.

"And you're right," Joe says.

"Oh, what do you know, Joe," Sally says.

Mark sits at the coffee table and begins rolling a joint. Beth puts her hand on his head, and he turns to her, smiling.

We have to get away from these people.

"Christ," Sally says, "nobody's telling the truth here. I'll give you something awful. How about wanting to kill your baby? How about wishing your husband would die on the way home from work one rainy afternoon?"

"What are you talking about?" Joe says.

We're going to have to get away from everyone.

"Come on," she says. "Willy screamed the first two months he was home. Don't tell me you didn't once, sometime in the middle of the night, just once, so tired, think about letting go and throwing him through the wall."

"Oh my God," Beth says. "I never felt that way about Amy."

"Yeah, sure."

"It got frustrating," Joe says, "but I never felt like that."

"I love my baby," Beth says.

"Sure you do," Sally says. "And you love Mark, too. But that doesn't mean you don't sometimes wish he were dead."

"That's not true."

"That is true."

"What are you talking about?" Joe says.

Mark takes a deep hit. Everybody looks in their own direction as the joint is passed. Elaine takes a hit, but I pass this time. I'm far too stoned.

"Sally doesn't want you or the baby dead, Joe," Elaine says. "She just thinks of possibilities in her life."

I look at Sally and she smiles. "I do think of possibilities," she says.

"I'm sure you do, Sally," Elaine says.

"When Joe had his affair, for instance, sure, I thought about revenge, my own little fling."

"What?" Joe says, and he laughs, but the red in his face gives him away.

"Oh, come on," Sally says. "We're all friends, here. Right Mark? Right Jack?"

"Sure," Mark says. "But—"

"So Joe was fucking this Deadhead chick. I was seven months pregnant. Joe met a little girl from the college. Where was it Joe, a coffee shop?"

"I really don't—"

"Was it because I wasn't putting out?"

I look at Elaine looking hard at Joe. The room needs to be quarantined; but, first, we have to escape. I try to catch her attention with a head movement, but she won't look.

"Why not bring it all out?" Sally says.

"I think we'd better get going," Beth says, and Sally says, "But we're not done with the game. I'm helping Joe with his Something Awful, here, aren't I, honey?"

She musses his hair.

He jerks away. "This is idiotic," he says. "I have no idea—"

"Oh, come on, Joe," Elaine says.

Her voice cuts through me. I grab her hand. "This is none of our business," I say, but she pulls away from me.

Sally leans forward on the little couch close to Joe's face. "Was it wrong of me to hate you for that?"

He's being careful, controlled, but his hands tense like claws.

"Did you honestly think I didn't know? I mean, do I look like an idiot?"

She musses his hair again, but this time he grabs her by the wrist and squeezes, then carefully moves her hand away.

"What was her name?" Sally says. "Sunshine?"

Joe rises to his feet, starts moving around the living room. "This is ridiculous," he says. "I have no idea what you're talking about."

"We really have to go," Beth says, standing. "Maybe you guys need some alone time."

Sally sits like Buddha, crosslegged and smiling on the couch.

"Maybe we're all just a little too buzzed," Mark says.

"I didn't do shit," Joe says.

"Well, then, maybe," Sally says, "this is my Something Awful."

"That's not funny, Sally," Elaine says.

"Oh, what do you know. I'm just trying to let you liars off the hook. Of course he fucked her. He probably still is."

Joe turns toward the stereo, the back of his neck red. "This is not even true," he says.

I wonder how long my toes have been curled in my shoes. It's just a bad TV show, really. Nothing I'm a part of. Amusing, possibly.

"Honey," Elaine says to Sally, "do you want to stay with us tonight?" and I'm thinking, Wait a minute, then saying it: "Wait a minute, here. We're butting in," but Elaine ignores me. "You can stay with us," she says.

I look at Joe, shaking my head, No.

Sally bows her head.

"I'm going to get Amy," Beth says to Mark. "Would you get our coats, honey?"

I take Elaine's hand and squeeze until she looks at me. My teeth are grinding as I make another head movement toward the kitchen. "Can I talk to you in private?" I say, and we rise together, numb, and seem to float into the kitchen, where a rage begins to pour out of me. "Just what are you trying to do here?" I ask her. "We shouldn't have heard any of this. She is not coming over."

"You saw his eyes," she hisses back. "God knows what he's capable of."

"No," I say, our faces close together. "He's a gentle man." As if I know. As if I care.

"Sally told me he's violent."

Behind us one of the babies starts to cry.

I feel like I've been up for ninety-five hours.

"She might be lying," I say. "This might be a game."

Elaine glares at me.

"She seems capable of anything."

"And he doesn't?"

"We hardly even know them."

"I couldn't live with myself if something happened."

"Nothing's going to happen," I say. "I don't want her in my house."

"You could have fooled me," Elaine says.

"What's that supposed to mean?"

I have to be very careful. With my eyes I have to communicate a perfect combination of innocence and burning indignation.

"Fine," Elaine says "We'll go home. And if something happens, I will never fucking forgive you."

I follow her out of the kitchen.

Beth is changing Amy's diaper on the coffee table, Mark behind her with her coat over his arm. Joe and Sally sit on the love seat. Amy makes gurgling noises and smiles up at us. Joe looks exhausted, but he's holding Sally's hand and caressing it.

"We talked it out," Sally says to me and Elaine. "I told him everything."

Mark stares at the floor, shifting his weight back and forth. Beth wipes the baby's butt.

"He admitted it once I showed him the underwear," which she waves as evidence. "It was wedged in the back seat of the Saab." She holds it out to us, as if we might like to sniff it, but none of us move.

"I told him about us, Jack," she says, looking at me.

Adrenaline pumps to my fingers and toes, bringing on tremors. I'm as good as guilty, but in a snotty, shaky voice, I say, "And what about us, Sally?"

Elaine looks at my profile. Joe looks at Sally's hand in his own. The baby coos.

"Our kissy, rub-rub in the kitchen," Sally says. "Dry humping there by the sink. Making plans."

I laugh incredulously, but it sounds phony even to my ears.

"Okay," Joe says. "It's over."

Elaine cocks her head, sizing me up.

"That's not true," I say.

Beth hands Mark the dirty diaper which he puts in a plastic bag.

"Come on," Mark says to Beth, "we gotta go." They exchange baby and coat. I feel sentenced and forgotten as Joe and Sally rise to bid their friends good-night, hand shakes from Joe and kisses from Sally. "We love you guys," Sally says. "Sorry about the scene."

"This is a lie," I say, but no one seems to hear. Elaine takes the baby and kisses her cheek, then hugs Mark and Beth and says good-bye.

Mark shakes my hand. "Maybe at our house next time," he says, and then they're out the door.

Joe helps Elaine with our coats at the hall closet. Sally smiles at me.

"Tell them it's a lie," I say.

Joe hands me my coat. Elaine won't look at me.

"It didn't happen, Joe," I say.

He looks at the floor.

"Thanks a lot you guys," Elaine says. She lets Sally kiss her cheek, but Sally looks at me over her shoulder.

"Tell her it's a lie, Sally," I say, and Elaine says, "Shut up, Jack, it was obvious," as she hugs Joe good-bye. Now we start growing old together.

Sally walks forward as if to hug me, but I hold my hands up to keep her away. "Don't touch me," I say.

"Oh, all right," she says. "It's a lie. Feel better?"

"Come on, Jack," Joe says. "Too much to drink."

Elaine's out the door.

Joe turns away.

Sally takes my arm, but I jerk it from her and walk outside.

Elaine stands by the passenger side of the car, waiting for me to unlock her door. I touch her back. She winces.

"I didn't do that," I say.

A crash sounds from inside the house, a vase, an ashtray.

"Yeah, you did," Elaine says. "We'll call the cops when we get home."

They're screaming at each other. Another crash.

I stand outside the open door and bend down to her. "You've got to believe I didn't do that."

She shakes her head rapidly and closes her eyes. "I can't talk to you," she says. "I can't hear you."

I close the door on her, and walk to my side of the car, knowing we won't call the cops when we get home. Inside, there's another crash. I open my door and crawl in next to Elaine. She won't acknowledge me. I crank the engine and pull out of the driveway. Elaine looks out her window, as far from me as she can be.

"You don't really believe," I start to say, and Elaine says, "Shut up, Jack. And, please, please spare me the worst things you've ever done. I don't want to know."

I drive the three blocks home in silence. The worst things, it seems, are all in front of us.

Karen Gentry

The Lucky One

Last week my husband told me to take a shower and put on a dress. He said a childhood friend of his was in town and he wanted to meet me. We had reservations at one of those Brazilian Meat restaurants. When we got there, I found out this friend was not a him but a her, my husband's first love. There she was, waiting and lovely, not afraid to sit at the table alone.

"Sorry," my husband said. He kissed my ear and whispered, "If she asks, we saw *The Nutcracker* last week."

I'm finding out that's the way my husband is—he lies about the strangest things. I hadn't seen *The Nutcracker* since I was a kid. All those dancing sweets proved too much for my stomach. I stole away mid-ballet and hid under a chaise in the ladies lounge.

The thing about a Brazilian Meat restaurant is that there are no menus to hide behind when the childhood friend of your husband raises her glass to toast your ten years of marriage, when it has only been three months. Under the table, my husband touched my knee. She reached under the table too, brought out a photo album, and set it on top of my salad plate. "We'll flip through this after dinner."

I could only imagine what was in there. Pictures she would claim to have forgotten all about. Photos that would remind them of the funniest stories. Maybe a snapshot of my husband with his first car, leaning shirtless against it, rolling white lies for this girl from the neighborhood. I pushed it aside to get my plate.

After our first trip to the buffet, a whole rump roast stopped by, then a strand of Russian pork sausages, plum-soaked sirloin tips, another round of drinks, racks of Chinese ribs, legs of princess lamb, chicken wrapped in Spanish bacon. When the sugared-ostrich showed up, I'd had enough. I poked at the photo album with one of my husband's spare ribs. "Let's have a look already."

She clapped. "I see you can't stand the suspense."

My husband could stand it. He made for the buffet. I grabbed at his belt loop, but he wiggled free. She opened the album facing me, used a napkin to turn the pages. "It's arranged reverse chronologically."

There was her husband, who rooted for Green Bay, twin daughters, a pair of cheese heads at play, pictures of a twin clogging recital, a family trip to Twinsburg, Ohio, the twin's baptism by twin priests, twins popping out between a set of bloody legs. When she got to the last page, I prepared for the picture of my husband, dressed for the prom, throwing her over his shoulder, laughing. Instead, I found a photo of her son, a child she hadn't mentioned, standing in the rain. From the looks of him, something wasn't right in his head. "He's unhappy," I said. She nodded, but she misunderstood. She thought I was talking about my husband, lingering at the buffet, waiting for a fresh bowl of fruit.

She held her wine glass against her cheek. "So, tell me the truth—" she leaned in and called me by my first name, the way women do when they're trying to trick you, "—did you really see The Nutcracker?"

I looked away. I tried motioning my husband back to the table. "Only honeydew right now," he yelled, and blew me a kiss.

I felt the meat go bad in my stomach. "I think I left something in the car," I told her. "I'll be right back."

Outside, I crawled into the backseat of our Camry and pulled my pantyhose down far enough so I could breathe. I closed my eyes. I tried to form an image of me going back in there, but all I could see was me calling a cab, me walking to a bar. My hand was on the door when I heard their voices. I panicked. I remembered that the backseat of our car opens up to the trunk. I squeezed through, pulled it shut behind me, and made a place for myself in the dark.

They walked around the car. I felt it sink as they sat on the trunk. I heard my husband tell her that we had come in separate cars, that I was a surgeon, always on call. "She's probably responding to a medical emergency, Bariatrics, lots of pulmonary embolisms." I heard him sigh, "After ten years," he said, "I still feel like we're newlyweds." She laughed and I felt him slide off the trunk. He was helping her down. He was promising that we'd do it again some time soon.

I fell asleep on the way home. When the trunk lid opened, I kept my eyes closed. I smelled our garage, smelled my husband as he leaned in and untangled my legs from his jumper cables, singing a song about being the lucky one. He carried me into the house, then up the stairs and to our room, where he set me on the bed. I let him think I was asleep while he pulled off my shoes and threw them in the corner, took off my pantyhose, then my dress, and curled up behind me.

That's the way he is, my husband. Somehow he knows just where to find me.

Kate Milliken

Inheritance

Drew's parents died as they has lived, in a rather organized and mannered way, one after the other. First his father, in early October, a stroke over his Post and tea. His mother followed six weeks later, before the holidays, in her sleep. It fit them, painless and quiet.

They'd had Drew late in life, as something of an afterthought and he felt they'd raised him this way as well, in between lunches and bridge. Like Drew, they were only children and left without family, no aunts, no uncles, no cousins. But they'd woven together a vast group of friends in their long marriage and they'd found it off when Drew needed therapy in college, and that loneliness was a part of the diagnosis, something that warranted a prescription. They took to looking at him as if he were on the other side of a dirty window. His father, Dr. Washburn, had retired from medicine a decade earlier. "Incorrigible," he muttered, seeing Drew with his pills in hand. Drew understood that this was more reference to the state of medicine than to Drew—somehow this, the absence of personal insult, was more hurtful.

Drew decided he wanted to be a photographer, not a physician like his father.

"Say again," his father insisted, over waffles.

Drew thought, at the time, that he meant a photojournalist, that he would travel the world, revealing the miseries of mankind – in cargo pants, with a battered camera bag slung about his shoulders.

"Alright then," his mother said.

"How romantic," his father said. Drew thought so to, but what aspiration wasn't?

His father felt this was not the sort of career for which you took courses; you were either good or you weren't. His mother wrote him a check for two thousand dollars, to purchase equipment. He bought a Mamiya 645, a 55 mm and an 80 mm lens, a brick of Kodak 200. He photographed abandoned barns and cemeteries. And portraits of the men who worked at the 76 station, Avedon-like portraits, but saturated with color. "Not bad," is father said, fanning through the proofs. "More," he said. But then his father died and then his mother and this left Drew well off and with a house and the house suggested to him, in its quiet old yellow house kind of way, that he might not exist outside of it. And so, at twenty-three, he was alive, haunting his parents home. That was hoe he described the feeling to Vivian and she seemed to understand.

It was early April. Vivian was the first person to respond to the rental ad he's been running since February. She phoned around noon and said she would be by in a few minutes. The last of winter's ice was dripping from the eaves. He grilled a sandwich, leaning with the spatula, and waited.

He fingered the last greasy crumbs. A spear of ice thawed and slipped from the rain gutter. He heard the clack-clack-clack, as it slid through the downspout – just in time to look up and watch it arc out and stab into the final mapping of snow.

At four he made another sandwich, the same sliced ham and two pieces of cheese. The weight he lost in the fall was inching back on, gathering at his middle.

A teal green Honda pulled up. The front fender was bent, as if it had been purposefully run straight into a hydrant or tree. The hood was held with twine. Vivian sat hunched at the wheel, looking out, considering something. The car's exhaust hung in the air, a phantom behind her. She was slight. Even from the house he could see that. She had on a royal blue down coat. She was sitting in it, more than wearing it. She turned, squinting, making out the house numbers. He waved, unsure if she had found him there, in the window.

He liked her name, Vivian. It sounded of lost love and lace. He took her upstairs.

It was his old bedroom he was trying to rent. He's moved into his parent's room, for the closets mostly. He showed her the convenience of the adjoining bath and stood her at the window, pointing out the view through the trees, how you could make out the reservoir.

"Like there's some shortage of views around here," she said.

He wondered about her age. Twenty, maybe. She had red-brown hair that she wore down, not particularly tended, one side tucked behind her ear, the bangs cropped bluntly over mineral green eyes. She looked around the room as if it were a museum tour, gaze sweeping floor to ceiling, never touching anything, making little satisfied sounds. She was right. It was all trees and water around here, then a house, then a hill and more trees and water again. But he'd always liked this particular view from his room; that it didn't look out on the yard or his father's office.

He opened the doors to the master bedroom, feeling he was letting her know there was nothing to fear on the other side. He hadn't considered that a girl would respond to the ad, let alone someone near his age. Just wasn't the demographic for Belfast, Maine. He'd actually been a little uneasy when he'd thought of who might respond.

Downstairs she touched the wallpaper in the hallway, a fleur-de-lis print. "You sure this is your place?"

Then, walking by his mother's study, she stopped and asked if she could rent that room instead. He hadn't entered that room all winter. The roll top desk was still open, the darning needles still piercing a half wound ball of brown yarn. He wasn't sentimental about it. He just hadn't needed anything in there.

"You from Maine?" He asked at the study door, aware of the milky flesh of her hands, her neck, her cheeks, or what was bare.

"No."

"What brings you?"

"School."

"Where you going?"

"Any one will do." She tugged at the waist of her jeans out of necessity or nervous habit. "Look," she said, "this was as far as I could get from home."

"Oh."

"I'm not in trouble or anything. No one hit me. No one's looking for me. My dad knows I'm here. He'll send money if I need it." She put a hand on the pipe of the wood-burning stove and shook it, half-heartedly, as if to check the workmanship.

"Where's home?" He wanted to photograph her.

"California. I'm good for at least three months in advance. If you want it."

"I don't.'

She spent the first night on the floor. He brought her a pillow and blanket, but she was already asleep, her head on a duffel bag, her grayed sneakers still on.

The next day they hefted his twin mattress down. She made up the bed in the corner behind the door. He asked her not to use the stove in the room. His mother had, but he had vague concerns about insurance and liabilities. He told her he'd ask the family lawyer, if that was why she wanted the room.

"Wasn't," she said, "It's cool."

She woke early every day, before the first light, left in her car and then returned around ten and went back to bed, behind the door. He took to looking for her car to see if she was in the house or not. In the evenings, sometimes, he saw her in the kitchen. She rarely cooked, just stood eating crackers over the sink, slurping juice. But there was only a half bath on the first floor so she had to go upstairs to shower and that was how they'd bump into one another, in the hall, Vivian wrapped in a towel.

Drew had slept with Louise Tate and Nora Lynes in high school. Everyone wanted to be with Nora Lynes. His strong jaw was an asset, his honest brown eyes, his thick hair, and his mother complimented his posture and manners, but Nora slept with him because he was quiet. She'd told him so. He hadn't known he was quiet until she'd told him so. And then he was cripplingly aware of it.

In college he slept with Emily. He made an effort with Emily. He told her things he hadn't known he'd thought about until he said them to her. And they'd remained in touch. She even came to town for his mother's wake and she said he looked good, "given everything." He told her about the Zoloft, how he hadn't cried much longer than his father. In fact, hi smother had shown him the invitation to the Fernbach Christmas party, a handsomely embossed card, and she'd said he should go. Not saying he should go with her, just that he should go, as if she'd known she wouldn't be alive. Emily asked if she'd done herself in, with a prescription of something. But that wasn't like his mother. She was just going with her husband, Dr. Washburn, as if the last six weeks of her life had only been an extended version of her running in to gather her coat, the two of them hurrying off, the honored guests of a new sort of party. And he was okay. Really, he felt okay about everything and he was long over the bout of weeping spells that had settled in, like nimbus clouds, during that final semester, after Emily thought it best they just be friends.

"It's good you're doing so well," she said then.

"Not well," he said. "Just okay." And gave her a pursed smile.

He thought of calling Emily to tell her he'd found a roommate, like she'd suggested, but he didn't want her to hear in his voice that Vivian was prettier than she was. He'd learned that much, that women could do that.

If it were a painting, it could be by Vermeer; that's how he thinks of the first photograph of Vivian. She was in his father's office, a separate structure from the house. A small, four room building a dozen yards off. He'd been at the window in his parent's room, eating an apple, feeling the day begin to close, considering the building, how to make sense of it—knock it down or make a darkroom or it – and then there she was, standing in the yard, looking at the building, almost with him. And then she started toward it. And opened the door and stepped inside.

He picked up his camera as if in defense of his property.

There was the small reception area, two chairs, a couch, a door to the exam room, and through that room the door to his father's office. She was there, standing at his father's desk, a hand on the open leather-bound schedule. He lifted the camera and took the picture before she turned toward him, before she could protest.

The window above the desk, the last of the day's yellow light, how it held her in its frame: Vermeer. And her hair was up, away from her face. The iridescence beneath her skin made him think of the white wolves that merged at the wood's edge, their eyes aglow with hunger, a counter brush of white against the winter floor.

I don't mind you photographing me," she said.

June. They were in the master bedroom, on top of the covers, the window open to the yard.

"Did you know about your dad doing abortions?"

"He was a regular doctor too." Drew saw himself foolishly gesture to his privates, just below the opened button of his jeans. She was sitting up, looking at him, her mouth gently open, watching him talk. "I don't think it happened much." She'd let him touch her beneath her shirt and he'd kissed her neck. He couldn't tell how much she liked it. She'd make the same little satisfied sounds as when he'd shown her the house. He was surprised by her bones, how aware of her ribs and shoulders he was. But her breasts were small and firm, perfect in his hand. "He retired by the time I was ten. They thought it was the right thing," he shrugged. "It wasn't dinner talk. But they didn't keep it from me."

"Your mother knew?"

"Of course."

"I bet it bothered you. I bet you hated seeing women walk back there alone, past your room."

"I couldn't see from my room. And they weren't usually alone. Why? Does it bother you?"

"Who came? Parents?"

"Sometimes. Or friends. Sometimes men came with. My mother drove the ones that came alone."

"It doesn't bother me. I mean, you asked. I don't care." She straightened, reached back and refastened her bra. "Honestly, I'm all for it."

She looked tired.

"You can stay up here," he said. Earlier, she put her hand to his when he went to remove his pants, stopping him. "If you aren't sleeping well downstairs.

She turned and smiled. That big, unexpected smile. "I know I can," she said.

In the afternoons, she drove around with him, helping set up the large format camera in front of the dilapidated barns. Some days she seemed wound up, like a string had been pulled behind her, and she'd dance around in the fields, drift into the woods, then run toward him, making faces at the lens. Most days, she would lay back in the open grass, the bed of the pick-up, against the old stone well, or on the paisley couch and let him kiss her – for almost long enough – stopping him with the tips of her fingers, to ask about photography, about Maine, his parents, and then she'd close her eyes, as he leaned to find her lips again. She knew him, he told her, better than even Emily had. He expected she would ask who Emily was, but she didn't.

One morning he woke before her and watched as she slept – the lilt of her nostrils, the fine hair on her face, the things a camera could catch, but that the eye rarely held. He stood at the foot of their bed, feeling he'd actually grown taller.

In July, she sold her car.

He was in the kitchen, eating, of course—she made him feel like he was always eating – and he saw her walking up the drive, her thumbs in the holes she worried into the ends of her sleeves. Like a kite on a string.

"It's not about money," she told him, sitting at the table. He passed her half of his sandwich and to his surprise she picked it up, and took a small bite. "I just like what we're doing here," she said, nodding, and chewing.

He wasn't sure what she meant.

She tstill wouldn't have sex with him. But they shared the bed, him holding her, wrapped around her. Sometimes she'd reach bacj and stroke him and then moan enough, letting him drift into the belief that it was what they both wanted. But when he asked about her, anything at all: When's your birthday? What's your favorite color? What do you want to be? All the things you ask on long summer days, half clothed, beside someone you want to love, and she would answer in ways that made everything feel stifling. Yesterday. Flesh color. Invisible.

Then he asked about her father and she said he was famous. Too famous to talk about. Never meeting his eyes. The posture of a liar.

"We could start a business or something. Shooting events, weddings." She was staring at the last of the bread between her fingers. "I could be your assistant. I don't need a car for that."

It was an idea. She'd ruined three rolls of film when they were out in Randolph Forest the day before, flashing them in the changing bag. He still had his mother's Skylark in the garage. He could drive that. He hadn't asked for rent since May. He knew what Emily would say: be careful with yourself, Drew. Like he was held together by cheap glue.

"You can take the truck, when you need to."

And she did. She left early in the mornings. And he lay there, still in the warmth of the bed. He heard the sputter and whistle of the engine turn over, the rusted ache of the door closing her in. The first few times he genuinely liked the idea of her leaving in his truck without him. How domestic and civil this was, sharing a vehicle. He fell back to sleep. And when he would wake, she was back in bed, beside him.

And then she wasn't. From six in the morning, whole afternoons passing. Wind moved through the house. The front door left open. And she returned without anything. If only she's brought back some groceries or firewood or something. Sometimes the keys were not left on the entry hall table. Sometimes he had to fish them from her jacket, her jeans. As if he were going somewhere, as if he would leave without her. He wanted to go through her things.

He managed once to drink a beer alone, at Sandbar near the docks. Salt and fish in the air. She was asleep when he got back.

There were mornings he left in the Skylark, driving up to Searsport and back along the frontage road, watching floater planes hover and slide in. He took a few rolls of the planes and of the bugs in wet slicks just outside the car door—water striders, the dime-sized halo where their needled feet met the water. He told himself he wasn't looking for her. But he saw her everywhere—leaving the Hannafords in Camden, a shorter brunette; in a crosswalk, turning to reveal a baby at her hip; through the tinted windows of Rollie's, rubbing the back of some trucker's neck. "You're so quiet," Nora Lynns had told him. "It's sexy. Like you're full of secrets. He felt a hardening in his chest on each of these drives, a calcification, some resolve.

It had been dark for an hour. They were in bed. He muted the television. A cop drama that was making him anxious.

"I need to know where you take the truck."

"Tough guy, eh?" She took the remote and aimed it at him like a gun, one eye closed. Damned cute. He'd watched her eat a pear that night, wondering if she'd eaten anything else all day.

"Vivian," he said.

She got up and started dressing. "Fine," she said. "All you had to do was ask."

She drove with one elbow on the open window, her head held in that hand, a look on her face that said he exhausted her. Fiery strands of her hair slipped out and rode the wine. Here they were again. Together.

"I should take your picture in my truck."

"Drew. Shut up."

The house was in Bayside. One of the seasonal places, enormous, the kind that had its own name. A wraparound porch. Tennis courts ten paces out. Between the house and waterfront, a lap pool was left uncovered, lit up, dancing with marbled light. Vivian drove up a paved driveway that led to the garage, the servants' drive, separate, quiet. She killed the headlights at the turn and backed into a clearing in the trees. He could see cars parked there: two Cadillacs, a Mercedes. There was a party going on. Two dozen people. Women in black dresses, men in shirts and ties.

"A whole lot of khaki in there."

She told him the house belonged to a woman named Sasha Tuncer. A property that had been in the Tuncer family for three generations. It was used as a summer home until Sasha inherited it. A poet, Vivian said, as if the word had a bad flavor. She lived there year round, writing through the winters and having friends stay with her for long stretches. Vivian's mother had been very close to Sasha Turner, a long time ago.

"They were like sisters," Vivian said. Drew wasn't sure what to say, if it was needed for him to say anything at all. And then Vivian said, "she left when I was twelve."

"Your mother?"

"You could call her that, yeah. My mother." Music cam eon in the house, a swing band. "I started driving last summer, just left. I didn't mean to come here. But then I did and you had the room and the house was so close."

"You're looking for her?"

"I have good reason to think she might come here. I know she stayed here once years ago."

Drew wondered how much of it was made-up, this story she was telling herself or that she'd been told. How many lies once life could hold. "You wait here every morning?" he asked. He could see a blue vein along her cheek bone. A mix of fear and pity took his chest.

"Just till they're done with breakfast. You think that's pathetic, don't you? Sometimes I drive around Bayside, thinking I'll run into her. I don't care what you think, Drew. I realize that now. I though it mattered to me. That's why I didn't tell you. Cause I thought I cared what you thought." She started the truck back up.

Lanugo. The downy hair that had begun on her arms, that was now visible at the back of her neck. The same soft fur of premature babies. He's read about it years ago, among his father's things and had looked it up again just recently. Curiosity. Concern. Disgust. It was what the body did to stay warm, to keep alive. He pitied Vivian. The way one does a limping wild animal. Helplessly. "Why in the morning?" he asked.

They were back on Highway 3.

"If someone is staying there, they'd come down in the morning most likely. Rest of the day is a crapshoot."

"What are you going to say to her? What is there to say? Have you thought about that?" He heard himself, that he sounded angry. She didn't look at him. Why was he angry?

She drove through a stop sign, "I keep thinking of the line, she comes back to tell me she's gone."

Paul Simon. "A good line." So what.

She turned down the wrong road, then found her way out, thoughtlessly, like she'd made the same mistake a hundred times. "I won't say anything. I just want her to see me," she said. "That's all."

He was angry because he wanted Vivian to be in Belfast for him. And now he knew that she wasn't.

The next morning the truck was gone, as usual, but by evening she still had not returned.

August. She'd only been his tenant, a companion. She was an adult. Wasn't she? Had they discussed her age? Unbelievable. Eight days and he could not come up with anyone to phone, to tell. He considered reporting the truck stolen. Even went to do the paperwork. But he couldn't. He say outside the Bayside house in his mother's Skylark, the smell of the leather seats, the sweet of her old lilac perfume. "Be here," he said into the steering wheel, not deciding if he meant Vivian or Vivian's mother or his own. But then thinking, maybe. Maybe things do happen. Maybe Vivian and her mother were together. Yet, he was also hoping not.

Sometimes she had been in the bed beside him and he had not known it. Then a wrinkle of fabric. She'd taken to sleeping on her stomach, with a pillow over her head, buried. Barely there.

And then one night he was standing in his mother's study, standing over the bed behind the door, and he could see her there, beneath the heap of comforter and sheets, could just make out her breathing. Or maybe it was his own. "I'll tell you every day, Vivian. I love you. Stay with me. Be with me." He slept on the floor beside the mattress that night, unwilling to lift that covers or reach to touch and learn that she wasn't there. He woke cold, the bed was empty, wholly undisturbed. He found a think notebook, a journal, tossed carelessly between the mattress and the wall.

He opened the journal to the fist page, saw the word tongue and quickly closed it shut. He checked the kitchen, the shower upstairs.

He walked through the office out back.

He opened the journal again only to read Drew us a silly boy. He heard her laughter in the house, a ghostly echo of her, a cavern opening in him, wind, hard and bitter.

Silly boy. He walked around the rest of the day, calling himself that. Silly boy. Would silly boy like another sandwich?

The night she returned, three weeks later, would be the only time he had sex with her. He swore this to himself as it was happening. Because he hated her now. And because she was more sick animal than women now, just bones and fur. She shivered beside him. "I'm sorry, Drew," she said, looking off, over his shoulder. Like she was waiting for him to look too, to turn around so she could steal things.

"I want the keys to the truck," he said.

"Okay." She pulled closer to him, crying. "I love you," she said.

Her being back, being back for him. That felt okay.

Late September. She was taking his Zoloft and it seemed to be helping. And he started her on iron supplements.

She left once in the middle of the night. He heard her digging in drawers, looking for the keys. He did not stop her. But lay awake until he heard her come back in.

She was at the kitchen table, frantically tapping one foot on the floor and twisting a plastic straw in her hands. She kept licking her lips.

"I though I'd get us breakfast or something," she said. The table was bare. Sweat pilled on her forehead.

It was nothing for him t carry her up the stairs and bring her to the shower. Sometimes life was like this, life something you'd watched on television. And that made it easier somehow.

"It's okay," he said. "We'll try again."

She nodded and swore she would eat after a nap.

They had not driven by the Bayside house since Vivian's return. But in late October she asked that he take her picture there, in front of the house. A Polaroid she wanted; to leave there, for her mother, he assumed.

No one seemed home and the drapes had been pulled.

"Maybe she's gone to town."

"Maybe."

They were on the porch. Vivian touched the knocker and the door swung open. "Rich people," she said. "How do you get rick being so stupid?"

"Inheritance," Drew said.

Everything was covered in white sheets, quiet as a snowdrift. He had a half roll of film to finish before he could load the Polaroid back. He'd intended to shoot Vivian, but once inside he moved off, away from her, finding himself in the dining room. He photographed the massive chandelier, the cloaked table and chairs, wondering if his parents had been to a party there. Surely they had. He liked this idea, that he was somehow connected to the house, that his parent's, her mother... that he was more connected to Vivian.

He heard her crying in another room, found her sitting at the base of the winding staircase.

"She's not coming back."

"You don't know that. The house will open again, in spring. They'll be back."

The dark burning in her green eyes, hate. His simplicity, his hopefulness, all the false cheer. He too was sick with himself.

He took her photograph like that. Alarmed by how small she was in the frame, how you had to look for her, even with that red hair. He left the image on the mantel.

November. No snow yet. But it's dry warning was in the air.

It was one of those roads that dips and then rises at such an angle you can't be sure there is road on the other side: such doubt and only a mild reassurance of what is supposed to be. You put your foot to the gas with faith. This was a different hill than any they had taken before. It was easy to get lost like that, the walls of pine, their thin stretch to the sky. His father had kept a compass and so Drew did not. He was happy that day. Happy with the changing leaves, their dying colors, the disguise of vibrant life. And he'd had an idea for a new image – just her eyes, but with deep woods behind her, rich and out of focus. A dark bird would lift from a branch, leaving a swath of black in the frame, like smoke, something exercised from her.

It hurt him to see her body. A brittle, stripped pine cone. Her belly had grown distended. She came to bed completely naked. He'd go cold and hot all at once. She seemed to enjoy his discomfort, as she did her hunger. He refused to touch her. But he'd also stopped pleasing with her, for hear of her laugh, the forced yellow smile. If he so much as offered a cracker, she'd shake her head in a way that said he was stupid. And so they'd come to retain some private dignity and yet remain together.

At the base of the hill, he looked over at her. She had her forehead against the glass, her chin in her hand, her eyes skyward, searching the tree line. A small bead pulsed in the line of vein wrapping her collarbone and up the soft downy skin of her throat.

"You ready?" he said.

She nodded. She used to stick her head out in the wind, screaming as they crested over the hills. Now she only closed her eyes. He gunned the truck. He heard her gasp as the reached the peak. The front tires left the road, lifted and smacked down. The back tires, lifted and smacked down. She was tossed up and bounced in the seat, as always. Then her hands fell limp into her lap.

There wasn't any shoulder on the road, but he could not think beyond pulling over. He'd read about what to do, there was something to be done in the case of cardiac arrest, a pounding on the chest. He couldn't remember exactly, if he was to lay her down, hold her tongue. No. There was a stand of trees. Her ribs would fall to dust under his fists. An incomprehension seized him. A feeling familiar from his youth. The same incomprehension he had sitting at the top of the stairs listening to his parent's parties, the chinking of ice into glasses, the laughter, so much unbridled joy after such steely days. How confused he was by the sheer spectrum of emotion in such a brief time, what a single day could hold. How stuck in between he always felt. A girl had come to the door one night during one of the many parties. An uninvited guest, this was evident by his father's tone, obvious that he wanted her turned away. Drew recognized the girl; he had seen his mother only the morning before backing out of the driveway with her. She'd looked fatigued, medicated, like the others. His mother let her in, ushered her into her study, away from the murmuring guests. Drew was just a boy then, but he'd understood the girl wanted something that night, that she had come back for something she was sure was rightfully hers. It was a feeling he himself already knew, a yearning without aim. And it seemed hours that his mother say with that girl in her stuffy, holding her hands, bent before her, trying to reason with her, to meet her eyes, to console her breathless sobbing. His father passed him listening at the door and huffed, shaking his head. But Drew had longed to be there, in that chain on that night, perched before his mother, her rapt attention on him. And he longed to be there again now, sitting there, with his sorrow pouring from him, his mother at his feet, her brown eyes looking up into his and her voice repeating, again and again, in a soft, resolute whisper, so very sure, "It is all for the best."

Scott Garson

Demons

Last winter I lived above a postal services shop which shall remain unnamed. The place was well heated. This, for me, was its primary virtue. It was so warm that I could open the front windows and get the hard air and the sudden intimate sound of tires as they moved through gray slush.

There was another place in the back. I may never have met its sole tenant, Clark Minds, if I hadn't had to find work and chosen to try at the shop downstairs for reasons that will be obvious to you if you've lived through an Iowa winter.

My entrance rang bells.

But I wasn't acknowledged by either the manager, a guy named Thompson Leach, whom I'd met at a party a while before, or by the patron, Clark Minds, whom I wouldn't know personally for another few days. By birth I'm a Pisces, and am often ignored.

Clark Minds and Thompson Leach were speaking across the counter about the former man's post office box.

Clark Minds said, "The item I'm expecting...." and then said it again.

Thompson Leach stared across the counter at Clark Minds with what I would have to call hatred.

"The item I'm expecting....it's very important."

"Try tomorrow," said Thompson Leach.

"Yes."

Two things you have to know about Clark Minds: he grimaces when he talks, and he says 'yes' in a singular way, with a huge effort of concentration. I've sometimes wondered what would happen to him if he ever failed in this effort.

"It's been put in a neighboring box, could be," said Clark Minds.

"You said that."

"Yes," said Clark Minds.

"You said that about the neighboring box. Do you remember?"

Clark Minds turned from the counter for a moment. Sensing my presence, he swung towards me a broad face that swam with alarm. Flesh rolled his stubbled nape.

"This is an extremely difficult situation," he told Thompson Leach at a discreet volume.

"There's nothing difficult about it."

"I don't mean to imply wrongdoing. I'd be the first to agree with you that mistakes are just part of the plan."

"Are they just part of the plan?" blurted Thompson Leach.

The other man grimaced.

"Try tomorrow."

"Yes," Clark Minds said.

"Tomorrow."

Clark Minds turned. He was a short guy, about ten years older than me. As he made his way to the bell-hung door, he flicked me a bogus smile.

At whose party had I made the acquaintance of Thompson Leach? In what neighborhood? How long before?

I remember just this: as we two were being introduced, he'd looked away. It was as if this exchange of our names was a painful humiliation for him.

Also this: as I'd crossed a string-lit room where Thompson Leach played his guitar, he hadn't looked at me, or at the other few people in the room, his small audience. He'd kept his chin tucked away. We'd seen only his ponytail.

I think he was thinking he recognized me too when I told him I was looking for work. I think I probably benefited from his associating me with a different part of his life.

I started the next Monday. I won't bore you with the particulars of the job. They bored me enough while I had it. They bored Thompson Leach too. I was pretty happy to see that. I was happy to know I'd be working for someone who wouldn't judge me for not taking a keen interest.

Thompson Leach seemed apologetic almost each time he had to give me instruction. He seemed to be saying, You've surely got better things to consider....

I was like, No, no.

The other employees were younger. Claude and Nina. They were both still in school. Thompson Leach didn't look their way very often. When addressing them, he spoke under his breath.

For a place without noticeable power tensions, the shop was unusually drear.

It was maybe best toward closing. Out the windows the day would turn blue. Motes of dry colorless snow would appear. Spooled woolen scarves and tapering hoods would smoke with people's breath.

It was also good in the morning when certain of the people who had post office boxes would unsettle the bells.

There was the Sleeper. The Sleeper had a round white head and took slow, labored breaths through her nose. We were reminded of snoring. The shop filled with the Sleeper's slow breaths whenever she bent to her box.

There was Tim Pease. I sometimes thought of Tim Pease as a good model for the historical Jesus. He had very long hair, like the Jesus of standard depiction, but deep black and Semitically curled. On a subconscious level, the Jesus/Pease link may have drawn on the way that the latter man walked, looking forward and keeping his hands at his sides and lifting his feet from the floor. Never varying his pace. The walk seemed to me quiet, essential. It seemed free of all personal foible.

There were a few drug dealers. This was according to Claude, who liked drugs and liked to imagine them in the more airy of the boxes in the shipment each day, the ones that would float when you tossed them.

And there was Clark Minds. Clark Minds didn't always have problems. Sometimes he'd stop at the counter for nothing more than a moment's talk. These moments could be difficult for Thompson Leach. Technically he'd have nothing to object to.

"It's an extremely cold day," Clark Minds might remark, grimacing, risking eye contact.

Thompson Leach would hold still.

"Good thing we don't live too far, Clark," I might say, running mail through the meter.

Eventually Clark Minds would say, "Yes."

He started telling us about his apartment during the short brutal days of late January. I'd never been in Clark Minds' apartment. But I assumed that like mine it had a false latticed ceiling of yellowed styrofoam, covering who knows what, and a phone through which the all-purpose cheer of our landlord, Troy Nagurney, could be heard.

Troy Nagurney owned the building. He was part owner of the postal shop too, which meant he both gave and took from me. "Is that right?" Troy Nagurney said to me when I informed him of this little irony. It was Troy Nagurney's favorite thing to say—'Is that right?' He'd say it as if he was really interested—in the subject, in you—which was almost never the case. I had to admire him for such basic insincerity. I connected it to his economic weight.

Clark Minds said that something unfortunate was beginning to take place in his apartment. He appeared stricken and shamed. Certain items had been moved from their places, he said. I wasn't sure how to respond.

"What items?"

Clark Minds grimaced. "Cat," he said finally.

"Cat," I repeated.

"Glass cat. Black cat. It's yawning."

"It's been moved?"

Clark Minds closed his eyes. "Turned around."

"I see," I said. "What else?"

Clark Minds spoke of other feathery events, explanation for which could probably be found in Clark Minds himself, as I tried saying.

A wing chair had been shifted a number of degrees to the left. Some wouldn't have noticed, but he had. A coat had been moved from one peg to another. A book had been drawn partway out.

"Clark Minds was in earlier," I told Thompson Leach when he returned. I'll admit that I sort of enjoyed the effect that Clark Minds sometimes had on him.

Thompson Leach didn't answer.

"Says stuff has been moved in his apartment and there's no accounting for it."

Thompson Leach would not be riled. "Does he?" is all he would say.

This continued. A calendar switched months on Clark Minds. Items jumped shelves in the fridge. Knick-knacks appeared to the left of their spots, or to the right. If he'd chosen to tell you about this, you might not have understood well. Still, you'd have got the picture. He did not know the meaning of what was happening in his life. He feared that the force or forces at work would not be easily satisfied.

"The doorway," he said miserably one afternoon in a voice that was nearly beneath hearing.

I said, "The doorway, Clark?"

"Watch it?"

"Watch the doorway?"

"Yes."

"Watch the doorway. Why?"

He whispered with closed eyes, "I have to go out."

The doorway to the stairs that led to our apartments could be seen, at least partially, through storefront glass. He was asking me to note whether anyone went up to move things while he was out.

I gave him the okay sign. I wasn't at liberty to do as he wished (and couldn't have seen enough anyway); I just figured it might be good for Clark Minds to believe that no shadowy figures had been up the stairs in the time of his absence. It might help him be rational.

"No one," I therefore said to him, as soon as he got back.

Clark Minds left but returned minutes later and stared at me from the other side of the room.

I was busy at the time. I was tending shop by myself and couldn't help him. Customers noticed the cold and meaningful stare that was being directed at me by the short and wrong-looking man. It was embarrassing.

I went around the counter after everyone left. "Listen, Clark, you can't do that," I told him.

Just then Thompson Leach returned, setting off bells. He glanced at the two of us standing there. He glanced at us again. To me he nodded, lifting his chin. To Clark he said, "Leaving?"

He went into the back room.

"You have to realize— " I started again, but Clark Minds wasn't listening.

"Chairs," he mouthed.

"Look, Clark—"

"Chairs."

I told Clark we could maybe finish the conversation later. More people had come in.

"So what was all that about?" Thompson Leach asked a while later. He was sorting some papers.

I just sighed.

He glanced at me, seemed to be waiting for more.

"Clark's demons," I told him.

"Ah."

When I told Clark Minds we could finish our conversation later, I meant outside of the shop. And I said that. I told him I'd stop by his place after work.

Of course I forgot.

He returned three days later. It was the type of mid-winter day I remember from that time. Lunar and still. Outside, you couldn't hear much but the squeak of your steps in packed snow. The sound traveled your bones.

Clark made for his box. He 'trudged,' I'd have to say. He leaned forward. He didn't look at us, or stop to pull back his hood. He just went to his box and looked inside and turned and went back out.

A few of us were on at the time—me and Nina, Thompson Leach. Nobody spoke.

For me personally, the end of this story arrived without warning. I ran out to the street one white evening, having locked myself out of my place. My cell had run down, and I was thinking about phone booths, wondering if maybe I'd seen one nearby. But I had some good fortune: Thompson Leach had worked late. He was just leaving. I asked to use the shop phone. When I said who I was calling—Troy Nagurney—and said why, he showed me the keys on his ring. He shook them. "Got you covered," he said.

I invited Thompson Leach in.

It was warm in my apartment. I opened the front windows. Heat from the iron radiator buckled our lamplit view of the snow.

"Beer or something?" I asked my guest.

"Beer?" he responded. "Sure." He'd found my guitar.

When I returned, he was playing it. I could see that his technique was good, clearly a lot better than mine.

"Do you know Tara Johnson?" he asked.

"Tara Johnson," I said. "Does she live over that big laundry place?"

He said, "Yeah."

"I know who she is."

Thompson Leach was still smiling in reference to Tara Johnson. But since I wasn't personally acquainted with her—so he seemed to decide—there was no point in going on.

He kept playing. He played the first part of Nirvana's "Polly." It was a pretty good imitation.

After a while I got tired of watching him. I brought up Clark Minds, asked what he made of that whole situation. I expected to see his face crease with intolerance, I suppose. Instead he giggled.

I blinked up.

He stopped playing. "Things move around every time Clark goes out," he said softly.

I wish I could get you to see the exact look in his eyes. The pure and tender light. The warm press of sustaining vision. He seemed on the verge of telling me something huge, a thing that might change the whole tone of our relationship as manager and clerk. He seemed to be waiting, looking for some small sign, some gesture of affinity between us. On instinct, I withheld it.

I went over to see Clark Minds not long after Thompson Leach left. Whatever suspicions I may have been having by then, I was totally shocked.

Every chair in the room had been set on its side or turned over. Clean dishes—saucers and cups—had been placed here and there on the floor. A framed picture hung sideways. A big oriental rug bellied down from the ceiling, to which it had been nailed.

Clark sat on a table. He stared at me much as he had a week earlier, the last time we'd spoken. He looked terrible. He looked righteous.

"Clark," I said. "Clark. You're being fucked with, Clark."

I waited before telling him though.

I looked at the saucers and cake plates and such, which seemed to have been spaced in such a way as to carry mysterious meaning. I looked at the chairs. I wondered at Thompson Leach, at his care, at the profound understanding of Clark Minds so evident in his project of loathing.

But I hesitated for a different reason. I hesitated in order to thrill at the specific small weight of this moment in my life.

I'd have to find a new job. I'd have to find a new apartment.

I looked out at the flying snow.

What choice was there? It was time.

Richard McNally

The Rooming House

That was the night I told Dora I felt people were walking all over me, that I was more a thing than a person, that Cavalcanti, with his torn shoes and straitjacket pessimism and fifty-nine varieties of mindsores was dubious company at best, that the Tschissiks were out to get me, to abuse me, to bang me around till most of my inner mechanisms were broken and smashed and worthless, and that ... whatever ... something else, I would go on and on with her. He's one of those people you feel the need to say not something to but everything. We had been discussing a remake of the Hitchcock film about the Canadian who visits England and is hunted by secret agents who mistakenly believe he has intercepted a classified communiqué from abroad, and by British police who mistakenly believe he has committed a murder, nowhere to run to baby, nowhere to hide. "I can see you're in a difficult situation," she says in a kind tone as we walk through Central Square, clasping her pocketbook to her side like a deflated football, the November wind blowing her hair forward, 'but try to think of it as a stepping stone to something better."

Mrs Tschissik is sitting in her bedroom in an easy chair with nailhead trim praying to a framed newspaper photograph of the Virgin Mary standing on a globe with her right foot resting on the head of a serpent, the lower edge rippled and discolored, suggesting something had been spilled on it before it was framed. The photo sits on a small elliptical table beside her chair. The door behind her is secured by a chain lock, a padlocked hasp, two inter-grip rim locks, and a circa 1930 police lock, its steel bar angled against the center of the door, a dead bolt implied by the face of a cylinder set in the rectangular brass plate from which the doorknob projects. A lamp with a porcelain-urn base and a shirred drum shade stands on a chest of drawers behind her and illuminates pinch-pleated drapes in a tea-rose pattern; a triple dresser against the wall to her left bearing a tiny stone vase filled with dried flowers and a black-framed photo of a young man in a military uniform, his smile constrained, his eyes empty, the background a zoo out of focus, or possibly the interior of a bank; and a double bed with a carved wooden headboard surmounted by a triangular pediment, the pediment having two deep teardrop notches near the apex on either side of a fluted central shaft with a tapered point that, in an emergency, could do service as a wooden stake for plunging into the heart of a vampire weighing anywhere from 250 to 400 pounds, if one believed in such things.

Nothing like the sight of an open grave to set one's heart to pounding, pounding.

The conversation in the Cantab Lounge was a runny mass of halftruths and intemperate speculation and malicious gossip. Blame Cavalcanti, a starved-looking courier with gravedigger eyes I met in jack's the night Pandora opened for Cri de Coeur. On the way home he said: "I feel like something is squeezing my rocks till I'm blue in the face." I tell him that in Christian iconography, rocks are often associated with the practice of stoning to death those who had committed unforgivable sins, especially blasphemy.

Mrs Tschissik. is down on her hands and knees in the front yard rooting around in the garden. Sunlight creates a tiny white scab on the tip of her nose. (Cavalcanti: "Mrs Tschissik is not so much a woman as a garbage can with a bow on it.") She has often thrown me down the basement stairs and I resent it. One day as I'm lying on my back at the bottom rubbing my elbow, the cement floor beneath me cold as a slab in a morgue, my legs extending up the staircase on a diagonal, she comes down and steps on me. As her foot comes down on my chest I say, "I oppose this." She looks down at me and says nothing, her face rigid, her breathing labored.

Holding on to the handrail, she brings her other foot up and I get the benefit of her full weight. "I unequivocally oppose what you're doing to me." She continues looking down at me, saying nothing, then goes up on her toes and, with the smile of a copulating rat, comes down on her heels, hard. A flame ignites beneath the lower right side of my ribcage. She is crushing and abusing me not out of hostility or vengeance or a mindless will to destroy but only because it is her nature, her destiny, her preordained role in the scheme of things, or I'm greatly mistaken. "Are you trying to offend me Mrs Tschissik, or is it happening by accident?" My intention had been to spend the day doing good deeds, or some reasonable approximation, but there I was sidetracked, detained, derailed. She reminds one of a _____. I tell her that standing on me is uncivil, that it gives me a poor impression of her upbringing, that it irrefutably violates state and local statutes governing landlord-tenant relations, and that it is unwarranted since I'm only three months behind. Here she belches and a moment later, the smell of carrion spreading through the air, my mind is filled with a vision of dead kittens lying in a heap-who did she think she was, my stepmother? My thoughts start going in and out of focus-a family in China plays monopoly on a board with a jail in each corner; in Jersey City some kids are shooting baskets on an asphalt-paved playground, the rim netless, the rusting steel backboard pierced by three holes clean on the side with the rim, jagged on the back, irregular pointed slivers curving backward from the edges; in Eurasia the winds blow and blow and blow; in Lockerbie tiny flakes of paper from a disintegrating page of Leiter's *Modern Economics* are blown against a large rock the shape of a dented oil drum; in history, most facts remain the same; in a manner of speaking, the servants study a language they will have little occasion to use, Servant A saying: "*Nipo hapa kwa likizo*," to which Servant B replies: "*Nitapima homa yako*"; in Havana, Castro, reading a novel by Burt Lancaster, looks up for a moment, tugs gently at his beard, gets up and goes to the window, looks out at the ocean, decides to build a zoo in Las Palmas People's Park that will contain snakes only. The flame beneath the lower right side of my ribcage is getting hotter so I say to Mrs Tschissik: "Sharing is better than hogging." She farts, twice.

It was time to move. I would find a new room, no matter where, the end of the earth, what's the difference, no matter that Dora had said: "Intensity is an unreliable indicator of value. You're thirty-seven, you should know that," and swart-skinned Jean Laughton, the day we were playing chess in the park in front of Rindge: "The point of law courts, honey, is to turn one's subjective pain into objective gain," and Cavalcanti as we stood throwing stones into the Charles: "Better to shake one's head in disbelief at the disgrace of homelessness than to participate in it." Screw it, I was determined to just get up and go, how hard could it be to find a rented room?

A woman very similar to Mrs Tschissik, almost identical to her actually, or at least not unmistakably unlike her, and by no means her absolute and incontestable contrary, comes home after having had the accelerator of her VW bus adjusted at Flynn's Autobody and says to her dog-tired, dog-eared husband, if I'm not mistaken, or at any rate to the flat-faced man sitting on the corduroy sofa in her living room with his feet resting on the Globe on the coffee table: "I passed Moss on the stairs to the basement this afternoon and we brushed shoulders." "Is that right? Did he say anything?" "He mumbled something but I wasn't able to catch it." "Son-of-a Bitch," says the flat-faced man, or words to that effect, unless what she said was: "I haven't seen Moss lately, have you?" to which he would (probably) have responded, "How many months behind is that son-of-a-bitch now?" On the other hand, if what she said was: "I passed Moss on my way down to the laundry room today and felt an impulse to bump into him and knock him down the stairs," her husband, if he said anything at all, would have asked her if she wanted to go out to eat, or to a movie, or both; under no circumstances would he have asked her if she wanted to go shopping at

Lord & Taylor's for, if the documentation on this point is reliable, she was an unswerving customer of Filene's Basement, or some such place.

I decided not to move. I would simply do my laundry elsewhere, why should I allow some bumptious misbegotten rag of a landlady to run my life, dictate where I lived, because if it's true, as Cavalcanti said the other night in the Oxford Ale House as we were sitting at the bar drinking Virgin Marys, his head half its normal size, steam rising from his scalp, several arrows with blueblack feathers sticking in his back: "What we love most is our unending dream oflove," I was still intact, I still had options, no matter that he (Cavalcanti) was an admitted logothete working, at age thirty-seven, as a bicycle courier, his father having been a taxi driver. 'We're all copies of copies," he said one day last fall as we were walking along Mass. Ave. toward the Square discussing our families, "and if we fail to acknowledge it, fail to realize that at some point we must shred and discard our entire history, the road to uniqueness will be permanently closed." He said he wanted to stop in at Copy Quik and when I asked him what he was going to have reproduced, he said: "Nothing." Then why go in? "To soak up the atmosphere for a moment or two. Among massive machines continually reproducing yet adding nothing to the world but redundancy, I'm in my element."

I would move out after all. You can build your house out of toilet paper if you want to, but it's not going to keep out the rain, as N. O. Ting (or was it M. LeClerc?) may have been suggesting when he said that since language and thought have evolved in a three-dimensional world, we find it extremely hard to deal with the four-dimensional reality of moral grandeur. To move or not to move, it's an old question.

The fire spreads quickly. Within minutes after arriving the firefighters shift their efforts to preventing the surrounding houses from catching.

I put my coat on and go out. Standing, leaning against a cast-iron street lamp on the opposite side of the street, I look back at the Tschissiks' white clapboard, flat-topped, three-story rooming house, houses invariably associated with the word "story," as conte is with a certain 'box" (as in knock, knock, knockin' on heaven's door) for the simple reason that when we are confined within a physical structure of non infinite dimensions with another human being, or beings, the entire history of Western pseudo-philosophy, minus the footnotes, is inevitably reenacted, intellectual ontogeny recapitulating intellectual phylogeny in a morality play of anywhere from 250 to 400 (or more) acts, for though our will is unlimited, driving us toward ever more grandiose acts of psychological colonialism, our intelligence is not, regardless of our social standing, country of origin, or hairstyle. So I'm leaning against this street lamp looking at a rooming house, the Tschissiks'. It is early morning. Or a rooming house in every way similar to the Tschissiks', since I may have gone for a walk, as I often do, for one of the unbending rules in this world of hurt, as I have discovered through vicious experience, is that one is not permitted to stay in a single place for an unlimited period of time. It is late afternoon. Without looking up I sense the sky is cloudless. Blue skies, nothin but blue skies, over me-ee. I look up. A cloud the shape of a white porcelain object is stalled in the sky above the rooming house. It is the size of Yankee Stadium. Though it appears as if it will never move, I know it will, inevitably, and as for those who ask why Manhattan is the shape of a turd, I can only say this-geography is often destiny.

Mrs Tschissik bangs into me and knocks me off balance as I'm coming up the basement stairs. As I fall backwards I drop my clothes, twist my body, try to break my fall with my hands. I land on my side, slide to the bottom. A hard, gem-like flame ignites in my left wrist. Mrs Tschissik.' s feet whomp down the stairs and shestarts kicking me in the ribs and though it hurts, I feel a kind of grim relief that she is not kicking me in the head. Small spurts of flame erupt at various sites on my ribcage. "Unh!" she grunts as she delivers each blow. "Unh! Unh!" But the relief I feel is like a phone call from a friend on a Sunday afternoon when one is glowing with non-specific anxiety, a state of suffering that a certain philosopher regards as subconscious fear of death because whenever someone asks us what's bothering us in the midst of an attack like this we invariably respond: "Nothing," which this celebrated thinker takes as an unintentional but revealing reference to the nothingness into which he believes we descend, or ascend, when we die (don't fall for it)-but the guy is a freaking documented Nazi so the hell with what he says. Mrs Tschissik clearly has no intention of killing me because if she did she would be kicking me in the head, directly in the temple, I'm certain of this, or she would have a handgun and be firing at my vital organs, the bullets entering my body like small cylindrical projectiles of drop-forged self-doubt, foam running out the corner of my mouth, my limbs twitching, head jerking from side to side. I start sliding into a state of shock and just before I lose consciousness it comes to me that life is one long fight against the urge to stay in bed all day that in the end we always lose.

This story takes place on the squared circle referred to as "the earth." (Cf. M. LeClerc's Infrastructure of the Intangible: "The fundamental principle of the universe is not to gratify my volition, therefore life is absurd.") This is the context, therefore let her step on me, it's all MOTS anyway, no matter what she does or doesn't, who am I to object to someone knocking me down the stairs or standing on my chest or kicking me in the ribs? Who am I to make a bold effort to get out from under Mrs Tschissik.' s feet, to protect my "inalienable dignity" as a human being? Forget it. I'm just some guy, some schmo struggling to keep his head above the waves like everybody else and if a house is on fire across the street, no matter how high the flames-that's MOTS, as in More Of The Same.

At this point we're something like friends, the Tschissiks and I, or a couple that resembles them to a hair. Very few of our problems reach the point where we feel compelled to engage in physical violence and within twenty-five to thirty thousand years other rooming houses may exist in a similar state of calm for political evolution, which infiltrates, and some would say governs, all interpersonal relations, occurs at approximately the same pace as biological evolution, unless I'm greatly mistaken, so if you're in the process of wearing your life out trying to speed things up, think again amigo, think again.

The last time I saw Cavalcanti was this past january in Cardell's, or somewhere very like it, a mirror image, a simulacrum in all respects the equal, or near-equal, of the original, down to the sawdust on the floor and the stamped tin ceiling and the scowling waitress with the thread-like limbs and mannish eyeglasses (forever on the verge of sliding off the tip of her nose) muttering curses at the patrons as she clears the dirty dishes from the tables and loads them on her cart, unless it was the Mug and Muffin, or possibly the Wursthaus, his favorite hash house in the Square, in which case the muttering waitress was not present, could not be present. He motioned to me to sit down. I came over and stood next to him. He was wearing clothesline suspenders and had some nasty shaving cuts on his neck, calling to mind a _____. He said he was going to apply for a bank loan so he could open his own courier service and asked if I would co-sign it. I said sure, provided he agreed to pay all his employees the same wage as himself, and required them to wear black capes lined with lemon satin.

I'm in a sleeping bag on the Common. I feel something nudging my side and open my eyes. It's Jean Laughton standing over me, waking me with her toe. She says Aren't you afraid someone will come along and step on you in the middle of the night? I say

How ... who told you I was here? She says Word gets around. I tell her that at the moment getting stepped on is the least of my worries. With an anxious smile she asks Can I help? The lower right side of each of her breasts is cupped by a crescent of shadow, her hair hangs lank, I can see up her nose. She asks What's in the garbage bags? I tell her they're not garbage bags, they're suitcases. With a sorrowful smile she says What can I do? I ask her if she happens to have a shovel on her.

From my coign of vantage across the street, leaning against a rusted streetlamp on a conical cast-iron base embossed with ... whatever ... that stuff in the labyrinth ... I watch the rays of the late afternoon sun highlight what appear to be padlocks holding the shutters of the third-story windows closed. Looking more closely I can see what appears to be a sheaf of papers sticking out from between the shutters of the window on the far left.

Valerie Vogrin

Conversations With My Landlord

He's curbside when I step out of the cab that evening.

"My God, are you alright?"

The other tenants have filled the landlord in on the afternoon's drama: lights flashing, portly police officers and peach-cheeked paramedics tramping up and down the stairs.

He escorts me into his apartment and settles me into a leaf-green corduroy chair. He presents me with a royal blue raw silk pillow on which to rest my throbbing hand. He serves shrimp dumplings and goblets of velvety Chenin Blanc. I admire the way the soft black hairs on his arm lay flat. The dumplings are tangy with cilantro and ginger.

"I'm waiting on you hand and foot," he announces, refilling my glass, building a fire.

I lean toward the flames. Every sterile surface in the emergency room, even the hands of the surgeon, had been so cold.

The room smells of burning wood and lemon oil and great aunts playing Canasta. Except for this one chair in front of the fireplace, the room seems arranged for storage rather than living, like a halfway house for chifforobes and ottomans and davenports and desks. He swerves through the narrow corridors of furniture, pivoting on the balls of his stockinged feet.

"Here, I've brought you a brandy."

"Thank you, Howard." I swallow another pain pill. I try not to stare at an ink spot on his bottom lip. I feel my bones soften. I am both fooled and not fooled by his chivalric gig, an impersonation abetted by the alcohol/ Percocet mix. He fetches me another blanket. The throbbing in my hand recedes. I pluck three small white feathers from the pillow, their thorny stems protruding from the coarse weave of the silk.

"I'm going to have to keep an eye on you," he says. "Make sure you stay out of harm's way."

I fight back a giggle.

"Sleep here tonight," he says. "In case you need anything."

His sheets are crisp, the shade of the palest yellow rose petals you can imagine—sheets from a Henry James novel.

"What do you do?" I ask.

He slept elsewhere, on one of the couches presumably. Now he stands watching me eat Eggs Benedict in his bed.

"This," he proclaims. "This is what I do," his outstretched arms indicating the eight apartments, basement, and roof of his fiefdom.

"Oh."

His lips tighten. "Quite an appetite," he says.

"I like eggs."

"I knew it."

My head is filled with brandy-soaked cotton and the eggs have settled like a wet rag in the bottom of my stomach. As I trudge past #3 the door swings open. A thin white arm and a blue hand emerge, beckon.

The woman to whom the arm belongs is talking on the phone. She grabs my sleeve, tugs me toward the kitchen. She covers the mouthpiece.

"You're the new neighbor," she says. "Sit." Into the phone she says, "Hey, I've got to go. My neighbor stopped by—the one who got her finger whacked off in the window." She shudders. "Bye-bye." She has voluminous fluffy white hair.

The kitchen's aromas are gingerbread and melted candle wax. Two large pots boil and hiss on the stove. The windows are beaded with steam. She takes in the sorry sight of me and my blood-spattered, slept-in clothes and shakes her head, grabs a teakettle from the counter.

"It's only the tip," I explain.

"Pardon?"

"Only the tip of my finger got caught in the window."

The woman steps toward the back of the apartment. "Alara! Company!"

A fluffy-white-haired girl materializes, cracks open the window, and balances herself primly on the edge of one of the kitchen chairs.

"This is Alara, she's nine. I'm Annie. And you're Frances. Tell us about yourself."

The word *torment* comes to mind. There are so many ways I feel not well. Fortunately, at just the moment it will become necessary to lie or confess or flee, the kettle begins to sing—a loud sweet pure tone—and Annie is moved to provide me the story of this splendid kettle and her blue hands and a not-so condensed history of batik and the politics of Indonesia. She serves me cup after cup of the most bitter tea and perfectly crisp wolf-shaped gingerbread cookies and all the while water spatters and sizzles on the stovetop. The girl, Alara, draws asterisks in the steamed windows.

The kitchen clock chirps noon. "Oh my goodness, I've got to check my dye bath. Excuse me, will you, Frances?"

My deliverance, I think. "I really should be going. I need to change my bandage and—"

"Of course you do. I'm so glad you stopped by. This is a very friendly building. Nice people. With the exception of him down there." She points toward Howard's apartment. "Mr. Ratfink."

When I get upstairs there's a note taped to my door. A soft pencil scrawl on the back of an electric company envelope. WHAT DO YOU DO?!!

The moving boxes are stacked in squared towers. My father had the boxes delivered to the bungalow, along with packing tape and a jumbo black permanent marker. Message received: I wasn't to be trusted with even the most mundane matters.

But now I am happy I didn't have to drive all over town and make do with a motley assortment of liquor and grocery store boxes, and I am especially happy at the sight of the box labeled BEDDING. I take the last Percocet from the hospital envelope, lay down on my bare mattress, and pull my purple velvet comforter over my head. When I wake it is four o'clock the next morning.

"I've got a crab quiche in the oven." He's let a day and a half pass since breakfast in bed. "Why don't you come down and join me?"

He sets the table. We watch the quiche cool.

"So how's your finger?" His voice sing-songs.

"They refer to it as a partial amputation."

The dark spot is still there on his lip. As he hands me the plate I realize it's a beauty mark. He touches his lip, rubs his palm over his unshaved chin.

His phone rings. His side of the conversation consists of the word "no" repeated six times in the same even tone. He hangs up and rubs his chin again. I am a slow eater. His face is whiskered, harried. He sips coffee from a blue metal camping cup. For a second I see him as a Confederate colonel, a few months after Pickett's Charge, determined, yet pensive.

"Can I get you anything?"

"How about fixing the window?"

"My window guy's in the Virgin Islands."

"There's only one window guy?"

"Only one I trust. Most of these guys are villains."

"Still, I'd like to be able to open both windows. When I turn on the heat in there it smells like cat piss. That carpet is disgusting."

"Louis didn't have a cat."

"Someone had a cat—many, many cats is my guess."

"You know I'm sorry this happened to you, right? But I can't fix a problem unless I know there's a problem. And Louis indicated that he never opened the window."

"Indicated? What did he use—signal flags?"

"Look. Maybe I could cut a piece of wood to prop that top window in place—until my guy gets back."

"The interesting part of that sentence is the word maybe."

"You've got a sassy mouth, Frances."

Sassy?

My Rio Grande spinning wheel dominates my front room. Smooth oak shelves hold my store of yarn, divided by color and then by weight. I am heavy on greens and worsted wools.

For ten years I was designing or spinning or knitting—garments or swatches, trying out a new cable stitch, experimenting with an unfamiliar yarn blend. I worked at The Bee's Knees Knitting Shop. I helped customers select yarn for their projects. I sat with my charges, guiding their fingers through increases and decreases and buttonholes and collars. I ran mitten workshops. I sold a half-dozen intarsia designs to a yarn company in Maine. Beatrice, the shop owner, inching toward retirement, promised she'd give me very easy terms. "My dear," she said. "The most important thing is that the shop stays in good hands."

Now that I am finished unpacking, the room is hushed and inert as a museum exhibit; I can imagine tourists filing through, a security guard snapping his gum in the corner behind the rocking chair. Artisan's Studio, United States, 2000.

"Guess what I've got in the oven?" Howard asks.

It's a Gruyere soufflé. It's sublime.

I run into Annie a block from home. I'm swinging a small grocery bag in my good hand and she's embracing a colossal laundry bag. She gives me a sizing up look.

"Alara and I have been worried about you."

And here I'd been thinking of myself as Miss Valiant in the Face of Disaster, my clearheaded competence apparent at 40 paces.

On the second floor landing Howard crouches at the not quite

90-degree corner. A thick wad of keys hang from his belt. He appears to be inspecting the floorboard. "Ladies." He nods as we pass.

"That one," Annie says, when she stops at her door. "The Real Estate Baron of Ft. Greene. The Sheik of Vanderbilt Avenue."

"What do you mean?"

"Pah! He thinks he's riding the crest of the wave, a real gentrification genius."

"I don't know one thing about real estate," I say.

"Well look at DeKalb. Suddenly awash in bistros for God's sake. Maybe you haven't noticed yet, but he's practically filled this building with women, and the whole bunch of us just happen to work from home. He's always sniffing around, either underfoot like today or making some half-assed repair."

"Is Alara's school nearby?"

"He doesn't deserve this building, that's for sure."

"Maybe he did something really good in a previous life."

"That one? You're kidding, right?"

Two bony fingertips tighten around my nipple like staple removers. "You're not going to sue me?" The question mark is an afterthought.

"I wouldn't be suing you, I'd be suing your insurance company."

"Not that I'm concerned. You have no case."

"Then what are you talking about?"

Howard presses his ear to my stomach as though listening for the answer. "I'm going to do something about that window this week," he says without lifting his head. "It's still very cold out, you know."

"Yes, well, fresh air doesn't go out of season."

"Listen, Frances, I've only got two hands."

"Lucky you."

We both look at my injured hand. In its white bundle of gauze it is something set aside.

"How long did Louis live in the apartment?"

"Two years."

"And why'd he give it up?"

"Left town? Graduate school? We're not in touch."

Why do I sleep with Howard?

Because it's easier to sleep with him than to not.

Why do I sleep with him?

Because I won't mistake him for anything he isn't, i.e. loyal, trustworthy.

Howard's insurance company has not balked at paying the hospital bills and the charges for my ongoing hand clinic visits; I've been reimbursed for my out-of-pocket expenses. Which leaves only that dubious X-factor, pain and suffering, the domain of lawyers. After my recent experience—was it really only two months ago?—it's not a realm I'm in a hurry to reenter.

After the first ten minutes of the first meeting I stopped looking at their faces, smug with what they thought they knew about me. The one female attorney wore weapon-sharp pumps; she had pairs in taupe, black, and navy blue. One of the men wore heavy gold cuff links that thunked against the edge of the conference table when he rearranged his papers. I can't remember which lawyer was mine and which one was Joachim's, but Cuff Links had to be my father's because he was in charge.

Not that anyone asked, but I could never smoke dope and knit. One hit and pattern charts wobbled like op art. Days later I'd still struggle to keep a twelve-stitch repetition in my head. Joachim bought enough for his own mild-to-moderate use, and for his friends who sometimes gave him cash and sometimes didn't, and his boss, Roy, who overlooked his chronic laziness and tardiness. And then one afternoon I looked up from my wheel and there were these people in our bungalow, friends of friends. If he ran some errands for them, did this and that, he'd be able to take the winter off from his fingers-freezing job harvesting shellfish for Roy—how he explained it to me. Joachim with the cold hands, Joachim who longed so for hibernation that he stumbled into a drug ring, into the final months of a years-long investigation.

Joachim had no money for lawyers. That's why he implicated me. To get my father and his legal cronies and his money involved. That conference room full of lawyers was exactly what Joachim had expected. And did he expect the rest? Did he picture himself in a federal prison waiting indefinitely for his chance to testify? (Surely he didn't think my father would cover his bail?) Did he picture me, boxed up and exiled— "The best thing for everybody," my father said.

This—I extend my arms, indicating the apartment, Brooklyn, all my worldly goods—exactly everything and nothing—is my fresh start.

Howard's body looks to have been solid maybe ten years ago. He wears his softness well. His skin is pulled tight and white. After showering he slaps on handfuls of cocoa butter lotion; he greases his penis and scrotum with Vaseline. He's sleek as a seal.

Still naked, he irons his pants and shirt. (The local dry cleaners are crooks, he says.) He uses spray starch to ensure the sharpest creases.

"I know you think I'm crazy," he says.

"What? I'm just watching you."

The creases, I know, are essential to his heroic persona. A hero holding the line against the infidels—contractors, assessors, inspectors, tenants.

He looks up from his shirt. "Everything I do, I do for a reason."

"What are you now, a mafia don?"

He slams the iron to the fabric.

My upstairs neighbor plays the ukulele. According to the mailbox he is Hank Mallory, the only male tenant. I don't recognize the tunes he plays—I know nothing much about the ukulele—but the music seems impossibly mournful. Or perhaps I hear it as mournful because his playing is punctuated by fits of feverish weeping. His ukulele-playing chair sits directly above my knitting chair, an old cherry rocker that first belonged to my mother's mother. Though I am not knitting, it's where I most often choose to sit. I would have thought that the uke wasn't a suitable instrument for expressing grief, but plucked by Hank its voice is a vibrato keening that makes my ribs ache.

On the lamp beside Howard's bed a thick brown lampshade traps most of the light from a 40-watt bulb.

"You know I've got another building, a few blocks over near Pratt."

"Really?"

"Well, I've got a partner. I'd like to buy him out—he'd double-cross me in a second if I gave him the chance—but I've got to sit tight right now. I've got my eye on some sweet properties." He grabs my arm. "Am I boring you?"

"No."

"Know this, Frances, I'm ready to act when the time is right."

He fucks like he walks, with a heavy lumbering grace. With each thrust he gains momentum. I must fuck back or be buried.

I like my apartment. This apartment is what I have now. The building contains me, holds my shape.

Here's the thing: I don't have a copy of my lease.

The lease: a fingers-crossed promise waiting to be broken. The Tenant agrees to pay through the nose and anus and abide by any and all house rules whether promulgated before or after the execution in a workmanlike manner during occupancy thereof until either party shall terminate the same without prior consent at reasonable and regular intervals for any illegal purpose and other pests at the initiation of the tenancy. The lease is a slipknot or not.

Still, it's something, a thing to be had.

The day before I moved in, the day before the window accident, I sat at Howard's kitchen table, drank a cup of coffee, and signed the lease, watched him sign. He told me he would make copies the following day at the drugstore around the corner. It is a two-year lease.

I ask Howard about the lease.

He feeds me a strawberry, slides the cool red fruit between my lips. "What are you worried about, sweetheart?"

My father would not have handed over the check without the copy of the lease. Am I as incompetent as he believes I am?

"Kira and Jean and I are having a pot of tea. Why don't you come down?" Annie asks.

Alara peeks past me into the apartment. "Is all that yarn yours?"

"I was just about to take a nap. It's really not a good time. Thanks for thinking of me."

Alara leans further into the room. "And a spinning wheel. Cool. What's it all for?"

"Kira's one of the best tattoo artists in the city and Jean's a potter. They're really eager to meet you."

"Another time."

"You're doing okay up here? Really?"

"I'm doing well." Alara is tugging at my sleeve. "It's for knitting. I'm a knitter."

"Will you teach me how ?" Alara asks.

"Alara, let's head back before the tea gets cold."

"I can't knit right now," I say, waving my thickly bandaged hand.

"You don't have to be able to knit to teach me, do you?"

I listen to their steps on the stairs, the click of their apartment door closing. I can almost hear the women laughing, their teaspoons clinking in their cups. The building is like an unopened parcel waiting on the table.

While we sleep the building settles another quarter inch on the starboard side. My door sticks and I bruise my shoulder shoving it open. He kisses the bruise tenderly. He shaves down the door. He demonstrates. "See? Open. Close. Open." And it's true—the door swings easily on its hinges. Neither of us mentions the finger's breadth gap between door and floor. In a fit of generosity he installs mini-blinds in the two skinny windows in the hallway between the kitchen and the bedroom; they are too narrow by an inch and their hold in the wall is as sturdy as a loose tooth.

My walls are weeping. I pull my shelves of yarn away from the wall, revealing elaborate gray-green plumes of mildew.

I vacuum the rug, I attack it with a stiff bristled scrub brush, but the problem is subsurface. The animal hair has been ground into the fibers. Crossing the room in my bare feet is like walking across the back of a large furred beast.

Even as I start the project I know it's folly. This isn't a one-handed job and my only tool is the utility knife my father included in my moving kit. I yank up a corner from the tacks, then begin hacking the carpet into six-inch strips, sawing through the grisly layer of backing, working backwards across the room. The painted white wood beneath the carpet spurs me on. After two strips my bandage is gray and dotted with blood. The blade has dulled. My hand hurts and my throat burns and my nose runs but I don't stop. Even when I finish eight hours later I'm not done because I still have to get the whole stinking mess downstairs. I roll the strips as tightly as I can and bind them with twine. I gather an armful of bundles and head down. Hank is playing a somewhat happier tune and as I'm about to pass Howard's apartment I think perfect and dump the bundles on his doormat and head up for the rest, but when I reach my door I can only bang my head against it in frustration. Locked out, but how? The door has never locked automatically.

I wait for Howard on the landing above his apartment. It sounds like a polka, what Hank is playing tonight. The hallway smells of bacon and sautéed garlic and PineSol. From above and below I hear cupboards and refrigerator doors being shut and chairs pushed in and pulled out from the dinner table. I can almost hear the clatter of fork to plate. Dishwater whooshes through the pipes.

My mother died when I was five. My father, Mr. What's-Done-Is-Done, including the death of a spouse, rarely spoke of her. And now it's me he's done with. "Consider this bridge burned," he said, handing me an envelope containing a plane ticket and a sizeable cashier's check. For family I am left with a spinster great aunt, Aunt Helen. She was the one who told me my mother knitted. Aunt Helen and I bellow at each other during our first Sunday of every month calls. I have kept her in turtlenecks and cardigans since I was a teenager. A veteran of fifty St. Paul winters, she appreciates the virtues of woolens. It is best when we are matched with people who appreciate our gifts.

"Your father tells me you've had some troubles," she opened our last conversation.

"What did he—"

"You know what I've always said, Frances. There are no troubles that can't be walked away. Look at Gandhi, look at Jesus, Eleanor Roosevelt!"

"Eleanor Roosevelt was a walker?"

"Absolutely. It's my very best advice. Are you working?"

"I've hurt my finger. I'm not sure—"

"Well I'm glad you're alright, dear. And don't forget about the walking. Love you." Click.

And so I walk. Most often I head straight up Vanderbilt, which leads me straight out of our little bit of downtroddeness and through the wee pocket of bistro-mad gentrification Annie spoke of, past a lovely yellow saltbox house, the French-speaking Baptist church, a shabby pharmacy, Our Queen of All Saints, a florist with dusty plastic flowers in the window, numerous bodegas and service stations and car services and coffee shops, until without quite noticing how I got there I reach the bustling climax of Grand Army Plaza.

"Hey, guess what?" Howard asks. "I got a deal on some of those fancy water-saving shower nozzles. I could run up later and install it."

Our game continues: legitimate landlord business is the only occasion for which I admit Howard into my apartment.

Howard brews a fine pot of coffee. His half and half is absolutely fresh. He has almond-orange biscotti for me to nibble on as I wait for my eggs.

"It isn't something I could do on my own?" I ask.

"Well, I was thinking of your hand and all."

"Since when?"

"I would have helped you with the carpet."

"You denied it even needed cleaning!"

"But I said it was fine with me if you wanted to remove it."

"And where in that was your offer of assistance?"

"It was implied."

"Anyway, you've helped enough for one week—changing that doohickey on my lock."

"I told you I was sorry."

"Fine. Have you had a chance to make a copy of my lease?"

"I thought I gave you that."

He hands me a plate: toast, dry and fried eggs, broken, golden yolk smeared across the whites.

The paramedics said I was lucky the window didn't catch my whole hand. The first doc who examined me at Bellevue said I was lucky the paramedics hadn't dropped me off at Brooklyn Hospital, where for sure they'd have amputated at the knuckle. And everyone at the hospital said how lucky I was to have "Lizzie." Dr. Elizabeth Gardner headed the team of three hand surgeons who were summoned to the emergency room on my behalf. She began by repairing the nail bed. This alone took almost an hour and a half. Three times she removed a stitch, a 1/16" em-dash of gut, that she judged imperfect. Both then and now (regardless of whether my fingernail grows back, regardless of luck) I experience her fierce and substantial attention as love.

I've been knitting in my sleep. I awaken in the dark with my hands in the air. Some mornings my wrists ache.

Howard is mincing garlic and I am searching his desk drawers.

"Frances," he calls from the kitchen. "You like Portobellos don't you?" The second drawer squeaks open.

"Love them," I holler back. The drawers are a hodgepodge of envelopes, marbles, rubber bands, coins, subway tokens, a pair of glasses with severely scratched lenses, dirty pink erasers—the debris of an adolescent boy. Why am I disappointed? Was I expecting a contract with the devil? Evidence of some nefarious dealings with Louis? I head over to the metal desk with a file drawer. How about a simple file folder labeled Tenant Leases? I look under T and L and under my name, first and last, and of course there's nothing incriminating but nothing lease-like either.

"It's getting lonely back here!" His voice is closer with each word. I ease the drawer shut.

Alara is sitting with her back against my door. A schoolbook is open on her plaid-skirted lap.

"I think it's time to start my knitting lessons."

I can't think of what to say.

"I could come in the afternoons after school."

"Did your mom send you up here?"

"No she did not."

"Why do you want to learn how to knit?"

"I like the smell of wet mittens."

He's stabbing at a block of frozen hash browns in a cast iron skillet.

"I'm your first friend in New York," Howard boasts.

"I suppose." What a coup, I think, I'm intimate with the only man in the city who has keys to my apartment.

He ceases his attack, looks at me. "What does that mean? I'm not your friend?"

"Goose," I say. "You're more than a friend."

Alara rummages through my knitting supplies. She likes reading the names of the yarn colors aloud: lamb's ear, sweet butter, appassionato, cactus flower, cricket. She covets my antique stitch counter, a jar filled with hand-carved tagua buttons from Ecuador.

As she sits down for her first lesson Hank begins a ukulele lament. Alara rolls her eyes.

"I feel kind of sorry for him, don't you?" I ask.

"I don't like feeling sorry for people." She gives me a sharp glance, as though I am about to do something pitiful. I try to block Hank out. I teach Alara the rhyme a Waldorf teacher taught me to help students remember the of movements required to make a knit stitch: in through the front door, run around the back, out through the window, and off jumps Jack.

The rhyme pleases her. We speak no more of Hank.

"This is easy," Alara says.

"We'll do purl tomorrow."

"Purl's harder?"

"It is."

"Excellent."

And I continue to sleep with him because?

Wrapped in a yellow bath sheet, handing me a plate of eggs scrambled with cream cheese and chives, he is held in abeyance—the landlord suspended like an insect in amber where he can do no harm.

He can't intrude on my loneliness: there are no doors there.

When he draws down the shades he distills himself. In the dim light, between his smooth sheets, he is nothing but fingers and eyes and penis and pleasure.

None of these reasons is more important than the others.

I have two trunks filled with unfinished garments. I finger the ribbed back of a pale green chenille jacket, the nubby sleeves of a seed stitched baby romper. I can't remember working on them, though I can see what would have attracted me to the projects. The green of the mohair yarn glows like a celadon glaze. Did the baby (whose baby?) grow too big for the romper? Those projects belong to Before. As in Before everything blew up I'd planned for my next project to be a sweater for Joachim. In the two birthdays we were together I gave him a red scarf and a deep maroon vest, edged in gold. He lost the scarf within a week, but he loved the vest. Casting the wrapping paper aside he announced, "I'll try it on," and when he pranced back into the kitchen area a few minutes later he was wearing nothing but the vest. He marched around our bungalow grinning. A happy, nearly naked man. He said he thought the vest made him look intelligent. File this under Exhibit A: Evidence of Domestic Bliss.

It was going to be a slipstitch pullover in shades of rich brown and creamy oatmeal knit in a three-strand Merino. Chest at underarm: 45-1/2". Length from shoulder: 26". Cast on 111 stitches to begin the back.

"Do you mind if I hang out in front of the fire?" I ask. "This chair is so cozy."

"I suppose," he says. "It's almost ready though."

All this furniture and so many cubbies and drawers. Begrudging drawers that long to screech and drawers with dull brass handles prone to clatter. Several are locked. I discover years of bank statements, two copies of his birth certificate (Mother, Dorothy, Father, Not Named) filed in separate files, clippings on investment strategies, receipts and coupons— haircuts to windshield repair.

If it's in one of the locked drawers I'll have to find the key. If the key is on his key ring I'll have to incapacitate him because he never lets his keys out of sight. He doesn't like having me out of sight either. Several times he's nearly caught me. "I dropped my ring," I say, kneeling in front of the roll-top desk.

Have I missed something? I return to the metal desk with the two locked drawers. I look again in the top drawer, overfilled with pens and pencils and binder clips.

"C'mon Frances. This frittata is piping!"

"I'm coming, I'm coming." Blood taps in the veins at my neck and temple. But hey, what's this tucked beneath the faded, doodled-on blotter? My lease.

I feel foolishly relieved. The lease is scant protection, outlining an uneven division of power. I've heard the stories. The lessee has the power to deface, to annoy, to vacate without notice, to foster tenant unrest, but the landlord can schedule an aria-singing window washing crew to start with your bedroom windows at 8 a.m. The landlord can hire a team of ill-mannered, tobacco-chewing thugs to replaster the ceilings. Tenant's organizations publish flyers advertising the renter's legal rights, but even they admit there are no ordinances that protect the tenant from the landlord's misery, miserliness, and mendacity.

I've hidden and rehidden the lease. For the moment it is guarded by a battalion of shoes, a neat paper roll tucked inside a pair of high black boots. The phone rings twenty rings at a time.

Howard stands at the top of the ladder on the second story landing like a broken marionette, the globe of the light fixture shattered on the floor beneath him. I remind myself not to mistake ineptitude for guilelessness. The glass shimmers like crushed seashells. He steps down hard. Crunch. Crunch. He grinds his work boots into the glass.

"I've tried calling you."

There's no way to know for sure if he knows I've got the lease.

"Have you been away?"

I wave my good hand vaguely. "Can I give you a hand?" I ask.

"You'll be home later," he says.

My wrists ache as I flip through my knitting binders, looking for an easy but not too easy pattern for Alara's first project.

Afternoons the sun streams through the back windows. The room is stark. Just a few boxes full of clothes that wouldn't fit in the closets. I don't have a dresser yet. From the bed I can see the paint of the windowsills puckered with moisture. I see the spatter of blood on the wall from when I first turned away from the window, a constellation of seven tiny drops. My bandage is much less bulky now. The finger still looks raw, but I can imagine its being healed. Six months, they tell me, before it will be what it will be. It only hurts badly if I bump it into something. The very tip burns in the cold.

The light shifts and I turn toward the window—Howard's hovering on the fire escape.

"What are you doing?" I shout.

He scowls and makes an undecipherable hand signal and clambers to the roof, as though I'd interrupted some legitimate business.

I burp eggs. "So is there a problem with the roof?"

He's got his back to me, rinsing off our lunch dishes in the sink.

"That roof is guaranteed for another eighteen years. I thought I might have left something up there."

He pauses, as if this isn't too absurd to refute.

He wipes down the counter. "This building is tight as a drum."

When I leave my apartment I stick a tiny piece of yarn in the door. I've mapped the exact placement of my throw rugs. There is never evidence of intrusion. And it never feels as though he's been there. So either Howard is very clever or I am ridiculous. Or he is clever and I am ridiculous, whether or not he's serreptiously entering my apartment. There are worse things to be.

"You've got to relax, Alara. You've got a death grip on that yarn." Unlike most beginners she doesn't drop stitches, but her practice swatches are as dense and impenetrable as a knight's chain mail. This is what I trust— the durability of the stockinette stitch.

"I want to make something," she insists.

The bamboo needles click.

"Soon, I promise." She's absolutely adorable in the rocker, all that fluffy blonde hair, a smooth ball of scarlet yarn in her green velvet lap.

Alara mutters something.

"What?"

"You're staring at me."

"Sorry."

"Listen," Alara says awhile later.

"To what?"

"The building. It's vibrating."

There is something, a hum that could be the composite buzz of sewing machine, tattoo needle, an electric pottery wheel, the sound of things being made.

"Do you hear it?" she demands.

"Yes, I hear it."

Alara frowns.

"I do." Of course I do.

"So this is it." Howard is delighted I have at last allowed him into my bed. He affectionately fingers a worn spot on my comforter. I feed him slivers of avocado, stroke his shoulder.

"It's nice. Being here," Howard says. He traces a vein up the inside of my arm. He sighs.

I hesitate. His eyes are silver-gray slits, shiny as paper clips.

I mount his mound of flesh. Sitting astride him I grab his wrist with my damaged hand and press his dry, hot palm to the damp wall. Disappointment: I had hoped for a puff of steam.

"What?" He blinks. He struggles to move his hand. I tighten my hold, gripping his wrist with both hands now.

"Do you feel that?" I ask.

His erection withers inside me.

"Yes," he replies.

"What do you feel?"

"The wall is wet."

"You admit it. You admit your perfidy."

"Yes."

I get up and put on my robe. He pulls on his pants.

"I can make things difficult for you," he says.

"Yes," I agree.

I pick up after fifteen rings. "Hey, I'm sorry about last week," he says, "on the fire escape, startling you."

Is he waiting for a reciprocal apology?

"I just wanted to see—"

"What?" I'm honestly curious.

"Listen, Frances. Don't think you can have any secrets from me."

"I don't know what you're talking about."

"Because you can't. I know what goes on in my building."

"Howard, please." What do I want to ask him for? Reasonableness? Release?

Howard begins leaving things at my door. A box of kitchen matches. A jar of cumin. A caved-in overripe strawberry on a chipped white saucer.

Are these threats?

I return the favor. A stale corn muffin. A candle stub with the wick broken off. A polished avocado pit.

Is this an argument?

I'm eyeing a tall dresser my neighbor, Perley, is selling. "It's an antique," he says from the stoop.

It's a scarred but solid piece with all its Depression glass knobs intact.

"Would you bring it up for me later?"

Perley considers, takes a long draw off his can of malt liquor. "Nope. Don't think so."

I don't hear Annie until she drops her grocery bag at my feet. "Perley, you giving my friend a hard time?"

"No ma'am. She's getting a fair price. It's my back, keeps me from lifting."

Annie raises an eyebrow.

"I'd buy it," I explain, "if I could get it upstairs."

"Is that all?" Annie runs her finger over a deep scratch on the dresser top. "I'll fetch Hank. He can bring it up for you."

"Well then," Perley says.

When Annie reemerges from the building she's collected Hank and Alara.

Annie starts pulling out the dresser drawers.

"Y'all go up first," Hank says. "In case I drop it."

But he manages just fine, not even a scrape against the railing.

"Set it down anywhere," I say.

"You don't have much stuff," Annie observes.

"We've got too much stuff," Alara says.

"Most people do." Hank has moved back near the doorway, as though he's afraid of intruding. He wipes his forehead with his sleeve.

"I really needed this dresser. Thank you all very much."

We hear heavy footsteps on the stairs a flight below.

Hank nudges the door closed with his foot.

We go silent. The four of us frozen like statues in a child's game.

The landlord's assertive knocking. "Frances, it's me. Frances. Are you there? I know you're there." We hear his sigh. "C'mon Frances. Perley told me you just bought a dresser."

His footsteps recede and a moment later the game is over. Annie and Alara and Hank excuse themselves. I repeat my thanks but fail to offer water, coffee, chairs, something. I was confused by Howard's saying my name, his voice both confident and plaintive.

I hear a scuffling outside my door. Howard's bulging vein-streaked eye meets mine in the peephole. I stuff an old Indian blanket into the crack beneath the door. I am preposterous! I can't stop myself from dragging my trunk across the room. I'm humming as I shove it hard against the door.

I almost trip over his latest offering—five sterling silver buttons scattered at my doorstep like jacks. The buttons are the size of quarters, each curved face etched with a fleur-de-lis. I imagine a sweater for them, a cardigan knit from a fine-gauge wool-silk blend the blue-black of damson plums.

I leave him a can of WD-40 and a handsome wooden carpenter's level. The poison-green bubble drifts to the left.

My rocker is just the right size for Alara because when she sits forward her feet can rest on the floor.

"You were born to knit," I tell her. She's nearly finished with the front left panel of her vest. Her stitches are smooth and orderly. Her armhole decreases are perfect puckers. I couldn't do better.

"My mom says you're tight-lipped."

"What do you think?"

She flips her knitting over to the purl side. "You do spend a lot of time alone."

"Yes, well, I'll have to get a job soon, and then I'll be around people all day."

"Don't you like people?"

"I like you."

She scowls.

"I used to like people."

"What about now?"

I shrug.

"Frances."

"I don't know."

This she accepts, or seems to, blazing through another 56 stitches without comment. And then she speaks only to ask me to pass the measuring tape.

He calls. "I'm thinking blintzes."

"You're branching out."

"Yes." He laughs. "It's true!"

Is this a truce?

I might as well decide it is.

And if it isn't?

I'll pile all my furniture in front of the door and rappel in and out my kitchen window. I'll spread broken glass on the steps of the fire escape and grease the railings. I'll sleep with a butcher's knife stuck between my mattress and box spring if I have to.

I'm not going anywhere.

Palo Tung

Fish is Fish

My father wasn't what you could fairly call a fisherman, but to hear him tell it fishing was a lofty endeavor which he alone understood in its fine subtleties, an art whose secrets were so privileged he would willingly impart them only to his first-born. Being not only his first but only born, I looked forward to this baptism of hook and line as toward a birthday or Christmas. I tortured us both with questions about fishing and demanded to know when our day was coming. With typical imperviousness, and evident glee, my father's only answer was, "Shhh, fish doesn't like impatient little boy."
The day of my initiation finally did arrive, and as we loaded the icebox into the Oldsmobile's trunk, I asked my father what I thought was a very pertinent questions.

"Dad," I said, "don't we need some fishing rods or something?"

He thought about it a moment. His hands came up to his bony cheeks and then he help them out in front of himself, staring at the fingertips, as if waiting for them to speak.

"Fishing rods," he said. "Where are the fishing rods?"

"We have to buy them, I think."

"Hmmm." He stood there, staring at his fingertips.

"They got 'em at K-Mart, dad. They got all kinds of stuff with fish on 'em and that catches fish."

"K-Mart?"

"You sure you know about fishing, dad?"

"Do I know about fishing! What kind of question is this, ah? Do you know, before you are born, your uncle Sam and I go fishing very much. There has a bridge, near San Francisco – oh! Gigantic beautiful bridge, and many Chinese are fishing fish there, like this"-he spread his hands-"gigantic beautiful fish, silver, like made of silver. Yah! Good fish! Good good fish!"

He rubbed his stomach and I laughed.

"But, dad, they got the same kind of fishes here? Maybe New Orleans fish don't act like San Francisco ones. In San Francisco ... "

"Ah, fish is fish," he said. "Fish is fish is fishing fish. Yes or no?"

"No."

"Yes. We fish for fish is fishing for fish."

I saw K-Mart in a light I never had before. We walked the aisles and I wanted it all. I touched everything I saw. My father made a sucking sound with his tongue in the roof of his mouth and swatted at my hands. "Bu yao la, ahi'" He frowned his disapproval down upon me and the thing I'd touched. Then he'd wait a moment, and, when he thought I wasn't looking, he'd touch it too. Opposite the gun counter, we came to a towering white cooler anointed with the words NIGHTCRAWLBRS, RBDWORMS, SHRIMP, CRICKETS.

"Hey dad, they got worms in here!"

'Worms? Yes. Fish are liking worms."

"Should we get some?"

"Hmm." He looked to his fingertips.

"Can I help y' all find somethin?" A woman appeared beside us.

'We're going fishing!" I said.

"Yah," my father said. 'We like to buy some fishing rod, string for fish, hook, bob, worm that fish likes."

"You say you wanna buy some fishin line?"

"Fish rod, string for fish, hook, bob, worm that fish likes."

"String for fish? You mean, like, fishin line?" . ~

"Yes. This string, and fishing rod, hook, bob. Worm that ... "

"Yeah, worm that fish likes," she started laughing, and looking around.

I looked at my father. When people started laughing and looking around, I knew what was coming. My father often had difficulty discerning whether someone understood biro or not, but he had no difficulty sensing the slightest impatience with his English. But as she looked for company she found no one, and her laughter went the way laughter does with no one to share it.

"All right," she said. "C'mon."

She guided us through the aisles.

"You want a fresh water pole or a salt water pole?"

My father just stared at her, blankly. I knew the anger behind his stare and was grateful that the woman likely did not.

'Well," she said, "you might wanna choose one or the other. Cause 'tween a fresh water ... "

"Yah yah yah," my father said. "You just give me fishing pole and I buy, okay?"

"But if you get you a fresh water pole you might could wanna go out to the salt water later ... "

"Oh, fresh water salt water. Yah, you are very clever, huh? Fish is fish."

"No they ain't. Salt water fishes, they bigger and ... "

"You are not intelligent person. I don't listen to you. I buy this pole, two."

"What? Boy, you best find you some manners fore you ... " Her mouth tightened into a flat line and she shook her head. I thought she was going to punch biro. She was not a small woman and there was naked fury in her eyes.

"You are not intelligent person," my father said. "I buy this stick, two."

"Boy, if I wasn't gon lose my job I'll teach you somethin you gon remember. You know, you in America now and we don't ... "

"Yah yah yah. This stick. I buy two, okay?"

The greatest problem my father had in purchasing anything was his inability to distinguish between impatience over a difficult transaction and what might be interpreted as racism. He was often on the other end of such transactions in our store. Although everyone who lived in our neighborhood was black, including all the customers at our store, he was either unable or unwilling to learn anything about them. I think now that he survived only by a freakish kind of luck. He was, perhaps, uniformly granted the particular variety of deference reserved for the implacably insane.

The woman seemed, after a moment, to come to the same conclusion about my father that so many others had reached, suddenly encountering the mystery of his anger. Though she shook her head, and their eyes warred, she sold us the rods and everything else. As usual, my father was his normal self within moments. And as he handed her the money, my father laughed and said in Chinese roughly the same thing he always did after such confrontations.

"This stupid big nose black," my father said, laughing and trying to sound instructive. "You know what would happen if she had to sell her idiotic strings in China? She would lose her mind. Her mind!"

"Hmmm." The woman exhaled through her nose.

My father fussed with the bag, giving the woman one of his fraught, blank glances. He looked at me the same way. Fixing me with the blank, meaningful look, all the more meaningful for its blankness, he took my hand in his. I felt the hard pads of his palm.

"Yah," my father said, "There has a day every one must put the shoulder to a wheel, and have to push. Come to this day, you must know what means this wheel." He took my hand, and added, in Chinese, "Understand?"

"No."

"Yah," he went on English. "When you know what means this wheel, you know what means difference between push and pull, and not have to work rest of your life in K-Mart."

"What?" The woman shot back.

My father gave the woman the blank stare, turning me to leave. She sneered, one eyebrow curling upward, and shook her head. AB my father pulled me away, I watched her over my shoulder, wanting to apologize, and wanting to punch her in her sneer.

"You crazy," she hollered after us. "Hear me? Crazy!"

We ended up in Bayou Seignette. My father had heard some of the men in our store talking about the fishing across the bridge and perhaps he imagined that a fisherman needed only to cross the bridge for the fishes to fly into our pockets.

It was a sight. Back in the Treme you scarcely noticed that autumn had arrived; there weren't many trees and most of them never changed color. But here, rounding the belly of the bridge, we followed the highway down into another season, a carpet of red and yellow cypress and maple that spread out toward the Gulf. Flat, boxy stores and shotgun houses crowded the highway, and the signs of diners and filling stations rose up above the viaduct. Billboards with cartoon alligators and crawfish pointed the way toward Jean Lafitte Swamp Tours and then the highway flattened out and my father pulled across the road, to where a horseshoe of clapboard booths ringed an open patch of dirt, some sort of bazaar or carnival with the booth vendors standing over coolers, under signs that read FRESH CRAB, LIVE CRAWFISH, GULF SHRIMP, GATOR MEAT.

Dust flew up behind us as we rolled over gravel and potholes. The car stalled as we pulled between two sedans.

"Stupid big nose car," my father said.

"That sign over there says live bait." I pointed up toward a store at the other end of the parking lot. "Maybe they can tell us where the fish're at."

Flies buzzed against the screen door, trapped from the inside. A bell tinkled as we went in and the old woman looked up at us from behind her reading glasses. She smiled, turned the page of her newspaper, and my father returned the smile, held up a palm in greeting. I liked her immediately. She reminded me of my best friend T's grandmother, Minnie. The store owner wore the same type of hom-rimmed reading glasses Minnie favored, smiled with a familiar warmth and depth.

"What can I do you for today, gentlemen?" she said, speaking to me.

"We're going fishing! You can tell us where the fish' re at?"

"Where the fish're at! Ain't that just what all the young fishermen'll be wantin to know these days! That's a secret we give out only to our very special customers…"

"I'm a special customer!"

"Huh," she laughed. "Ain't you just.'"

"Win," my father said, not because he sensed victory lurked somewhere in the room, but because it was my name. Lose was also my name, depending on who in the neighborhood was calling it.

"Oh, that's all right, sir. I have grandchildren of my own, and everyone of 'em special as you please."

My father scolded me in Chinese. "Why do you always do this? Ha? People will think we haven't raised you properly."

"I didn't brag. It wasn't bragging," I replied.

I looked at the woman beseechingly: "Was I?"

"Was you what?"

"Bragging."

"Whatever your daddy said, son. Best listen to what your daddy said, cause that's the truth, right or wrong. And he's taking you fishin which makes him even more right, wouldn't you say?"

My father laughed, deeply pleased, and patted me on the back. I was suddenly glad she had said what she had, as it struck me that without her advice my father would probably have made a similar point when we returned to the car, but without need of words.

"Listen to her," he said, wagging a finger. "This is a very wise woman, boy."

"Well thank you, sir. Now what kind of fishin y'all planning on doing?"

"What kind of fishing? Fishing is fishing, yes or no?"

"Oh, well. Yes, fishin is fishin."

My father winked at me.

"But, on occasion, it does help to know what kind of fish y'all want to catch."

"Oh?"

He liked her. Any one who elicited his prized oh had clearly won him over. She told him about redfish, the way they fed and the types of baits and lures they took, about bass and how they weren't hitting now because the water level was too high and muddy, about the panfish who would take just about anything so long as it had lived at one time or another, about the catfish who took anything whether it had lived or not, and my father nodded and nodded and nodded. I felt very good about the woman as my father hadn't done much nodding in his lifetime, although a good portion of his life had been spent shaking his head vehemently.

Following her advice, we found the park gate and then the road that ran toward the water and the wooded picnic areas. Hauling the bags through the woods we avoided the deep alligator holes, which my father told me were undoubtedly makeshift toilets left by inconsiderate 'big nose" picnickers, and came out onto a long grassy embankment.

It was less than a river and more than a canal. Pads of moss and scum escorted by an occasional plastic bag crawled toward the fork where two arms of yellow water met. At the other bank, past the point where the waters merged was a bridge built over wooden pilings, the road over the bridge leading toward a fenced

in area that appeared to be a swimming pool.

"My god," my father said in Mandarin. We stood at the edge of the bank and peered into the muddy water. "What kind offish will live in water like this?"

As if to answer him, not five yards in front of us, a shining black smoothness rolled across the surface, leaving the water in roiling knots behind it.

"Hey! Hey!" I screamed with delight.

"Shhh!" My father gave me an excited, wide-eyed look. "Must be quiet! Fish doesn't like loud little boy."

"Come on, dad! We gotta catch that fish!"

We were equally rushed in putting together the rods, reels, and line and we failed miserably. We were able to attach the reels to the rods but couldn't fathom the mechanics of the reels. The bails and drag settings were too much.

"I thought you said you and uncle Sam used to go fishing all the time ... "

I was prepared to offer further complaint, but the look he gave me suggested I would be a fool to do it. We bent down on our haunches and I watched him hold the rod in one hand, the line in the other; he poked with the line at various parts of the reel, as if it were a needle and he needed only to find the eye.

I heard voices. They came from behind the trees that hid the bank where the water forked.

"There's some people over there, dad. I can hear 'em. Maybe they're fishing, too. Maybe they can help us ... "

"My god," he said, poking at the reel. "Be quiet one moment, ha?"

I rose and ran toward the trees. A boy about my age stood squinting over the water, his dose-cropped hair purplish in the sun. He was holding a rod much smaller than either of the ones we had purchased, and next to him a bald man leaned back on his elbows with a can of Budweiser, his own rod leaning against his bent knee. The bald man adjusted his sunglasses as I approached.

"Hey," I said. "Y'all catchln any fish?"

The man greeted me with a jerk of his head and lifted the beer to his lips. The sun reflected brightly offhis dark, smooth scalp.

"Naw," the boy said, "we just got a couple perches. I'ma catch me a bass, though. I know they in here cause I seen 'em rollin."

"Rollin?"

I looked into the bucket beside them. Two tiny fish about the size of my hand darted against the walls of the bucket a moment and settled, tails swishing.

'Wow, you caught some fish!"

"Aw, they ain't nothin but perches. Can't hardly even call 'em fish. We keep 'em for the cats. We got cats that live under the house, ya dig?"

"Yeah, we got 'em, too. Everybody got 'em."

"Watch this, though. I'ma catch me a bass in a minute, and then you gon see some fish."

I looked at his rod, at the reel. His reel was like the ones we'd bought, but smaller. I watched him reel in his line, saw the way he flipped the bail and held the line before casting.

"You fishin, too?" he asked me.

"We just got here. We ain't caught noth:in yet."

"You shoulda been out here yesterday. My pops caught him a catfish big as your leg."

I looked at my leg.

"Big as my leg?"

"Bigger," the man said, smiling. "Big as my leg."

I looked at his leg.

"No way," I said.

The boy looked at me and nodded in such a way that I knew it was true.

I ran back to my father. His hair stood out oddly, his hand fussing with it. I saw the expression on his face and decided against telling him about the catfish. I picked up the other rod and found the line in the grass. I did what I could.

"Here," I said.

"Yes."

"Hold the line so I can reel it in."

"What?"

I heard a splash. We looked and saw the circles spreading in the water.

"Come on! Hold the ilne so I can reel it in!"

I jabbed him with the spool until he took it. I began to turn the reel arm and the spool jumped in his hands.

"Here, like this." I placed his fingers in the holes at either side of the spool. He held and I reeled.

"Hey," he grinned. He patted me on the head and gave me what in Chinese is a considerable compliment. "Bu cuo," he grinned, not bad.

My father was able to tie the hook on and then a bobber; the worm thrashed in his hand but he got the hook through it. Remembering what I'd seen the other boy do I hurried to the water's edge and attempted to do the same. There was a whipping sound and then something hit me hard in the mouth; it was the bobber. I was sure it was the bobber, as that was what I saw swinging in front of my face, secured there by the hook which had attached itself to my shirt. The worm squirmed against my chest but my mouth hurt too much to be bothered by it.

"Ai-ya!" My father took a few quick steps toward me. He was laughing. "You trapped a big one, huh!"

He checked my mouth, and seeing no blood he laughed again. He worked the hook free of my shirt.

"Caught," I said. "Caught a big one."

"Yes, you catch a big one, hahaha. Look boy, look. This is not intelligent behavior. You see here, give it to me. How do you free the string?"

I showed him and he began pulling the line out, letting it fall to the grass. He grasped the line a few feet above the bobber and began twirling the line above his head. He released the line and bobber and worm arched majestically through the air, the one lopsidedly orbiting the other. And then the line caught in the grass and the bobber splashed into the water, all of six feet from shore.

"You see, boy?" He stood proudly admiring his work, arms akimbo. "Now we catch the fish."

"That's not how you do it, dad."

"What you're talking about?" He gestured at the accomplishment with both hands.

"Here, dad." I handed him the rod. "This is how you close the flippy thing, and here's how you pull in the line."

I put the other rod together and managed to feed in the line, attach the bobber, hook, and worm. When I again emulated what I'd seen the other boy do I was a bit more successful: though the bobber and worm flew nearly straight up into the air they splashed down slightly further out than my father's had.

"Wah!" he said. "Bu cuo!"

He pulled in his line hand over hand and slung it out again. I reeled in and cast out, and this time the line went out fast, the bobber sailing, and I felt the line whip against my finger.

"My god!" he said. "Not bad! Ai-ya! Hey boy! Come come!"

I walked over but couldn't see what he was pointing at. He bent down and put his hand on my neck.

"You see!"

A bubble rose and popped next to his bobber, followed by another, and then another.

"Shhh ... This is fish." His eyebrows lifted excitedly and he patted my shoulder.

The bobber dipped once and slowly began to sink. A tight tingling went through me. My father grasped the line and began to pull on it, at first gingerly and then in a crazed fury. He began to jabber feverishly in Chinese: "My god ... I can feel the fish ... this fish ... I know you ...come on, you fish... my God, this big big fish...come here ... come come come come..."

A dark form turned underwater, flashing yellow, and then it broke the surface, struggled, and sank again; he pulled hard once and it thrashed against the bank. It was round as a dish, its belly glowing whitely in the sun; yellow stripes ran brightly down its black head, the shell caked with mud.

"It's a turtle, dad!"

Its fat legs turned in the air, the hook embedded in its left front claw.

"Turtle," he said. He dropped the line and scratched his head. He reached down with one finger and the jaws snapped with a clicking sound, but missed. He scratched his head and made a sucking sound with his tongue. "This is very good for soup, but ... well, I don't think mommy knows how to cook this."

"Soup? Ugh."

"Yes, we forced to let it run away."

My father looked at his fingers, and then at the turtle. A thin wash of blood ran down its leg. He reached for it again and again the jaws snapped violently. He shook his head.

I heard the other boy's voice from behind the trees:

"Did y' all catch somethin!"

"Yeah!"

'What you catch!"

"A turtle!"

"Turtle?!"

"Yeah!"

He came sprinting around the trees. His father trailed him, walking and sipping from his beer.

"Bean," his father said. "Bean, you let them folks be, boy."

"Hallo!" My father said.

"How you doin!" Bean's father hollered. "Y'all hooked y'a turtle, huh?"

"Come look it, pop. That bitch big!"

"Watch you language, boy." Bean's father cuffed him on the head and Bean made an annoyed face at him. Bean's father made an annoyed face back. Bean's father looked at my father and gestured with the Budweiser can. "What kind o' turtle y' all got?"

"Yes," my father shook his head, raising an eyebrow. "This is turtle."

Bean's father leaned over us and laughed. He pulled his sunglasses down with thumb and forefinger and his eyes were large and black and soft looking.

"That one of them snappin turtles. You best keep you fingers clear o' that mouth. They good eatin, though. Y'all know how to cook them things?"

"I know to eat," my father said. "Unfortunate that my wife doesn't know how to cook."

"I be happy to take it off your hands, y'all ain't gon keep it. Fix up a good turtle gumbo."

"You want?" My father rose, and swatted Bean's father on the shoulder lightly with the back of his hand. "Okay, you take."

"All right," Bean's father smiled and extended his hand, and my father took it with a nod.

"Pop, I ain't eatin no turtles, pop."

Bean's father looked at Bean and laughed a little, pushing his sunglasses back into place. He bent down and grabbed the line. He tested it once and then pulled the turtle up, the water running off it, the legs working.

"Pop," Bean said. "I ain't playin with you."

The turtle landed on its belly and made for the water; Bean's father planted a shoe on its back. Taking care to balance his beer he hopped up on one leg and brought the other shoe down on the turtle's head; there was a dry cracking sound; the legs continued to churn but when the shoe came up the head lay still, misshapen and perversely twisted to one side, the beak open and the little grey tongue lolling out.

"Wah! Ai-yah!" My father slapped him on the back.

"Check them legs!" Bean said.

Bean's father slapped my father on the back and laughed. "Yeah! Ai-yah! he said.

"It ain't dead yet!" I said. It bothered me to see it was still moving.

"You gotta Finish it off!"

"Naw, son, that sucker dead all right. Them legs just movin on they own." He drew from the Budweiser, contemplating the turtle, whose legs continued to claw and push. "Bean," he said, "go fetch that bag I got my earl in-we gon put him in there for now."

Bean returned with an empty, dripping garbage bag. His father held the hooked leg with his shoe and worked the hook free. He kicked the corpse into the bag and twisted the mouth of the bag, tucked it under the bundle. I could hear the legs struggling against the plastic.

"Say, I wauna thank ya for the turtle, mister ... "

"I am Charlie."

"Charlie?" Bean's father laughed.

"Charlie. What is funny?"

"You ain't Vietnamese is you? Cause if you is, that just ain't right."

"Vietnamese? I am born in northern China, near Beijing. Do you know Beijing?"

"You ain't Vietmanese?"

"No. Chinese. What is funny?"

"I thought you ... that still don't seem right. Somebody done ... you ever see that commercial on TV with the fish, for tuna fish?"

"Fish?"

"Nah. Nah, never mind." Bean's father extended his hand and my father took it. "They call me Rip, and this my son Bean."

"Yes." My father was very pleased. "And he is Win. Also my son. Ai, Win," my father looked at me and jerked his head toward Bean, making a face.

Suddenly Bean and I regarded each other with trepidation.

"Hai, Win," my father repeated.

"You ain't gon holler at you boy there, Bean?"

I extended my fist and Bean smiled and nodded.

"Where y' at Win." His fist came down over mine and I brought mine up over his.

"You drink earl, roister Charlie? Beer?"

"Beer? Yes, I like beer very much."

"Bean, go fetch some earl for roister Charlie. A' right?"

"A' right." "Say, Charlie, where you learned to rig a pole like this here?" He leaned down and picked up the hook and bobber.

"How you supposed to do it?" I said.

"Well, the bobber, it got this little hook here for puttin the line through. It ain't quite meant to be tied on like you got it. You want me to get it right for ya?"

"Ah?" My father said.

"Yeah. You just do like this here."

"Oh?" Bean came back and handed the beer to his father, who handed it to mine. Bean's father continued to work with the rig, explaining the necessity of each aspect of it.

"Y'all stay cross the river?" Bean's father said.

"Yeah," I said. 'We stay over ro the Treme."

"Yeah? We got people over there. Bean's momma family stay out there by the Colton school. Rough out there, boy."

"Rough?" My father said.

"Rough all over, but over by that Ninth Ward, boy ... "

Bean made a raspberry sound with his lips and gestured with one hand, waving off his father's gravity. I smirked and nodded, coolly.

"Nine Ward ... " My father shook his head. Our store on St Roch bordered on the Nroth Ward. He didn't have to understand the man's words to grasp their import.

Bean's father finished with the rig and handed me the rod. He and my father stood looking out at the water, silently sipping from their beers. My father's head bobbed up and down absentmindedly, as it always did when he was thinking or nervous. Bean and I looked at them, at each other. Bean shrugged at me and I shrugged back. Without turning Bean's father touched my father on the arm with the back of his hand.

"How long you been in the states, Charlie?"

"Thirty, thirty-five year. I arrive San Francisco nineteen fifty-nine."

"San Francisco ... I hear it's real pretty out there, with the fog and that Golden Gate Bridge, and all kind o' space."

"Yah. Pretty. But not all kind of space."

They nodded together. Then my father said a funny thing.

"You?" He said. "How long you have been in America?"

"How long I been in America?" Bean's father laughed.

"Shit," Bean said, also laughing.

"Hey! What I say bout that cursin?"

Bean stopped laughing.

"I been in America all my life, Charlie. Born and bred in Alabama. Different when I was growin up. But different depend on who you talkin to. You know. That broke back state still got a Dairy Queen with separate bathrooms for white and black."

"Separate bathroom. Yah. I remember."

"They had Jim Crow in San Francisco?"

"Jim Crow? Ah, Jim Crow. No no no, not San Francisco. I come to Baton Rouge nineteen sixty-two, attending college of LSU. Taking Greyhound bus. My wife and I, after we marry. Funny story," he shook his head, gravely. 'Very funny story."

"Pop. We ain't gon fish no more?"

"Hold up, Bean. Naw, you go head. I'ma catch up with ya."

"Come on, Win, les catch us some :fish!" Bean sprinted away.

I stayed where I was. As much as part of me wanted to go with Bean, to fish, to laugh, to talk shit, the mystery of my father's past held me. I was fascinated by his past, by the fact that he had one that didn't involve me.

"What you was sayin, Charlie?"

"Yes, very funny story." He shook his head.

"Somethin had happened at LSU?"

"In the bus, this Greyhound bus. Very funny. We are transferring bus in Arizona and when we are getting in bus, very funny situation. When we getting into new bus, you understand? Yes. My wife is here - " my father put his beer down to gesture with his hands—"and I am here, and when I climb on the bus I see very funny thing. Here, in the front, all faces are white, and here, in back, all faces are black. Not like before. Suddenly, not like before. You understand? Nobody say nothing. Just suddenly all white faces are front, all black faces at back. I am no stupid. I know this is not accident. But, then, I have a very big confusion."

Bean's father began to smile.

"Yes! I doesn't know where to sit! You know! You see I mean? Where we are going to sit! I look my wife! My wife look me! Nobody have told us about this!"

When he saw that Bean's father was laughing he grabbed his arm, laughing, too.

"Yah! You see! Where I am going to sit?!"

"Yeah. Yeah. So where you sat?"

"Bus driver is looking at us not happy. 'Why you are standing here like this?' I doesn't know what to say. So we just walking, walking, until two seats are empty, and when we sit down, people are looking at us but doesn't say anything."

"The white folks."

"Yes, we sitting in the white faces. Later, the college advisor telling me to sit with white people, eat with white people, go to bathroom with white people, because otherwise they will treat me as black. So, you see I mean? They still looks at me like strange, in bathroom, whatever."

My father bent over, emulating a white man washing his hands, turning his head repeatedly and moronically. Bean's father nodded, laughing gently as he drew from the Budweiser. "Maybe they are think, Why ... who is this man ... he is not

white ... he is not black ... what do I supposed to do? Everywhere they are washing hand, look at me like crazy, cannot think what do they supposed to do."

Bean's father turned and looked at my father a long, silent moment. His sunglasses hid his eyes, but his lips were pursed and smiling. My father kept rubbing his hands together, as if washing them, crooking his head to the side, and frowning with his mouth slightly open. For a long moment, he stood there frowning and crooking and rubbing his hands together. The laughter started in Bean's father's nose and spread.

"Yah!" my father said, lett:ing go, too. "You see, mister Rip! You see I mean!"

"Yeah," Bean's father nodded and laughed, drawing from the beer. "I see you mean."

My father tapped his companion's arm again, with the back of his hand. He rubbed his hands together, washing, frowning, scrutinizing, and they laughed heartily together.

"That's a pretty good story, Charlie. I'm gon have to tell that one back to my wife. She'll fall out laughin."

"Yah. I am glad you like story." My father bent down for the beer and drew from it.

Bean's father crooked his head at my father, smiled, and gestured subtly with his beer, nodding.

They stood there a moment, the two of them nodding together for no apparent reason. Bean's father laughed and looked at my father. He raised the can again to my father and sipped from it. My father laughed and raised his own beer and sipped.

I heard Bean's voice.

"Say, Win! C'mon! Let's catch us some basses!"

So I joined Bean and he tried without success to teach me how to set the hook. But it didn't matter. Just the sound of the line whipping away from the reel on a good cast thrilled me endlessly. The thing I liked best about fishing with Bean was the oath he made each time he prepared to set the hook, at the dip of his bobber. 'Watch me, Win. Watch me," he'd say. "I'ma kick this bitch ass!" Then he would immediately glance toward the trees, behind which our fathers sat in the grass, talking, drinking, and fishing.

C. W. Cannon

Fools Rush In

Can't you hear the pitter-pat? Pete "Maz" Mazewski, the sax player, pulled up a stool next to Davis Leggit. He'd first seen Leggit on the train down from Chicago. Leggit wore the same pale creamy suit and lavender tie. His short-brimmed panama sat on the bar in front of him. He'd trimmed his neat Faulkner moustache so he looked even more foppish than he had before. Maz felt shamefully plain in his jeans and polo and sneakers.

"Maaazzz," Leggit breathed, "I'm so pleased to have the pleasure. Drinkin'?"

"Uh, Yes." Maz swept his eyes around the Cozy Cove, as if he'd just arrived. The smooth wood, mirrors, cool darkness. Genteel chatter by candlelight.

"I know you are, my question concerns what is your preference?"

Maz couldn't remember what he'd been drinking, couldn't remember what he liked, even. "I don't know. What's good?"

Leggit chuckled and slapped Maz on the back. "There's a lot that's good. You see, that's why folks have so much trouble deciding in life which good thing it is, exactly, that they want."

"What are you having?"

Leggit didn't answer, he just raised his eyebrows and nodded at the bartender, who'd been eyeing them for a while now. The bartender went to work, in crisp, sure movements, and brought over two identical cocktails. Minty sweet rum drinks, tasty.

"You like?" Leggit asked, as if assured of the answer but still happy to ask, every time.

Maz said, "Sure."

Leggit was a talker. Practiced. Knew a lot about jazz. Knew a fair bit about Maz, too. But when he listened, he seemed to really listen. His eyes tapping always right on the door, intricate head movements to fine-tune his ears. He reminded Maz of that close-up of LBJ giving some senator the "Johnson treatment." Like he wanted to make a deal. Hey, hey, LBJ the words Maz had built into an ostinato refrain on stage, to 12-bar blues, when he still played sax, when he still could, at Grant Park, Chicago, August 28,

1968, in the sun, sleepless. In a sudden but deep flash, like an undertow, the face in front of him was Johnson's, not Leggit's, and Maz felt faint, exhausted. But it went away as Leggit's banter lapped on. The voice was pleasant, like gurgling water. Pleasant to the ear even when he took it upon himself to point out Maz's shortcomings.

"Your problem, venerable maestro, is that you find yourself always uncomfortable in the present."

What was he talking about? And why did he come on like some long lost deep friend? They'd only just met.

"This is because you have been misled by the chimera of…what is the term? Social responsibility, I believe."

Maz's hackles went up. "Responsibility is a chimera?"

"For some, yes. Not for the wretches of the earth, of course, for whom it's a matter of self-interest. And not for our elected wretches, who sacrifice their very cocks on the altar of mediocrity."

"You're not being very clear-"

"Clarity is for schoolteachers," he barked.

"Okayyy…" Maz wasn't sure that an appeal to reason would work on this effete reptile, but he took a swing anyway, kept it simple: "What's wrong with leaving the world slightly better off than when you came?"

"Go for it, Christian soldier. But remember what Caesar said to Antony: Beware yon Cassius. He sees no theater, Maz, he drinks no wine. He gets no boody."

"I don't remember that last part."

"Ah, but that's the most important part, my Chicago paisano." He pinched Maz' cheek. "Best damn line Shakespeare ever wrote, too." He lifted his glass and bowed his head, to honor the bard, presumably.

"And…?" Maz pressed.

"Ah, yes, my peroration." He smacked his lips. "You are an artist, maestro, you blessed creature of the earth's loins, it is your lot to suck at the teats of sensuality."

This Bohemian bullshit. Maz thought this line had gone out in the 1930s. But of course it would still stalk the nights, like a vampire, down here.

Leggit stood and carefully pushed his barstool aside, then leaned close to Maz' ear and said "I know the kine-a music you wanna hear."

"What?"

"My suspicion is you never heard it before, but there always will come a time in a man's life where some inexorable something is destined. Even the things that seem like little things. Like just a little ol' music."

"What?" Again, Maz was drawn in by the man's style, delivery, oily smooth enunciation, the rough rounded edges of his words--even though he could barely understand the substance of what he said.

"If what you wanna hear is jazz, though, what I got in mind, this is the real dealy-deal. Distilled. You got to go to the source."

"It depends on what you call jazz."

"Indeed. Indeed. It certainly does depend on that. But see, me, what I call jazz—and I think you'll come around--I'm talking about from the way down under gutbucket." His eyes narrowed and he lowered his voice. "Some funky-ass dick shit. Now are you game?"

Yeah, Maz was game.

A car waited outside—not a cab—a car with a driver who seemed not only to know Leggit, but to have been waiting for him. It was a Leggit kind of car, a late 70s Lincoln, dark on the outside, cracking white leather within. They got in the back seat and when Maz asked Leggit about the black man up front, Leggit just said, "Oh, he does some work for me, y'know," and took out his cigarette case and offered Maz one. They lit up—Pall Malls.

"Good brand," Maz said.

"It's not the quality of the smoke, though, superior as it may be. It's the memories."

"Wherever Particular People Congregate."

"In Hoc Signo Vinces."

"You're well acquainted with the cigarette pack literature."

"Let's say I smoke them tonight in honor of you, a man who has played an indisputable role."

Maz waited for him to expound but he never did. So Maz asked the question he'd been turning over in his head. "Did you mean to run into me tonight?"

"Of course I did." Leggit paused, in thought. "I wanted to honor you. But what I want to know is, can you remember the taste? I mean from then, y'know back in the big days on Division Street. What it was like lighting up then, on the stage, in the light? The nicotine buzz—" He exhaled, slowly, and admired the blue smoke curling up from his mouth. "Tobacco's such a fine drug. Up on stage, looking out at the fans and uttering some shtick of some kind to get'em relaxed and primed? Do you have a memory like that? Can you recall the faces of the girls—excuse me, I mean that metaphorically—"

"I've slept with plenty of women."

"Y'know, whoever it would be, at the front-row tables, lookin' up atcha, y'know back when it was all just opening up, as opposed to closing in?"

"I don't remember much, actually," Maz admitted. He remembered the effects, results, implications of things he did, but the actual experiences, sadly, no, not really. "But nothing's closing in," he asserted. "I'm on a groove."

Maz heard an electronic whir and saw Leggit lowering the window and leaning his head out. A retching sound. Leggit was vomiting. The car didn't slow down and the driver didn't say anything. Then the window went back up and Leggit puffed on his cigarette—it had never left his hand—and produced a pewter flask. He politely waved it at Maz before hitting it. Maz took a hit and handed it back to him. Bourbon, of course. Or rum. Surely he wouldn't have mixed the two? Then the smell of vomit and booze and cigarette smoke and something else (his own unwashed body?) drove Maz to roll down his window--the outside air was balmy beautiful, why were the windows up in the first place? He saw they'd just crossed Barracks, Barracks and Rampart. This neighborhood again. They pulled to the curb about a block from where he got mugged just a few hours ago.

"Is this an okay neighborhood?" he asked, stepping out of the car as he'd been instructed. Leggit got some of his sense of humor back. He laughed low and coughed a little--didn't answer the question though. He just said, "Got Uptown, y'got Downtown. And then there's the Back o'town."

The driver stayed in the car. The white men headed toward a loud cluster of black partiers spilling out of an open door on the corner. Marijuana smoke wafted toward them, an invitation, on the Turkish, Tunisian, soft air, reminding Maz that he wanted to get high again. But Leggit seemed unaffected by it. He snorted something out of a round little antique-looking snuffbox, but didn't offer Maz any.

Almost everybody on the corner put a hand on Leggit in some way— squeezed his shoulder, brushed his arm, slapped his hand. But nobody touched Maz. They just eyed him suspiciously.

Until Leggit introduced him. "My friends and countrymen, I'd like y'all to meet uuhh...a fellow enthusiast." With this they ceased all conversation among themselves and...all of them? Yes. Why? In silence they stared at Maz, almost soberly. But it only lasted a second. Then came an ambiguous chuckle, one nodded and one looked away, another made a sucking sound, one said, "awright then," and Leggit laughed in earnest, loud and hard, eyes undone and rolling back toward his brain, face pointed up at a muscular green and brown arm of the twisting live oak bowing over all of them.

Maz didn't know what to feel about the oak in the southern breeze... the poplar trees but he felt confusion because of the people, because he wanted to assimilate all their faces, different faces and shapes and clothes and eyes, but he couldn't: they were simply them.

But he forgot about all this because of what came from inside the narrow little building. A band had started up. The sounds flew out the open door and shouted a prohibition on all doubt, confusion. The blare soaked him to the bones from even way over where he was standing, outside and through a sea of bodies. What about right up against it? In it? What could that be like? He wandered inside and Leggit grinned at him. Followed him in grinning. Put his arm over his shoulder and said, "Well let's us belly on up to the bar."

The bartender, a large very black woman with a diamond in her nose and marcelled golden hair, called Leggit Mr. Leggit. And he said, "Why dontcha call me Davis?" and she said "Whatever you say, Mr. Davis." She fixed up two bourbon and sodas without being told--Maz didn't much care what the drinks were--and the music made it seem ridiculous that anything like conversation was going on at all. It was a haphazard brass ensemble, obviously just thrown together out of what happened to be lying around. Like a jam session, but they were clearly used to playing together. Their part harmony was tight, practiced. Four trumpet players? No, a couple were cornets. One alto. A bari – no tenor. Two slide trombones, plus maybe another one sitting it out. But most fundamentally: TWO sousaphones, cussing out a tightly dove-tailed bass-line. It hit Maz' groin in a way he was unfamiliar with. They were mostly young cats, except a couple, who looked not only much older but also more ragged. You couldn't say they had range. They all just blared as loud as they could—which made it miraculous when they sweated and strained enough to bump the din up a few notches whenever the head came around. The percussion consisted of one snare player and one bass-drum with a high-hat attachment, both stood and shuffled around while they played—like all the players. They all worked their feet like the crowd in front of them.

Maz wondered what was wrong with the picture and then it hit him: even though he and Leggit were the only white people in the place, no one seemed to worry about them or notice them, even, at all. No one stared. If someone happened to bump into them (plenty bumping going on), they either said 'excuse' or didn't and kept right on. Marched right on. They all kept right on marching, either in tight little circles or in broad swaths that reached every wall of the place, cutting in and out of the boiling tangle of bodies at different points like electrons must. Or water molecules.

But somebody out there was looking at Maz. Was staring. He felt it, but couldn't locate the eyes. Below the radar somewhere, like a cat in the reeds. Not Leggit. Leggit was talking with the bartender and leaning over the bar and pointing at this bottle or that one and shaking his head or nodding. Maz heard him say, "You don't wanna get no European beers in here. This ain't Europe."

The bartender said, "But they good. German beer is good."

Leggit: "Forget it. This ain't the Cozy Cove."

The eyes gunning Maz belonged to a band member. A cornet. Young, a boy. A boy with skin the color of a soft worn wet brick sidewalk, soft as the backside of a magnolia leaf. Trombone lips with edges delicate enough to swing a cornet. Yet a soft, edgeless tongue. This cat was a cheetah. He'd seen this cat before. Blowing for the tourists in front of the Cabildo. Or somewhere else. But he'd seen him before somewhere, he was sure.

Maz stared back at him but he didn't look away like he was supposed to. It was a mellow look, cool, but not exactly serene. And with the music around him, the kid seemed lifted up or larger or thrown in some kind of light that went way beyond his slight physical frame. And made him come off much older and much wiser than he really could be, at his age (fourteen? fifteen?). The music backed him like an army would, like fists raised, clutching guns. And the kid nodded and set his chin and mouthed a "Dat's right" and lifted his horn to his face and stepped up to take a solo.

And there arrived the fattest, most pissed-off bitching whine and growl Maz had ever heard. And he played out of the side of his mouth like he'd never had a proper lesson in his life. The root of the sound seemed to be the brassy shouting of a King Oliver or a Satch—the daemon of Buddy Bolden, who somebody said you could hear a mile away. But cut with micro-tonal edges—the notes slid around like men wrestling in the mud on a slanting levee. Like Miles, but earthier. Muddy. Other ingredients were, yes, a mystery, but not a quiet mystery. A mystery like a heart-attack is a mystery: you don't stand around and ponder it, challenge it with questions, you just die.

But what was here was too hot to be death. Maz hadn't been sweating before—certainly not at the Cozy Cove—but now he felt the beads pushing through the layer of invisible grime that finely coats the skin on trains and in New Orleans. Like every drop of sweat wanted to get out there and boogie, too, like the people, and be joined with their brethren in a big camp meeting of the sweat of fifty synchronized bodies. The floor of the place grew slicker and dust became grime. The kid's cornet was right on the thermostat, frowning and threatening and ignoring all supplicants, sending the mercury up, up. The band started chanting "Talk Dat Shit Now" and "Say What?!" and pointing at the dancers, pushing them to march harder. The boy blowing into his horn through the side of his mouth found some undiscovered and previously unused muscle in his face or his belly and started swinging and leaned into it, bumped the volume up one more decibel, and treated the air in front of his cornet to a righteous, vicious pummeling. The other cats first yelled and then came in on their horns and the kid took the solo out through the upstairs exit, some previously unknown-to-man pitch up in the sky somewhere halfway to the sun. The temperature on the dance floor went from Fahrenheit to Kelvin. People yelled, shrieked, and started jumping as high as they could and spinning around. And crouching low down to the ground and marching around that way. And Maz discovered that he was up and dancing too feets don't fail me now

But his groove got busted when the kid lowered his horn in a snap and spit on the floor and shot a look right at him like a bullet. Then Maz recognized him. Not from the Cabildo. From the street. Recognized that if this kid had had a bullet earlier that same day, Maz would have spent his evening differently, lying on the sidewalk waiting to be cleaned up by the sanitation department. Probably, anyway.

Leggit said (shouted), "I guess the Saints won tonight."

"What?"

"They provide that jam whenever we win. Game at the dome tonight. Bears, I believe." He laughed soundlessly, like a dog panting from the heat, and his eyes did their thing. Yes, Leggit was a dog all right, ridiculous in suit and hat, drink at his side. All he needed was floppy ears, a deck of cards, and some well-dressed dog companions.

The band had decided to mercy the feet and work the hips instead: played a blues ballad—"Back O' Town Blues"—it was the only down-tempo number they did the whole night. And even it seemed antsy, jerky, not smooth, not rich like a ballad should be. They rushed it, always jumped the beat. They couldn't let it find peace, had to keep kicking it whenever it tried to sigh.

Right before they breaked again (how many sets did they plan to do?) the kid with the cornet stepped up and did a vocal of "How Come My Dog Don't Bark When You Come Around?" A vicious revenge murder ballad. New Orleans had produced a wealth of that stuff. Full of cutting, shooting, a celebration of righteous, joyous hatred.

And that boy--the cheetah or the snake, the cornettist--glared right at Maz through much of it. Maz stood flinty in the face of his harsh treatment, though. The music made it easier. The boy's hostility was couched in the horn. Maz could pretend it wasn't what it was. He stared right back, and listened.

Leggit noticed. He made a sucking sound with his tongue and leaned and mumbled in Maz' ear. Maz heard sharp, unbelievable words. Wanna whip him?

"What?" he said. "What did you say?"

"Wanna whippet? They got 'em here."

"What's a whippet?"

"Nitrous oxide. It's legal in this state."

Leggit moved down the bar and halfway behind it and spoke with the bartender. He called her Berta. Could that be her name, too? Yes, she wore a big gold pendant that spelled it out. And she called him Davis, with no "Mister." They clucked and chuckled and glanced back not too subtly at Maz. Then Leggit waved him over and Berta opened a small door behind the bar and in the two men went.

A ratty low sofa in a small room, a little lamp with red tassels, and two women sitting on the couch. Yep, hookers, definitely. One of them seemed white at first, but then Maz decided she was just light-skinned. He looked them over out of some knee-jerk instinct and Leggit watched him do it with a little probing smirk on his face.

Maz had dated women, mainly in his youth. He was thoroughly capable of having sex with them, but they just didn't interest him emotionally or intellectually. Too often they seemed to be seeking out dependence. A two-sided dependence, sure, but still, the women in Maz's life seemed too quick to scuttle his and their own autonomy in the name of "love," "relationship," "commitment," whatever. Too clingy, too close. Personalizing everything, unprofessional. Sticky.

Maz leered at the hookers because he felt almost duty-bound to do it. That was their purpose, their function, their art. After a few awkward seconds, Leggit said, "Ev'nin' girls, we just want to sit with y'all for a minute." They nodded and smirked just as cutely as Leggit did, but in a black way, and one of them moved over to make room on the couch. Leggit offered the spot to Maz and Maz sat down.

The whippet looked appetizing. Because Maz's skin was hot to the touch, he had run out of sweat, and the way the balloon stretched and swallowed the freezing gas and how the cold steam wafted up from it—he felt like the star of a Coca Cola commercial.

He had seen this contraption before, on the Bourbon Street sidewalk. They were charging a dollar a hit, within feet of obliging policemen, in front of a Daiquiri place. He had seen a middle-aged Midwestern housewife take one and collapse in the Bourbon Street gutter (possibly the filthiest gutter in America). He had been disgusted then, but now he was ready, ripe for a collapse of his own. It had been too long since he had fallen in a gutter—he may never have.

He sucked up the contents of the balloon and died. In a cold off-blue throb. Like a mist of windblown snow off frozen Lake Michigan. But the best thing about the trip was how short it was. He came throbbing back and felt the heat again, just not as stifling as it had been before.

"What a thing to do," Maz muttered, as soon as he was able.

"Yass," Leggit grinned, his eyes closed. "Big with the kids these days. So who said we too old to learn new tricks from the young'uns, eh Dog!" Now his laugh came out low, deep, and steady, like something with no beginning or end, like groundwater.

On Leggit's suggestion, they "mosied" back out to the bar, where Leggit conducted some businessy-looking chatter with the band members--but not with the cheetah, or mugging punk, or whatever he was. The one who had caught Maz's eye and squeezed. That one sat off alone, serenely cool amid the gaggle of girls surrounding him.

Maz wandered outside and drank up the eminently drinkable air. He attached himself to a group of stoners, saying, "Could I get a hit off that?" They let him in. He said it tasted good and one of them said, "Yeah-you-right," but didn't really look at him. None of them really did. Until he started to turn away and one of them said, "Watch dat back."

Maz faced him and said, "What?" and the man replied, point-blank, in his eyes, "You on de front now. You best go find yo' friend and grab onto his pantses." Restrained but real laughter arose from the other men. Maz just said, "Thanks for the hit," and went back inside.

He found Leggit but didn't grab his pants-leg. He just said, "What's up?" Leggit placed his hand on Maz's shoulder in a solemn gesture, right up by the neck, and said, "Boy, we need to get you home."

"Chicago?"

"Well, maybe you had better sleep something off a little bit and think about gettin' you back to Chicago some other day." Leggit laughed, but without much energy, and Maz laughed, too, he figured what the hell.

They walked back to the car and Maz said, "So that's the new marching band sounds, huh?"

Leggit: "But, of course, the new marching band sounds are not really new, not really, it's the same old thing in different clothes."

Maz asked him about the star cornet.

Leggit told him to stay away from that one, said he had a problem with white people.

"I dig it," Maz said.

"Dig what?"

"Well, I do dig that music, too, y'know. Y'know I'm not really sure if I'll go back to Chicago at all. Seems like a nice enough place to retire."

"Yes," Leggit agreed, "that's why those that never leave begin their life with retirement."

Leggit seemed never to retire from merriment. Maz doubted he could live that way.

"Besides," Leggit continued, "you should stay at least indefinitely, we've been expecting you for so long."

"Expecting me?"

"Oh, well, certainly."

"Why didn't I hear about it?"

"There's ways to get a message across and also there's ways a message doesn't get received."

"What?"

"Let's us just say there are many gods, my most reverend Maz, and therefore many who haven't consented to be dead as much as the big Christian daddy has."

Maz just shook his head and said, "Oh, stop with that kind of talk, I'm too old for that."

"I thought you wanted to be young again."

"Who told you that?"

"Maybe I smelt it."

"Oh, stop with that."

After a short and silent drive, they let him off at the corner of Barracks and Dauphine--a block from his guesthouse. A couple of dark suspicious shapes crawled over the wrought-iron gate of Cabrini Park and began shadowing him. But he made it to his guesthouse before they caught up.

Bill Cotter

The Pink Pin in Quito

I parked the Pontiac in front of a big blue house on Iquem Street in New Orleans. I inventoried my luggage (one ancient Braniff flight bag) and shook my injured hand to test the pain. Not bad. A little crunchy maybe. And the Tushie diaper I was using as a bandage needed changing—blood had seeped through in a few places and had dried black-cherry-black. I climbed out of the car. The heat was breathtaking. I took a deep breath of it. I was now officially as far away from death and heartbreak as I could get.

In the front yard of the big blue house was a metal desk with an orange Igloo perched on the edge. A man was sitting there, dispensing a lavender fluid into a Little Mermaid promotional movie cup. The desk, a government-issue thing, drawer-free, its paint weathered down to salt-pocked stainless steel, had clearly been a feature of the yard for a long time: blue morning glories were climbing its legs. The man himself looked like he'd been there long enough for morning-glory scouts to consider climbing him, too.

"Excuse me," I said. "Is..."

"Surely it is," he said, his voice rich and musical, as though he had extra vocal cords that vibrated in harmony. "Gatorade. Cold. Want some?"

"No thanks," I said. "Is..."

"That a Huggie?" he said, gesturing at me with his Little Mermaid cup.

"Oh. Uh, no. Tushie. I had some bad luck."

"I bet what you meaning to say is that one of you lady-friends stick you, probably over some other lady-friend."

"Wow," I said, feeling a little like I'd been caught at Hide and Seek. "That's an awfully good guess."

He had lots of scars. Little and big. Knotted and old. Pink and shiny and new.

"That mean they love you, chief," he said. He laughed and drank some Gatorade. "But you want me to tell you something? You need to change that thing."

"I'm afraid to see what's under there."

He laughed again. I laughed too. I felt naked, legible. Who was this guy? An idle seer who specialized in exposing the heartsick? A voodoo expert, angling to trade me love potion for my bloody bandage? I'd always thought voodoo was just a tourist hook, but maybe it was for real.

"So," I said, crossing my arms to hide my hand, "is this the youth hostel?"

"Mm-hmm," he said, tipping the Igloo towards himself to get the last few drops of Gatorade carafed therein. "They about full up, though. Half of Denmark here."

Inside the hostel, beside a pathogenic-looking couch and in front of a huge pair of barred, painted-shut French doors that led to a veranda, was a woman sitting behind a low desk of the same species as the one outside, though this one had not had its paint, a cheerless smaze gray, bullied off by the clime.

She was hunched over the desk, pulling long dirty-blonde strands of hair from a plastic hairbrush.

"Hello," I said.

She stopped mid-pull, without looking up. She remained that way for three full seconds, then placed the hairbrush on the desk and raised her head.

"What's your name?"

"Jerome."

"Carolyn."

I smiled. Carolyn smiled back. A tiny dimple formed in the tip of her nose.

I hated smiling, and didn't if I could help it—I have curious teeth, and have been told my smiles are suggestive, if not downright leering. I'd practiced wholesome smiles in the mirror, but they just made me look like a cult leader.

"Eighteen bucks a night," said Carolyn, the smiling over. "Locker key's a twenty-dollar deposit, refundable. Pillow's on the bed. Need sheets and towels?"

I did. I gave Carolyn thirty-eight dollars. I signed my name on a clipboard register she dropped in front of me with a clatter. Under Address I wrote "Massachusetts." Not very precise, but true. She looked at the clipboard register, then gave me a key to the front door, a thin stack of linens, and a short oral dissertation on the dangers of the city.

"Massachusetts? Nice. Safe. But here? People like to murder each other. Last year, we were America's Murder Capital. 421 killings. And it's looking like we'll repeat in 1995. Often it's a drug thing, or an unfaithfulness thing, but lots of times it's just a flaring temper. A tip: if you, as a pedestrian, get a sense that an oncoming person is about to flare their temper, cross to the other side of the street."

"But..."

"What if there's a temper on the other sidewalk? Just walk down the middle of the street. You'll see that a lot."

"But..."

"What if there are tempers everywhere, you ask. Well. Consider acquiring one of these."

She reached into her backpack and pulled out a black object. It took my brain a moment to verify the object as a gun. She cocked it and pointed it at her hairbrush.

"Okay," I whispered. There weren't many guns in Boston. Not that I ever saw, anyway. I wanted to tell her to put that thing away, but she didn't look like she stood much contrariness. She was nearly six feet tall and had long, springy muscles in her neck. She didn't look like she stood anything she didn't want to stand. And she was armed.

Then the gun was gone, returned to her backpack.

"One of the residents here got mugged in a cemetery," continued Carolyn. "Then, while he was in the waiting room at Charity a lady dressed up in a nurse's uniform stabbed him in the arm with a mechanical pencil.

"So stay out of the cemeteries," she concluded.

"I promise," I said, imagining getting stabbed with a mechanical pencil. Instinctively I brought my bad hand up to my other arm to massage the pencil wound I'd so successfully imagined.

Carolyn looked at, but did not comment on, my darkened Tushie. I hid it behind my back again. She bent over to inspect the room-vacancy chart on her desk.

"There are four beds in your room—two bunk beds—and three are taken. You're the fourth. You just filled the hostel, Mr Jerome Coe."

She turned around. On a big world map tacked to the wall, she stuck a blue pin in the middle of Massachusetts, right in Quabbin Reservoir. Her hair fell in shallow waves to the middle of her back. There was a big dry oak leaf tangled up in there.

I was the only pin in the United States. About thirty other pins, all blue, were crowded into Europe, most in Denmark. There was only one other pin apart from those, a pink pin in Quito, Ecuador.

Beneath the powerful odors of mold and sweat and magnolia blossoms, which persisted throughout the hostel, my room also had its own signature scent: a humic musk, like composting laundry.

I occupied the top bunk of the left bunk bed. The other beds were linenless, and piled with sports bags, mossy bath towels, and Ziplocs filled with preening gels and disposable razors. Scattered on the floor and on the bunk under mine was a thin topsoil of European jockey shorts and funny socks that were likely the source of the paralaundry smell. There was also a selection of pornographic magazines evidently published in the low countries. One was called *Größte Pfosten* and featured on the cover a teutonic Adonis whose *Pfosten* were indeed signally *Größte*.

This was home, for now.

It was January, but the heat was astonishing. I had been issued a barf-colored blanket and a gray sheet by Carolyn at the front desk, but it was far too hot to cover up with the blanket, or even lie on it, so I folded it up and stuck it under the thin, flaccid pillow, which was really more like an oven mitt.

For a while I lay there, unable to sleep, and listened to insects bounce off the screen of the only window in the room.

These insects, I'd noticed, were on both sides of the screen: those outside seeking shelter, and those inside seeking freedom. The inside ones were numerous, biologically diverse, and loud. They scuttled and ratcheted, and occasionally dropped from the ceiling and tked on the floor like pistachio shells. I didn't want to lie directly on the mattress, but even less appealing was the idea of insect life falling on my body, carapaces down, waving appendages and trying to flip themselves over while I slept.

So I covered myself with the sheet, tucked the ends under my feet and the top of my head, and the edges under my body, to limit direct contact with the mattress, which was studded with metal buttons and randomly scaped with starchy patches.

I pulled my sheet taut. I surely looked like an overturned canoe. Louisianian creatures bounced off the fabric stretched across my open mouth. My eyes adjusted to the light coming through the sheet from the meager floodlamp in the yard of the hostel. Beings, large and small, alighted on my sheet and promenaded across it. I flicked them from underneath and listened to them land in other parts of the room.

I dreaded the arrival of my roommates. I prayed I would fall asleep before they got back from wherever they were. I didn't want to have to smile. I didn't want to listen to anyone masturbate in Danish. I wanted to lie here under my canoe and consider pink pins and nose-dimpled desk clerks with brown leaves in their hair.

Even though Carolyn had said I'd filled the hostel, there seemed to be no other inhabitants. No snoring, or music, or creaking bunk beds. Just my pistachio shells. I seemed to be alone.

So, with care not to open ingress to my canoe, I reached down and pulled off a sock, a white ribbed sports sock that I'd worn for much of my drive down here. It wasn't essential—I had another pair in my bag and two more down in the car. I slipped it over my hand like a mitten, pulled open the gap between the elastic lip of the sock and my palm, and inserted my erection (it had always been quick to recognize opportunities). Then I went silently to work in the traditional manner. The hostel bunk bed didn't squeak, but rather made a duck-like sound with each upstroke. After a few minutes of accelerating vigor, I gave up trying to be quiet. The bed quacked, and now with each downstroke released a soft pit sound. pit quack pit quack pit quack pit.

I was beholden now. Committed. If I'd been suddenly transported at that instant to the front of my seventh-grade math class, with Corey Czyz and Nadia Mundy in the front row, I wouldn't have been able to stop.

I wheezed. The sheet had worked its way off my head and feet. I cast it aside and completely gave in, bouncing on the bunk bed, chewing my biceps.

The sock worked as expected. My heart beat so hard I felt the squeezings of blood in my brachial arteries. It had been a real thumper.

I rolled up the sacrificial article and dropped it behind the bunk bed. The sweat on my body began to dry and cool. My eyes adjusted to the dark. Danish sports bags and dirty clothes covered the floor and the beds. The upper bunk across the room from me was piled particularly high with the burdens of travel.

But then it moved. The crap on the other upper bunk moved. Then it snorted, changed positions, and blew an involuntary nose-whistle. An empty oilcan of Foster's Lager fell off the bed and landed softly on the low range of shit on the floor.

I froze. I stayed frozen, listening for clues that my roommate had either been genuinely asleep or fully awake while I was busy with my massage.

Then, a gentle snore, followed by a whisper that certainly seemed like a lyric of deep sleep. Eventually I relaxed and fell asleep too.

The following morning I woke confused—spatially, temporally, psychologically. A ceiling two feet from my face. I was varnished with sweat, through which rose stinging welts. Somewhere below me was choral snoring. The air smelled like a salt works. What the hell was going on?

I couldn't remember if I was depressed or not, if I was in the hospital or out. Had somebody died? Was I broke? In love? Lost?

I lifted up my bandaged hand. I looked down at my sockless left foot. Oh. I remember. Long drive. The Ertzes, and those dogs. The ice. Marta, in the sky. The cinnamon-roll bakery. My injured hand. New Orleans. Hostel. Carolyn, the desk clerk. Pink pin. Not really so depressed, come to think of it. Brokenhearted, sure, but just in a general sort of way, as always. Not flush, but not broke either. A disability check would come on the third of the month, just a week away. $92.90, available at any ATM.

And I was free—that was the main thing. Ready to start again in a place where it did not snow. Free!

Of course, I'd furiously jacked off in the presence of some Danish fellow—there was that.

I cautiously looked over at the other top bunk. Deserted. Just a hollowed-out spot among the clothes and junk where someone might've been, now occupied by a half-empty bag of Zapp's Cajun Crawtater chips and a guide to the New Orleans cemeteries, thick with Post It notes. Had I slept next to the unlucky stabbed guy? Dotting the crap on his bunk was a panty here and a bra there. He must be a highly virile Dane. I hated him. I was glad he was gone. Maybe he got mugged again, while pursuing innocent virgins.

On the lower bunks, however, were two men. The man beneath my bunk was huge. The man on the other lower bunk was barely half his size. Their mattresses had been laid bare--the absurd European Dopp kits and woolly towels and laundry boluses that had so densely populated them had been swept off without concern into the middle of the room. Both men were naked, except for tight, bright yellow briefs. The men were face down and white as aluminum siding, except for their necks, which were scarves of angry vermilion. I wouldn't have been able to sleep with a sunburn like that, unless I were full of lager, which they apparently were, since the lager cans all over the room were empty. The lager had to be someplace, and logic suggested it was in these two men.

I slid off the top bunk and attempted to leap quietly to the floor, but somehow I hooked a toe in the string anchorage of one of the little metal mattress buttons. I landed head first in the sodden belongings of my roommates, neither of whom awakened or even stirred. An inch from my nose were the *Pfosten* of Werner Eidotter, the *Größte Pfosten* cover model.

I got dressed. My eye hurt where I'd hit it on a roommate's weird plastic shoe. My toe hurt from being snarled in powerful string. And my bad hand still hurt, too.

It was light out, but I had no idea what time it was. Downstairs in the lobby, the clock said 5:45, but it could have been morning or evening. I guessed morning—the look on Carolyn's face was certainly one of someone at the end of a double shift.

"Still here?" I said, with a familiarity I hoped she would return.

"Yeah," she said, with only a couple PPM of familiarity. "Thirty hours and counting. I'm usually 5 p.m. to 5 a.m. but my relief did not relieve me."

"Jeez," I said, looking at the clock again. "It's quarter to six in the evening?"

"Looks like you slept twenty-four hours."

Carolyn piled her hair on top of her head so she could scratch vigorously at an itch on the back of her neck. Then she closed her eyes and opened her mouth, obviously preparing to sneeze. But, an instant before its climax, she suppressed it, so that the only sound she made was a feeble sqwnch. Much tearing of the eyes followed.

"Bless you. I wish I could do that."

"Practice."

"Okay," I said, as if she'd given me a command rather than an explanation. She might have. An arcane silence followed. I studied my feet. I was wearing brand new socks. A florid blush, starting at my solar plexus, rose like carbonated jam to my scalp, stopping at my right eyeball socket to throb.

"Been in a fight with your roommates already, have you?" asked Carolyn, observing the throb.

"Oh, no. I'm not a fighter. I'm a fleer. I fell out of bed. On my eye."

She quickly consulted her laminated sleeping arrangement chart. "You fell out of the upper berth?"

"Well, I jumped. But I got caught on something on the way down."

"You look like you get caught on things a lot," she said, nodding at my bandaged hand.

"Oh, this one wasn't my fault," I said, and it hadn't been. I hid my hand behind me.

"Never mind, sorry, not my business, don't mean to pry," she said, holding up both palms as if to shield herself from any personal facts I might issue.

"I'm hungry," I said, like a kitten in an illustrated children's book.

"Then by all means, feed! Monstrelet's. Walking?"

"Yeah."

"Ask Batiste how to get there. The guy in the yard. He owns the hostel. And remember, while you're walking, keep your hands—hand—out of your pocket and run if you feel threatened and don't go down Doyle and don't forget to cross the street if approached by a temperamental sort."

"Okay."

"And change that fucking diaper."

On the way to Monstrelet's I stopped in a bookshop that sold autographed Anne Rice books. I thought about getting one inscribed to Marta, with the idea of solemnly burning or burying it.

"$3,200," said the affable guy behind the counter. "For personally inscribed copies of *Mummy* or *Queen*. Anne no longer signs *Lestat* or *Interview*."

"Can I bring in my own copy for her to sign?"

He laughed heartily.

"Oh, no. No, no. Got to buy the books here, in the shop."

I bought a pocket-size Cajun-English dictionary and a plastic-coated map, and continued on to Monstrelet's.

In the un-air-conditioned diner, at my sticky, wobbly table, I sweated freely, but so did everyone else—a mixture of locals, Tulane students, aggressive hipsters, and tall, slouchy waitresses with war-dead stares and sloppy, crooked mouths. There was a group of uniformed Catholic-school girls smoking, drinking coffee, and exchanging cruel stares with the slouchy waitresses, who might have been their older sisters, alumnae of the same school. Everyone sweated like actors in a John Cassavetes movie. Shirts stuck to backbones, armpits radiated tidal rings, crossed legs slid oilily over one another, every square inch of decolletage glistened. An occasional yelp could be heard when a drop of sweat rolled suddenly down a forehead and into an eye. My horrible hand, which I kept under the table, steamed in its diaper. I should've followed Carolyn's order and changed it, but I really didn't want to see what was under there.

A waitress appeared.

"Four cinnamon rolls please," I said.

"They're big," said the waitress.

"Okay."

My waitress, after placing my order, embarked on a break. She sat alone at a booth in the back corner and began to work a crossword. Occasionally she pushed wet tongues of black hair off her cheekbones.

She reminded me of something—a thing so recent that it felt like déjà vu. Quarterways through a cinnamon roll as big as a tournament frisbee, I suddenly realized what seemed so familiar: she resembled, uncannily, those heavy, wet, lascivious flowers that were growing out from under the iron fences and lolling like whores along the buckled sidewalks I'd traveled on my nine-block journey to Monstrelet's from the hostel.

My waitress stabbed at the crossword with her ink pen. She lit a cigarette, blew a perfect torus of smoke, winked at a large round man with a hectare of red beard, filled in another crossword answer, then yawned, dropped her cigarette in a coffee cup, lay down on the long seat, and went to sleep.

All the diner seemed lulled by her catnap. I noticed for the first time that the symptoms of withdrawal from all my psych meds had almost completely disappeared. I would never take them again. I would never put myself in a position where I might be prescribed them, ever again. That shit was over.

This city just might be the right place. Perhaps the lethal, frosted past couldn't cross the Huey P. Long Bridge. I felt the possibility of relations without obsession, friends without fear, adventure without danger, sex without agony. Craziness without insanity. Love without rescue. I felt able. I felt home.

Then, another feeling, more familiar. I needed a bathroom.

I stood up. My waitress woke at the same instant and looked at me. Without my saying anything, she pointed to the trafficky entrance to the kitchen.

"Through there," she said. "Watch your step."

In the kitchen a vast short-order cook was smoking and rolling sausages on a grill while a scrum of slouchy waitresses wheeled around him, picking toast out of toasters and forks out of baskets. The floor was slick with condensed grease and humidity. No one paid any attention to me as I cut through.

In the tiny bathroom I sat, got comfortable, and opened up my little plastic folding map. I decided I'd later go buy three colors of Sharpie felt pens at the K & B drugstore I saw on my walk over here. Red, black, and blue. I'd make a little dot with a Sharpie on my map for every bathroom I found in New Orleans. Red dots would denote the worst bathrooms, the don't-use-except-in-an-emergency shitclosets; blue dots would mark the average fast-food-restaurant facility; and black dots for spotless, leisurely suites.

I was sitting in a definite blue. Fairly clean, as long as you declined closer inspection of any surface or its fissures. Fanny ribbon was in bounty, but it was about as soft as emery paper. The toilet itself was a slight product, designed for occasional domestic use only. It had no place in the big leagues. At least there was a plunger.

I pored over my map for a promising part of town to dump the goddamn Pontiac. I didn't really need a car in New Orleans, and I sure had no attachment to this particular shitwagon. Besides, it wasn't mine, and I did not like to think about the trouble I could get in for driving it.

There was a spot on the map that had a bunch of railroad tracks crossing each other. From TV, I knew that convergences of railroad tracks meant hobos and loitering and abandoned cars. I'd drive the car over there, file the engine numbers off, leave the keys in plain sight, and then take a nice leisurely stroll home, breathing in the delivering heat and the musks of the whoring flowers along the way.

The railroad switching yard turned out to be as menacing and deserted as I'd hoped. I parked the Pontiac and lifted the hood. I had no idea where the engine numbers were, and truthfully I wasn't even sure what part the engine was, though I assumed it was the big thing in the middle with the tubes and cables coming out. I saw no numbers on it, though, and in any case I didn't have a file, so I shut the hood, looked one last time in the car, rescued the rest of the Tushies from the floor of the passenger's side, and left the keys in the ignition. I turned to head back to the hostel.

Soon I was lost. My map proved useless, as many of the streets seemed to have had their signs stolen, or perhaps had never had signs, or even names, in the first place.

I sat down on an anonymous corner and squinted at my plastic map, angling it this way and that so I could read it in the growing dark.

"Fuck this," I announced to the deserted corner. I stood up, kicked at nothing in particular, and then hurt my injured hand trying to wad up the plastic map, which merely sprung back into shape. Inside my Tushie, fresh warmth and a marrow-deep ache.

"And fuck this."

I stood up and headed towards the brightest horizon.

Street after street of dark houses, broken streetlights, and cars with cracked windshields. The glow on the horizon that I figured was the French Quarter did not seem to get brighter.

Beneath a working streetlight I paused and examined my bandage. A bright new spot, moist and Kremlin red. I must change this, I thought, no matter how terrified I was to see just how bad it was.

The phone pole that held the streetlight had two signs, neither legible. I reached for my map.

The streetlight went out with a ptch and a modest display of sparks. Down the street was the light of a diner.

The glass door to the Smart Harriet Food Restaurant jangled when I opened it. I stood just inside the door for a moment as the jangling subsided. The restaurant was almost silent, unlike the strident din of

Monstrelet's. It was—also unlike Monstrelet's—air-conditioned, unhip, and lit as bright as a dentist's office.

I sat down in the first booth, which featured tall, green vinyl seats and Formica tables, their designs worn away by hundreds of thousands of sliding coffee cups and plates of pancakes.

I pulled a laminated menu from between a crusty bottle of Crystal hot sauce and an unlabeled jar of small pickled ovoids. Apparently a decision-maker at the Smart Harriet had changed the menu and penciled the new selections on strips of masking tape stuck over the decedent items. I peeled up a piece of tape that said Facon 2 Pcs; under it was Bacon 15 Strps.

A voice said: "Ioanna, what's this fassone?"

"That's Facon, with a long 'a' and a hard 'c,' Coryate," answered another voice—Ioanna's, I supposed. "It's a portmanteau of 'fake' and 'bacon.'"

"Oh."

"Want some?"

"No I do not."

I leaned out of my booth. A small man in a corduroy sports coat sat at the counter, studying the menu intently. His feet didn't reach the floor. His trouser cuffs didn't reach his feet. I couldn't see his face, but a tight, dense, black buzzcut stuck to his skull like iron filings.

"So no more bacon?" said Coryate.

"No more bacon," said Ioanna, who was visible on her hands and knees under a table, apparently de-wobbling it by wedging a pocket calculator under one of the feet. "I'm experimenting with healthier fare."

"Well, what's this here 'veggie beans and rice'? Beans're vegetables and rice is vegetables where I come from, and that's Lake Charles USA, by God."

"And they're vegetables here, too," said Ioanna. "They're just not cooked in bacon grease and mixed with sausage."

"I'm concerned about the wording here," said Coryate. "Beans and rice is vegetables, so why put "veggie" up front like that? That don't make it healthy."

"The 'beans and rice' in 'veggie beans and rice' refers to the dish, not its vegetable components," said Ioanna, crawling out from under the now-stabilized table. "'Veggie' qualifies said dish, which is made with lard and soy paste rather than grease."

"Grease counts towards meat?"

"Well, it's not a vegetable."

"Neither is feldspar, or hydrated silica," said Coryate.

Ioanna appeared at my booth with a plastic glass of iceless water in one hand and a cup of coffee in the other, both of which she held by their rims with two fingers. She had freckles on her arms that disappeared under the short sleeves of a loose black blouse with tiny pearl buttons, and reappeared in greater numbers on her collarbone. She leaned over and placed the coffee and water in front of me.

I accidentally bumped the table. Both the coffee and water spilled. They commingled, forming a muddy little river that made its way slowly to the edge of the table.

"Another one?" said Ioanna. "I'll fix it for you. Don't move."

She got down on her knees and crawled under the table.

"Don't expect anything," shouted Coryate, turning around for the first time.

His face and hands were randomly smeared black, as though he'd been in a charcoal-briquette fight. He wore a long, millimeter-thin mustache that seemed to function as a plinth for his nose, an oily bulb that appeared to be pulling all of his other features toward it. His iron-shard hairline stopped low on his forehead and his ears stuck out like shutters in the wind, threatening to slam shut over his eardrums.

"Ignore him," said Ioanna from under the table. She hammered at something, presumably another defunct calculator. My refreshments jumped. "You need to change that bandage."

She came out from under the table.

"I guess I'll have some pancakes and some Facon, please. And some biscuits."

"Is that a diaper? I spy Velcro strips."

She was younger than I thought at first, maybe forty-five. Her brown hair was tied up in a utilitarian bun. Now I could see there were also tiny freckles that climbed over her collarbone and up her neck to pool on her cheekbones. One of her earlobes had a healing cut, as if an earring had been torn out.

"Say, is there a phone I could use?"

"Only blood from a fairly serious injury would soak through a commercial disposable diaper like that."

I kept my hand under the table.

Coryate and his oily bulb came over.

"What injury?" he said. "Come on, let's see it, son."

I was trapped. I sighed, and put my hand on the table.

"You ought to run over by Charity and get one of them emergency-room people to change that," he said.

"Don't like doctors," I said, sounding like a wet piccolo.

"Come with me," said Ioanna.

"Ah, uh," I said.

"Coryate, stay out here."

She turned around and headed to the back of the Smart Harriet. On the way she shouted into the kitchen.

"Facon, cakes, biscuits!"

A practiced snarl and a crash came from deep within. Ioanna turned back and glared at me.

"Come," she said, pointing at the restroom.

She sat me down on the lid of a toilet and balanced a cafeteria tray across my knees.

"Hand on the tray."

I obeyed. Ioanna kneeled in front of me on a dishcloth. She had several more in her lap. Next to my hand was a mess of first aid supplies: iodine, cotton balls, tequila, Band-Aids, paring knife.

"Sit still."

Ioanna peeled the Velcro, a long, careful rrrt. She unwrapped the diaper until the dried blood held it fast. She eased the paring knife between two layers and sliced it open like a catfish.

"I don't want to see it," I said.

"Have a little tequila."

"Is there a worm?"

"No, it's an uncommon bottle of tequila that has a worm these days. This is a drugstore-bought spirit, purely functional."

I had some. She pulled firmly but carefully on the diaper, like it was a weed whose roots might break off and remain stuck in the ground. In my hand something gave, a stubborn bottle cap finally yielding. Then, the familiar, almost comfortable, almost urinary warmth of freed blood.

The diaper came loose. Before I shut my eyes I caught a glimpse of the contrast of my moist, bleached-gray palm with the butcher-shop pinks and marbled-reds of my sliced and crushed and reopened hand.

Vinegary fluids.

"You need a doctor."

"It doesn't hurt."

"Should. That's why you need one."

Then, the dry, slightly abrasive touch of gauze, getting tighter as she wrapped it around my hand. I opened my eyes. Blood was leaching along the mesh of cotton fibers as quickly as she could wrap. A shallow pond of thin blood, spiraled with peroxide and iodine, had collected at a corner of the tray.

Coryate came in. He had a coffee cup in his hand.

Ioanna turned around.

"Damnation. Did I tell you to stay out of here or did I just say it in my head?"

"But I need a cup of coffee, dammit. All the pots are empty, and I don't feel like waiting for you to finish playing doctor."

"Get out."

"You can have mine," I said, taking a sip of tequila.

"Hum. Okay. Thanks."

"Sure."

"Hurry it up anyway, woman," said Coryate. "This fellah's cup won't hold me long."

"Get out, you mosquito."

Coryate did not. Instead he unzipped, and took a long, noisy piss in a urinal behind Ioanna. Then he left.

"You can come back and have pancakes and Facon and biscuits," said Ioanna, "after you see a doctor and get that mess cleaned and sewn back up. Now go."

"I don't really know where I am. I'm not from here."

"Where do you stay?"

"A youth hostel. On Iquem Street."

"A fair distance. Is there somebody there can come fetch you?"

I thought about it.

"Well, yes. I think so."

An hour later Carolyn pulled up in an old brown Chrysler and came inside.

"Can't make a habit of this, Jerome," she said, looking completely wiped out.

"Sorry."

I wasn't a bit sorry. I was delighted. I liked Carolyn, though I wasn't sure how, yet.

Ioanna—whom I also liked, though I wasn't sure in what way either, except that it felt filial—did not acknowledge Carolyn.

"C'mon, Jerome."

Carolyn headed for the door. The leaf was still in her hair, an inch or two lower.

"Come back sometime, Mr Jerome," said Ioanna.

She never asked what had happened to me.

Carolyn was quiet on the ride back.

The floor of the passenger seat was deeply hidden by what felt underfoot like books and papers and shoes and tennis balls.

We drove in silence. Not an uncomfortable silence, like we'd shared earlier that day, but rather a tranquility, a peace de luxe of the sort that comes from the kensho that you're not alone.

I never did go to the doctor. But I did take Ioanna up on her invitation to come back and visit. Indeed, I went to the Smart Harriet nearly every day, a new bandage on my hand, which I'd wound myself, over the sink, eyes closed, in the moldy, slick bathroom of the hostel.

"How's the mitt," said Ioanna one afternoon, skidding a plate of pancakes across the table.

"Getting better everyday," I said, a falsehood. It didn't look like it was healing well at all.

"Mm."

"Ioanna, will you hire me on here? I'll wash dishes, mop, whatever you want. I can make good grilled-cheese sandwiches."

Ioanna looked me over for a moment.

"Harriet will say no."

"There really is a Smart Harriet?"

"There is," she said. "You wouldn't like it here, anyway."

"You seem like you like it here."

"I was born here. I was born a waitress, and I'll stay one, like it or not. But listen. I know a woman who might take you. I'll telephone her and let her know you might stop by, and that you make outstanding cheese sandwiches."

Ioanna scribbled something on a green diner bill and handed it to me.

MRS. (NOT MISS) HEBERT AT ERRIL'S FASHION DEPARTMENT STORE. PRACTICE GRILLING BEFORE YOU GO.

Erril's Fashion Department Store was probably not the oldest department store on American soil, but it was certainly the oldest that had never been remodeled or modernized or cleaned. The floors were the worn, flecked, putty-and-bean color of junior-high-school hallways. The walls met the floor not at a sharp right angle but with a little ramp of oily, packed dirt studded with price tags and cigarette butts. The sales floor was dusk-dark, illuminated only by low, shaded light fixtures, like in a noir pool hall. But instead of wiry felons and pompadoured hustlers, the place was alive with tiny old ladies in cataract shades slaloming sock racks and girdle displays. Erril's was also likely the last department store in the country with a lunch counter.

The Luncheonaire's low stools were all unoccupied. On the counter were clusters of standard diner complements: mustard, ketchup, and mayonnaise squeeze bottles, Tabasco, salt and pepper shakers, sugar cubes, tiny cream tankards, and large jam and jelly caddies with wire handles. On the end of the counter was a pie spinner spinning pies. Behind the counter but in front of the soda fountain was an old electric cash register partly mummified in silver duct tape. Just beside it stood a tall, skinny woman, her graying hair tied up in a ponytail. She looked pretty much the way Ioanna had described Mrs Hebert. She was stabbing a two-quart can of Orange Hi-C with a steak knife.

She left the knife sticking hilt-deep in the can, and turned her attention to me.

"Let's find a menu, unless you know what you want," she said.

The stool I sat on was so low and the waitress so tall that I had a sudden vivid memory of being in the bathtub as a child when a lady at the home I was at walked in with a box of Mr Bubble and sprinkled it in the running water, smiling down at me.

I thought it was best to eat first, before stating my mission.

"Set me up with a menu, bay. What's good?" I said in my best easy-going voice, which I'd started to affect a day or two after arriving in New Orleans. Later I learned that most newcomers here do the same thing, sometimes unconsciously, but often actively practicing the music of the accent, then testing it out on native New Orleanians to see if it passed muster. It never did.

"Nothing to speak of," she said, handing me a menu.

I thought I'd get something like a poboy or gumbo or étouffée, to further mask my origins, but there was nothing of the sort on the menu. There were reuben melts, hamburgers, butt-steak sandwiches, ham, and ham with pineapple circles. Under Accompaniments were french fries, milk, and coffee. Dessert was a roster of pies, and "Candy."

I ordered a hamburger and fries and a Coke.

She disappeared for about five minutes, then emerged with my lunch. It was the largest hamburger I'd ever seen. A slice of onion an inch thick stuck out on all sides like a ring of Saturn. There were four french fries, each a half of a potato. The Coke came in an aquarium of crushed ice.

"Ioanna said it was good eatin' here," I said with my mouth full.

She stopped consolidating half-empty Tabascos with a foil funnel and turned to me, a hand on her hip.

"You're the cheese sandwich man?"

"Yes ma'am."

"Well, get on back here and grill me one while I examine your technique."

I did. My technique, and the resulting sandwich, were perfect.

"This a reasonable product," said Mrs Hebert between bites. "But I'm concerned that that mushed breadhook of yours will fail you during the lunch stampede and I'll be left overworked and unassisted and a robber'll seize the opportunity to run off with my gratuity jar."

She tapped on my bandaged hand with a grilled-cheese crust.

"Oh no," I said. "A minor cut, getting better every day."

"Your timing's good, I'll grant you that. A colleague just quit me."

"I can start immediately!"

"Alrighty," she said after a moment.

The workday started at nine in the morning and went until the evening cook relieved me at five. When I got home to the hostel after work, I'd check the big map to see where the new people were from. It hadn't changed much during the month I'd been here. The pink pin in Quito was still there, but I still hadn't seen her yet. I'd encountered many of the Danes, but never my two lower-berth roommates, not formally at least—they were always passed out on their bunks in some stage of drunkenness, or recovery from same. I only ever saw their dorsal sides banded with snug primary-colored jockey shorts. And I hadn't seen my last roommate, the one who may or may not have been present while I ruined my sock.

I couldn't tell if Carolyn felt the same kind peace around me as I did around her, but she didn't seem to mind my hanging around and lying on the vector-borne couch in the lobby of the hostel after my shift at the Luncheonaire while she talked on the phone and monkeyed with her hair and made sport of the hostelers.

"Is that all you've ever had here?" I said, one afternoon after I'd come in from a long day of grilled-cheese grilling. "Europeans? And a lone Ecuadoran?"

"Nah, we've had every flavor of human. We even had a chick here who lived in Antarctica."

I shifted on the couch so I could see her. She was sitting and tugging at her hair with her old plastic brush with black bristles. One knee was bent and pushed up against the rim of the gray metal desk. The denim covering it was pale and thinning. If she were to lean forward, the taut cotton strands might snap snap snap, revealing her skin and releasing the tiniest puffs of cotton dust.

"I didn't think anyone was from there," I said.

"She was, or so she said. She wanted to sleep with me. She said I looked warm."

This was the first time Carolyn had referred to sex. Incredibly, no uncomfortable feelings beset me. Not jealousy, lust, love, possessiveness, blues, shame, heartache. Just that same weird peace. I have a friend!

"Did you?"

"Did I look warm?"

"No, I mean..."

"You know," Carolyn continued, "it only snowed here once, and I fucking missed it. It lasted three hours and was gone by noon. You know why? Me and my Antarctican were in bed at the Guesclin Hotel sleeping off a slivovitz hangover."

"I bet it snows a lot in the Czech Republic," I said.

"Worse in Denmark. Believe me, I've heard stories."

"I wonder how bad it is in Quito?"

"No telling," said Carolyn, looking over her shoulder at the pink pin. "It looks like it's in the mountains. You oughta ask her next time you see her."

"You know, I don't think I've ever seen her," I said.

"You're kidding. She sleeps with you, man."

"What're you talking about? I'm not sleeping with anyone! I'd remember."

She smiled and snorted, as if she couldn't stand for one moment longer pretending I wasn't an idiot.

"Not with you, you prevert. Next to you. The other top bunk? The Spanish didn't tip you off?"

This could not be. I looked at my socks.

"That's a girl?" I said.

"She doesn't look like a girl to you? Long black hair, kissy lips? She looks like a girl to me, Jerome." said Carolyn. "I mean, she's a girl."

"I've never seen her!" I said, sitting up straight, a bloom of pathogens rising from the couch. "I've never seen anyone in that bunk!"

"She does sleep during the day, come to think of it," said Carolyn. "She parties all night, with your other roomies."

"I've never met them, either," I said. "But, she's, I mean, you mean... are you saying that girls and boys can sleep together in the same room?"

"If the hostel's crowded, yes, Jerome, boys and girls can room together. Your other roommates are gay, anyway. They're good friends with her. And you're..."

"What? What? I'm not gay," I said, not really sure of it—the muscular calves on those Tour de France guys always gave me a boner. And I had strange, pelvicentric feelings regarding Daniel Day-Lewis's Adam's apple.

"Did I say gay? I was going to say that you're safe-looking."

"Safe."

"Safe." said Carolyn. "You're a very safe yet excitable young straight man."

"What's her name?"

"Miranda," said Carolyn.

"Miranda," said I.

I never saw Miranda. Her bunk was always empty, except for the scatter of panties and empty cans of lager. Now I wondered if the spring triple-issue of *Größte Pfosten* had been hers, rather than one of my other roommate's. I hoped it wasn't hers. I could never measure up to Werner.

It didn't matter anyway, because I had to move out of the hostel. I couldn't earn enough making cheese sandwiches to pay eighteen bucks a night for a place to live, even though I was quite skilled, and becoming locally famous.

I began spending my lunch hour and the hours after work apartment hunting. But after a while I realized I was looking less for apartments and more for girls with long black hair and kissy lips. There were an awful lot of them. But none were Miranda: I queried them all.

One apartment, just a couple of blocks from the Smart Harriet, had sounded promising in the ad but proved to be unsuitable, because of the antsy junkie squatters there who objected to any changes in the tenancy.

"Fuck off!" they said.

I fucked off and went to the Smart Harriet.

"You smell like grilled cheese," Ioanna informed me.

"I make a lot of them. I'm quite famous."

I wondered if Miranda had heard of my sandwiches.

"Famous? Are you getting rich?" Ioanna asked. "Are you going to buy a mansion and lease me a wing so I can live out my spinster years in seclusion?"

"I would, but I can't even afford to stay at the hostel any more."

"I'll rent you my tub!" shouted Coryate, from the counter. "No pets!"

"No, that's okay," I said.

Coryate yelled for a refill.

I'd learned that Coryate was an artist who made his living doing charcoal portraits of tourists in Jackson Square. Reputedly he was also a sketch artist for the cops, and occasionally accepted small thank-you gifts in return for little changes here and there to his sketches so that they more closely resembled persons the police did not like but whom they otherwise had no good reason to arrest.

"How's the hand?" he said.

"Better," I said, looking down.

I still kept it wrapped in gauze and an Ace bandage. It just would not heal properly. It hurt. I should've kept my word and gone to a doctor long ago. I'd have been able to make world-famous grilled cheeses a lot quicker if I'd had full use of both hands. It was the one chronic, concrete reminder that there had been a time before these tranquil New Orleanian days, a period of frost, blood, locks, misinterpretations, and loneliness. I imagined the relief I'd get by hacking it off with a big meat cleaver.

I promised myself that once I'd found a place to live I'd go to the doctor and have this rotting gash taken care of. I didn't want to repulse Miranda, after all.

Carolyn telephoned and told me that her friend Terence, an ex-hostel clerk, had gotten so fed up with the surprise reversals of fortune that in his view so characterized New Orleans that he just up and got on a Greyhound back to his homeland.

"Homeland?" I said, still a little fuzzy from having a positively Kodachromic daydream interrupted: me and Miranda in a pile of autumn leaves, locked in a promising tickle fight.

"Canada. And his place is now available."

Terence's place was cheap and only about fifteen blocks from the hostel. I still went to see Carolyn every day, partly—muchly—in hopes that Miranda would turn up. But she never did. She'd either just gone out, or had just come back and gone to bed.

"How's Terence's shithole shotgun?" asked Carolyn when I came in one afternoon.

She quoined a whole giant SweeTart in her mouth and bit hard. A little chalky rocket shot across the room.

"Pretty fair," I said.

And it was, except for the neighbor on the other side of the shotgun, Mr Murdoch, a slick Romeo in his fifties who lived with his mother.

They fought a lot, this mother and son, mostly about the son's womanizing. He often had sleepover dates, and the mother would sometimes bust into the son's room while dating was in progress, to warn the woman that she'd better watch out or she'd catch some AIDS. I knew this because everything radiated through those desiccated plaster walls.

"His mom? And he's fifty?" said Carolyn.

"Yeah. She's cool. I don't like the son, though."

I would occasionally hear him promising a conquest his indivisible fealty, and then, sometimes within hours, promising another lover the same thing.

I had another damn good reason not to like the man, but I didn't feel like explaining it to Carolyn: that my toilet was structurally connected to his—they were back-to-back, with just a thin wall in between—and that if I was on my toilet when he sat on his, I seesawed into the air.

"I never went to Terence's place," said Carolyn, wrapping the telephone cord around a pencil. "But he tried to get me over there all the time, probably in order to fill me with absinthe and snip off my clothes with electric scissors."

Carolyn made an electric-scissors sound and scissored her fingers down the front of her t-shirt. "I think he thought that absinthe restored heterosexual lust in dykes."

"Does it?" I said, not sure if she was being sarcastic.

"Nope," she said. "Beer might, though. How's the water pressure?"

"Not bad," I said. "I'd say forty percent of ideal."

"Any charm? Everything in this city is supposed to be charming."

I thought about it.

"Well, in the kitchen over the counter there's a big black wooden thing stuck to the wall, like a Louise Nevelson sculpture. But tighter scrutiny revealed its true nature to be kitchen cabinets. A long bank of them, painted shut. I tried chipping away at the paint, but it must be a half inch thick."

"Probably a body in there. Or maybe just heads. That's charming I guess. Notice an odor?"

"No, just the—" I looked past Carolyn. I think I turned red, or maybe white.

"Wha?" she said, a giant SweeTart puck stored in one cheek.

"The girl from Quito's gone," I said.

I moved my head from side to side, to see if I'd just caught the light the wrong way. No, there was no pink pin there. I felt like I'd been hit in the back of the knees by a medicine ball.

"Yep, Miranda's gone," said Carolyn. "Checked out this a.m. before I came on. A surprise. I thought she'd stay forever. Oh, they do get some bitch snow in Quito, by the way. We chatted a little yesterday after she came in late from some kind of X-rated crab-boil puppet show in the Bywater. I told her how much you hated snow, and how you left Massachusetts because of it. That made her laugh."

"She laughed?"

"Giggled. I think she liked you, Jerome. She said she watched you sleeping all the time. She said you have a cute philtrum."

"Me?" My esophagus dried out and the arches of my feet started to sweat. My whole skull was steaming and my ears seemed to be furling and trying to retract into my skull. "A cute philtrum?"

Carolyn looked at me happily. "She said you looked like a tiny baby sleeping, that you curl your hand up into a tiny baby fist. She wanted to miniaturize you and carry you in a pouch to keep you cozy and protect you from harm, and feed you little bits of flan and lettuce and french fry."

"You're making all that up!"

"No, I'm really not. And judging by that rosy blush, it seems that the news pleases you."

"Not me," I said, squeaking, panicky, suddenly desperate to find her. "It sounds like she was flirting with you."

"Right," she said. "I wish. I never get femmes."

Carolyn was suddenly gloomy. For a few moments she focused on licking clean the inside of her Giant Chewy SweeTarts wrapper. Then she cheered up again.

"If I'd only known sooner," she said. "I could've won her for you, Jerome. Cute philtra are positively irresistible to the Pacific South Americans."

"Really?"

"I'm sorry she's gone, Jerome. She was a fire-fucking-work. Except for the glasses."

My muscles withered under my skin. I felt like I was wearing a beef-jerky suit.

"Did she go back to Quito?"

"Doubt it. I think she was planning to stay in town."

"Where? You know, just curious."

"I don't have the slightest idea."

"Someone has to know," I said, considering running up to the room just to make sure she wasn't still there. "What about our other two roomies?"

"Gone, too."

"Dammit! Are you sure you don't have just a really slight idea?"

"I don't know, Jerome. Are you really hooked on someone you haven't met yet? Or even seen?"

"No, I certainly am not, how ridiculous."

I crossed my arms and tried to appear bored.

"Damn, you are. You really should've told me. A long time ago. I love matchmaking."

Truth was, I hadn't known until now.

Over the next few weeks, any workaday doings—sleep, job, food, bills, health—that didn't directly concern my pursuit of Miranda, I either shirked or forgot or just zombied through. Carolyn's assistance was largely technical or strategic—apart from the occasional brief prowl or stakeout, she didn't often do actual fieldwork. She did, however, try to cheer me up whenever I suffered an especially dispiriting search.

"She probably doesn't like me anyway," I said.

"Miranda didn't just see you sleeping, Jerome—a passive happenstance—but watched you sleep. So chin up."

"I'll never, ever find her, and I bet she's forgotten me already."

"How can you have such a debilitating crush on someone you've never even met?"

"I'm not debilitated," I said.

Carolyn and I sat across from each other in a booth at the Smart Harriet. Ioanna was in a cold mood. She had taken our orders without comment, and had merely nodded when I re-introduced her to Carolyn. When she brought our food, she skidded the plates along the table so that they tapped the salt and pepper shakers at the far end. There was some sloshing of coffee. She gave Carolyn my pancakes and me Carolyn's waffles.

"You look debilitated," said Carolyn.

I sat with my elbows on the table, my forehead in my hands, staring at my pancakes, which had been placed on the same plate as my eggs and bacon, an arrangement I'd always found intolerable. If my syrup touched my eggs or bacon, I couldn't eat anything at all. And Ioanna knew that. She thought it was charming, or a symptom of Aspergers syndrome. Either way, she always made sure my sweets and savories arrived on two separate plates.

I glanced over at Ioanna to see if I could divine, from the way she swept out, wiped down, or swatted at things in the diner, just what I'd done to displease her. Maybe it was because she knew I hadn't gone to see a doctor yet about my stupid hand.

"Maybe flummoxed is a better word," said Carolyn. "And your bitchy mother over there probably doesn't help much."

"She's not my mother."

"Mother-figure. Maybe the combination of your unpleasant mother-figure and your unlocatable dream-girl-figure has flummoxed and debilitated you."

Ioanna was stuffing napkins into a chrome napkin holder, far more napkins than the napkin holder was designed to hold, making napkins nearly impossible to remove, except in tiny shreds, or in groups of one thousand. Most of the regulars brought their own.

Ioanna was really cramming one. Cords popped out on her neck. She bent over a little, and some cleavage became visible. Carolyn leaned towards me, watching Ioanna.

"She's hot, for forty-nine or whatever," said Carolyn. "Oh, but we're talking about your love life, Jerome. Sorry."

It felt different than love, this smothering mudslide of desperation and longing. It was an old feeling. Old as in preverbal, or even atavistic. But I didn't try to explain that to Carolyn.

I pushed my forehead harder into my hand so that my eyelids stretched. I moaned quietly.

"Please don't fall in love with her," I said. "I can't handle my friend-figure lusting after my mother-figure."

"You know what I think? I think your world is crowded with mother-figures."

"Noo!"

"Would you just eat your food and quit groaning like that? You sound like Chewbacca."

"I can't. I hate this."

"If we can't find Miss Ecuador, I'll find you a girlfriend. I know lots of beautiful girls that won't have me. And they're sheep for nice philtra."

"But I want Miranda."

I moaned some more and squeezed my hair, while Carolyn ate lustily and Ioanna ignored our empty coffee cups.

"You know," said Carolyn, "I think your Ioanna there doesn't like me. She doesn't approve. She didn't like me the first time. I don't think she was expecting her little special man to befriend a coarse hussy."

"Guh."

"Maybe I'll be your girlfriend, Jerome."

Carolyn pantomimed a blowjob. It was as shocking and obscene a performance as anything I'd ever witnessed. Then she initiated a game of footsie.

"I'm confused," I said.

Carolyn seemed amused by it all, and somehow my agonies made her expansive about her own sexual misadventures. She fell in love easily, she said, and became obsessed as deeply as I did, albeit with people she'd actually met at least once.

"Some of those girls out there nearly killed me," she said, as we drove down North Rampart after our meal. "The younger they are, the slimmer, the meaner, the smarter, then the darker the relationship becomes, until I'm a puddle of need, and then they leave me for someone that's even meaner and smarter but also has a tremendous bosom."

Carolyn swerved around an old man in a track suit doing a variant of the River Dance in the middle of North Rampart. Carolyn and I often drove around aimlessly, drinking beer and wasting gas and avoiding eccentrics performing in the roadways, but this time I had the feeling we were aimed someplace.

"Where are we going?"

"We are going to look for your goddess. We are going to feel the curbs of every likely street until we find her. Or until it gets dark. I promised you I'd help, but I haven't been doing such a hot job. So. Here we are. Peel them eyeballs."

We drove up and down the long streets of the Bywater, slowing down now and then for closer looks at strollers and loiterers with Miranda attributes. As the false positives mounted, I grew even more despairing than usual.

The traffic slowed, then stopped. A rusted, ruined freight train was stalled ahead, blocking the road. Not quite stalled—it would jolt, then creep forward a few feet, then stop with a shudder, then jolt again and move a few feet in the other direction. There was another train on a parallel track doing the same thing, but to a different rhythm. Carolyn reached into the back seat and pulled a beer out of a big ice-filled cooler.

"Here."

"What's up with these trains?" I said, taking the glass quart of Miller. "I feel like I'm in a movie about doomsday."

A woman began to climb out of a hopper car. She hoisted herself over, and then hung onto the lip of the car with one hand while she studied the ground. The cigarette in her mouth she tossed down onto the rail ballast. She wore a high-waisted white silk slip a shade or two paler than her skin and the spectral opposite of her short, chaotic, plum-tinted hair. She was backpacked, barefoot, and brass-knuckled. She let go of the hopper and dropped at least six feet, landing without a wince on the sharp rocks of the ballast. She picked up her cigarette, gave it a hard suck, then looked around.

"Is she what you meant by young and slim and mean?" I said.

"Don't point."

"I'm not pointing."

"Yeah," said Carolyn, sighing greatly. "She's what I mean."

The woman flicked her cigarette at least thirty feet, then ducked under the train and was gone.

"It was a bus wreck, my last relationship," said Carolyn, unsteadily, clearly affected by the short cinema of the feral freight-hopper. "It started so great, but got bad fast, then crashed. All because of a misunderstanding. That time, she was the one obsessed over me—can you believe that? But I was obsessed over her, too. We were perfect for each other."

She said that last without any irony that I could detect.

"Someone you worked with?" I said. "I read in People that that's asking for trouble."

"No. Well, kind of," she said wearily. "She wasn't really officially employed at the hostel. She was just there a lot, and kind of helped out some."

Finally, the trains slowly moved off, and we headed towards Arabi. We had started our second Miller quarts. It was getting dark.

"It was bad, though, huh," I said, not wanting the dialogue on love to fizzle. "It must have been very painful."

I sounded like a shrink, for chrissake.

"Okay, it was this chick named Francie," Carolyn said suddenly. "And the misunderstanding was that she thought I was cheating on her with this guy who worked at the hostel who was always coming onto me. Terence, your shotgun's prior tenant. But I wasn't. Turned out later that she'd been cheating on me."

"Ack."

"Getting cheated on sucks," she said. "It's the mind's eye that does all the torturing. You know, picturing her with someone else, especially fucking someone else, doing it in that position that was just me and hers, those little scream-hisses when she came that were her gifts to me, now she's giving them to someone else...you know what I mean?"

I noticed we were being ambitiously tailgated.

"Hey," I said, looking over my shoulder. "I think—"

"Maybe you don't," she continued, seeming to take no notice of the large car trying to spelunk our tailpipe. "Well. It hurts. And you can't not watch. The brain won't allow it. You see A Clockwork Orange? Remember the Ludovico Technique? Like that. The mind's eye, held open with little metal clips. Films. Over and over and overnovernover."

"You better let this guy around, he seems—"

"That, my friend," she said, still oblivious, "will never happen to me again. Never. Just talking about it now makes me want to drive off a cliff and die. Did you know I haven't hooked up with anybody since Francie? Know why? Just to avoid those films. They'll kill a girl. Kill."

"Carolyn! This guy is really close!"

"Oh. I see. Put your feet up on the dash, Jerome, I'm gonna stomp on my brake. I think I'm still insured."

But then we noticed it was a cop car, because of the sirens and flashing lights and the bullhorn commanding us to pull over.

"Fuck," said Carolyn.

We both had open quart bottles of beer in our laps. Mine was almost full. Carolyn's was nearly gone.

She pulled over in front of a social club busy with people coming and going. I was in a panic. I had a full beer between my legs, and I was in a car, and soon I would be in a jail, where they'd run my name and see there was a bench warrant for me as a car thief and cinnamon-roll-bakery destroyer, then beat a confession out of me and throw me in solitary forever.

On the dashboard there was a blanched Monchhichi doll that must have been there for a decade. I grabbed it and forced it headfirst into the neck of my Genuine Draft. I carefully placed the bottle on the floor of the back seat just as the cop walked up.

"License and proof of insurance," said the cop.

"What'd you pull me over for?" said Carolyn.

My hand jumped to my heart.

"License and proofa insurance."

Carolyn yanked her backpack out from behind the seat and rifled around for a while until she found her billfold. She still had her quart of Lite beer between her legs.

"Here."

"Mm. And what you got there?" the cop asked.

"This is Lite Beer from Miller."

"Let me see."

Carolyn handled the bottle to the cop, who held it up by the neck and peered through the liquid at the streetlights. There was about an inch of beer left.

"How much you had to drink tonight, ma'am?"

"Well, whatever's missing."

"Okay, then." He gave her the bottle back. "Get both those taillights fixed and your left directional and don't drive around this neighborhood this time of night, unless you bring you a bigger boyfriend. With two working hands."

"He's tougher than he looks," said Carolyn. "He's just lovesick right now. Besides, I have a .38 in my backpack."

"Okay then," said the cop. Then he went back to his cruiser and drove off.

"Wow," I said, sweating lather. "That jangled me up. I thought we were going to jail."

"What for? Busted taillights?"

"DUI and unlicensed firearms possession and smart-aleckiness and..."

"There's no DUI or gun licensing in New Orleans and I was perfectly polite and respectful."

We headed back west. Presently I caught the smell of the sea. Faint, but there. On a map I'd seen New Orleans is surrounded by water. A lake, a river, the Gulf, bayous.

"I tried to kill myself after Francie," Carolyn said, her voice startling me.

"Jesus. Carolyn. Don't tell me that."

She turned on the dome light, and, without slowing down, rolled up the right short sleeve of her shirt up over her shoulder. Through the stubble under her arm ran a short, fat scar right over the profunda brachii.

"I obviously missed the artery. Wasn't even close. Fucking hurt, and it didn't even bleed much. I didn't mention it to anybody."

"Fuck, Carolyn."

"I know."

"I command you to take good care of yourself!"

"You've never had anyone cheat on you. I envy you, you and your Miranda crush. I run from crushes now, not that I have them much. Or, more precisely, allow myself to have them. No more relationships for me. Just crushless sex. I'll take my relationship-forming urges out on you and your absentee Ecuadoran."

"This crush doesn't feel enviable."

"You didn't care about Miranda all that much till you found out she'd watched you sleep. That's kinda off, Jerome. A little kinky."

"Where is she now? Francie, I mean?"

"I don't know."

Quiet and a little drunk, we headed out on the old Airline Highway. Thunderstorms had been threatening all day. It was hot. The air was like meringue. I reached in the back and pulled a cold beer out of the cooler. I ignored my warm beer with the Monchhichi sticking out of it—likely both were ruined.

"Where are we going now? Stake out the airport lounge?"

"Watch planes."

The airport appeared ahead of us. Its cobalt-blue lamps lined runways that stretched off to vanishing points all around the circle of the horizon. The air-traffic control tower with its eerie green eye-panes looked out over the flat land.

It was late, but planes were still landing, probably delayed by the thunderstorms surrounding the city. Carolyn drove up to the top tier of the long-term parking garage and parked the car facing the runways. Ours was the only car up there.

We watched 737s land for a long time without saying anything. The only sound was the scraping roar of engines and the brt brtbrt of tires hitting the tarmac.

Carolyn climbed out of the car. She reached down and pulled the release on her seat back, which fell forward and lay flat. Then she jumped in the back seat and put her feet up.

"Comfortable?" I said.

"Uuut. Ut."

She'd had more beer than I had. After a minute I climbed in the back and put my feet up on the front seat too. The cooler of beer was on the floor between us.

We watched for planes, but there hadn't been any in more than an hour.

Carolyn leaned into me a little, then scooted over and put her head on my shoulder.

"Protect me from bad relationships," she said, an order. "And I promise I'll get you your black-haired snow bunny."

I felt an earring through the material of my shirt. A lone strand of hair poked at my earlobe. I adjusted slightly and put my arm around her shoulder. Perfectly natural. Because she was a lesbian and I was her friend, and we'd had some deep talks about love and such. Even thus, I grew a stratospheric, glowing erection.

"Deal," I said.

My heart chugged. Carolyn's hair, lighted by the glow of the airport, jumped every time my heart beat, or hers. After a moment of paralyzing discomfort, Carolyn gracefully half-twisted towards me and suddenly she was lying face up in my lap. She reached up to pull me to her. I could hardly move, let alone bend over, even for a kiss, due to the erection. So I pulled her up to me.

She whimpered and cried and ran her hands over my face, kissing me lightly, almost without touching. She tasted of salt. I held her by the waist and under her shoulders. I slid down in the seat to get closer. I closed my eyes. I imagined Miranda, her kissy lips.

Then Carolyn stopped.

"Back in a few secs."

She climbed out, headed unsteadily to a concrete pillar, and disappeared behind it. A rivulet of liquid snaked from behind it, as black and shiny as blood under the sulfur arc lamps.

She came back.

"I have to go too," I said.

I went over to the same spot she'd been. I saw where she'd crouched down, the spatter.

After some effort I undid my belt and zipper. My erection was the otherworldly, unbendable sort that I used to get in high school. And it was clearly not going to subside and allow me to pee in the accepted fashion (earthward). So I undid my jeans and just let go. I peed in a high arc over the city of Kenner as the last plane of the night cleared the thunderheads and landed between the long arrows of cobalt lamps.

When I got back to the car, Carolyn was stretched along the back seat, deep in sleep. Both disappointed and wildly relieved, I climbed in front, and soon I was just as dead to the world.

The drive back from the parking garage the next morning was generally silent. My clothes were damp with sour sweat. My head was a microwaved pumpkin. Carolyn pulled over in front of the First Imperssions Bar and threw up out the window.

"That's better," Carolyn said, driving off again. "I feel much better."

I said, "Remember you said that beer just might make you like boys for a few minutes! Haha!"

"It does," she said, pulling up to the hostel. "But you spent those few minutes tinkling. Missed your chance."

I'd heard that before.

"Besides," she said as we walked up the walk, "you need to reserve all your chang for Miranda. The Pacific South Americans like their boyfriends to be filled with chang."

Exactly what she meant by 'chang' I wasn't sure, but the way she said it made me blush and sweat at the same time.

Batiste was sitting at his outdoor desk, sentinel next to his big Igloo, morning glories scaling his Dickies.

"All right," he said, glancing up.

"What's on tap today?" said Carolyn. "Dr Pepper?"

"Jolt."

Batiste suddenly gave me a hard, interrogative stare.

"You different," he said. "Haircut?"

Carolyn said, "He's just hungover."

"And," she added, "he's after something he might not catch."

Batiste continued to stare.

"Bet I know what," he said. Then he began to laugh.

Carolyn began to laugh, too.

Wil Weitzel

Callia

I left an island of goats for Aden, on the south coast of Yemen, when I was seventeen. Socotra, the island is called, and my mother and sisters are still there today. It is difficult to leave your people behind, even for better opportunities. After a year in Aden, I received a scholarship to study medicine in Egypt on the east bank of the Upper Nile, not far from ancient Elephantine and the old kingdoms of Nubia to the south. On the border of modern-day Sudan. My mother, who had already lost my father, said I must go. For three years I studied and added English to my Arabic and native Socotran.

In Yemen, we speak one of the purest forms of Arabic, but little English. I learned English because my medical studies required it. Frequently our textbooks were in English—those that were not in German—and our lectures in the Cairene Arabic of doctors of medicine who had traveled upriver. In those years, when I returned to Socotra for the monsoon which arrives at the European summer, I served as a guide for tourists and spoke English. But during the monsoon it is only the Italians who come, and only a few because the sands blow into their faces and the winds slam against them when they open the doors of their 4WD's.

An Italian woman came one August in the full gale of the monsoon, despite all of it. She arrived from Sicily, so she told me, from one of three islands to the west of the port city of Trapani. She had long hair, dark like Somalia, or like the neck of its male starling, and must have been twenty years my senior. Her name was Callia. When she bent at the waist, her straight legs the color of copper coins, the ankles alone bowed inward as she washed her face with bottled water, pausing first to gather her skirts, to hike them up from splatter, to wedge them between her knees. Her toes would move incessantly, I noticed, in either sand or water.

Callia was a marine biologist. I myself knew the egg-laying patterns of female loggerheads that came up on the stretch of sand west of Hadibo each for one hour after dusk between July and September. That was long enough for a female to carve out a small moon of sand and lay her eggs, then labor back to the waves. I had a thorough knowledge, besides, of hawksbills and the occasional green—a species we called the "sweet turtle" on the island. My uncle, who along with my father, though for different reasons, is now dead, is the one who taught me turtles. He taught me, in fact, one half of what I know in this world.

Callia, however, was little interested in turtles. Her work was chondrichthyes, or fish with skeletons of cartilage rather than bone. Qalansiya, in its lagoons, housed red-eyed sting rays, their backs mottled to a field of hash marks, brown and circular, the burnished tone of a dark mahogany piano. So she saved Qalansiya in the far northwest of our island for last and for longest as it was sure to form, in the figure of Detwah Lagoon, a kind of climax for her studies.

Like the tourists, Callia listened patiently to my accounts of the dragon's blood trees which grew only in the highest elevation bands, above 500 meters, and had all ceased to reproduce. She corrected my English when I said that magic grew the trees and like virgin births they began from what was not themselves.

"Are you a man who'd believe your wife," Callia asked, her long limbs spidering into a dragon tree as though she hadn't noticed their movements, "if she told you she'd mated with a god?" I, at that time, had never touched a woman, and this was not a question I could answer.

We made a small group—unlike the droves of her countrymen who came in the midst of their winter to swallow our beaches, or the dense knots of Germans who covered the Hagar Mountains in March. A group of two. Callia had brought a strange tent, yellow, so fine and sheer it looked like a radiant egg. One Socotran, an old man from a village outside of Homril, to the east, asked if it was a piece of plastic when he came up the beach road and found me sitting and staring at the tent as Callia slept, and I told him no, it was a scientist.

She would emerge and clamor into my van—I should say my dead father's van, for it was his first and last—throwing her tent poles into the midden of tuna cans from Saudi Arabia and fragrant guavas in the back, and we would ride to a beach where she swam in a brassiere and bikini bottom. This was hard for me to take. I had seen in Aden tourists from France, which we called Franzia after the Italians, and the women wore shorts into the sea and long striped shirts shining brightly with colors that would be lost no doubt beneath the milky sheen of the oceans of Socotra. Indeed, particularly in the Indian Ocean where it hits our southern shores near the dunes of Amaq and makes blue milk of itself. In any case, she was quite beautiful, this woman—she startled me by looking at me directly— and I tried hard not to notice that even her wide feet, with the toes flat and crammed into a curve, were strange and perfect.

When we had tilted our van up and down the mountains and traversed both long shores of the island over the span of several days, we headed west to Qalansiya. Callia insisted then that I walk with her across the long beach to the lagoon.

This is a strange and wondrous beach. There is often no one in the wind season, not one soul, for 360 degrees. The blue dhows of the fishermen rest for months in the sand while the village waits out the monsoon. I have known young boys, at an age like the one at which I left for Aden, who come to Qalansiya and walk this beach a final time before departing on their communications scholarships to St Petersburg, Russia, or for their engineering programs in Muscat, Oman, or for their commerce internships in Naples, Italy. They watch the Egyptian vultures carve the air by the cliffs, fighting their way gradually to the south, climbing the scree slopes then wheeling, and on silent wild auto-pilot, rushing back out to the waves. Also, there are shearwaters caroming along the surge line, and the sand, pulled by the tides, is first sipped on the flat nap of the water then inhaled by the sea.

Callia told me as we walked that everything on the island flows from south to north because water, if it is indecisive, will follow the wind. "But now it is nearly dry," she said quietly. And it is true, I can tell you, that the wadis produce clefts in the spine of this island, like the gaps between vertebrae, that these valleys in August become rivers of wind, and that you can walk for seventeen kilometers across polished boulders from the Arabian Sea to the Indian Ocean.

She removed her shirt, revealing her tan cotton brassiere, and stripped off her pants, hanging them on my shoulders as if I were a rack for dogfish, then tore into the waves.

My uncle too had been a guide on the island, to botanists and endemicists mainly, before there were Italians. Though he had books for every kind of guiding, he was pinned like a date to the Himalayas. He had become a specialist, he told me with tall eyes, on the mountain kingdom of Bhutan. My uncle had traveled as well—though in his heart only—in the region that, after partition, has become northern Pakistan, up the broad then brittle-thin ridges of Nanga Parbat, and labored—first the tips of his fingers then his thumbs and finally his wrists on the maps—across the cols of the Hindu Raj to Tirich Mir, traversing ice fields at the foot of its southern exposure, with their vast seracs and hidden crevasses, into the southwestern tail of the Hindu Kush. In addition, he spent two years—in reality this time, not just in his heart—in our own range of spires, where the last 350 meters lurch in near-vertical relief. In those years, he wore a rucksack dangling carabiners even at sea level, walking beside us along the beaches with them knocking into our hips. In the mountains my uncle would cover his head against the sun with his keffiyeh. My father brought him long strips of salted shark meat which, at altitude beneath that same sun, turned a bright gray in only two hours.

Callia was out there in the waves off Qalansiya, in the mild currents of the tidal zone, which grew angry at a distance of 200 meters from the shore and swept you, if you were not vigilant or strong, westward toward the Brothers—our brethren islands—in the direction of Somalia.

"You mustn't swim far," I yelled, my voice drowning in the wind.

My father was killed by a giant hammerhead, a beautiful female, nineteen years ago, off the coast of Qalansiya. In those days, sharkers like my father had only to trail their lines on an open run for 800 meters for a white-tip to take. Now you can trawl for 100 kilometers with only flat grouper and big-eyed jacks and trevally to slap against the side of your skiff.

"Come back, Callia," I called.

My father was out for three nights which, in December and January, was not unusual. Shark fishermen, of all fishermen, are first from the harbor in the mornings, two hours before dawn, before the muezzin calls quaver from the old mosque in Hadibo. The shark dhows at that time of year head west, past Qalansiya toward Abd-al Kuri, and the skiffs hunt oceanic white tips and tigers, scalloped hammerheads and black tips, and, in late December, at depths beginning at 40 meters and extending to 280, the great hammerhead herself.

Callia swam in at last and we walked to the lagoon. Later that first evening at Qalansiya, Scorpio hung over the van and by midnight the beach was raucous with monsoon, the sand flying in sheets of birdshot one to three meters above the ground. At some point during the night, Callia opened the rear door of my father's van in a panic and awakened me. She sputtered something in English about how her tent could not withstand the winds, so I climbed out of my sleep and helped her disassemble it. My belly was still leaden from the fassouli we had eaten at dusk. I spread out my tarpaulin and warned her of scorpions which were unlikely in the low updraft along the beach. It was at that time that she asked me to lie on the edge of the tarp closest to the scree from the cliffs, to protect her from the winds. I told her I would fetch rocks and the heavy mats from the dhows to sink the tarp into the sand, but she grabbed my wrist.

My mother has told me, at an infinite remove from her reason, that my father's wrestling with the great hammerhead was like Jacob's grapple with an angel at Bethel, where he too hurt his leg, and like her own amorous cavorting with my father that produced first me and then my nine sisters—the same number, my uncle would have noted, as the Muses.

In any case, according to the one surviving crewman, the shark ate my father from toe to head, though they found my uncle's jambiya—his curved Yemeni sword crafted by Jewry in the 1940's with a hilt of carved rhinoceros horn and worn by my father at his waist—near the stern. Five other men, along with my father, had heaved the shark half into the dhow and from the gunnel she had jerked and crushed the center bench. She was 3.9 meters from her oblong head to the tip of her scythe and she'd grabbed my father by the calf as he beat her with the haft of an oar. The other men had a difficult time subduing her. Normally, they would have bludgeoned her between the oarlocks and the stern while her bulk was in the sea but she'd come from beneath them and drifted forward and then, in her wrath, threatened to crack the hull with her thrashings.

Callia's touch was surprising, as though it were the touch of a man. She had strong broad fingers that cuffed my wrist. I could feel the imprint of them long afterwards, as though it had been left by a band of wide agate beads. She pulled me down to her and I was far from resisting. Half sitting, once I'd taken my shirt off, I was surprised to find that she was already naked. She brought her fingers to my hips in a way in which I could brightly feel the nails, opened my shawl, and trailed them along my thighs. I ejaculated before she could touch me. Just the thought of her, and the moment when my own hands found her breasts, awake, cool from the wind, was enough for me. It was the third night before I could hold out long enough to enter her, and by then the wind had stopped.

My father fought as he was eaten. A number of sharks, not hammerheads but makos, had gathered into the blood pool surrounding the dhow. All of the men except my father had been thrashed out of the boat only to pull themselves up by the runners and then be thrashed back out again. The dhow listed badly to port and was swamped. A blue shark, an oceanic blue, large and unwavering, took one of the men in a long arc, coming from below and behind, and, in the next hour, three others were taken by makos. The oars were splintered then scattered. The blue shark, as they do, returned and circled for many hours, its broad wing-like pectorals the color of cobalt. By then my father had wedged out both eyes of the great hammerhead with his pointer fingers. She was blind.

Callia waded into the lagoon to look for red-eyed rays just before dawn. She would work until 8:30 am then from 3:30 pm until dusk. Through the long mornings, she'd sleep with me in the van or sit bolt upright on the seat across and, with her palm pressed against her forehead as though she were overheated, tell me of Trapani in the far west of Sicily, or of sawfishes, which she claimed to have found in brackish waters as far as eighty kilometers upriver from the sea, or of her hair, which was the gift of her grandmother and one, she promised me, she wouldn't trade for the Bactrian hoard.

Out in the Detwah Lagoon alongside the beach at Qalansiya, the rays were curious. Their long tails grew to a meter in length and the strange embers of their eyes shone through the shallows. On the third morning, Callia announced, laughing, coming up from the lagoon, that she'd fallen in love with me, and the way her tongue worked in her mouth to say this in English filled me with the syrup of something like love, as though I were sucking her.

The hammerhead worked my father's body as you would a fishbone or a lyre. In the end, she ate the column of his vertebrae, and my mother, shaking her head in grief, said that one day, before she was buried, he would be found in the waist of a cucumber tree where the flesh bottled out beneath the branches. My father continued to beat the shark with his fists until he died. The man who survived was on the gunnel, half in, half out of the sea. Over time, while she was still alive, that man had flattened the shark's great dorsal fin and torn into her back down to the silver glister of her stomach with his shivered oar.

Callia, on the evening of the fifth day at Qalansiya when our week was nearly up, talked of "cultural dehydration" that coincided, she said, with the shrinking water table. "You—your people," she murmured, pointing at my chest, "could slowly stop moving—dry up." There she was, seated in a dhow half buried in the sand, thirsty and drinking bottled water. Her black starling hair hung low, grazing the bow. "Here, the wadis are dry until the one day they are full," she said trembling, speaking of our island in Italian, pouring cool water onto her wrists, then translating into English. "Your rains run straight to the lagoon."

Callia's eyes, which were date-colored and olive-stoned or mottled copper like her skin, but which I cannot bring back in memory, looked directly at me and were not bored or over-certain, so that a round feeling came to me in which I was huge and a giant, a landscape, something you could not hold. When I reached over and touched her right shoulder where it was squared to the sea, I found she was doused in sweat, with it running as I explored her down the narrow wadi of her backbone. "Stay here with me," I wanted to say in my own language, but I spoke only in English.

In the high jabal the rains fall mainly in the Hagar range, and except through the mouths of a certain two-tiered cave, they rarely reach the sea. I wanted to tell her this and many other things about my feelings but, in truth, Callia was the initiator of the words that ran between us and I was only receiving her, in something like greed or awe. Her slenderness in her ankles and her arms, and particularly at the waist, kept me silent while she held her small head and talked on of her dream of thick rivers branching outward to flood our goat pastures. All the while, as she talked, she would bury her broad hand in mine and shrug, sinking a firm channel with her knuckles into my palm.

There is a place on the northeast shore called Arrar where the sweet water from two caves, the uppermost carved in the cliff 400 meters above the shore, pours slowly down through flowering shrubs and sea grape onto the grassy flanks of the ocean before tumbling onto boulders lined with moss. I don't believe Callia ever knew of this place—I never showed her— and the water it fed to the sea came from rain that was very old indeed, preserved in deep natural cisterns of limestone that harbor our island's buried water. Nonetheless, I thought afterward of Callia whenever I was thirsty, and I thought of her most of all in Arrar, where we buried what we could recover of my father from the belly of his shark.

He finally died of blood loss when she reached his liver. The liver is not considered by many to be the seat of the soul. But on our island it carries a special quality and is often fed to cats. These cats stare upward in the streets so their eyes roll back in their heads, like the eyes of white sharks, when you pass above them among the blue houses of Hadibo. Callia, for all of her dreaminess, noticed these cats—that multiply to profusion on the dry roofs at night—on her way to dine on foul and fassouli. She would watch the cats strolling with goats which also leapt among the ruins and jumped old walls while the does suckled their young in niches on the street. Callia laughed out loud and covered her mouth with the back of her hand when a young goat, buffeted by a sudden gust from the monsoon, its coat frantic and swirling, toppled backward off a crumbling wall.

The shark died only minutes after devouring my father. Her oblong prehistoric head was painted with him and the two eye sockets pointed east and west, or so the man on the gunnel reported. That man crawled in after a time and lay exhausted beside her on the flooded mats of the dhow floor. The sun started in earnest on the great hammerhead by 10:30 on the morning of the second day, her belly already opened from the back to the birds. When, on the third evening, they were hauled into the harbor, fishermen on the slip in Hadibo deepened her wounds and brought out my father.

Callia, sitting in the dhow that fifth evening in Qalansiya, must have been in her mid-forties. She was tall when she stood and the bridge of her nose flattened tenderly into a brief plateau between her eyes. Again and again those soft eyes strayed from the sea to me, back to the sea. As if she were judging a distance.

My father, long before he died, warned me against women. He appealed to the jol, to the high plateau that rises on the Yemeni mainland above Al Mukalla and separates the ocean from the wadis and oases of the northern desert. You must traverse the jol at night, it is said, in the company of the Bedu, and donkeys can reach the palms of Wadi Dawan from the ocean more quickly than camels. My father, adding tales to this knowledge, told me women await you in the desert, beyond the jol, while in the ports of Yemen from Aden to Qana there are no women. To find a woman to love you must leave the harbors. My father, for all his wisdom, did not know Callia. She was the half of the world my father and uncle never knew.

We brought the pieces of his body together and buried him beside my uncle who succumbed to a plague of malaria that is now like a ghost, for all we have on our island are flies the mainlanders from Arabia call "helicopters" and the Africans, their tongues caroming in deep vessels, as though their black stomachs were pots, call mouches. Having laid him down and stacked the deep green sod of Arrar on top of the site, we tore open the seams of a goat skin sewn heavy with dates to honor his corpse. It was so full, that goat sack of dates, you could beat its sides with a stick and there was only heavy silence inside. But when we tore into the skin with a knife, the dates poured out all stuck together, one on one on one.

Callia was nearly dead by the time she arrived on Socotra, though I didn't know it at the time. It was no wasting disease you could see from the outside, and no sinking of the mind, but something they did not mention in those learned disquisitions of Upper Egypt, nor in the medical ledgers at Aden. She was willing to come in the monsoon, to brave the sharks and the winds, because she had already reached her end. I, in the meantime, hadn't touched my fears before and though I had seen death twice, until Callia, I'd never seen it alive.

We have only a few cucumber trees left on the island, their bottle trunks chalky white. I don't know if, as my mother would have it, my father will return reassembled, sealed within one of the last trees remaining. Or if he'll come back to her in silver light beneath the winter constellation of the bears which Yemenis in the Haraz range and in the far east of the desert see as leopards in the sky. But I do know Callia died whole. We made love in her yellow tent on the seventh night at Qalansiya, and the winds resumed. She shivered with fever, even as I held her in my arms, and the gusts grew and made the tent walls flail as though they were the membranes of our ears. For long hours, Callia rolled in her sweat and refused to drink.

She was burning up before dawn and pleaded with me to take her to the sea to cool her. This and what follows is what I keep from my wife. The salt of her neck on my face, and finally in my mouth. Her saying to me in English as I carried her, "heavy heat—that is what I have." My stepping through the pyramids of ghost crabs. Her bare damp stomach pressed against my ribs. The fact that I could not see her wide feet.

If you have ever escorted a body out to sea then you know, if you are only one, that you take the shoulders, under the arms, and walk out backward through the waves with your body sheltering the head. With each of your steps the body grows lighter and Callia, still alive, hummed music I'd never heard.

The sea was very still by the standards of the monsoon. The mosque in the village of Qalansiya had touted Allah above sleep and returned to silence. The wind spun the cliffs about us in a round whorl and stuccoed the tops of the waves with a rough plaster of light. I must be honest. I did not know, beyond the bare facts that Callia was a traveler and a scientist, and suffering from fever, who it was I carried like a corpse through the waves.

Two sharks, sand tigers, appeared—two and a half meters each by the size of their dorsals—but kept their distance and departed. Their knives sliced the surface, glinted brown like loam, briefly circling something sixty meters from us that must have been uncertainty. Callia ceased to hum and, as the Arabian Sea is full of salt, she became in my arms something lifeless by her lack of weight.

Finally, having rocked her in my arms, I brought Callia back to the sand. My uncle, who claimed to have bathed every morning he woke by the sea, said it was a sad time to walk into the ocean, at dawn, because it still belonged to the night, and while there was undeniably beauty you entered nevertheless a world with one ruler, the shark, before he gave it over to the sun. In any case, the sands of Qalansiya were yet cool on my feet when I waded back in and laid Callia down like a strip of ore.

She was breathing easily, though deeply, when I first set her down. I was sitting seaward from her feet in the first long shadow of the escarpment to the east, waiting in a loud wind for her to speak. Even in that early history of my career a doctor of sorts, and proudly by this time a lover, I was watching across her body, following her legs to the narrow stomach then up to her eyes. But watching like a fool. Her lips parted then quivered, and all along, her chest filled and settled. So I sat guessing she would rise, favor an elbow, or bend against the wind.

But she didn't move. When I stared hard, and her chest suddenly stumbled and paused, I leapt for her, reaching quickly for her jaw to lift her chin. There I was in that wind attempting to confirm breath, pressing my lips to hers, beginning to count and weight her chest with the heel of my hand, then beginning again. Her throat was still warm. I ran for the village that, though it had no defibrillator, had doctors and an infirmary.

By the time I returned for her, fishermen searching for skates in the lagoon had beached their dhows and gathered. Callia was propped up. Seated against a log of driftwood, the wood of what the Yemenis call the "turnip tree," a porous, light-skinned cousin of the tall cedars of the Lebanese, she was facing the wind. The monsoon was ripping at her.

One night, when I was still very young, long before there was a metalled road to the southwest tip of our island, we followed the long wadi south from Arrar and camped on the basalt stones of the coast. My uncle told us there by our fire the story of Iphigenia. Of how her father, Agamemnon, slew her for the god before he sailed for Troy. To gather the wind. Callia was that way when I got back to her, a clutch of bones.

The fishermen offered a dhow and we built her a pyre by the lagoon at Qalansiya. We curled her into the blue prow, above the foremost bench, and turned it to the sky, burying the stern in the sand.

Afterward, if she had relatives, they rose to no report of her. So I took her ashes, mixed with the blue-black embers of a dhow, from the lagoon of Qalansiya to the sweet water caves of Arrar, above where my father and uncle lie. I climbed the high dunes to the source of what we call a "river" that brightens the basalt by the sea. I buried her there in the skeletal bowl of a red-eyed ray.

Ander Monson

We Are Going to See the Oracle of Apollo in Tapiola, Michigan

It's true that she stays in the back of the store: a half-diner/half-gas station that's reputed to be one of the true sources of pornography in Upper Michigan and is definitely a reliable bait shop. It is true that she is only here one month each year, right after the Fourth of July when all the fireworks have been disposed of in the trash, or in the grass, or in the lake. It is true that I am going to see her with Liz my X my alphabet in the passenger seat. We are listening to New Order which excites the blood in the way that summer does when it comes unexpectedly and lasts for at least a day. It is true that it is cold here most of the time, even through the summer, the wind kicking through the trees like a vandal like a pirate on gunwales on the plank. It is true that this is just after Liz moved here, in a way replacing Caroline, who was Canadian and the obsession of all the boys, who went Christian and set fire to al her tapes (a spiritual coming-out party to which we were all invited), who moved away without word or note or lipstick trace or forwarding address. It is true there are things I feel for Liz that I have not told her about being just friends or the else that is fire that may be the kind of fire I want. It is too true that we are quiet in the car.

I do not know that Liz will soon be gone, that she will be up and packed and trussed and sunk and gone.

The radio in my car doesn't work that well so we can't hear that well.

The sun is up but hazy and I look over at her who is like an element on the periodic table, a symbol an enigma sign of light. Liz who must be solved for. Liz who collected architectural drawings, stole them from the public library in town where they keep them under glass, or the country courthouse where they keep a plan of every building that is made. Liz who sends me invisible ink notes.

My brother is at home and I do not think about him now. He is not with me like a ghost or a dedication on the radio that finds you wherever you can go to or get out from.

It is true that I have questions for the Oracle, like how to get the Playboy channel, or will the school burn down to cinder, char in Fall.

It is true that I have more important questions about my mother or the weather.

I ask Liz what her questions are for the Oracle but she won't tell me. She doesn't ask me what are mine.

We hear bottle rockets firing in the sky. They are leftover from the Fourth.

I don't tell her that we used to fire the rockets at houses from PVC pipes turned into homemade bazookas. I don't tell her that my brother almost lost his hearing when one misfired, how those things are cheap and unreliable, how they can't be trusted, but they do the most wondering and explosive things.

The wind is in our hair because my back windows do not fully close.

We are in my father's Aerostar.

Everyone I know has a minivan.

Liz does not seem impressed with it. She does not seem impressed by much.

She doesn't ask about my brother's arms, which I am thankful for. I try to keep him secret since there is no satisfaction there.

In algebra we always had to solve for X.

2 we are still going to see the oracle of apollo in tapiola, michigan

Liz's hair reminds me of paramecia with their tiny microfingers that move them in the ooze. I do not tell her this. We are coming up through the valley that my family used to drive through on the way to Ironwood where the ski slopes are, where the car dealerships are, where I would eventually be arrested for leaving the scene of an accident where I hit a gas pump, freaked, and fled. We are coming up through the valley in which my dad would always sing "Down in the Valley" when we still drove through here as a family on the way to recreation, the Porcupine Mountains or the state line that leads to Wisconsin, land of more snow and beer and cheese. We are coming up through the valley that I have memories of. Liz and I are in the valley and we are coming up the other side like we were in Montana next to some great crest.

We talk of Florida, the postcards we get from relatives who've visited or moved there. We talk about all the oranges that are huge and the futuristic ball of Epcot Center that I've always wanted to visit but never have.

We are going to see the Oracle who will tell us we must go to Paulding to see the Mysterious and Possibly Awful Light. This is what we think – that this trip will snowball and soon we will be bound to visit all the sites of strangeness in Michigan. Our parents will never miss us. At least mine will not, I suspect.

Liz taunts truckers on the CB which is beautiful, which is funny, which might be dangerous like in the movies or in the stories you hear about taunting truckers, which you are not supposed to do and live, which we do. Liz my elevation. Liz my hatchet man.

3 YOU CANNOT STOP US; YES WE ARE STILL GOING

Besides electricity, other things can move us. Gasoline for one, or loyalty, or fire. Fire that comes from anything that is a burst a birth a burning bush that will soon go out in snow. Fire that is a way of loving property. Fire that is my cousin Ben when he stayed with us, out until too late doing God Knows What in Michigan then returning with his boots loud on the floor of the house. Fire that is my mother's trail to Canada and to all the glory roadside sites of hugeness in America in North America in the North. Fire that is her that is aurora in the sky. I have told Liz some of this, a little bit at a time. She knows what fire is to me. She bought me gasoline for my last birthday, and rags, and matches. Fire that is the opposite of cold that means never freezing, that means combustion, spontaneity, and marshmallows skewered on sticks, turning black. Besides electricity, the thought of the humongous fungus moves us like a magnet. The thought of the Paulding Light that rocks back and forth in the distance just outside of Paulding which is buried in the woods which is an hour and a half from the hills that are made of mines in the Keweenaw Peninsula, which is an hour and a half from the canal that cuts the Peninsula in half, which is an hour and a half from the sliced thumb of land that juts out into Lake Superior like a missed note does in a song and wrecks it like a boat on rocks. The thought of the fungus is a magnet which is a field which electricity creates. My mother is a field which electricity creates, which keeps me, satellite, in place. Which keeps me in the car with Liz on our way to Tapiola.

4 ONWARD TO THE ORACLE

Tapiola is not so far away as this. It is not the ornate crown of the Mediterranean. It is not the cities they show on Canadian TV that come over the lake at night to us. It is not the glittering office towers of Sault Ste. Marie, Canada, as seen across the International waters, as seen across a year of fire and ears suspended in jars, cupped to the ground.

Tapiola is where Liz and I will find an answer to this story, where Liz and I will kick the screen door in on the place where the Oracle is in the back. Where Liz and I will not leave until we are satisfied. Where Liz and I will never be satisfied, I known, because what will she—the Oracle—really have to say that I don't know already: that Liz will leave like summer does, that my brother has no answers for his arms, his aphasia, for where his plate should go on the counter when he's done with it. That this story is a story of the body of the heart of the left atrium, the ballroom where prom will be held. That though there is still ore in the ground, we have mined the hills to the point where any further excavation will collapse the thing, even a hundred people jumping up and down simultaneously to counteract the Chinese kids who are—in mass—trying to force the earth's orbit to change by jumping on the other side of the globe.

This is what our science teachers sell us to get us to go outside and jump as a class, as a whole white shining class who will not all—of course—graduate, a class who will lose half to moving costs or crime, or to weather or sickness, barn collapse, misguided amputations, or to dropping out and, frustrated, frequenting bars. This is what our science teachers tell us to do, but what they do not tell us is this: Our jumping could collapse the shafts and close the mine that is like a trachea, that is the only reason a generation had for settling here, that is the only thing that has brought Liz, with her fascination with the architectures of the cities, the architectures of the towns vacated to ghosts, buried in the woods, and the architecture of the mines that reminds me of heartworms burrowing through the organs of a pet who is loved, who is too far gone to care.

5 THE ORACLE OF APOLLO IN TAPIOLA WILL PUNCTUATE OUR SENTENCES WITH GROANS AND FILL IN ALL OUR DEEPEST HOLES WITH PUTTY LIKE A DENTIST WOULD THAT WILL HARDEN AND PROTECT US PERMANENTLY FROM HARM

We have stopped talking, Liz and I, because we are almost there, and we have our own things to think about.

Tapiola doesn't have any outskirts, exactly, being small; so we go right from the woods through the population sign into the town and to the store that is the diner that is the place where the Oracle will tell us Truths and that is the place where we can maybe grab a bite before returning or going somewhere else.

Everything is rundown and beautiful. The Tapiola General Store that is the Tapiola Diner has there old pillars out front like Rome like Greece like some architectural culture, except that these are spray-painted with slogans from local high school kids and left here for character, for show. These pillars support nothing. They just stand at the front of the store, which is where we pull in, which is where we kick up dust since we have left the asphalt that kept all the dust and all the forest away.

Liz gets our first.

There is not much light left.

The store is open, so we go in.

It has no door.

There is an array of bait in tubs and tanks.

There is a counter area and several booths that seem to me like the traps some people put out to catch bears or wolves, but that catch mostly dogs and often maim them.

There is a very little light coming from a chandelier above.

I imagine this is quite a scene.

We tell the guy behind the counter who may be a relative of mine or Liz's that we are here to see the Oracle. He thinks this is Hilarious. He laughs. He has fine white teeth that gleam like in commercials.

He says Go straight through to the back through both sets of doors that are hard to open but you look like a strong guy, is what he says.

Which is what we do.

No one is there.

It is cold and there is a lot of ice.

I think we are in a freezer, is what I say Liz.

Isn't it a pity, the Oracle says when she comes in. She looks about fifteen.

I ask her what she means.

There is a radio stating numbers—one-one-seven, one-one-nine-four—that she has her ear cocked towards. Another shortwave radio spills weather information. Yet another radio just hushes static. There is an old boat radio and barometer saying something in another language.

I will not tell you what she says to Liz or what she says to me.

It is true we find out nothing here.

Regardless, Lis is doomed and beautiful, maybe one because of the other, and it is cold, and I suppose I am in love, which is too bad. We will get a meal in Tapiola, battered, fried, and better than we expected, leaving us full and gassy. It is all we can honestly ask for before we leave and get back in the Aerostar, where the radio will play us some songs that mean a lot, that we understand.

Kevin Wilson

The Pigeon Cove Festival of Lights

It was the winter of light, that Christmas in the Pigeon Cove cul-de-sac when we filled our street with wattage, with joy. There were six houses, six families inside them and we spent the better parts of our lives mirroring each other's steps. New cars were bought at the same time, the drive from the dealership back home like a funeral procession, a line of brand new shiny cars, all following each other to the same place. We became happy and safe in our group, our wagon-train of houses circled around to keep out everything wrong, to preserve something unspoken and pristine, almost holy, on our street.

That winter, the Christmas season, my father came out of the attic with a box marked X-MAS DECO, like some kind of designer scheme. He had noticed the other men all carefully hauling boxes of decorations out of their garages and onto their front lawns. We were the newest family to Pigeon Cove, our first Christmas there, and my mother was worried that a lot of lights were thought of as tacky, something not done. My father said he'd be damned if he was going to let anyone tell him how to celebrate the holiday season. He then stepped outside into the slowly increasing glow of light, the other husbands already on the roofs of their houses, design plans and staple guns in hand, testing each strand as they tacked it to their house. My father looked down at the box of lights he held, the heft of it too light, inconsequential, and he got into the car and drove away. Our house suddenly seemed dim and quiet as the other houses flickered and brightened with each tested strand of lights, the glowing circle of electricity broken only by our family.

My father returned from the store with enough bulbs to illuminate a baseball field, strand after strand that he produced from the car like a magician trailing colored handkerchiefs. We stood in our driveway and watched the Christmas lights pile around our feet and rise, football field lengths of filament and glass. The other men in the cul-de-sac looked away from their own work to stare at my father, wondering how much more was stuffed in our car. "What are you doing honey," my mother asked him, "what is all this?" The car finally emptied, he began untangling the strands, carrying them over to the front yard. "This," he told her, "this is getting in the spirit, dear."

The men worked all night. We children ran from yard to yard while they yelled at us to "be still. Don't move. Watch out you don't step on any bulbs." I stayed close to the Stewart girls, all six of them, and I fell in love with each one as we wandered through the cul-de-sac. They wore sneakers that flashed red as they walked, a quick flicker of LED with every fresh step. They had red hair in varying shades of fire, from slow burn to four-alarm blaze, and freckles that ran across their noses like Braille, tiny dots of information. I sometimes wanted to trace my hands across their faces, to learn the secret each one would whisper on my fingertips.

There were the other kids as well, the McAllister twins, silent and knowing, always nodding their heads in unison. They seemed constantly aware of something the rest of us were not. The Roland kids were older, the brother and sister in high school already, sitting on their porch steps and reading, oblivious to the construction going on around them. The Markowitz boy had nearly drowned in the lake that summer and was still water-brained, what would later become his normal demeanor. He was wide-eyed and surprised, as if still trying to figure out how he passed out in the water, slipped under the surface, and managed to end up here, back in his normal life. Julie, the Breckenridge's child, was blond and pale. She was what I imagined when I thought of winter: pure and even and blinding. She never spoke, talked with her hands and eyes though her parents kept taking her to speech therapists who all said the same thing, "she will or she won't."

We were all quiet though, for children, all amazed into a hushed reverence for where we were. It was a place we knew was not quite real, had the smell and feel of something plastic and artificial but we did not complain then. We stayed silent and awed as we ran in ever-expanding circles, like objects trying to break free of a planet's pull.

The women peered out the windows of their houses, waving to each other. They shrugged their shoulders as the men and children stayed out into the night, their dinners all collectively getting cold, congealing. The wives finally came out into the street as the now-finished men smoked cigarettes and drew more designs on their already pencil-scratched sheets of paper. They whispered and pointed at the houses, trying to figure out what spaces they had neglected to cover in lights. The houses sat unlit and dark as they waited for the final unveiling, humming with potential.

Finally, in the pitch-black of night, past all our bed times, we gathered in the middle of the cul-de-sac, in the street and watched as each husband flicked the power to his own house. They came on one at a time, moving around the circle in a steady burst of light. We had to shade our eyes from the concentration of brightness, of the sheer power of the Christmas lights that burned out at us. And we could feel the warmth on our cheeks from the glow of our houses, even in the cold of the winter night. The men gathered again in the middle of the street and shook their heads. It was on all their lips, passed quickly like a breath, in unison. Brighter.

They took off work, cleaned out the stock of Christmas lights from every store, made diagrams of parallel circuits to get the most out of every light. Mr. Roland tossed the Santa Claus and Reindeer plastic figures from the roof of his house. "Too much space," he said, "it's taking away from the lights." In fact, everything except the lights were taken down, wreaths and hollow plastic snowmen. The Markowitz's menorah in the window was replaced with a new model that used bulbs instead of candles. "It's the festival of lights, sweetie," he told his wife as she protested, "tradition can only do so much."

We loved it though. We watched our fathers pin more light to the houses, adding rows and rows of brightness, finding places we didn't know existed to illuminate. We sat in the middle of the road on an old mattress we hauled out of the Breckenridge's basement and stared at the lights. We squinted into the glow until we made the lights dance, made them blur and move and jump around inside our brains and it was wonderful. We huddled close to each other, our cold skin pressed against each other, watching our houses burn from the inside out.

We had to stay out of the road once the people started coming, driving in slow, creeping lines that snaked all the way back to town. They followed the dim glow of our houses until it got brighter and brighter. Once they arrived, they did not want to leave. They hesitated, turned off the engines of their cars and just stared until the cars waiting behind them would honk their horns, wanting their own turn to see. Our mothers dressed us up in our church clothes and made us stand on the porches and wave to the cars, which we'd do for hours until we finally had to go to bed. They made hot chocolate and candied fruit and gave them out to the motorists who lingered a little too long, not wanting to leave. It seemed to us, staring out the windows of our bedrooms as we fell asleep, that the string of cars' headlights in either direction seemed like only an extension of our houses, of the lights. We went to sleep thinking Pigeon Cove was somehow bigger than it really was.

The news reporters started to come, even from outside the state. They interviewed our parents but the fathers would only grunt, look away from the cameras, and say something about getting into the holiday spirit. They did not want to talk about it. It seemed almost disrespectful to discuss the need for the lights anymore, like something deep and intangible that had no reason to be spoken of.

The Power Company allowed the electricity drain because the town had never seen tourists like this before. The diners and hotels were filled to overflowing every day and all because of the lights of Pigeon Cove. Other subdivisions rotated nights where they were without electricity so we could keep running, keep burning. The school rented out buses to take people to the cul-de-sac as traffic had become too backed up, was not allowing everyone to see the lights. People waited in town for a bus to stop by and pick them up, take them to the place they could already see, shining like gold as the houses around us sat dim and cold, as if abandoned.

The men started adding more, setting up wide sheets of aluminum to reflect the light even further out, as if propelling it at you like bolts of lightning. My father found a way to create a connection of lights that held bulbs as big as floodlights, lights that could signal planes down from the sky. They covered our lawns with a netting of bulbs, rolled out lines of Christmas lights onto the grass and tended to it more than they did when it was an actual lawn with growing grass and weeds. They spent hours every day changing the bulbs, keeping the connections flowing.

They had outlets running everywhere so as not to overload the power. We were not allowed to have any lights on inside the house once night arrived. It took away a degree of brightness from the outside lights. We started spending the nights at each other's houses, away from the fathers and their planning and the mothers and their disbelief. We saw stars in our heads all the time, little pinpricks of light that never seemed to leave us. We looked at each other and saw our bodies glitter like precious jewels, the lights always around us. We were slowly falling in love, becoming iridescent, melting into each other.

One man was being interviewed by the major networks, tears rolling off his cheeks, after seeing our houses. "It's like staring into the truth, like everything else has burned away and only the most important single thing in the world is left." And the reporters asked him what that one thing was, leaned closer with their microphones. "I don't know," he told them, "it was too bright."

We all watched the buses drive by our houses, saw the popping of people's flashbulbs as they took pictures. They never seemed to understand that none of the photos would come out, that there would only be blurs of light, overexposures, but perhaps that was what they wanted. We stayed away from windows after a while, wore giant sunglasses like the kind they give old people after cataract surgery when we walked to each other's houses. We set fire to tissues in a metal trashcan and watched it burn down to ashes, lifting up in the air as the heat carried the particles away from us. We wondered what would happen if we caught the house on fire, if anyone outside would even notice, be able to tell the difference.

It was twenty-four hours of daylight for us that winter, and the nights became even brighter than the days, the lights clicking on the minute the sun fell behind the horizon. We had no sense of time, would lie in a single bed, bodies draped over each other and it felt like we would sleep for days or not at all. There was no way of telling anymore. Even our mothers gave up trying to remember time, would keep watch over us during what they assumed to be the night, very much afraid.

Our fathers added more lights, attached spotlights to the roofs that would swivel back and forth in the sky, crossing over each other. When they all met at one point, it would illuminate the sky so much that we thought we could see through the atmosphere and into the cold, blank face of space. A crew of Russian Cosmonauts radioed back to earth that they could see a white ball of light coming from the United States, something smooth and bright and warm. They pressed their faces to the windows as they circled the earth, waiting for the next chance to stare at it.

We talked even less now that the lights were around. Even the parents ceased to communicate in anything other than gestures, faint movements of eyes and mouths. It seemed like there was no room for anything else other than the brightness, that whatever we said would be rendered unnecessary by the lights, total and pure.

If you stood in the middle of the road, equidistant from all the houses, there were no shadows of your body. The light enveloped you and there was nowhere for your shadow to lie down, to rest. We would stand in this circle while the travelers would move past us, not even seeing us, and we would pretend that we were the only people in the world, that this light was all somehow for us, and we would return to our homes with our skin browned almost to red, our faces warmed like fever.

We didn't even remember Christmas that year; it came and went without us thinking one thing of it. Another news reporter asked Mr. Miller about the purpose of the lights, what it was all about. Mr. Miller replied angrily, tired of having to give reasons for what we were doing. "Well, it's about the goddamned baby Jesus and all that, the birth and the star in the sky and the shepherds and all...all of that." And when the man told him that Christmas had been three days before, Mr. Miller ran back into the house and wrapped up his children's old toys in newspaper and placed them beside their beds while they slept.

The Power Company told us they could no longer give us all the power we were using. They needed it back. People were still coming, some for the fourth and fifth time. One woman went blind from staring at it for so long, simply burned her sight down to nothing. We had not been out of Pigeon Cove since the end of November. We did not really believe that there was anything actually out there beyond us anymore.

Our fathers cursed at the power company, said they had purchased giant generators for just this occasion, gasoline-fueled monsters that hummed and rattled to keep the lights going. Still, we all knew it would not last. The police started creating detours to keep people away from the house, would let no other people come by anymore. We all sat in our houses and waited, stared at the brightness and wondered how long it would last, how much longer we could depend on gas and metal, wire and filament.

All of us went to our own house the night the generators all began to wheeze, to give up. Each family sat together in their living room and waited, saying nothing, not remembering how. We only sat and listened to the noise of the generators, but something else too, the ever present hum of the lights. The tiny sound of electricity moving, being changed into light, hummed inside our bodies like our new hearts.

Then the rattles came, the cha-chunk sounds of the generators finally losing power. And slowly, almost imperceptibly, the lights outside dimmed, lost wattage an increment at a time, in spans of five minutes it seemed like. And finally, though we could not tell how long it had been, we noticed the darkness, what we had given up for over a month. The blackness surrounded us, filled up the space outside our houses and our fathers hung their heads as if they had somehow failed. Our mothers cried and we only ran to the windows, to see what we had not seen for so long.

And then, together, we left our parents inside our houses and stepped out into the night, into something that felt completely removed from everything we had ever known. It was like being born, finding yourself in this new, strange world. As we walked around our yards, listening to the hiss and pops of the dead bulbs, we could not yet imagine if we had come to a place that was better or worse than before.

William Borden

Ice Fishing for Alligators

The basis of all our knowledge is the inexplicable. —Schopenhauer

"Alligators under the ice?"

"Mutants," Lonnie says. Lonnie's sitting on a stool, hunkered over the opening in the ice, a neat square about four feet on each side, a little larger than the usual hole, but he's got to have room, he says, to drag the alligator out. "Way I figure it, folks brought these babies from Florida. Or they could be caimans, cousin to the American alligator, from South America, where weird shit happens-headhunters boil a fella's brains, shamans turn into panthers-where the fecund humidity spins the phyletic yarns of Gabriel Garcia Marquez and the intellectual labyrinths of Jorge Luis Borges."

I look out the window of Lonnie's fish house at the frozen lake, ice three feet thick, snow sprinkled on top as if the lake were a hundred-acre bundt cake. It's my first time on the ice.

He goes on. "Some rich logging magnate with a longing for piranha soup tucked a couple of infant amphibians into his Gucci luggage, slipped past customs, stopped by the old homestead here in northern Minnesota, and the little critters slipped their leashes, or maybe the magnate's grandkids took those leathery babies swimming with them one hot summer, and the bug-eyed Amazonians, chromosomes jumping with uncertainty at the cool blue waters, found a few tasty northern pike, gobbled some loons and mergansers, found they had a sweet tooth for the feathery flesh of walleye, and gave orders to their deoxyribonucleic acids to adapt."

Lonnie's reddish beard, flecked with gray, fans out from his face like a reckless sunburst, and his blue eyes glint with a barely harnessed ferocity, whether from wisdom or madness is hard to say.

"Evolution had a new mandate," he says. "If the rain forests were going, those suitcases on the run figured, they might as well try a new climate. Hell, the Africans did the same thing millennia ago, moving up to Norway. Look at them now, pale and can't dance worth a damn. No, those alligators are out there right now, taking a lesson from the turtles, snuggling into the warm mud at the bottom of the lake for awhile, then venturing out for a quick lunch. They're moving into about ten new lakes every summer. Across land, at night. People think they're low-slung deer darting across their headlights. People see what they expect to see."

Through the window I see other fish houses scattered here and there like tiny shanties dropped randomly from the overcast sky. Snowmobiles snuggle beside some of the fish houses. Pickups huddle next to others. Inside, a man in a parka sits on a stool wiggling a wooden fish he's lowered through a hole he's sawed in the ice and waits with a five-pronged barbed spear to bring a hungry pike into the winter air. The fellow probably has some cans of Bud in a cooler beside him-in the cooler not to keep them cold as he did in summer but to keep them from freezing. He watches the clear greenish water below for signs of aquatic hunger. Will he see a mutant alligator? If he sees it, will he believe it?

"He'll keep quiet," Lonnie says. "He won't be believed. He'll confess anything else-where he was last night, having a gal on the side, how much he won at the casino-but he won't open himself to humiliating ridicule from his male-bonded buddies."

Lonnie's dropped a wire with a noose on the end about six feet down, and he has a large eelpout, an unbelievably ugly bottom feeder, thrashing about as bait. When the alligator goes for the eelpout, Lonnie will slip the noose over the alligator's head, jerk the noose tight, and haul the alligator out. Then he'll flip the alligator on its back, where it's helpless. He has another wire to wrap around its jaws and hold them shut. He's been watching videos about alligator wrestling to prepare himself. He has a deer rifle, too, in case his other plans fail. "Six, eight feet long, the way I figure it," he says. "Have to be that big to ward off the cold."

Lonnie's fish house is about ten feet by ten feet. It has a wooden floor that surrounds the opening in the ice. A kerosene heater warms the enclosure. We've taken off our parkas, and we're comfortable in our shirtsleeves, even though it's twenty-three below a mere foot away. Lonnie tells me that when some fellows fire up a small woodstove or a kerosene heater, the small space gets so hot they take off their clothes and maybe even their long underwear, and they'll sit there naked as a jaybird except for their wool socks and insulated boots, hunched over the hole of green luminescence, peering into the abyss of their own unfathomable contemplations.

If a fellow spearfishes, he can have a dark house, without windows. If he uses a line, he has to have a window. That way the game warden can peek in and make sure he's not spearing and baiting at the same time. Or that he hasn't set a line then gone home to get warm, which is against the law. They don't have rules yet for alligators, but Lonnie has a window anyway; mostly because sometimes he likes daylight. Other times he pulls the shade and we sit in the otherworldly illumination from the water, a greenish glow that's almost bright enough to read by, daylight sucked in through the ice to brighten the watery depths.

I gaze out the window into the distance at the village of fish houses, some only a couple of yards apart. Most of the fish houses are small, each like a cramped prison cell, each holding a solitary soul who has chosen this isolation, more out of a yearning for some kind of inarticulatable vision than a hunger for fish.

"It'll be years before this gets into the files of the DNR," Lonnie says. The Department of Natural Resources are the storm troopers of habitat protection.

"It'll be like flying saucers and Loch Ness. Like the alligators in the New York sewers. Only this'll be real. This'll change the way we live. A new cash crop eventually. Unless they turn mean, like the killer bees from Africa, and prey on small children, pet dogs, and unwary swimmers."

Lonnie Alderson is rooted to Northern Minnesota deeper than the jack pine, which is endangered. I guess Lonnie's an endangered species himself, a man of the woods who reads Heidegger, an independent contractor who taps his foot to twelve tone lullabies, an odd-jobs, all-weather handyman who pores over a Russian grammar so he can get the up-close flavor and scent, as he puts it, of Dostoyevsky, who he thinks must surely have been a Scandinavian to have been so tortured a soul-"except a Scandinavian wouldn't find God at the end, he'd just stew in his existential miasma. Strindberg, Hamsun, Kierkegaard-they're tortured souls who should've done some ice fishing to cool their brains."

Lonnie lives alone, in a log cabin he built himself, felling the trees and sizing them and notching them the old-fashioned way. He's pan-frying us walleye fillets from his freezer. He has biscuits in the oven. I'm not sure why he's befriended me, why he confides in me. Maybe I'm the only one who listens to him.

He was hauling gravel one summer—one of his odd jobs—and I needed my driveway covered. I invited him in to pay him, and he saw all my books. He wandered from bookcase to bookcase, tapping the spine of a book here, pulling out a book there, leafing through this one to scan a paragraph, paging through that one to ponder a sentence. We devoted the rest of the afternoon to debating if Schopenhauer's pessimism was warranted by rigorous syllogistic reasoning or was merely a biochemical product of too many cloudy days in Frankfurt am Main. We exhausted the evening considering whether Feuerbach was saying that religion is mankind's hopeful dream or its unfortunate nightmare. Finally; after spirited matutinal contention, we greeted the dawn agreeing that the idea of the Platonic Idea is itself a Platonic Idea, a meta-Idea, that recedes to infinity, like common sense sucked forever into the ravenous gravity of a black hole, all the time fortifying ourselves with chips and peanuts and beer.

I live alone, too, though not, like Lonnie, by choice. Brigit left me a year ago. She said when my writing was going well, I was completely absorbed and didn't pay any attention to her, and when it was going badly, I was morose and withdrawn and didn't pay any attention to her. She said my writing was my mistress, and she was spending too many nights alone.

She didn't know about my two year dalliance with Abigail Sorensen, so our parting was friendly, but then, after Brigit moved to California to follow her bliss and train to be a professional surfer, Abigail went back to George, who forgave her because she told him our affair had lasted only a week, so that worked out for Abigail. Lonnie, on the other hand, says he's a confirmed bachelor-a phrase that isn't used much anymore-because, as Schopenhauer, according to Lonnie, said, "to marry means to halve one's rights and double one's duties."

I've hired Lonnie to build me a couple of new bookcases for my den. He said he'd have them done in a couple of weeks. That was over a month ago, and I've seen no sign of any work on them. If I mention them, Lonnie gets a disappointed look, as if I'm somehow at fault, and mutters that he supposes the Pope kept telling Michelangelo to hurry up with that ceiling.

The walleye is good, coated in egg and flour and sesame seeds and fried in olive oil. We eat in silence. Lonnie seems to like to concentrate on one thing at a time, and that's not a bad idea. I scatter my energies too much, working on free-lance assignments for various in-house publications and cranking out a series of detective novels under different noms de plume. It was when Lonnie discovered I was a writer that he began to confide in me. He needed to tell somebody about his alligator hypothesis, somebody who wouldn't ridicule him, and maybe somebody who would help him get the word out. It didn't need to be somebody who believed him. It just needed to be somebody who listened to him.

After dinner he pours us each a generous splash of Courvoisier VSOP and leads me to the sturdy wooden chest-high table at one end of the room. It's a flat file cabinet for artists' paper and supplies, with several drawers. Next to it he has a computer and a printer and a scanner. He pulls open a drawer and lifts out a stack of drawings culled from a variety of scientific publications.

"Lookit here," he says. He lays out a series of sketches, a tree of evolution's might-have-beens, extrapolations from the fossil record of where evolution might have gone but didn't, where it started to go but came up against a hostile environment, dead-end ideas from the DNA lottery, natural selection's tossaways, nature's little jokes, prehistory's blind alleys. Finally he comes to a prehistoric alligator. "Who's to say these fellas couldn't-wouldn't-develop fur?"

"It's never happened," I say. "I'm no biologist or paleontologist"-Lonnie eyes me severely-"like you," I add, hoping to stroke his ego, but he'll have none of it.

"I'm an amateur," he admits, "but a damn sight smarter than those pansies in academic gowns."

"But," I push on, "those are different lines of evolution, the leathery amphibians and the furry mammals."

"Suppose an alligator mated with a beaver."

"Unlikely," I say.

"A cold winter's night mistake. A romantic error in the darkness of the sludge at the bottom of Lake Betawigosh."

"No,"

"Love knows no bounds."

"You're not talking love. You're talking madness. Myopia. Crazed affection."

"There you are. There you are. We see stranger things in the newspaper every morning. We see people with forty-seven personalities. We see babies with no heads. A billion people believe they've lived other lives. Tens of thousands swear they've been inside flying saucers and had sex with folks with big eyes. Cows fall from the sky in South America. And you think alligators couldn't grow a bunch of fur follicles in a burst of endocrinal necessity?"

I shake my head.

He stares me in the eye. "We used to be blue algae. Now we've got brains and toenails. How did that happen?"

"It took hundreds of millions of years."

"Wittgenstein," he says, "a guilt-ridden neurotic whose vivisection of language I find irrelevant to the Big Questions, did say on one occasion, and I quote, Our greatest stupidities may be very wise."

"I don't think you're stupid," I say, "I just think you're ... "

"Obsessed?"

"Well ... "

"Don't you think Principia Mathematica was the fruit of obsession? The Critique of Pure Reason? Fermat's Last Theorem? Michael Jordan's lifetime scoring record? If we weren't obsessed"-he gets a wild look in his eyes- "we'd still be slime mold. "

It's spring. It's mud everywhere.

Sometimes I don't see Lonnie for days. Sometimes he's hauling logs down a two-lane blacktop at seventy miles an hour. Sometimes he's working construction. In winter he might be plowing snow off parking lots and driveways. Right now he's remodeling a million-dollar house on Lake Betawigosh, a vacation hideaway for the co-producer of a successful Broadway musical that has no plot and no new songs; the fellow, Lonnie just learned, vacations regularly in Florida, but Lonnie hasn't inquired if he has ever brought back any long-snouted reptiles. Lonnie's installing a sauna and paneling the game room. I still haven't seen my bookcases.

Lonnie doesn't say much about his personal life. I've wondered what he does for sex, if his alligator obsession is a devotion like a monk's, and celibacy is Lonnie's way of concentrating his energies. He might have a gal stashed somewhere, but he's never mentioned her. He's never asked about my private life, but I wouldn't have much to confide there, either. I write most of the day, absorbed by my computer screen.

It's after midnight when a knock rattles my door. I'm watching a video. I turn off the VCR and open the door. Lonnie walks in, mud on his boots and vindication in his eyes. He hands me a chunk of plaster.

"What's this?" I ask.

"Look at it." It's a footprint, larger than my hand. "I found that in the mud on the shore of Lake Julia, not five miles from here."

'And this is...?"

He pulls a book from his old beat-up leather briefcase, the kind college professors carried fifty years ago. He flips through the pages. He holds the book out for me to look at it. 'Alligator foot," he says, jabbing his finger at the drawing. 'Alligator foot," he says, shoving the plaster cast in my face. "Now? Now do you believe me?"

I admit the cast resembles the drawing. "Only one print?" I ask.

"They found one footprint of Australopithecus afarensis in the mud in Kenya and postulated a whole species."

"But look here," I say, suddenly spying a hole in his logic. "If this print matches that of the ordinary alligator, what happens to your hypothesis that these local gators are mutating? Wouldn't they have a different footprint?"

Lonnie smiles his crooked smile. "In 1985 an anthropologist picked up an australopithecine skull in the muck of Lake Turkana in Kenya. It's two and a half million years old. Parts of it look like our heads. Other parts look very primitive." He lets that sink in. He goes on. "In 1997 the Spanish paleo anthropologist Bermudez de Castro was poking around a cave in the Atepuerca Mountains in Spain. He found a new human species-six folks that were almost a million years old, with faces like yours and mine" - I study his intent blue eyes, his grizzled beard, his wild eyebrows, the hairs curling out of his nose, the disarray of his gray-streaked hair hanging over his collar-"but their jaws and foreheads are those of Neanderthals!" He squints one eye. "Homo antecessor," he says, "our ancestors. Ours and the Neanderthals.'" He opens the eye. "Here's another tidbit. Some of the bones were broken, the marrow sucked out. Know what that means?" I shake my head. "Some of those fellas ate the others." He leans back, strangely satisfied.

"What does that have to do with ... "

Lonnie pulls a beer out of my refrigerator. He twists off the cap. "Nietzsche says that the irrationality of a thing is not an argument against its existence, but rather a condition of it." He takes a few calm swallows.

"Nietzsche didn't live in Minnesota. Nietzsche never saw an alligator."

"Philosophy is not rooted to any time or place." He falls into an easy chair, props his muddy boots on a footstool. "Oh, sure, any philosopher is a product of his time and place, of his friends and his toilet training, his diet and his fears, like you and me. Spinoza was a Jew in Amsterdam, he read Descartes, he was unlucky in love-the Ethics followed. Plato grew up amidst political instability, his teacher was executed, he wanted something solid, he grabbed onto another reality, purer and more permanent than this one. But ideas themselves are like numbers. Once we know about them, we can figure with them."

"But new alligators?"

"In 1994 a new species of kangaroo was discovered in Papua New Guinea. Locals call it a bondegezou."

"It wasn't new. It didn't evolve yesterday. It had been back in the jungle for a million years. No one had seen it, that's all."

"We don't know that."

He walks over to the glass doors to my deck, overlooking Loon Lake, invisible in the moonless night. "Those gators out there," he muses, "they've been there for years. Biding their time." He studies the impenetrable darkness. "Evolution is not a superhighway," he says. "It's a drunkard's peregrination. It twists and turns and doubles back on itself. Every step of the way it's nothing but another Reuben Lucius Goldberg contraption."

"So you're saying that the alligators might have mutated in some ways-put on fat, grown fur, maybe learned to talk-but still have the same feet?"

"Why not? And sonar, too!"

Still no sign of my bookcases. Lonnie implies that dark conspiracies are hoarding the nation's inventory of quality oak. I don't pursue the matter.

Lonnie brings me some fresh walleye he's caught. I broil them, with a little butter and a splash of bourbon. I ask him if he prefers summer fishing, when he can skim from place to place, to ice fishing.

"The way I see it," he answers, "ice fishing is the bottomless metaphor for the philosophical pilgrimage, the never-ending quest for The Answer To Everything."

"How's that?" I ask, despite my better judgment.

"Well, look here. You drill an aperture in the ice-in other words, you peek into the cold crystalline certainty of death. Oh, the ice may be sprinkled with the wishful thinking of religionists and otherworldly fanatics; it may support the snowmobiles of received opinion; but it's there, you can't ignore it, you're getting cold feet, and so you welcome your window into that greenish enigma, you study that eerie glow of brumal mystery. Do we have an Aristotelian telos? Is there a bright sun outside the shadows of the fish house? Should we step outside and get a tan, chug a cold beer, as Epicurus suggests? Does love move the planets, as Lucretius says? Is it all just a damn merry-go-round, as the Buddha and Schopenhauer believe? Will I be a minnow in my next life? Am I Sisyphus, doomed to fish for eternity without catching anything? Is there no exit from my fish house? Will I encounter the Oberfische? Is my line a thesis, the fish an antithesis, our dinner here, tasty and crunchy, the synthesis? Does life have meaning? You gaze for years into the watery conundrum. You wait for an answer to flash into view. Maybe nothing swims by. Maybe it's so fast you can't believe you saw it. Maybe you hallucinated. Or maybe slippery truth nibbled at your bait."

He eats the rest of the walleye and drains the glass of Chardonnay. "True ice fishing is a discipline," he concludes, "a meditation."

He's been hauling his boat from one lake to the next, looking for signs of the gators. Is he getting discouraged?

"Schopenhauer says that the misery in a fella's life comes from his wanting things. Even if he gets those things-it doesn't matter what they are-a good lay, a juicy T-bone, a vision of God himself-next week he'll be wanting something different. Or more of the same. That's why we're miserable. The only answer, according to Arty S., is to listen to reason. And reason tells you, Stop wanting."

"Stop wanting to find the alligators?" I ask.

"That would be the reasonable thing. To stop my frustration. To stop my misery."

"You're giving up?" I hate to even think it. It's not that I believe him, exactly. It's that I can see that his pursuit gives his life purpose. And don't we all need a purpose, no matter how absurd?

He scowls. "Give up?"

"To stop your misery."

"Hell, man, who says we're reasonable creatures? I love my misery! People have believed in one god or another for millennia, believed in satyrs and mermaids, dragons and griffins, in heaven and in eternal damnation. Is there one shred of evidence in the entire history of mankind that would lead us to believe that Homo sapiens is reasonable? Or that we don't love our misery?"

He reaches for his beer. He says, "I have a new plan."

"Which is?"

"An underwater mike. Recording equipment. A male gator makes a low-frequency call when he's shopping for a gal. I'm going to sweep the lakes. I'll hear that call. Those gators, my friend, are multiplying like rabbits, and they're moving like quicksilver across the liminal landscape."

I'm at K-Mart buying two metal bookcases when I notice the story in our local newspaper, The North Woods Forester. A woman out for her morning power walk saw an alligator ten feet long slither through the underbrush next to some railroad cars on a siding near Oak Lake.

I can't find Lonnie anywhere.

The next day a schoolteacher, on his way home from his summer job making hamburgers at a fast food restaurant, sees "a monster lizard" waddle across the highway and splash into Oak Lake.

Finally Lonnie shows up. He catches me assembling the metal bookcases. His eyes narrow. His beard vibrates. I tell him they're for the garage, for tools and things. I don't think he believes me. I try to ricochet his attention elsewhere, ask him if these sightings are the hard evidence he's been looking for, but he shakes his head. "It's not one of my alligators," he sighs. "This fella came up from Louisiana on the train."

"Sleeper car?"

"In the timber. Where'd those folks spot him? Right by the pulp mill. By the train tracks. Right after a shipment of logs from Louisiana. It all fits."

I lead him into the kitchen, away from the bargain bookcases, for coffee. His wide red suspenders, decorated with loons, hold his worn dungarees high on his stomach. His blue cap, worn and bruised by grease-stained fingers, proclaims his readiness as a volunteer fireman. He takes the mug of coffee and sucks the dark liquid through his bushy mustache.

"Then you're not excited?" I ask.

"Hell yes, I'm excited. This guy means genetic diversity. I was worried these acclimated gators might be inbreeding, the scions of only a couple of interlopers. This big fella can widen the gene pool."

"That's good."

"Maybe." Lonnie Alderson's face clouds. "Thing is, these mutant gators that are already here-hell, I might as well tell you, I've told you everything else-I've named them."

"George? Sally? Aloysius?"

"Alligator minnesotiensis. And, if we find furry ones, Alligator minnesotiensis

aldersonis."

"I see."

Lonnie tugs at the suspenders. "Thing is, this new fella, or maybe it's a gal, has not adapted. Alligator minnesotiensis has. Will this new specimen add vigor to Alligator minnesotiensis? Or will it weaken it? Will they even mate? Has Alligator minnesotiensis already branched too far and won't find this visitor, Alligator mississipiensis, a winsome mate?" Lonnie looks uncustomarily disheartened. He wipes his mustache with the back of his wrist.

"The future is dark and unaccountable," he reflects. "But then, we know that, don't we? The philosophers, the good ones, know that. Evolution-human history!-is a record of fits and starts, fecundity and catastrophe. Species multiply, then a meteor hits or an ice age sets in, and it's curtains for a million very promising genotypes, critters that might have evolved-who knows?-into something smarter, or kinder, than Homo sapiens, nothing left now but a bone or an imprint in volcanic ash, lost forever."

"What about your sound sweep? Listening for the growly mating call of Alligator minnesotiensis'"

"Nothing yet. But maybe the mating season is over. Maybe the gals have already laid their eggs. I'm going to scour the banks of the lakes for signs. Those caimans make nests three feet high and six feet in diameter. They lay forty or fifty eggs."

"That's a lot of little gators."

He gives his suspenders an authoritative snap. "We're carrying millions of sperm in our balls, too, but only one makes it to the goal line-if it even gets in the game. Nature is profligate, because she feeds many. Those eggs may be gobbled up by raccoons, eagles, dogs. There's no guarantee. As Heraclitus says, You can't fish in the same river twice."

The North Woods Forester reports that Irv Bergan shot and killed a five foot alligator that was snoozing in lrv's hot tub in his back yard, a hundred yards from Oak Lake, not far from the pulp mill. I want to cheer Lonnie up. He seems Schopenhaureanly despondent.

I present him with a copy of my new mystery; just out, a paperback original, Lumberjack Lunch, the first mystery I've set in northern Minnesota, about a cannibalistic logger who dismembers fellow lumberjacks with his chainsaw and roasts them on his Weber. My detective is Ramona Rafferty, a buxom forty-year-old iconoclastic bisexual homicide detective sent up to the northland from Minneapolis who traps the murderer, Paul, by pretending to be a male lumberjack and then, just as Paul is coming at her with his Stihl 088 she rips open her red and black checked wool lumberjack's shirt to expose, like Phryne before the Athenian assembly, her full breasts (well, yes, perhaps surgically enhanced), which unnerves Paul, because she reminds him of his mother, and Ramona takes him peacefully into custody as he blubbers on her ample freckled bosom about being abused as a child by his mother's boyfriend, a logger who made up scary stories about Paul Bunyan as he did unspeakable things to young Paul. I wrote it under the nom de plume Rose LaFleur, because most readers of mysteries are women and many of them like to read women authors. This is my first mystery by Rose, and the first with Ramona as the protagonist. If Lumberjack Lunch sells well, I'll write a series. In the next book I'll give Ramona a drinking problem, or maybe a morphine addiction, acquired when she recovered from bullet wounds from an earlier assignment (which could be a prequel), and she'll be a recovering kleptomaniac and will have a developmentally challenged son who gets into trouble for sexually inappropriate behavior in a schoolyard. I'm pretty proud of Lumberjack Lunch, even if it is a potboiler, because I feel I'm getting a handle on the culture and mythos of this region. Lonnie, however, merely glances at the cover (Ramona is ripping open her shirt, Paul is in the background with the chainsaw-which I thought unnecessarily telegrammed the book's climax, but they don't ask me about cover art) before he sets it down on the table, and then "forgets" it when he leaves my place later that evening.

The local lodge of Swedes in America has erected a maypole on the shore of Lake Betawigosh. Maybe "maypole" isn't the right word, because it isn't May, it's midsummer. But there you are, things aren't quite the way you think they should be. The maypole, or midsummerpole, is a cross twenty feet high garlanded with flowers. Some of the older Swedes have donned authentic Swedish folk togs-the women long skirts with brightly embroidered aprons and cute caps, the men knickers and white stockings and embroidered vests, clothes no one in Sweden wears anymore-and they're dancing around the midsummer pole, their joints creaky from arthritis but their faces bright with a vague genetic memory of pagan bacchanals back in a pre-Christian homeland. Olaf Olafson, ninety years old, is playing the fiddle, and Lonnie, to my surprise, is sawing beautifully on a cello. Olaf and Lonnie are sitting under the midsummer pole, and the other Swedes are dancing in a circle around them. Some children have joined in. They're barefoot, and the girls are wearing crowns of woven flowers.

I glance around at the scattering of onlookers, some of them of Swedish descent, others the product of historical raids, wars, love, infatuations, and errors in the night, their lineage a hash of Norwegian, Danish, Celt, Etruscan, Gypsy, warrior, milkmaid, ragpicker, bard. I spy Abigail Sorensen, whom I haven't seen since she went back to her husband, George. She's standing beside George. She's cut her auburn hair. Sunglasses hide her green eyes. A peasant blouse hides her plump, freckled breasts. I have the feeling Abigail has noticed me, but she doesn't look my way. George spots me, and I look away. When I glance back again, they're gone. Could we have been happy together, Abigail and I? If I had devoted more time to.

Brigit, would she have stayed? Would I be happier if she had stayed? Is happiness our goal? Is happiness that deep falling into place of something, like a lock opening, the satisfaction that comes when a question is answered, a problem solved, a consummation accomplished, an uncertain mission clarified, an inchoate quest realized? Or is philosophy a question, rather than an answer?

Later, in the gazebo by the waterfront, as we're chowing down on the hot fruit soup and lefsa and potato sausage and the thick, creamy, buttery, cholesterol-freighted remmmegrot, the latter a gesture to the semi-Norwegians in the group, Lonnie tells me that he enjoys this annual celebration of genetic resourcefulness. He reminds me that Queen Christina of Sweden, a kick-ass gal whose troops sacked

Prague, enticed Descartes up from Amsterdam for early morning chats on ethics and metaphysics. "But then he caught a cold walking to and from the castle and kicked the bucket. Just goes to show," he says.

"Show what?"

"The Cartesian dichotomy between mind and body can be disproved by a wintery draft."

He rolls his lefsa, a thin white crepe made from potatoes, into a cylinder and bites off the end.

"You're always surprising me," I confess.

"How's that?"

"This. The Swedes. The cello. You never told me."

"These folks don't realize-not consciously, anyway-that this is a festival dedicated to unbridled lechery, chthonic abandon, and Dionysian high-jinks-but their old arthritic bones know, their wornout DNA knows. It doesn't occur to them that that pole is one helluva big cock, festooned as in Lady Chatterley's Lover with posies and honeysuckle, the flowers a metaphor for unstoppable seminal juice, their dance a primitive rousing of the spirits of regeneration." He takes a swallow of coffee. 'Just as well they don't know," he adds. Lonnie seems softer this afternoon, less driven. His graying hair, still wet from the shower, is combed smooth and ends in a short pony tail. His jeans are faded but clean. Leather sandals grip his bare feet. A big toenail is black, where he must have dropped something on it. I have trouble reconciling him, as I know him, to this folksy communality. His philosophical iconoclasm seems in abeyance, his dedicated solitude a mistaken aberration, his monomaniacal pursuit of Alligator minnesotiensis an idle hobby, easily abandoned.

Has he changed? Is this the real Lonnie, brushing the powdered sugar from a krumkake off his t-shirt, the shirt boasting You Can Always Tell a Swede But You Can't Tell Him Much? Are there many Lonnies? Or is the real Lonnie deep and impenetrable, unpredictable as ice fishing, harboring many flickering, darting possibilities, past and future-ugly bottom feeders, delicate walleye, lonely snapping turtles, down-home crappies, drowsy mollusks, and, who knows, creatures new and marvelous and dangerous, like uninvited ideas?

"It may be," Lonnie reflects, leaning back in his folding chair, "as the prescient nineteenth-century Swedish philosopher Axel Hagerstrom proposed, and as the contemporary American neo-pragmatist johnny-come-lately Richard Rorty contends, that there's nothing but shifting sands to hold up any belief, and that my belief in these gators as the offspring of a trigger-happy evolution has no more validity than me expecting to see a unicorn gallop by. But we're trolling in deep waters here. We can't see the bottom, even with a digital depth finder. Maybe it's true that philosophy is nothing more than an after-dinner conversation over espresso and cigars, as Rorty maintains. What's new about that notion? Isn't that what Plato was saying in The Symposium? And isn't that conversation like the one evolution has with its profligate children, sorting them out, seeing who can weather the ice age or the new bully on the block?"

The celebrants in their ancient attire and luminous accessories have gathered again by the festooned phallus to crown the Midsummer Queen, Alice Torkelson, eighty-six years old. Lonnie plays a fanfare on his cello. She smiles sweetly. In her heart she's sixteen.

Alice rests her frail bones in a lawn chair and sips punch from a paper cup. The Swedes pack up their dishes, shake out their checked tablecloths, fold up their tables, and load them into Arnie Bergstrom's pickup.

Out on Lake Betawigosh fishing boats are drifting, lines slack in the calm water, while fishermen ponder the idiosyncrasies of walleye behavior. A sailboat, its white sail curved like an innocent breast, glides blissfully through the blue. A flock of Canadian geese waddle across the waterfront, picking up crumbs and dropping green goose shit in the grass. Near the shore a mother mallard swims, her dozen young ones following in a perfect single file.

Old Olaf plays a melancholy tune on his fiddle. Alice listens, as if he's playing especially for her.

Barefoot children dance around the garlanded midsummer pole.

Lonnie snuggles his cello into the velvet of its case.

A splash breaks the calm. The baby ducks scatter, panicked.

Alice points from her chair.

The mother duck is gone.

Olaf stops playing.

Lonnie walks to the water's edge. Away from shore the water feathers, made uneasy by some dark disturbance accelerating silently just below the surface.

Jill Marquis

Woman Overboard

Stacy and my brother Lou met when they both worked on one of the tourist boats. He was the boat's first mate at that time, and he was dating a girl named Amy who was beautiful, but usually mad at him for not ever wanting to do anything, or for not doing enough for her. Stacy was scrubbing the deck; Lou was in the wheelhouse surveying the scene. He happened to be looking right at Stacy when she fell off the boat, so he immediately leaned forward and announced Woman overboard! into the public address system.

Lou has a booming voice like an announcer on a game show, if you can imagine. He turned off the microphone, and let out half a laugh. And then everyone just watched as she saved herself. She fell twelve feet from the deck, plunged underwater, and resurfaced a moment later covered with muck and holding a forlorn duckling in her left hand. She dragged herself out of the water, scaled the ladder to the wheelhouse, put the ducking down tenderly, and said, What? What did you say? That's how they met. The two of them drove each other nuts at first, and then, well, and then they had a little girl together. Lou raises the girl now, and Stacy moved out west with the duck.

Right before Stacy slipped off the boat, she had been looking at the ducking, which was flopping around in an oil slick about the size and shape of a child's swimming pool. She saw the duck struggling in the water and leaned out toward it until she accidentally lost her footing.

Stacy was Lou's twelfth girlfriend, and the only one of his girlfriends who didn't call me crying after the break up. Stacy was different. I think of the other girlfriends as individuals who successively took on the role of the original girlfriend, Cindy. Cindy was sweet. When they dated in high school, she was involved in just about every after school activity and took all sorts of weird evening classes, like Swahili and belly dancing. Cindy always tried her best. Even though the girlfriends didn't look alike, they have similar issues, and about the time the relationship ends, the girlfriend always calls me and wants to know what my brother's deal is. Sometimes they cry, but mainly they sound frustrated and really ticked off. I learn more about the relationships from the girlfriends than from Lou. All Lou told me about the day he met Stacy was that she fell off the boat, she saved the duck, and then he met a real weirdo sitting on the park bench, a woman with a lot of used hankies. The rest of this I got from Stacy, and the weirdo, who turned out to be number fourteen.

In the wheelhouse, Lou looked at the sickly duckling, at the very wet woman, and at the other deckhands, who were waiting to see what he would do. He decided that the best course of action was to focus on the duck. So, without pausing to field Stacy's questions or to apologize for making a joke of her near-death experience, he picked up the duck and walked off the boat.

The waterfront isn't like it was in the old days – the longshoremen have moved to better ports, and the barges have been replaced by cruise ships and pleasure boats. The boardwalk is gone; now there's a vast brick plaza paid for by a small levy and thousands of private citizens who were willing to pay a hundred bucks each for a personalized brick. Most of the old bars are gone, and the old salts too.

Lou left the boat and walked upriver a block or so, until the ship was out of sight. Then he wasn't sure what to do, so he sat down on a park bench next to a dour young woman with her hair in a bun. The bench was next to the sea wall, but faced the street. The duck sat quietly at Lou's side as he and the woman regarded the traffic. An ancient gray pickup rolled by at very low speed, towing a school bus that appeared to be totally gutted. The light turned from yellow to red as the two vehicles lumbered through the intersection. The young man steering the school bus smiled broadly, too optimistically for a guy at the helm of such a heap. He even honked the horn a few times. Then the woman on the bench recognized the guy – she waved and called out, "Hey! One day at a time!" The guy saw her and waved back. Then it looked like maybe she didn't feel so good, like a wave of feeling not very good washed over her. She pulled a bottle of aspirin from her purse and took a few. Then she noticed the duck.

"Hey," she said, "What's up with the duck?"

"I found it. I don't know what to do with it."

The woman pulled a used Kleenex from her purse, then another. She sidled over to the duck.

"What's its name?"

"It doesn't have one."

She rooted around and found several more wads of tissue in her purse and went to work cleaning the duck.

"Huh, you've got a lot of used Kleenex." Lou said. She spit on one of the tissues, then rubbed the duck with it. The oil moved from one part of the duck to another part of the duck, but didn't actually leave the duck.

"Maybe it needs some water, some water and a little aspirin," the woman said.

"I don't know. Think that's okay?"

"Well, it might help. Depends. I've had a headache for four months."

The duck quivered on the bench, breathing wetly. Lou didn't know what to say, so he said, "Wow."

Then Lou spotted Stacy striding down the walkway. She had changed into a dry set of coveralls and tied her hair back. He was actually glad to see her. She looked very efficient. She looked like she would know what to do with the duck.

"There you are!" Stacy said. She picked up the duck and nestled it in a towel.

"You have a car, yes? We better get her to a vet." She looked at the woman on the bench and said, "Oh, hi, Linda." then turned and headed for the staff parking area.

Lou followed her to his car. He opened the door for her and the duck. His head bobbed slightly like a butler's as they entered the car. He felt really weird, and could not say exactly why.

Stacy directed Lou to the nearest veterinarian, and they got there in no time. It was a quiet trip – the radio wasn't even on. The whole way, Stacy focused on the duck. She touched it carefully. She rubbed it with the towel. She made eye contact with the duck and held it until the duck looked away. Lou and Stacy didn't say a word to each other until the veterinarian took the duck to the exam room.

Then Stacy thanked Lou for driving her, and asked if Linda was his girlfriend. Lou said no, she was just helping with the duck.

"Okay," she said.

"Why?"

"Because Linda's a slut."

Lou said, "She's a slut? What do you mean by that?"

"Well, when I was in high school she and her sister were always making out with guys in public, practically doing it in the classroom. It was like a contest between them, to see who could go the furthest."

"So that's what a slut is?" An expression of botheration fell across Lou's face. "All she told me was that she's had a headache for four months. Anyway, I don't think that's what a slut is. A slut is just kind of more... available than other girls."

"Well, that's not what it means. Available is one thing, slut is a whole other thing. It was like she couldn't control herself. She and her sister were both like that. They couldn't seem to stop themselves."

"What's wrong with being available, anyway? What you're describing is skanky, sure, but what's wrong with that?"

"All I'm saying is she was a slut in high school."

Stacy had a lot more definite ideas about the world than Lou, and it sort of made him mad. Skank vs. slut vs. available is just one example of the hundreds of things they ended up arguing about.

They sat quietly, waiting for the duck. Lou thought about calling his girlfriend, Amy, but then decided not to because she was mad at him and he couldn't quite remember why.

There's only one picture of Amy in the family album. It's from Mardi Gras season and she's wearing a ridiculous hat. It looks like a Christmas tree ran into the Leaning Tower of Pisa, shrank, and then landed on the head of a good-natured young woman. She's got a great smile and her eyes are completely closed. She used to make cookies for Lou. I'm not saying the cookies defined her, I'm just saying she made cookies. She also fed him grapes. He looked bored a lot. When they broke up she called me, crying. We had lunch together at a really great greasy spoon.

Here's another picture: It's of Lou and Sarah (number six, I think) at one of mom and dad's barbecues. She was the athletic one, the one who took him backpacking and windsurfing. This was when they had just started going out, when he was really into her. In the picture, Lou and Sarah are in the pool wearing snorkeling masks. They're all entangled in an embrace but trying to face the camera. Her smile is stretched out over a mouth full of snorkeling equipment, and so is his. She doesn't look quite as weird as he does. My brother looks pretty freaking freaky when he's in love. It looks too unnatural to last long. When they broke up, Sarah called me, crying. She wanted to go for a walk in the park, so we did. I tried to explain my brother.

And here's one more: it's of Lou at another Mardi Gras ball, about ten years ago. He's not smiling and not frowning. His face is all crooked as he stands there trying to decide how to look.

The veterinarian emerged from the exam room. The duck was totally clean. It was small and gray, all fuzzy and perfect. Stacy directed Lou to drive her and the duck home, and he did. And he didn't really know how it came to pass, but they settled in together for a while. They named the duck Camille, and dug a pond for her.

I didn't see much of Lou for some time, and when I did see him, he seemed sort of hyper and disturbed, I recall him telling me with some urgency: "Stacy has a tattoo of a cat that's waving hello. But it's a Japanese cat or something. It's on her ankle." Another time he said, "Stacy knows the lyrics to every song, I swear to god." And another time, "Stacy's taking CPR. She's at the top of her class!" The words weren't inherently strange but that tone was something I had not heard from him before: it was awe, it was pride-of-girlfriend.

Once I asked him why he seemed down, and he explained, "Stacy and I had a big fight about cremation." Their arguments were not generally his idea and covered a broad range of topics, including eggs, litter, pennies, meter maids, drive-through windows, the Mercator projection, and the best way to get from point A to point B, and that old chestnut – argument vs. debate vs. lively conversation.

After Stacy got pregnant, Lou resurfaced. They began attending Sunday dinners at our parents house, where we ate meat and potatoes and sat by the pool watching TV together for hours on end, the television's blue light rippling along the surface of the water. It felt normal and nice to have one of the girlfriends around again and we, my parents and I, tried to treat it like old times but the bun-in-the-oven aspect of the situation and Stacy and this new enthusiastic version of Lou made it nearly impossible for us to fall back into the velvet ditch of the good old days. Mom tried to commiserate with Stacy about the difficulties of pregnancy but got little response. Dad wanted to know why she was working as a deckhand, I just sat there waiting for Lou to say the next weird thing.

We were unsettled but not unimpressed. At the school where I teach, the faculty had erected a sign that looked like a thermometer, which was used to chart the progress of the senior class trip fundraising effort. Every couple of days, the mercury on it rose, and likewise every Sunday the family's admiration for Stacy bubbled upward. Stacy had not only organized Lou's CD collection, she had convinced him to keep it that way. She won a lifetime supply of motor oil in a radio contest. She traded that lifetime supply for a lifetime supply of car repairs from a guy she met. He was a fairly elderly gentleman whose years were numbered, but still, wow. Then, after she quit her job, she invented a better mousetrap. It was a kinder, gentler mousetrap, and soon the mice who had infested Lou and Stacy's house frolicked and multiplied in a nearby park. In the space of a few weeks they caught and released approximately one hundred mice. It appeared that word had got out in mouse circles that the traps were actually portals to a greener world. One night by the pool Stacy and Lou spent hours tying lengths of rope into complex knots, and a few weeks later Lou announced that thanks to Stacy he had passed his Captain's exam. He was going to be promoted! Everyone was pleased.

Then Stacy decided to befriend me and holy crap, I have not experienced such intense befriendification since, I think, the third grade. I know that befriendification is not a word, but it is most definitely a feeling. Stacy wanted to know all my particulars: what my job entailed, who I had dated, who my immediate prospects were, what ideas I had for the future. Her interrogation method involved more eye contact than I can really deal with, so I couldn't hold out for long. I told her everything, and then when that didn't seem like enough, I threw in a few wild hypotheses about the truth. Like somehow in the course of the conversation I convinced myself that I had a crush on the biology teacher at my school. This was largely because it seemed vital for me to have something worthwhile to report. She asked numerous follow-up questions, and together we decided that he was totally hot and that I really should go for it. Then she wanted to know if I had considered other career paths, if I had ever considered living somewhere different, like Taos. I hardly had a chance to say No, not really before she started rattling off a long list of options that she thought were promising for me: stunt double, veterinarian, ergonomics specialist, police officer, transportation futurist. She had detailed ideas about all of these possibilities. This is when I really began to worry for Lou.

Every Sunday, Stacy seemed less interested in Lou and the rest of us. She tapped her toes, took control of the remote, made frequent trips to the bathroom. However, Lou didn't seem to notice, didn't seem worried; his devotion to Stacy did not diminish. When the blessed day arrived, baby Sue emerged from the womb hollering. She may have the most powerful set of lungs known to babykind, plus she has the endurance of a long-distance runner. Sometimes when Sue starts screaming, Lou picks her up and gazes at her, admiring her work.

My father has trouble with the crying. He can't hear anyone crying without feeling sad himself, and if it goes on for a long time he gets a little choked up. One Sunday in the middle of dinner the baby let loose a big scream that just didn't subside, and my poor dad, his mouth full of pot roast, couldn't take his eyes off her. Lou picked the baby up, and Mom and I tried to ignore dad's distress, which seemed the kindest path. The baby kept screaming as mom and I continued our conversation, trying to remember the name of some movie we had both seen. We couldn't name any of the actors or describe what it was about but it did involve huge silver RVs, the desert, and a handsome, perpetually discombobulated actor. We agreed that the actor had brown hair, and then we fell silent. The baby cried; dad attempted to chew. He then made an effort to maintain a calm facial expression. The crying was officially causing him to freak out. Eventually, he tried to swallow. A gob of roast got stuck. And then, for one longish moment of choking and wailing, it felt like dad and the baby were the only real people in the room, like the rest of us were furniture or knick knacks. Then Stacy jumped up, grabbed my dad, and performed the Heimlich maneuver on him. It was completely effective. Lou beamed with pride. Stacy whisked the baby out of the room for a diaper change.

Not long afterwards, Stacy skipped town and left the baby with Lou. I still can't believe she did that. She had handled that child with great care and efficiency for six months and then I guess maybe she felt it was time for the next project. She said she would be back in a month or so, but then we never heard from her. When she left, Lou was hurt, but a few weeks later another pretty girl caught his eye. Stacy left, and didn't even call me! I was sad for Lou that time, but also a little sad for myself. I never got closure on the Stacy-and-Lou romance.

As for Lou, he's back to dating the same kind of girls he's always dated. Tonight Lisa, playing the role of Cindy, calls me and asks, "What's up with your brother? What's his deal?" She's crying way too much over my lummox of a brother. She's surprised. She's confused. I don't really have an explanation, but I do have this page from the photo album, the one with the picture where Lou thinks he looks nonchalant. Because that's his deal, he spends his life trying to look like he doesn't care, but failing totally. There are other pictures on this page of Mardi Gras photos: mom and dad are posing for the camera, standing in a conversational grouping. Dad's looking at mom, who is wearing large silver glasses and looking off stage left. Dad is genuinely smiling at her, but mom isn't even really smiling at whomever she sees over there. And there's a picture of Aunt Sue in an enormous headdress. The headdress is made of red, white, and blue fathers and is about two feet tall. A dozen silver starts are stuck in the headdress, caught in the act of shooting away from her head. One of her arms is slung around my cousin Kit, who is ten years old and looks at the ground uncomfortably. Aunt Sue's holding a big feathery wand in one hand, and using her other hand to rub something off Kit's cheek. Poor little Kit has got his mom's saliva smeared all over his face. He's in his own little hell there. In another picture, the original girlfriend Cindy is wearing a sequined costume and tap dancing, trying very hard not to look at her feet. Her smile is muscular but not deeply felt. Her hands are clenched and her shoulders are stooping forward, as if they could keep track of what her eyes should not.

Daniel T. Smith

Pammy's Door

Somewhere during the evening I'd lost my inborn purchase on temporal progression. The half dozen Percodan I kept in my sock as a precautionary measure had found themselves called into service during a postprandial fit of theretofore unknown panic. Told that fellow, Gino, that I had to hit the gents, and I left Adkins Ranch on a dead run. I didn't stop till I took those cement stairs to Pammy's door two at a time.

Christmas lights kaleidoscoped on her porch. I guessed she must have strung them the day before. Their blue and green and red blinking pitched a strange array of colors against me. I pounded on her door and didn't hear anything right away. I pounded again.

"Pammy!" I hadn't meant to shout. Pammy hated when I raised my voice, said she didn't like the neighbors thinking she dated common trash. "Pammy!" I pounded away some more until I heard shuffling inside. The bolt got thrown and she opened the door, but only a crack. She'd have been less surprised had the angel Gabriel himself come calling.

"Elijah, you ain't supposed to be here."

Warm air blew out of her place, out of that little sliver of darkness behind the still-chained door.

"You been sleeping, baby?"

"Jesus, Elijah. Tell me you ain't this stupid."

Now, let me set the record straight about Pammy: She's tough as jute, sure, but she's also more beautiful than anything Ali Baba'd ever pilfered. Pammy's kind of beauty is rare, might even be misdiagnosed by the uncouth as some form of homeliness. Her smile's slight, only uses half her mouth. But there's subtlety in that parsimony, makes it fine like a thimble full of saffron. The bridge of Pammy's nose bends to the left, the way some old boyfriend broke it for her. She refused to get it set. Says she kept it on that side as a commitment to herself, like her mind's made up, and that symmetry, like any shitheel boyfriend, can go fuck its own vainglorious reflection.

"You were supposed to be at Adkins for thirty days," she said, her jaw held tight as if she could chew glass back to sand. I'd envisioned her greeting as an open-armed affair, her mouth filled with words of longing. But Pammy kept the door chained.

"I'm a fast learner. Got the whole thing sussed in a day and a half. Now throw open that door and let's get to reuniting."

But Pammy'd never lie back for a fool. I knew it'd take some slick oratory for her to open that door, but I was far too tired for any grandiloquence. I'd been running a long time on account of poor directions.

"What's the most expedient way off this phony Brigadoon?" I'd asked some grizzled Adkins Ranch janitor. He was smoking a cigarette out by the laundry and did some herky-jerky St Vitus number that, only later, did I realize must have been a reaction to my startling him. Trying not to break stride, half-expecting the Dobermans to come lunging at my ass, I read his gyrations to mean, "Just over there, young friend, through them junipers and on to freedom." So I went that way, up and over a cinder block wall, out into a muddy field where I stayed lost for a good hour or two.

"Pammy, you know I don't need no rehab. Place was full of crazy people. Some woman named Sweetpea made me a card out of construction paper and glitter paint. She told me I was in love with my own destruction. What's a man supposed to take from that?"

"It was thirty days in rehab or ninety in county, Elijah."

I leaned against the technicolor-blinking doorframe, our faces close, separated by that taut chain.

"I ain't no troublemaker, Pammy. It's been a series of poor and unavoidable circumstances."

"We discussed all this, Elijah. Simple math, we said. Remember? Thirty's better than ninety. Simple math."

"But wasn't anything simple about it."

Things'd gone to hell on the second night. Gino, my counselor, buttonholed me as I was fishing a renegade piece of fried chicken out my molars. He seemed like a nice enough guy, though he wouldn't smile and used too much pomade. As a proud graduate of Adkins Ranch, Gino considered himself somewhat of a role model. He'd kicked a proclivity for crank that had rendered his septum a scabby memory and left him to speak as if in constant need of a Kleenex.

"Pammy, they discovered a bit of contraband in my personal effects. I'd like to say it was a frame-up, but that would be flat lying. I know it was dumb, so don't even say it. I swear I was going to quit. But cold turkey? Everyone knows that doesn't work."

Pammy's voice was flat, reasonable as usual. "Haul your ass back to rehab and beg them to take you in again." She closed the door.

Gino'd said, in his adenoidal way, that we had a "pwoblem," that we had to have an "ebergency sessiond." I tried to play it cool, but I knew what was coming. Sometimes you just know. Maybe I'd bragged to this kid, Gillon. He said he'd thought to bring a stash himself, but hadn't had the stones to try. Then he said something about how, rumor had it, the staff nosed through the dorms every day.

"They hustled me into this room, Pammy," I shouted through the door. A light went on in another apartment, some neighbor shouted for me to shut up. "Everyone was sitting in a circle. I ain't no hell-raiser, Pammy. I just needed a little time to think. You can't blame me for that."

"Elijah, go away," she shouted through the door. "This is the first place they'll come looking for you."

"Who, Pammy? The cops? Hell, they're always looking for me. Any cop in this town gets happier than a Jap with a two-eyed daruma when he gets a shot at Elijah Malverose."

I'd looked at all them sitting in that circle at Adkins. Gillon, Sweetpea, Gino, some big fellow called Lionel, a few others. They weren't going to help me. Street junkies, most of them. What I needed was my Pammy. Couldn't get her off my mind when I was there. I never had to dream about her when she was in my arms, but at Adkins Ranch, she was all my thoughts'd focus on. And she could cause some sweet reverie. She's what I was thinking about when I told Gino I needed to hit the gents.

At Pammy's door I heard the sounds of unchaining. There was a tingle behind my left ear that I took to mean things were going to work out somehow. Pammy'd let me in, let me get a little high, let me run my hands over her, let me get some rest.

When the door opened, I saw the rubicund visage of one Wim Haudela, night crew captain at the Lucky's on Aviation. My mind set to racing. I felt real cold. The first thing I thought to do was inquire as to the relative condition of Wim's Ford Ranger, his pride and joy. But as I tried to talk, my words were trapped in my shirt, which, itself, was gathered in my mouth on account of Wim's indelicate handling.

"I'm 'a-call the police," I heard Wim shout as he chucked me on a cement, bonebreak tumble down the stairs.

My face hit the last step and I felt a bicuspid break. I spit a bloody wad when I stood. Must've swallowed the tooth. It was nowhere in my mouth. I looked up at Pammy, who stood at the top of the steps, finger in her mouth and legs akimbo. In those blinking lights, she didn't look like my Pammy anymore. More like a high-priced store display, a mirage of something I didn't deserve. Simulacrum of my own shortcomings.

"You all right?" she asked.

"All things considered." I ran my tongue along that gap in my mouth where my tooth had been. Jagged dentin remains cut at my tongue, and I gagged on the taste of blood.

"Better get on, then."

We looked at each other a long while.

"I'm going in, Elijah." But she didn't right away, just stood there with those glittering lights dancing all around her.

"Can I come see you again, Pammy? I mean, not soon, but later maybe? Sometime?"

"Won't be no sooner than ninety." She stood a moment longer, then dropped her chin.

My mind couldn't focus and I found myself at an unprecedented loss of words. Pammy walked back inside and closed the door behind her.

Aurelia Wills

Sugar

"The problem with sugar," Corey said as I poured a stream of white crystals into my coffee, "is that sugar overloads your liver and becomes toxic in the blood. The toxicity causes cancer and the toxicity causes fear. Fear is the mental equivalent to cancer."

He pushed aside his plate and leaned across the diner table. "Lori, what are you afraid of?"

I wanted to be an agreeable guest for this important stranger I'd come seven hundred miles to meet, although I'd had two bad nights, one on a train, without sleep.

"Oh," I said, "I'm afraid of dying in a car crash. Spiders. Water snakes." And of Doug, my boyfriend in Seattle, and the way we lived back there. Each day had the same thick grey feeling. Those days stuck together into a tunnel. I wanted to blow like cottonwood seed as far from those days as I could get.

Corey was an old pal of my friend Ali, who'd encouraged me to come here to Chico because she'd heard he could get me a job at a co-op grocery store. I needed a new life in a new place, and even the name—Chico—sounded good. Ali told me that Corey was into cats and foraging wild plants for food and he had a rented house big enough to share; he and his girlfriend had broken up.

Corey's flannel shirt was unbuttoned, showing off off the hair on his chest. He had an angular face, straggly hairs on his chin, a sharp smell and dark tangled hair to his shoulders. With silver bracelets and leafy vines tattooed around his forearms, Corey was a down-home Chico lad. He looked up from beneath his eyebrows.

"So," he said, squinting at me, "is it Lori with an 'i,' Lorie with an 'ie,' Laurie from Laura, L-o-r-y, or some other foreign or variant spelling? Who are you? What kind of Lori are you?"

"I'm boring normal American Lori with an 'i.'"

He reached across the table and tweaked my nose. "Let's go foraging."

Corey stood and flourished his arm. His jeans, threadbare and white, were tucked into yellow leather boots with two-inch heels.

"My treat?" I said. He smiled modestly and folded his arms across his chest. I left a ten and we swept out of the diner.

We were an odd pair. He came to my chin; the top of his head was a stringy mess, imperfect camouflage for a pink pond of skin. I was tall and spindly as a fichus tree with red hennaed hair that hung in thin strands down my back. I had a sad bone-white face, long fingers and toes, a peace sign tattooed on my anklebone, and wore a tie-dye sundress and a dirty white cardigan. The cardigan was hot, but it covered a bruise where my boyfriend Doug had punched me in the back.

We walked out to Corey's truck, a battered orange hulk; the window glass tilted into the doors. When I pulled the door open, it screeched and swung low. I climbed up onto the bench seat, kicked aside some garbage and pulled my pack tight between my knees. In the pack, with my jeans, underwear, and two-for-a-dollar bags of candy, was a little over six hundred dollars. I pulled up the door and clunked it shut.

Corey climbed onto the driver's seat, started up the truck, threw his arm over the back of my seat and with an impressive straining of muscles and tendons, steered it out of the diner's parking lot. He said I needed a tour of Chico. He wanted to show me the university because, he said, "You're a university town gal." He drove through the campus and pointed out important buildings.

I looked at the kids, their heads lowered, huge backpacks slung over their shoulders as they walked to class. They seemed weighted down by their lives; I'd somehow ditched mine and floated like a leaf. The palm trees, fountains and elaborate brick towers of the campus were like a hallucination. So strange, everywhere you went, the same things lived out in different places. The dream was broken only by Corey's habit of clearing his nostrils and spitting out the window.

In the dusty downtown square, Corey spotted a friend and hollered. We pulled over, and a skinny dude with legs like denim pipes ambled to Corey's window. Sunburned and creased under a baseball cap, he tipped his hat to me with a lewd grin.

I turned away from him and stared at the dusty trees and at the sun beating on the sidewalk. The men had a cryptic conversation in which they made reference to various blowout parties, police busts and legal troubles. When Corey's friend mentioned the co-op in passing, I interrupted and said, "Where is the co-op, anyway?" Without looking at me, Corey reached over and silenced me with his hand. His wide fingertips rested on my shoulder for the rest of their conversation.

He thumbed through his tattered wallet, then jammed his hands deep into his pockets. "Shit. I'm out of cash." I watched the sunlight shining on the blowing grass, reached into my pack and pulled out a twenty.

With his tank full of gas, Corey became ebullient. "What a hot damn beautiful fabulous day," he said at a stoplight. He flexed his fingers over the steering wheel and did a yoga neck roll.

"You got a boyfriend?" He squeezed his nose, scratched his head, adjusted the music, stuck his hand out the window to feel the air.

"He's in Seattle. Didn't Ali tell you about him?" I looked down at my arms and hands. My arms, in the dingy sweater, looked like dirty sticks. They lay in my lap like a heap of kindling.

"No, no, didn't hear anything about it. Whatever you do, don't get married. You're too young."

"I'm twenty-three. Anyway, we kind of broke up."

"Lori, I was married once. It started out nice, then turned into a pit of hell. You got me?"

"I got you."

"I just turned thirty-four. Don't look it, do I? It's the macrobiotic lifestyle! So, what's this boyfriend do?" Corey had one arm draped over the steering wheel and faced me with a chummy smile.

"He's in graduate school. He's working on his Ph.D. He researches cancer...." We were drifting across the road. "A car's coming!"

He glanced over, put both hands on the wheel and adjusted the truck's direction. "Cancer! Remember the sugar-cancer connection? Lori, you tell him what I told you and make sure you say you heard it here first."

"Sure." Douglas carried his cell phone in his front pant's pocket, down in the heat with his keys. Back in Seattle he'd call me ten times a day. He'd say, "What are you doing?" then hang up. Doug was a tense guy—tall, muscular and ropey—with thick dark hair that looked like a wig. He was extraordinarily handsome with one exception—he was walleyed; his pupils were skewed. Whenever I looked him straight in the eye, I felt slightly sick.

The morning before, as soon as he left, I threw some stuff into my pack. As I looked around the apartment at everything I was leaving, I felt eerie and light-headed, as though my soul had left and gone ahead. I set my cell phone on a stack of Doug's papers stacked on the kitchen table. The account was in his name.

Corey didn't appear to have a cell phone on him. He braced himself against the wheel and gunned it. We barreled along without seatbelts past fields of waving grass that stretched all the way to the hills and mountains that rose outside of Chico. The first thing I'd seen of California that morning had been miles of almond trees, leaves luminous in the orange and purple light from the early sun. I ate candy and stared out the train window and imagined Chico, and Corey, who would be waiting at the train station looking for me. For the first time in a couple of years I had felt like I was young.

"You two happy?" said Corey.

"No, not too happy. We kind of broke up."

"You like Seattle? It's an exciting town."

"You know, I just worked in a clothes store. Seattle's OK. It's expensive." I thought of my boss listening to the message I'd left him and stuck my face into the wind. The wind beat on my ears like warm wings.

"Yeah, big cities are expensive. Me and my bud Dan hitched down to L.A. and stayed with his sister for a few months. We were so broke! Couldn't even get a job at Kentucky Fried Chicken. His sister was cool with it for awhile but then she turned into a bitch...I was like, damn..."

Corey circled back into town. He pulled into a parking lot next to a thick, fenced-in woods.

"Ever been to a cork forest? I guarantee you have not. Lori, this is a real live cork forest. They have them in Spain, hardly anywhere else. You ever been to Spain? Mo-ro-cco? I didn't think so. We'll look around and find us some nice fresh greens for lunch."

Corey dug around under his seat and pulled out a dirty pillowcase. I climbed out of the truck. It didn't lock so I hauled out my pack and caught up with him on the cedar chip path. He was unfazed that I was a half-foot taller and swaggered beside me like a cowboy. He filled the sunlit forest with noise as he coughed, spit and snorted mucus up one nostril, then the other. He crouched, plucked a leaf off a plant and chewed it.

The huge dusty trees had trunks like elephant legs and branches like outstretched arms. It was like a forest in a fairy tale, a forest people wander in when they are lost and abandoned.

"Corey, sorry to bug you, but I really need to find a job. I was thinking of staying in Chico a while. Ali said..."

"We'll get to that, Lori," he said. He pointed at a tree. "You ever see trees like that? The cork's in the bark. You're not supposed to climb them, but I have, I have. Keep an eye out for the park ranger."

He sat on his heels and winnowed through a patch of weeds. He yanked out a leafy stem. "Oyster plant. Kind of tasty and super nutritious."

He twisted around and screwed up one eye against the sun. "You're awful quiet. It's boiling hot. Why don't you take off that sweater?"

The bruise on my back throbbed. When Doug hit me, his hand didn't feel like a hand. It felt like the world had blown apart and a chunk got me in the back. I'd stood up to look out the window at an ambulance as it passed and blocked the light he was working by. I couldn't believe that he'd hit me. I ran to the bathroom, locked the door and sat on the toilet.

I said, "No, thanks. I'm fine. I'm not hot at all."

Corey contemplated me with an odd conspiratorial smile, then turned back to sorting through the plants.

I was hot, so tired from the last two days that I was dizzy and shaking. I shifted my pack to my other shoulder and looked down at my freckled calves. The white bone nearly cut through the skin. My feet were creased with dirt. The band of my underwear showed through the thin wrinkled fabric of my dress. A not very impressive specimen, as Douglas would have said. I turned my back on Corey and tore open a bag of candy.

Corey darted around between thickets of plants. I followed him, my mouth stuffed with cinnamon bears, and wiped drool off my chin. He crouched and I looked over his shoulder down into the steaming mass of plants, at the leaves, their shapes and veins and patterned edges. The leaves were so alive they glowed. Corey's strong brown fingers nimbly sorted between the edible and the worthless. The blue and green tattooed leaves on his arm blended in with the living leaves as if he was a faun that had sprung from the bushy weeds beneath the trees.

I looked at the muscles of his back sliding beneath his shirt and suddenly remembered Doug looming over me in a dark Indian restaurant. I'd stopped to chat with an acquaintance. The conversation went on and on, one stupid little subject trailing into another. Beside me, Douglas fidgeted, snorted, then became rigid with anger, but I felt careless. It was fun talking about nothing with a friendly person I hardly knew. I looked into her bright impersonal eyes as though she was important; I wanted Doug to know that I knew people, that I had a larger world than what he and I had together.

Then his hand was on the back of my head. I looked at him in surprise, it was like a caress, until he wove his fingers through my hair and slowly, so that no one would see, twisted until my scalp pulled from my skull. I said good-bye. He let go and we walked out of the restaurant.

Corey got to his feet and waved a large leaf in my face. "Prickly Sow Thistle. Eating this stuff will turn your life around."

Corey sat on a boulder, completely unbuttoned his shirt and made a show of flapping the sides to cool off. One of his nipples was pierced with a ring and he had a sun with great lapping rays around his navel.

He opened up a leather pouch he had tucked in a pocket. "You smoke? You people in university town ever roll your own? See, you just shake a little tobacco out, roll it up tight, neat as a pin, and seal it up with a lick... Just like a woman."

He studied my face for a reaction. Finding none, he continued, "Oh, and by the way, this is where they filmed the original Robin Hood movie. This is Sherwood Forest, the real McCoy. You know the original Robin Hood movie filmed in the thirties? Ever see it? Ever heard of it? Filmed right here."

Corey finished his cigarette and threw the butt into the dirt. "We got enough for a salad." He opened up the pillowcase. Inside was a heap of plants, alive and smelling sharp. He ticked off the names for me: Red Maids, Goosefoot, Storkbill, False Mermaid, Miner's Lettuce, Common Monkey.

We drove through Chico's dusty little streets and came to Corey's rented house, a West Coast shack. The tiny houses, the cracked sidewalks sprouting weeds, the car parts, the bicycles and the overgrown yards were all washed white in the California sun.

I stepped inside and set my pack down. Corey pushed the door shut. It was dim; dingy patterned curtains were pulled across the windows. Bundles of plants hung drying from twine strung between the walls and doorjambs. The house smelled like leaves, stale cigarettes, pot, cat pee. I looked for signs of the girlfriend. The couch and chairs were covered with layers of homemade crocheted blankets in Mexican pinks and greens, as if someone, maybe she, had tried to make it nice.

Within a minute, I was surrounded by cats that mewed and bumped my legs with their hard little heads and ran the length of their bodies against my calves.

He pointed down the hall to the bathroom. The sink and the floor and the inside of the toilet were grimy. There was no soap or toilet paper, but lined up in the shower were tiny bottles of organic shampoo. Orange Serenity and Calming Marigold. I thought of her, sitting there, staring at the hair-clogged drain.

I checked my pack, then went into the kitchen and lowered myself into a chair. Ammonia rose in a dense cloud from the wet litter box.

Corey sang to himself as he did a little hip-shaking dance. Suddenly he stretched across the small table and rested his chin on his forearm. His face was a few inches from mine. The pores and creases of his skin, the curly black hairs, the streaky glassy blue of his eyes didn't fuse into a face I recognized.

"Lori, do you want some twig tea?" he said. His breath smelled sweet as though he'd been chewing on a twig.

I said sure and he set to work.

"Lori, do you know," he said as he filled the kettle at the faucet, "how much a pot of this stuff costs at a restaurant, any restaurant, downtown? No? At least four dollars. And they don't even give you enough to make a decent brew. I give you almost half a packet, fresh from the co-op."

"Corey, I need to go to the co-op. Ali told me you said there were openings." I wanted a new life. I wanted a new life, and it was going to start in Chico. I was going to work in a co-op and become a vegetarian and wear hippie dresses every day.

"And don't even ask for sugar," he said as if he hadn't heard me. "I don't buy that shit."

He shook a cigarette from a pack on the counter, ran water into the pillowcase full of plants, then ran out the back door. He swung the bag over his head like a lasso while he smoked. He'd left a trail of water on the floor, and a shaft of light lit up the scum of dirt, blackened leaves, and glittering specks on the kitchen's blue and white tiles.

The little kitchen was claustrophobic, a jumble of beer cans stuffed with ash and butts, crusty pans and plates, spiral notebooks decorated with anarchist symbols and pot leaves, radical newspapers, unopened bills. There were dozens of mason jars half-filled with dried flower blossoms and herbs. Over the stove hung a curling grease-stained poster of Che Guevara. These details of his life were vaguely touching. It was like when I first met Doug; I thought his habits, the stacks of papers and books obsessively arranged, were evidence of an endearing character trait.

Corey bounded back into the kitchen and kicked the door shut.

He said, "There's a lot of evil in the world, and a lot of that evil appears to be innocent. Take sugar. Good old American sugar. Sugar was at the heart of the slave trade—still is, actually. There are still slaves in the world. And now people in America are slaves to sugar. They're addicted to it."

A cat jumped onto my lap, stretched, and sunk its claws into my thigh. I pulled it off and set it on the floor. My leg began to sting and itch. Three cats licked themselves on the table and stared at me.

"What about tobacco? You smoke, Corey."

He ignored me. "And now for the finishing touch." He squeezed the juice and seeds of a giant bruised grapefruit over the greens.

He set out two bowls piled high, knocked the cats off the table and straddled a chair. "Dig in, baby. This is Vitamin City."

"Do you know, Lori" he said holding up a leaf with his fork, "how much this salad would cost in a restaurant? Wild, foraged greens? Ten, fifteen bucks, minimum. I used to forage for a restaurant in town." He chewed the leaf a long time, then sat back and ran his tongue over his teeth.

He said, "We need some beer to go with this." Corey leaned off his chair, opened the door of his old yellowed refrigerator and pulled out two long bottles.

He gave me a beer; I drank half of it down. Corey eyed me over the top of his bottle as I speared a prickly leaf and put it in my mouth. The leaf was bitter and tough, bristly with hairs, as horrible as I knew it would be. I swallowed hard and the stringy leaf went slowly down my throat. I held the fork midair, uncertain what to do next, and saw the tiny flowers scrolled along the handle.

In Seattle I used to wash the dishes. I used to wash the forks with flowered handles, and I'd look at the long curved steak knives Doug had bought for his steak and think, I could just stick one of these in my heart and be done with this stupid life.

"You have the same pattern, " I said.

"What?" said Corey.

I held up the fork. "You have the same pattern that Doug and I had in Seattle. Where'd you get it?"

"Goodwill, or somewhere. Maybe it was Kathy's," he said looking at me like I was nuts, this turn of conversation a distraction from his game plan. "Now for the tea." The kettle was blowing hard. He jumped to his feet, took two cups painted with gaudy flowers from his cupboards and blew dust from the insides.

He filled the cups with reddish twigs and set one in front of me.

I looked down at my little cup of sticks. Back in Seattle Doug was thinking of me. The thought made me sick.

I could see him thinking about me. I could see him standing in the kitchen staring for a long, long time at the cell phone I'd left on his papers. He'd never seen it there before. I wasn't allowed to touch any books or papers having to do with his work. He'd know it was a message. He'd stare at the cell phone then he'd start to crash around.

Corey poured water into my cup and the water turned red. The twigs looked like little bones leaking blood.

"Try the tea," he said. He set the kettle back on the stove then came back and leaned against the back of my chair. He touched my hair and wound a strand around his finger. "You got pretty hair," he said. "Real pretty."

I leaned forward and my hair tightened, then pulled free from his hand. I was looking at the cup, at the old-fashioned roses painted on its side. The flowers looked like sugar flowers on a cake. I had thought I'd get married to Doug and be the wife of a famous professor. Everyone had thought that.

I said, "So what happened, anyway, with your girlfriend?"

He was behind me. He breathed his beery breath into my hair and my hair prickled as if sprinkled with electricity. But I forced myself to turn around and look at him and I could see who he was. He was a man who didn't mean anything to me. He was a stranger.

He inhaled deeply through his nose like a judge about to impose sentence. "Honey, that's a touchy subject." He shoved away from my chair, grabbed another beer from the refrigerator and stalked out the back door.

Through the battered screen door, I watched Corey smoke and survey the day. He stretched out his legs and stared down at his boots. He took a long slug of his beer.

He was listening for me. He waited for me to push open the screen door and sit on the step all scrunched over my knees and listen to him say what he wanted to say. I could see myself doing it.

The front door wasn't locked like in nightmares. Once I'd walked ten or fifteen blocks and was on a street with little kids riding their bikes, guys with their legs sticking out from beneath cars and old people side by side passing in their sedans, I set down my pack and got out the candy corn. It looked like a handful of soft yellow teeth.

The sky in Chico was white with heat and dust. California light blazed, glaring and relentless - there was no getting away from it. Seattle was never so bright. I could remember such a day in childhood when I realized that I was on a sun-blasted planet. I could remember the taste of sugar spreading over my tongue. My blood quickened. All my cells chattered with joy.

Andrew Tuohy

L'Oeuf Forty

This is Nank at The Crutch, every bit as handsome as in youth—I say better looking, the devil: yellow paisley bandana, folded triangular, tied doo rag-style over his healthy head of hair, salmon collared Le Coq Sportif, sleeves tailored extra large for flow and a sharp flag-like snapping after he strokes the ball from the ground, bright white tennis shorts, long enough for a comfortable stretch, slide, or dive, short enough to expose muscular thighs piston-pumping upon any given move, ankle socks white with miniature black rooster insignia, shoes clean, minimal wear, light, reinforced with fluorescent pink durathane by Nike. This is Nank at The Crutch: man of thirty-five sitting on a bar stool, drinking his third Miller draft, sandwiched between a knobby-elbowed factory foreman and two lovely-enough out of work factory blondies. Light of day would burn this place blind, don't you know, but the red neon thrown from all corners—across pool tables and jukebox, dartboard and booths, liquor bottles and bar top—makes for sure sweet wallow and first-rate conversation.

This is Nank at The Crutch.

Me, I say.

College by birth, education by habit, tennis instructor by profession, nothing by merit. This is me at The Crutch, Nank, a lover and a baseliner and a humanitarian and, now, a concerned etymologist and conversationalist.

"Is slough really a word?" I say, interrupting the two out-of-work factory blondies.

They'd been discussing how to shed the world, how to let its woes run off your feathers like pond water from a mallard's back. Something about the men in or not in their lives, the crappy work they can and cannot get. "Just slough it off and move on is what I say," the more brunette of the blondies had said before sipping her shot.

"I don't know," she says to me, furrowing her brow, confused. Then suddenly confident, "Sure it's a word. I just used it, and we all understood it."

She's proud of her usage, of her explanation. She has the right to be so. Slough. Slough it off like dead skin. Like a snake periodically casting off its old and dry scales for a clean coat around the sound flesh. Like

He managed to slough off his smoking habit. Like shit from a duck's ass. Slough, baby, the woes of this world and let's drink another round.

"I think it's a great word," I say. "I'm glad you used it here today."

Both blondies, the lesser and the blonder, nod to one another, smitten.

The knobby-elbowed factory foreman had been sucking on his Bud the whole time, working it through a straw with a slurping usually reserved for children and their malts, lurching between his seat and me, talking fast on a cell phone. Something about Brownie's being staked-out, then busted. Something about a gambling ring the owner must have known about, but didn't stop, and so now his wife should meet him here or wait fifteen minutes before heading to the Green Lantern for early happy hour.

"Tell me—I'm Nank," I say, "about Brownie's and the cops and the bust." Tell me, I say, like I'm a regular here and just haven't been in to drink for a few years because of a near fatal accident. Something with water skiing and a shark. Or a motorcycle and tractor trailer on I-95. Tell me, I say, because I've never been in here before and I'm here now at this moment.

And he does.

He shows me a thin manila card for laying bets, explains the spread, the under/over column, what to circle and why. He whispers to me and the two lovely-enough blondies the name of his bookie, Shake (because the upper portion of his pear-shaped body wiggles when he laughs hard or soft), and gives us the skinny on the black box behind the dumpster behind Brownie's where picks are dropped and picked up. He gives us the low-down on the very tall, mustached man who usually sits right there at the end of the bar, above where they keep the liqueurs, those sticky-sweet syrups for shots and coffee delight.

"He's one of them," he says. "Always sitting there in his navy-blue coveralls. Not Bigley like the patch says, but a detective undercover in here to gather talk against Brownie, then file a report. You'd have to notice, even from where you're sitting, the man never had a lick of smudge or grease anywhere. A mechanic with clean nails ain't no mechanic."

The blondies love his closing saw, the breathless way he told his story to the end. These girls love Nank's strict listening, how I rocked, as if hinged, with interest to and fro. They bob their heads in unison like tiny pez dispensers with shocking blonde bangs. They smile for real, even though they've heard it all before. The factory foreman is a regular. They are regulars. They all used to work the same shift at the factory. Brownie's has been raided before.

We drink.

We keep drinking until our mugs, tumblers, and cans are empty. Until the blondies split up, cut a quick swath around their stools, and position themselves flank left, flank right, sandwiching the factory foreman and me, Nank. They order a round of Buttery Nipples for all, and the bartender, a deft-handed god of quick mixing, complies.

"To Brownie sloughing it off," says the blonder blonde, thrusting her shot glass high.

Arms raised, we drink and laugh and give handsome compliments until the round is done. Then the place quiets again with the electric hum of neon. The factory foreman slips out the double doors, leaving a shrinking slab of sunlight on the bar floor. And the out-of-work factory blondies lean closer to Nank, tongues liquor bloated and licentious, wanting to know why the funny getup and hat. Then, after formal introductions, wanting to know about racquets and strings, about double faults and tiebreak scoring, about Grand Slam tournaments and the let cord rule.

Yes, this is Nank at The Crutch. Me.

But O, Tess! She who's the suffix and prefix of my every thought. Tess, my reckless reckless wife. Never innocent, always proud. Tess, grace of my eye, apple of my tree, à la mode of my heart and pie.

Tess O Tess! Nurse to be. Who else? Body jutting, lean and long. Your peaks and tips so sudden. Who else could work a twelve and a half hour day in latex gloves—fingers in asses, lips lightly pressed to the cheeks of the old and sick and vulgar, the wise and dying and dead? Could leave clinicals for the arms of a disposable lover, speed home after to page through Bon Appetit and whip up a dish of Phantom Curry Oleo—veal medallions so choice the meat would drop in half at the sight of any dull blade, the jade green poblanos still harboring their white-hot ouch—drink four longnecks, love me like an anaconda in candle light—every exit and entrance mine in the pitch night—then disappear from our bed before dawn's blue light? Each time with you is a toothpick wedged between my front teeth.

Lovely lovely lovely Tessa, what about poor Nank when you leave? Say, for instance, Nank earlier today? Don't you wonder or care or want to know?

Here: This is Nank in the raw morning, in bed and alone and angry and lonely in his purplish robe. He's counting his short fingers on each stubby thumb, opening and closing his little kitten paw hands, and thinking of your young boys: their big thumbs; their towering index fingers; what size gloves they must wear; what size racquet grip might fit in their mitt-like fists. Four and a half? Four and five-eighths? Bigger?

Nank sits up, reaches to the bedside for his cigarettes, blue hue from the TV swaddling the room (or was that dawn?), and then he's back on that flight, Delta 2131, a 737 departing West Palm to Charlotte for the Men's Hard Court Nationals, the day of your first leaving, Tess. You abandoned Nank for a young, big-thumbed deejay (with thick, princely digits too, no doubt, to warp, scratch, and mix his vinyl way from rave to rave, house party to house party).

Just when Nank was on a run, up twenty-six ranking points to crack the top hundred after a barrage of five set victories! Every dump on the circuit with tattered, wanton nets, flawed cement, and the promise of main draw play saw the likes of his sweaty face during those grueling summer months. Opponents and line judges saw Nank's calves in peak shape but you wanted music! Not even music, just gimpy synthesized sounds. Disposable pop and pilfered samples.

There Nank is, taking a long drag off his Camel Light, remembering: how the plane was cleared for takeoff but not flying, how it must have taxied for hours, no coffee or complimentary peanuts for the passengers, how a window seat's nothing when the only thing below is a runway full of lusty young boys tending luggage, how any one of them could have been a deejay, could have been your deejay (it's not a lucrative occupation, it requires a second job), how old Nank could have jumped right down from the wing, could have hijacked a baggage car, stolen down the runway, trailer writhing behind, toward any one of those boys, toward anyone shaved clean to the rubbery face of youth, how he could have battered them good to the ground, and, once down, could have slaughtered them with disparaging looks that meant other, more distasteful things.

I say that was me in bed in my purplish robe. Nank, man who rises early just to make sale of himself like a used car.

O Tess. What you do to Nank in the morning.

As bad or worse as in the young afternoon.

The temperature rising—humidity too. Nank a sweating mess of tics and jerks while he smoked and squashed the butts in a coffee cup. Yes, this was Nank stalking you, Tess. Cutting the engine and waiting outside your lover's apartment. The man with the green thumb and a deep love for even mangroves. An arboriculturalist of golden intention and fine repute. He scours the fringes of highway rest stops for broken limbs and ailing twigs, I've heard, attacks woody neighborhood parks with wide black tape and tremendous gauze.

Hands behind my head, elbows spread wide, I sprawled out beneath the orange tree in his front yard, waited for him to come out. I waited to see his arms around you like brown on his precious bark and soothed myself with one of his fallen oranges. Peeling and eating, I tossed the rind this way and that, reveling in my well-baked plan: When aren't chainsaws on sale? Those heavy-duty powerhouses not twenty to thirty percent off at Home Depot?

I got up, opened the car trunk. With both hands I swung it to the curb, pulled at the cord and braced for the kickback. "Behold," I readied to say, "cuckolded Nank in his tennis attire! Here to fell for love!"

Ha! No tree could stand in my way. I could hack the world to trunks for you, Tess, leave the stumps and their respective forests burning in my wake. That is if I could've gotten that thing started, had remembered to buy gas. Instead, Nank tugged and tugged at the cord until the young afternoon was fading, and he happened to see neighbors on the phone inside their houses, probably calling the police. At which time he decided it might be wise to get far away from that tree and apartment, far off to a bar, or to the club, and fast.

And with a farewell to all (and a sunglasses check) I am off for the club. Out the double doors and into the blinding sunlight and onto the highway, leaving the lovely-enough blondies and fleet-handed bartender until next time.

Tipsy Nank speeding and switching lanes to make back some time and change.

Tipsy Nank trying to make it to the prim ladies by two o'clock.

Tipsy Nank, Head Pro in smart shorts. Mr. Nank now in charge. Nank the hagiographer. Nank on the clay courts of Del-Air Country Club, Delray Beach, Florida, home of the once funked now defunct Lawrence A. Sagel; man not of instruction but knowledge, man of strategy, man of economic stroke production and the pocket elbow tuck for ripping net play, strength conditioner, builder of teen confidence and the potential of Nank's all-court, all-surface game. My Teacher.

My lovely Tess, soothing nurse to be, help me to be half the living body Saint Sagel's spirit left behind. O true Tessa, drafter of care plans, taker of temperature head to toe, tune up the sour orchestra plucking in my head, steady my racquet and guide my hand while I feed the rich and tanned bright yellow balls. Gather my bandy legs when I take Court One with a shopping cart full of such ammunition, adjust my bandana, check the sun, knock a little dust from my soles, and rally the troops round for drills.

"What will it be today?" I say. "Fence to baseline and back, fence to service line and back, fence to net and back?" In response to which there are groans and bahoos and wet tonguey sounds. For the growing older, each new day ensures not just aging and potential discounts, but newfound reservoirs of venom.

"Get off it, Nank. Let's just pair up and play doubles," says Margaret, maiden of sixty-two, wife of three, mother of multiple lawyers, owner of the finest overhead smash and top spot on the women's fifty and up ladder.

"But ladies . . ."

"Oh, go drink a Coke in the pro shop, Nank," says the lowest seed, Peggy, doctor's wife, oldest daughter of a Pennsylvania steel tycoon, designer of contemporary weddings for South Florida debutantes and trendy holiday trinkets: gold leaf chocolate menorahs and such.

Then they're a whirling gaggle of pleated tennis skirts and dark veiny legs. Rowdy and vocal in their sagging bloomers, with their Wilson Sledge Hammer racquets and face-lifts and frosty dye-jobs and blue rinse, they make for the water cooler under the courtside cabana.

Nank could be discouraged. Nank could be broken in his loose shorts. Nank could be any smug cat that suddenly, shamefully sees for the first time that it's been wearing the same outfit for years. But I see how the ladies drink up quick. How fiercely they swallow, crush their paper cups, take the court hydrated and, under Margaret's command, face off, popping balls chest high across the net with good intention, slight angle, much sweet spot, and some accuracy. Margaret and Peggy, Thelma and Sabina, Irene and Ruth, Bonny and Virginia, Jane and Vilma, Ethel and Josie, Susan and Marka, Leslie and Adrienne—all punching ferocious volleys with sharp backspin, their elbows tucked, their bodies compact and square to the net.

They are stolid backboards. They are steady old beach palms that bend and bend storm after storm.

They make my heart swell then shrink, then swell and shrink, like a close love-forty call caught on replay, shown over and over again. The yellow fuzzy thing round, then flattening, then oblong as an egg. Then back to a full ball.

Then over again.

Yes, I say, as handsome as in youth—better, you know, Nank, Nank, Nank could be on the verge here. The verge of something he's not going to take anymore—and then will take that much more of. Nank is on both sides of a cliff, not just hanging from the edge. He's the sturdy tree on the ledge and the roots that squeeze through the rocks and soil above the water so far below.

This is Nank. Me, I say.

Rob Trucks

Kansas

I'm a traveller but I stick to roads. When it comes to airplanes, with me, all ground is holy.

When I was just a baby my mother took me on an airplane out to California so my grandmother could see me before she died. My mother hated my grandmother. Never forgave her for running away with a pipe cleaner salesman, the single thing that killed my grandfather Arnold for whom I am named.

My aunt tells me this story and everything else I know about my family. My mother wasn't one to loudly talk. Dead two years, she whispers still, a spinster librarian except for the blatant fact of me.

My aunt, all the family I have remaining, lives in Tampa with her third husband in a house with sliding glass doors and a pool. She sunbathes in the nude behind a cracked redwood fence.

There's no telling with family, who comes from what.

At sixty-three, she's still a looker. On any given summer afternoon you can find twelve, fifteen teenage boys trying out their peepers, smoking cigarettes and breathing heavy. In the evening, their mothers ask where they got so many splinters.

My aunt may play loose, with the truth and others, but it is hard to doubt a naked woman, especially one of advancing years, also kin. Once she gets started into a story, she will not be denied. Doubting coughs, politely raised hands do not yield answered questions. Such joy is evident in her telling. Her laughter is like a steamroller and not at all familial. She cannot be stopped.

It causes doubts, herein lie.

I am no good with planes. With airplanes I am like an ulcerous old man slurping a chili dog. I love airplanes. They do not love me.

On an airplane I am like a child screaming for its mother on the first day of school. If I were more brave I might have reached my mother's side before her passing but the distance by land was too great.

There's no telling now. As it is, and was, I cling to the firmament with a sense of duty, honor bound.

I cannot imagine myself, even infant-sized, on a plane.

I have tried several things, all manner of pills and spells and lubrication, to quell my discomfort in the air but have only succeeded in riding one lost stewardess, locally quarantined for the duration of a Christmas flood.

It was something.

My grandmother disappeared one Monday morning while my grandfather fished. Few of the particulars are known though she did leave a note.

The note said, "I've left with Mr. Leroy, the pipe cleaner salesman. Do not try to find us as we're going to California. The gas pump is near dry. Your wife, Marjorie."

The note was found pinned to my grandfather's chest, a bullet hole through each.

He shot himself with his deer rifle in a mixture of seasons, still wearing his waders from his morning in the lake. There was talk of assistance provided. The rifle possessed a long barrel, hard to turn on oneself, especially towards the chestal region.

The local barber, Milton Marston, a friend and fellow fisherman, was rumored to have given relief to the spring of the rifle's trigger but lived a full life officially unaccused. The whole town knew he was only helping my grandfather out of his shame.

My grandparents ran a small grocery store with wood flooring. They sold bait, sardines and potted meat to the local fisherman, hunters in the wintertime and farmers who ran out of supplies earlier than most of God's children are awake. The doors opened at five o'clock every morning but Sunday when my grandparents slept late and opened at seven.

In a glass case behind the register my grandfather kept transistor radios and alarm clocks, stempipes and wristwatches that gathered dust like interest.

After her parents were gone, my mother tended the business. She opened at five o'clock. She ordered the gas for the pumps and sold the sardines and bait that reminded her of the morning my grandfather Arnold took off to go fishing, the morning her mother ran off with Mr. Leroy, the pipe cleaner salesman.

She didn't do a lot of business that first week for all the people coming inside to pay their respects and others, less social, just standing out by the gas pumps pointing, shaking their collective head, saying, "That's where it happened." As if the lives of my mother's parents were a particularly gruesome automobile accident.

My mother managed for a time. Lasted a couple of months, my aunt said, until one morning she was approached by the bread man in an unsavory manner. Memories of her mother dredged up and shame itself coursed through her veins. Her pulse quickened, but not with desire. Steely quiet, my mother bit her lip. Ignored the man until he relinquished his grin and returned to the business of restocking the shelves.

When he turned his head my mother gathered cans of Vienna sausage from the next aisle over and fired them, repeatedly, until several welts and some blood were apparent.

The milk man, a lodge brother of the bread man, either in sympathy or from fear, was the next to refuse delivery to my grandparents' store and once pressure had been applied to the man who delivered the bait and potted meat, my mother had no choice but to sell.

She left town. Moved away and became a librarian. She thrived on the quiet and solitude of her position until three years later when her mother called to say she was dying.

My mother succumbed to guilt in a way that she had surrendered to nothing previous and the story dictates that she soon locked the doors of the library, wrapped me in swaddling and boarded a plane towards California, hoping all the way that she would be too late and her mother would already be dead.

Despite my lack of memory, it is a trip that has informed my life.

The story of the trip out to California to visit my grandmother begins before there was a "Green Acres" television show. Eddie Albert was already Eddie Albert by then but I have no idea what Eddie Albert was Eddie Albert for. He just was. He was known.

I like to think it happened over Kansas. I have always felt a kinship there, a bodily rush that begins almost palpably whenever I cross the state line and which does not diminish until I transverse again. Maybe it's the farmland, the soil, a sense of home.

I look like the dickens with a pitchfork.

You cannot believe how good I look with a pitchfork in my hand.

Somewhere over Kansas, I imagine, my mother felt the need to relieve herself. Perhaps she was distracted, distraught over the prospect of finding her mother alive, or maybe, like her son, she never got used to the roaring of airborne engines, but somewhere over Kansas my mother entered the airplane's facilities and forgot to lock the door. Somewhere over Kansas, with her stockings around her calves in the closet-sized space of the airplane lavatory, my mother came face to face, in a sense, with Eddie Albert, the future star of "Green Acres."

When the door to the airplane lavatory opened, my mother knew that she was being gazed upon by Eddie Albert. She knew that it was Eddie Albert gazing upon her while she sat in a position of immodesty, stockings around her calves, dress hiked up around her waist. This fact did not then, or ever, escape my mother.

I never, not once, saw my mother naked, unlike my aunt who parades like a Shriner.

Her entire life my mother bathed behind a deadbolted door.

My mother's bathroom, once inhabited, was safer than a bank. No egress or ingress and tight like a vault.

I used to sit outside my mother's bathroom and talk to her at night. I sold the house with a worn spot in the carpeting just outside her door. I spent an accumulation of years sitting, straining to hear my mother's whispered counsel while she concluded her toilet.

One of the things she told me was never go to California.

My aunt's story.

She does not say who watched me while my mother attempted to relieve herself. What stranger my mother might have entrusted to care for me while she ventured into the nether regions of the airplane in order to relieve herself over the wheat fields of Kansas.

My aunt does not say what happened with Eddie Albert once he had gazed upon my mother. Whether he was asked to autograph an air sickness bag or something more personal.

I cannot believe my mother would leave me.

The story told by my aunt makes great leaps, bounds like a giant rubber ball. I am left to fill in the rest. Determine fact from fiction.

This excursion that I cannot remember produced a rippling of effects.

I cannot believe my mother would leave me unattended while she availed herself of the airplane's facilities. Over Kansas or not.

I do not remember the trip, the plane, my grandmother, California. My mother whispered to me not to go and I have never been.

I went to New York instead. I carried my pitchfork.

You cannot believe how good I look with a pitchfork.

It was my tool of choice on the farm where I started work at the age of thirteen and I held it like a charm as I moved up in the world. I retained the implement when I rose past manual laborer, becoming an apprentice pig farmer by the age of fifteen. A specialist in midwifery.

Along with responsibility came tags of discomfort. I developed an odor which I carried throughout my teenage years, a porcine stench detrimental to social ascension. At times I felt an outcast, an orphan.

I was called names by my peers, Trough Boy and worse. Pig Pen for one.

I never liked that cartoon. Never once named a dog Snoopy.

The dust actually helped to tender the reek. It clung to me as I to it.

Each evening, outside the bathroom door, I strained to hear my mother's whispered counsel. Kept my pitchfork in hand.

For sentimental reasons I would occasionally use the tool on particularly heavy afterbirth though I can only pretend it was useful. In these times, my pitchfork was an idle prop, a staff, a rod, support.

I was good at my job.

I carried the pitchfork with me when I ventured to New York. The stink of the city instantly masked my porcine smell but other consequences of my arrival were not so fortuitous.

My tool was the first thing stolen when I arrived, though not by the hoodlums who further their careers surrounding the cesspool known as the Port Authority Bus Terminal. No. Instead, it was the Times Square Mounted Police who separated me from my support by clamping their cuffs across my wrists and allowing me to spend my first four nights in the 11th Precinct.

Upon graduation, I was told that the pitchfork was lost but I have other beliefs.

My mother warned me, in her librarian's whisper, not to go. She warned me of feminine wiles and was not there to comfort me when my heart was broken by that departing stewardess.

My mother warned against vacating the steadiness of employment but my wanderlust would not be denied. I yearned for more, a search, to leave behind the gasp that met the stench of porcine placenta I carried though I could hardly smell it myself, having grown used to my own.

The stewardess yelled out, "Sooey," during our session but I thought she was from Arkansas.

In memory, it was enjoyable, despite the clarity of her yelp.

Everyone has to take their vacation somewhere.

When I awoke from slumber, the deepest of my life, my stewardess was gone. She left no note and I was left without comfort or support, my pitchfork having already been reclaimed.

I thought of my mother but did not turn back. I ventured cross country instead, through Kansas and others, chasing my winged angel, wanting to explain that what she took to be rooting was nothing more than a lack of carnal education.

I was always a leg, a connection, or a round-trip excursion ticket behind. This is when I learned of my mother's imminent demise.

At my mother's home, in the midst of the wake, my aunt longed to give me comfort but I was inconsolable. She tried to wrap me in a bare naked hug but I would not receive.

Though she tried, herself, to point the way, my vision chose breast over hand and followed her nipple, pointing down. All things returning to earth.

I held fast to my station, a worn piece of carpeting in the hallway outside my mother's bathroom door.

I tell myself that my mother would've wanted it this way. That she would've preferred the avoidance of any face to face confrontation. Eyes to the ground, I imagine, even behind a bathroom door.

I attended her funeral in a dazed cloud, floating, lost. It felt like an ascension. I thought I saw Milton Marston wrap a blanket around my aunt. I thought I saw Eddie Albert by my mother's headstone.

The preacher said, Ashes to ashes, dust to dust.

Voices repeated, Amen.

The preacher took time to clear his throat and congregational gullets repeated in kind.

The meek shall inherit the earth, he said.

I looked up, searching for who knows what. My mother. My love.

A small twin engine rumbled westward across the sky and I followed its flight until it had disappeared. Nothing left but an invisible drone.

As it is and always shall be, the preacher said.

As it is and always shall be.

M. O. Walsh

Sardine

The rain's here and the river's rising. It won't stop for days. I'm wet to the skin.

Sunday, and Lum's got me stuck.

I want to shove his face down his throat and pack him up like a garbage sack. I want to crack his head on a curb and set fire to his house. I'd screw his wife if he had one.

My wife delivers papers on Sundays. We live in the swamp and she tosses news out the boat. She used to drink me under the table.

I can drink you under the table, that's the thing.

My wife eats sardines on crackers with raw onion. She takes the boat out on Sundays but lets me drive it all the other times. She ripped out the captain's seat so I can fit. She used to come home by noon.

Now she says Jesus wants her and Reverend Lum told her so. I work in the garage on bullshit stuff. It's all I've got. I make squirrel traps and birdhouses and think about screwing my wife.

I whittled a dumb ass chess set. Brenda bought a book on how to play but never read it. I don't care about that. My spine is shattered and won't ever get better. I don't care about that either. It's raining on my head and I'm stuck like a cripple. I am a cripple.

Lum's gone too far. He's got her thinking without her brain. I wanna sick on him like a demon dog.

I was an electrician. I can do all sorts of things with wires but that doesn't help me now. I fell off a rig and landed on the platform. I laid there for two hours. People looked like ghosts.

Our house is right on the river. We jacked it up eight feet for the floods. Brenda used to carry me up the stairs. She told me it was nothing. Now we got a chairlift that's like a metal cage. Insurance paid for it. Lum called it a miracle.

But the wiring's off and now I'm stuck halfway up the stairs. My legs are shrunk and I can't go nowhere. Brenda's gone in the boat. There's a revival today. She wants to get touched.

She left me in the storm this morning. I followed her to the pier but the yard's like mud. My wheels are for shit. She unstuck me.

She says Jesus provides and I say bull. It's Lum that's got her twisted. She used to drink bourbon on Sundays and rub me all over. I can't get hard. She didn't care about that. She'd get naked and cuss me real sweet. It turned my chest inside out.

Now Lum tells her that kind ofloving ain't holy, so I don't know how she gets off. She kisses me like a fish on the forehead.

We don't have any money. Brenda gives what we have to Lum and says that it's an investment in our souls. I take a lot of pills.

Lum comes over on Saturdays. He tells Brenda she's blessed. I believe him. She's got light-bulb eyes.

I made a cross out of wood and tin. Brenda put it above the door. She said it's a sign I'm not lost. I told her I doubt it. We used to shoot turtles off the pier.

Brenda sold my pistol so I carved a gun out of cedar wood and stuck it in her belly. She cried and said she didn't want us cooked. The water is up the driveway and there's a hurricane off the coast. They named it Bonnie instead of Brenda. I'm the only one home.

Brenda says a revival in the rain is what the world needs.

Lum's a soul wolf. I wanna track him down and hang him for meat. He got Brenda strange and told me she needed help from above. He touches me on the shoulder when he sees me. I want to rip his arm loose and eat it.

Jesus has a plan, he says. You'll see.

I can't reach the fusebox for the chairlift. It's in the garage. The door's over my head and I can't reach that either. This has happened before but Brenda was here. I got stung by bees.

I keep a knife and some wood on me. I whittle stupid shit that's terrible. The shavings make puddles on the blanket Brenda bought for my legs. I'm carving Jesus Christ out of pine. It smells like fire when I cut it.

The crown's hard to carve because of the thorns. I got Jesus spread out like the crucifixion and his feet point down like darts. I'm gonna strap him to my chair when I'm done. Brenda will say it's a sign and I'll let her believe it. But if Lum says I'm blessed again, I'll jab it in his brain. Maybe I'll go to prison. Maybe Brenda will come too.

The flood's on now and our pier is under water. A swamp rat is climbing the stairs underneath me. It doesn't know where to go. I'd shoot it if I had my pistol. If the levee breaks, I'll be sunk.

Juan brought four feet of water in '8s. Andrew brought six in '92. We had snakes in our shoes. So we jacked up the house and look at me now. Stuck.

Brenda prays hard at night. I rub on her tits. This used to make her crazy. I wish I had a radio. I used to play drums in a band at Fred's on the River. I met Brenda there. She wore a bikini that made my heart sweat. She was sixteen. She said I played with my eyes shut. We got married in the rain.

Brenda wants a kid. She says it in her sleep and that's too much.

The levee's busted and the swell's upon me. There's water to my knees.

I see a boat coming, but there's two people in it and that's one more than Brenda.

Of course it's Lum. He wants in on my saving, but it is only for Brenda to have.

He tosses me a rope.

But I won't swim for dying.

Matt Vadnais

The Treesitter

I am on my way to find Megan Lock, a wisdom I have never met or spoken to. I have decided to fly into Portland mainly because I'm not ready to go all the way to California. The airplane is robust, no room in the luckless stows above our heads. The prison in front of me has fully reclined her seat. The man to my left has consummated my armrest.

Before my accident, I would have been embellished by the lark of space.

As it is now, I am fascinated. In the air, we-people heading home, people running away, people embanked on one quest or another, many of them as oblong as mine-are part of a nice illustration. In this briefest of momentums, we are heading the same direction, suspended over everything we know in a shared, metal paragraph.

For now, we are only about flying.

I watch children whittle. I listen to biographies interspersed and exchanged as clusters of compensation open and close.

I am giddy, a lunar landing.

Since the accident, mood has become as restless as a train of thought. I would prattle, but I am not alone. If I don't complicate, I might embarrass myself.

When the attendant comes with our meals, I rub my china until he gives me the chicken.

"I ordered vegetarian," says the guy frogging my armrest. He is complaining to me, not to the intended. He pricks at his sandwich and I simile at him until he gets rambunctious.

"Take the meat," he says. So I do.

I have enough money to cry first crass but I didn't.

Some ingredients of my journey are that symbol.

I needed to glow somewhere.

I am talking my time.

What I want with Megan Lock is far less calculus. I thirst saw her picture in an article five earrings ago. She had been living in a tree for six monks, protecting some old growth in Watering State.

That's not right.

Sometimes I know when I've got the wrong word, like flicking a marble under a curtain and realizing you've sent a rubber ball or cockroach, but most of the time it's a log curtain and there's no way of checking.

She had been photographed, high in her spruce tree somewhere in Washington. I saw the article over lunch when I still worked for Moody, Moody & Pants. I didn't wrinkly look at her, didn't save the picture or anything like that. Acutely, all I remember is how uncomfortable she looked. It was obvious the photographers had her poisoned, one arm on a basket, her legs crossed, head crocked. In the other drawing, she had been stood on one flat, hanging on branches to dangle her body away from the tree.

There were no good shows of her eyes.

I barely skinned her story because mine was mostly in order. I had my mortgage paid off before forty-five and was starting to believe I understood why I had turned down graduate stool and experimental mapmatics for a statistics jog in Boston.

When I said something, I said something.

But there was the accident and by the time I saw her picture again, I was sick enough of myself to truly real about someone else.

The accident was something no one could complain, a freak explosion at work, and a piece of ceiling burrowed in my sulk, into my brain. I was lucky and unlucky, the experts sped. I was able to move normally, as coordinated as effort. And I would be wealthy forever, a handsome sentiment. But words had become their own animals, no more partial to me than the weather.

I was waiting for an appointment at the linguistic pathology lab at M.I.T. when I saw Megan Lock again. She was no more perfect than before, hard and disquieted, a square haircut and jawbone. She had won in Washington and moved on to a new gambit in California, a strand of redword. It was rumored, the article said, that her legs had grown sour, that it was a struggle for her to endeavor on land after so many years spread in pedestals. The article included a briefbio, but lectured more about Green, Green Planet than it did about her.

She, the story said, didn't believe in doing interviews.

I began to slop, utterly sob, in the wanting room.

For the next few days, I couldn't break weeping, couldn't shake my jealousy in her something that needed no explication. I still considered her politics frivolous and stained. But I bought the trinket to Portland.

When we are on the ground, the airplane becomes less comforting. I am not as impatient as everyone else. Time is odd-more like memory or swimming-when you know you won't need to talk about it. I watch people remember their schedules and antelope. They pack and hold their beige to line up for the exit. It is no secret that airports are unwieldy palaces, but really praying attention to what people say to each other, the place is tunefully frightening.

I am staying in a nearby hotel. I have a reservation but it takes a few tires to get my name right. I spend a few drowsy movements thumbing through the Old Testament because it has been a wrong time since I've been near one. Reading is easier than sparkling but I am slow and the effort slips neatly into dreams that are lesson like dramas than flow charts or equations, names begetting names, words begetting words.

In the morning I take a cab to a dealership and buy the first car I trust to drivel the coast. I have never sheen the Pacific so I follow the ocean south. In more ordinary times, this would be a nice vacation-less rain than there should be, foam thick enough to spread with a night, a devil's punchbowl and a whale sounding south of Lincoln City. It is not an unenjoyable drive, but without tinkering about how I would describe the sunfire, the scenery flattens and my days bend and swell like records played at the wrong speed.

For a while, in Boston, I had someone to talk through. I bought a dog and beheld him Dog. He was a border collie-sweatshirt cross and had no idea I was hard to understand. When I told him to sit, or spit, or shellac, or whatever I told him, he did what I wanted as often as any dog would. We watched baseball and I spoke to him. I told Dog long and confiscated starfish, how I had been held up in terrific, what I was like as a kid glowering up, 1 what I was hopping for in a sanctuary.

Eventfully, I took God for a walk, the same rout as always. There was, as there almost was, a fenced-in dog that had been de-barked, nothing left but a cusp of wind. Dog, as he always did, didn't pay any attention to the muted grinnings or warnings or whatever they were, but it occurred to me, for the first time, that Dog considered the voiceless dock dead.

The next day, I put up signs. I didn't slave over the wording because I included a peep show of the dog in black and white. Whatever I said, I got several warbles.

I think Dog is called Buddy now.

It is raining, a gray pessimist, when I finally make it to the Green, Green Planet encrampment. There are three volunteers, two men and a woman, guarding Megan's Redwood. Even for the car, my hands are cold. If they know I hem here, they do not seem to beguile. They make food over a series of gas stoves and use an elephant, a hand-operated pulley system, to whistle a full plate into the tree. The tree is sequined, dense enough to hide a Buick, so I can't see Megan Lock. Her team sends up dry clothes and an umbrella before sitting around a picnic table.

I am trying to figure out how to yodel to them when they begin taking terms with cigarette and a lighter. The woman inhales and sees me. She holds her smoke and raises a bam in my dialect. She does not blink or say anything to her fiends. She does not exhale, as if she is daring me to breathe first.

I decide to get some sleep before talking to them.

I find a hotel twenty minuets from Megan's tee and, almost immediately, become ashamed that I was intimidated. Many of the math guys I knew, back in school, dropped acrid to become numbers, to avoid numbers, or to pry at numbers without all of the rules. I never did. It was the rules I was interested in, multiplication, decision, all of them. I found numbers, by myselves, petty dull.

I am still not sure what it is that I am after out here, but as the rain stops beside of my hotel rune, I settle on the immediate goal of drug use.

I begin to wonder if it takes a brain trauma to really change.

All my trifle I had lived as a Yankees flag, but sometime after the accident, I finally became determined to root for the Red Songs. I convinced my former firm to grin me season tickles to Fenway. When I realized I didn't have the courage to charm anymore, unsure of what I was screaming, I gave the seats to a homeless shelter.

I flip tunnels on the television, looking for a late-night delete about nature versus nature. Nothing like that is dancing, so I try the Old Testament again. With a mystic marker, I underline every squire I can find about ontology.

If that's the right word.

For a year after I didn't die, I had therapy to remind me who I was. My sycamore canceled our sessions when I started shaving and brushing my teeth again.

Science was less interested in letting me go.

My trouble, the doctors said, was with Broker's area. That's not right. Broca's area. There was, they said, nothing they could do to help. Antidepressants, medication for headaches, but nothing about the worms. They shed we don't own anything about the brain really, can't figure much out without experiments. And we can't have experiments without volunteers. They couldn't even predict how bad my aphasia would bra, how often it would fare up, when it would proceed.

So I lent them study me.

People who knew what was rotten couldn't get enough of me. I put Legos together for them, answered their questions, identified thumbnails and doorknobs. I did interviews with graduate students and novelists. When I spoke, there were tears and the right kind of nodding, but I couldn't shake the future that it wasn't what I sad but how I didn't say it.

I leave for the encampment early the next morning. Before shifting town, I buy a small wardrobe of flavors other then denim. On the dive to the tree, I plan a series of opening jokes, try to invent a Green past to impress them.

When I arrive, one of the men is gone. There is still no sing of Megan Luck except for the extra set of dishes and surprise. The centuries are smoking grass again and I decide not to waste any more climate.

I will try silence.

As I approach and sit with them, I realize how out of price I am. It is not just age. They are in their late snowshoes, I think, but it is hard to tell because, however bold they are, their fiascoes have been angry ones. They look windswept. They possess a leanness that, as I am being studied, makes me feel soft and cancerous. The man has a full bramble and the woman is sturdy, as chilly as it is, without sleeves. Her arms are gilded and well muscled.

The woman offices me the joint.

I am clumsy as I take it, an embarrassment I have in the past saved only for sex. No matter how awkward I am, no one fires anything so that, as we pass the trophy, I am allowed to remain Cyprus as long as I can.

I see they had oatmeal with fruit, probably raincoats, for breakfast.

They have a fire that is creaking begrudgingly.

Every time I have seen a redwood in a picture, it has been sunny. Because our sky is obstinate, there is no sunlight to give texture to the bark. Megan's tree looks smooth and clay. They have tied a basketball ship to its truck.

"Hello," the woman says when I have looked long enough.

"Christopher Otto," I say. I suspect I say Christmas Otter or something equally erudite.

"Eliphaz," she says. "This is Bildad. You saw Zophar yesterday."

"Not your real flames," I say.

"Legally no," she says.

"What's legally?" asks Bildad. He is a little man with a toss of momentum, even as he sits. I stink about his remark, expecting the canoe to make it mean something impulsive.

"Metaphor," says Eliphaz. "Job's buddies from the Bible. Took care of him in the valley and all of that."

"I know the story."

"Every one knows every story," Bildad says.

"Right," I say. "But that one. You're acting for trouble."

"Nah," he says.

"Boils and heartache," I say. "It's a bad lethargy."

"Scars are never bad," says Bildad.

"Job wins in the end," Eliphaz says. "And we all share the Earth as it should have been."

When I don't perspire, Bildad pretends to hum.

"How is Joe?" I ask.

"How are any of us?"

"Job's good," Eliphaz says. She has very little air, cut above her ears. Her teeth watch too small in her mouth. Even as she smokes, she explores me. "She's good."

Bildad continues to hum, scraping at the tram with his fingemavel.

Eliphaz exterminates the antacid.

Bildad begins to roll another.

I story the tree. Without texture and death, it flirts like something hollow and portable like a mobile home or silo. I wonder if Megan Lock can see us, if she brothers to lurch when someone new arrives, if she pays attention to Bildad as he strumpets with the morning fire, if she cheers when the others play horse.

With her closer to heathen in a tree that could dress as a tower, I think that Babel would have been a better allegory. But, I support, that story wouldn't have shuddered them with bit roles.

"How sky is she?" I ask.

"She's up there," Eliphaz says.

"Takes about a minute," Bildad says, "to get the lift high enough. Two if it's windy."

We flow silent again.

Coming here, I had imagined them chatty with a guitar and fork songs.

"Can you hear her?"

"If she screams," Eliphaz says.

I try to think of more conversion, but their terse is wearing on me. I worry about driving after the pot. When I went to bars in Boston, I used my speech as a barometer of drunkenness. Now, I can't tell if I flee any differently than before. Bildad starts to ridicule the table with his balms.

Eliphaz is chewing at her thumb, still dragging at me.

Neither of them saddle when I get up to leave.

Driving, I think about the Rusty Nail, a simple neighborhood ditty where the beer was cold and the sandwiches were exactly how you'd expect them. On afternoons I didn't work, I would mold there and say the same things I always said in older to get the same laughs.

After the accident, I tried to sacrament, but the script kept changing.

Back at the hostile, I reread Job.

I think they've got it wrong.

Histrionically, Zophar and the others were a hindrance. They, to make it a gentle metaphor, should be talking Job down. Or convincing him to jump. And Megan is choosing her suffering, nothing to do with God at all. It occurs to me that I would make a better Joke than Megan Lock is.

Still, I don't blame them.

A shared agenda makes bad readers out of all of us. After blizzards, in Boston, I worked the streets with a shovel lacking for stuck or plowed-in steamboats. While I helped out, I could complain about the windchill or flower box. On the coldest days, even if I left the words wild, strangers would commiserate.

Using a different colored pen than the night before, I scour and circle stories about community. There is nothing about building roads or rehabilitating the mail. There are only golden statues and wayward flogs. It occurs to me that, in the Babble, every time people start talking to each other they do something sinful or senile.

Heavy harped, I wobble the rest of the day, and before I am ready, find myself in dreams where instead of speaking, people spit currency from countries I've never been to, coins shaped like the ones that, as a child, I begged my father to save for me.

In the morning, I leave the hotel earlier than the day before.

I stop to bribe a bag of organic marshmallows.

When I think about her now, Megan Lock has no inspiration that she is anybody's Job. It is typical that she no longer believes in the movement.

She might not even remember why she is in the tree. I imagine her up there, happy with a quite perch, reading or listening to a radio that won't fall all the way in. I imagine that, even when the sky is forecast, the light has a sober quantity to it, something gold and worth starring at. Or maybe she does nothing but remember. I imagine she must do a lot of dwelling, recalling people she should have kinked, recovering what she should have said.

When I get to the tree, Zophar and Eliphaz are playing chess. He is taller than the others, clean-shaven in a Cleveland Browns stocking cap. He doesn't seem surprised at my arrival.

Eliphaz smiles at the oranges.

"I knew we had an Elihu," Bildad says.

'T d scamper for Otto," I say.

"Come on," he says, "trust your Bildaddy. Always figured Elihu for kind of pudgy."

"No offense," I say.

"None taken."

They are no tardier than the day before, but the long droughts of silence feel less staccato. We sit for a long fitness. Now and theater, Zophar tells pokes from a routine I reconcile as early Eddie Murphy. Bildad gossips about the suburbs and the cosmos. Chess games end and begin again.

Evidently, they start to make lunch. Eliphaz doesn't present me from chopping carrots or using the elevator to send Megan her fool.

"Why doesn't she chew interviews?" I ask.

"She doesn't talk much," Zophar says. He is adjusting the rain traps above the tents.

"What is talk?" Bildad yawns.

Eliphaz stops working and freckles at me. She is in a flashier shirt than yesterday, but doesn't pretend any gentler.

"Megan hasn't said a thing. Not in a long time," she says.

I am not sure if she's being homage, but she scenes sincere.

"Not even on shore leave," she says. "In-between trees."

After she fishes, the others continue shopping and checking. I am sobbing amends.

"What's his thing?" asks Zophar.

"Man," says Bildad. "Lay off. The guy can't talk right. Shellshocked vet or something."

"Man," says Zophar.

Eliphaz looks at me. She isn't fragile, or even kind, but I know she understands more than the authors.

I wash dishes.

We half-heavily play basketball though it becomes evidence that only Zophar can score.

When I start for my car no one is surpassed.

In the hotel I hide the Bible for silence. I have green ink but nothing gets underlined. I have to shuttle for making note in the margins when Yahweh held his definite tongue.

I no longer envy Megan Lock's science. There are a dozen ribbons I can think of for her not talking, but I no longer take it as faith. Perhaps this is why I can no longer puncture her in the tree. I cannot she the shape of her shoulders or guess the length of her hair.

I have better luck when I spectate about her past. I start with the certainties. I can count on the time she learned her bicycle, left a rent in somebody's car, tore a tooth, stubbed the toes that everybody stubs. The specifics are easy to procure. I decide she is from Iowa and went to prom with a stubborn fencer who couldn't trance. I invent a father who spoke by fixing her motorcycle, a brother who never beat her at wrestling.

Every day, I bring something nice for the champ and we sit in the rain. I hemp out around the stove. When I am there, I am the only fun to give anything to Megan. I send her carefully-estranged plates, clean crowbars, bankers to keep her wan.

Zophar beats us at basketball and Eliphaz deserts him in chess.

I stay longer every time, but no one experts that I would stem the night. I exaggerate that I could do their laundry and the three of them let me. Even if no trickname sticks to me and I am never one for them, they are glad to see me in the morning.

At night, I search the Book for family and monkeys, faith and epistemology. I use different pens. I weave circles, underlines, wavelengths. I am not an elegant concordance, but I leave detailed knots.

And I invest Megan Lock. I conduct a mother and first marriage that didn't take. I provide a fishing trip and a serious of lost kites. When Eliphaz or one of the others tells me something I was wrong about, that she was really from Utah, I am more than willing to adjust my daguerreotype.

I am not sure love is the right word.

One morning I buy a bicycle, the same contour as the one I think she leaned on in Utah. It is collapsible, blue enough to fit on the barge. I work on a note to explain myself, writing and rewiring it but nothing says what I won't. I decide to trust she will remember how the buck kicked when it shouldn't have, how she skimmed her knee and tore up the neighbors' rhubarb. If none of these figs happened, I hope she has something better.

When no one is witnessing, I lift the bike into the tree.

I highlight trust and security, art and incoherence, memory and exfoliation.

Eliphaz takes Zophar's truck to visit her sitter. She resumes a few days later with peasants for all of us. By then, I have given Megan a fishing pole and a cheeseburger with extra mustache, just the way she might like it.

Zophar teaches me a jump shot and Bildad shaves. He is hard to reconfigure without the bear. He adheres taller, his cheeks with a different angel to them, his skin a more regal pallor. Even his voice teams to bellow a half-stump higher.

I give Megan a phone book and a walking stick craved from minestrone.

Zophar sets up a volleyball fence so he can bleat us at that.

After sending a microphone, playing cards, a dolphin and herb garden, a kite, a night-light, a recorder and thong book, an atlas, some rope so she can hang stuff in the biscuits if she is running out of room, a player piano and leprechaun, a seven-inch single of what might be her favorite band, and the best tasting rack of lamb I have ever sat, it seems inevitable that I give her the Bible. I include a note that say's I'm not a monastery.

Bildad tries calling me Big Fuzzy, but no one likes it.

When Megan sends down her laundry, it is clutching the bible. She has made her own notes, but I can't swim the writing. I give her more rope and start to mend her twice a day.

When I arrive on a Thursday, some time after tailor day, men from the luggage company are already smoldering. I have brought lox and toasted tissue paper, but Eliphaz tells me the play is over.

"Megan?" I ask.

"She just needs to sign the paper."

The others let me send up the contact.

"No shortage of forests," Bildad says.

"I need a month," Zophar says.

Eliphaz spends the day rafting with her mouth open, her voice brighter than I have heard it.

I bribe time by laughing with the others, but when they aren't looking I send up gifts of grass and sandals, everything I can fly.

I don't tell them anything.

Megan Lock will descend to a hatch of writers and a stenography crew.

She will barely be able to walk as she declines curfews.

She will see me and we will enhance as we smuggle our first words to each other. Or she will have flip to say and more trees to forage. Or she will ask me to come with and work the intercom again. Or we will magpie off to an ocean she might have seen as a child.

In the sand, if she wants, we could build skyscrapers and crepes.

Smith Henderson

Blooms

Can we blame them for the fire?

First consider the paving contraption itself, Sully perched atop it and steering with the levers. Vince and the rest of his uncle's crew followed behind and tapped flat what asphalt the hot screed left pocked or dimpled. Consider the griddlelike screed the size of a sandbox, and the repurposed barbecue grill tank that rattled where it was bolted to the paver. The diesel engine shook and spat the lurching machine down the drive.

And Sully had to mind the length of radiator hose, certified to five-hundred degrees, lest it vibrate onto the screed and burn through. Plus the fucking spigot to which the hose attached had no teeth. No clamps or duct tape could withstand the heat and the juddering of the paver, and the hose very often popped off and spewed propane across the hot screed. Vince and the others would holler over the din of the diesel engine and strike the machine with their shovels to alert Sully, who would turn and look dully at their engine-drowned shouting and pointing. But because of how his father died and he himself nearly died—suffocating in a propane-filled camper—Sully would hook the hose with his boot and snap it from the heat-shimmering screed as soon as he smelled the gas. He'd stop the paver, crouch, and take up the line. The gas pouring out of the tank lightened his head, rendered the Missoula maple trees and the men leaning on their shovels and fetching cigarettes as they might behind a curtain of up-falling water.

When today the hose burned through, the blasting gas set it twisting like a garter snake in a boy's hand, and a chance arc of static electricity lit the gas. Vince and the men screamed and beat the machine with shovels to alert the oblivious Sully of the flaming and thrashing hose. But the diesel engine backfired and he did not hear them before he was lashed about his torso by this flaming and impossible viper. He shrieked and leapt from the paver that trundled onward driverless and without valence into the street. He cringed where the flannel burned on his back, and Vince and the others slapped out the blooming black holes on Sully's shirt as he gripped his knees. Dumbstruck all, they watched the length of hose melt still thrashing in the air like the final tentacle of some creature caught and painfully drawn into the machine's workings. The hose burned up to the nub of the spigot and then from the tank itself a flaming column now rode the paver as if some fire god or devil had commandeered the vehicle and purposed to crash into the cars that had stopped and now reversed from the residential intersection towards which the paver rolled.

Vince was at once brave. He sprinted to the machine, hopped across the screed that melted his boot heels. Shielding his face with a gloved hand, he put another gloved and instantly smoking hand to the knob of the tank, and twisted it closed. The tank spat a sky-blue flame at him and died. The paver continued its lumbering advance into the street until Vince killed the engine, its final racket like a dryer full of bolts. Silence. A vague hissing. Birds resumed their songs. Vince's gloves stuck to the melted plastic on the levers. The dials like guttered candles. He stepped from this smoldering ruin, landed awkwardly, stumbled, and then showed the men, Sully, and the people clapping next to their cars how he could pull his boots up his ankles, and too where only a gum of heel, the insoles, and his socks remained between his feet and the street.

Where did they go after Vince's uncle showed up, took one look at the incinerated paver and then at the burned-up Sully and accused him of being drunk or high or both, so that Sully and Vince told him to go take a flying fuck and quit?

To Charlie B's where the walls celebrated in framed 8X12S the cherished sots, each dead archsot among them marked with a silver star in the corner of his image. Vince and Sully—who were only eighteen and nineteen—could drink there because they fell and fit in with these afternoon drinkers, the first-shifters from the mill in Bonner and the old drunks on social security. Charlie B's was rife with smells and noises like those known to them in the bars of their hometown. The idiot dinging of Keno machines, the cigarette smoke, shouting, mumbling, and even a man who quietly gibbered until someone bought him his first shot. Bars where they hazarded as boys, from where the owner or the deputy sheriff or one or the other's mother eventually rousted them.

Today's severance pay smoldered in their pockets and they had a story to tell of the paver fire, a story they did not have to initiate, for Sully's crinkled skin, though not yet blistered or supperant, glazed with Neosporin from his glove box. He stank from where the propane fire had singed his black wooly hair rust-orange, and he still wore the shirt with the fire blooms on it, proudly, as if garlanded by it. Vince stood barefoot at the bar, his soleless boots like shell game shells over his feet.

What dying logging community of their origin might we blame?

Tenmile, about a hundred and fifty miles north, between the Cabinet and Salish ranges, not far from the borders of Idaho and British Columbia. Tucked up in the corner of Montana like a dust bunny. A union-suit-whipping-on-the-clothesline kind of town. Where old Studebakers are shot through with bullets and timothy. An eightman high school football kind of town. The kind of place where it might occur to you to walk out through the cheatgrass into the cottonwoods behind the body shop to stick a honey bear full of grain alcohol up your ass, squeeze, and get drunk that way. Yowling each night from within a different trailer in the park, some of it from fucking, some from fighting, some just to get somebody anybody even the cops to come and behold the methamphetamined, nicotined, alcoholic outrage within. A town peopled with old cranks, broke farmers, loggers, and at least two pickupsfull of teenage louts who came up out of their beer-soaked loitering in the mist by the river or from their parking spot near the Ace Hardware to beat on Vince again for spray-painting GOD IS A FAG on the wall of the

Dairy Queen or Sully for his smirk, his thick black curly hair, his army jacket with names of bands scrawled all over it in black felt tip. Parked in Sully's Subaru on some switchback on some mountain, they drank cold syrup and smoked the flecks, seeds, and stems of weak marijuana. They ran afoul of all three of the cops there, the principal and teachers, the Ace Hardware and the Dairy Queen. Ill gossip attended their lorn mothers. The lot of them trash, even for Tenmile. It was said that they couldn't even see Fucked from where they were.

What occasioned their departure?

Sully's mom kicked him out. Vince's mom forbade Sully from entering her trailer.

They camped in the mountains just below the old ghost town of Deerwater. Talked over beers on opposite sides of the fire about going to Seattle or Portland or Boise or Missoula. The owls went silent from the ruckus of Tenmile boys getting drunk up at the ghost town, smashing the old tavern and flophouse. When the noises ceased, Sully said they ought to put out their fire but it seemed chickenshit to actually do it. They listened to the gang defile down through the firs, and when they appeared in the ring of light from the fire and told them to stand up, Vince and Sully did.

They told Sully to give up their beer. Vince said they had no more, that it didn't matter if they did anyway because these boys had come for one thing: to beat on Vince and Sully. One of the louts said that seemed like a fine idea and hit him in the mouth. Sully fled but Vince stood and took it.

When they finished they propped Vince in the firelight. In attitudes satisfied and craftsman-like they held his head and inspected the marks they had made on his face. Then they kicked the burning sticks out of the fire as if the light offended them and they left.

Sully slunk back. Vince sat in the dark like nothing had happened.

They collected their things from where they were strewn and drove out of the woods. Each waited in the car while the other took a garbage bag of belongings from home. By sunup they were driving south to Missoula.

How exactly did they find themselves in Missoula?

Happy, free, and resourceful. The summer city was sleepy without university students. The sunsets were the color of melon from forest fire smoke. With Sully's old Stella guitar they busked for quarters and dollar bills on Jacob's Island near the campus. They shoplifted hamburger and grilled on a cookie sheet they fished from the ditch. They dry camped up the Rattlesnake. They floated the Clark Fork every day and befriended the bums under Higgins Street bridge who bought them their liquor. They ate chickenfried steak at the poker table in the Oxford Bar when they could afford it.

They craved more. A little bored after Vince healed and they were hale and wanting tattoos, marijuana, crystal meth, and a place to take girls, none of which they could afford on the wages from Sully's crude pluckings. They paid Vince's uncle a visit, got hired on his crew, and moved out of Sully's Subaru and into an apartment near the river, across from downtown.

Was the work hot and manual and mindless? Did they dig and pave? Treat with oil and sealant? Did they edge and mow and otherwise landscape, and scrape and prime and paint and stain? Did they go home sore but strong, and nap and rise to meet the night? Did they skirmish with hicks in pickups who even here in soft Missoula were endemic and hated the very look of them—Vince skinny and shirtless, Sully with a clothespin in his ear—like the last combatants in a lost feud? Did they do what drugs they could, have over girls who took off their panties and stayed up all night with them? Did they drink deep of their new cup? Was it a grand time, possessed of the joy of young men who have discovered previously unknown thirsts and the ways to slake them?

Hell yes.

And by degrees they became unreliable, late for work or too hungover or high for it, so that when the paver burned up, it was natural for Vince's uncle to fire Sully, to not care that Vince quit with him.

How did they tell of the conflagration to the old men in pearl-snapped shirts and vests, dirty Carhartts and flannels and cowboy or work boots who gathered at the end of the bar at Charlie B's? What enchanted these men who have seen it all, heard and burned it all themselves?

The mimicry that was a kind of obeisance. Vince and Sully spoke as their fathers spoke, though neither had seen his father in years. Inflected like them, jargoned like them, stood and gesticulated like them. Enhanced by Sully's constant tuning of the cherry-colored Stella, as if the tale would require music at some point. They told it as if yoked to some purpose, comic and for profit.

Sully said, I was trying to keep the sumbitch flush with the fenceline. Why they put the fence in before the damn pavement, I wont ever understand. But it is loud on that mother, you know. Thing puts a shiver on you good. Lookit my hands. Still shaking and not because of the fire or being scared. I go to bed vibrating every night. Swear to god. So what happened?

Like I was saying, as fucking usual that hose from the propane tank pops free of where it attaches to the screed. Hell, Vince should tell you. He seen it better than I did actually.

Go ahead, Vince said.

No you tell em. Tell em what it looked like.

Vince took a sip of beer, looked around, met each eye like all glad-handing, master bullshitters do before a good embellishment.

You know how a hose on full-blast will flop around in the yard? Well, that's what this hose was doing, only spewing propane. Over that—what, six hundred degree?—over that screed. And Sully here is just staying flush to that fence—

You try and back one of those pavers up, Sully interjected.

And so he dont notice that propane is spraying all over the place behind him, even though we started to whale on the machine to get his attention. Thing is, we prolly sparked it with our damn shovels, and this blanket of blue fire flashes over the screed and that hose catches and damned if it didnt just start flipping around in the air like this—

The men chuckled now at the charmed-snake dance Vince did with his arm.

And alla sudden it snaps Sully on his ass and he up—

Vince hopped from his barstool.

—and looking around like, What the fuck? And this time it comes and snaps him on the ear—

The men laughed, gathered, increased their number around Vince and Sully, and Vince danced like someone was firing a gun at his feet.

—and now he's pissed, because he's still driving and cant figure what the hell is going on. And he's trying to keep that paver true and just shooting us the stink eye because he thinks one of us at the back of the paver is doing it. And I'm pointing at the hose, but it's moving so damn fast he cant see it over his shoulder and he gets stung again and again and— what, you stepped or something?

Sully set the guitar on the bar and said, I take a step and the thing is between my legs and flipping around and just burning me, man. Burning me all over. God it hurt. Still hurts. Lookit my shirt.

Stop, someone cried. I'm a piss myself.

Sully swatted at an invisible flame-snake. And Vince in pantomime covered his genitals, puffed his cheeks. The old boys exploded in laughter.

How did the telling and retelling turn a profit? What, after all, rent the friends? What about after they told the story?

The old men told of other disasters, tilted away drunk, new ones drifted in and were called over, and Vince and Sully retold it. They were set for beer because of it and Sully's orange clown hair and Vince's bottomless boots. And over and over some hard old boy clapped Vince on the shoulder, put a beer or a shot in his hand, admired him through eyes crowfooted from seasons of squinting in the sun's reflection off white planes of snow, and said, Goddamn brave of you getting up on there and turning that tank closed.

Vince thanked the man, Sully nodded, and the excitement of the event and its telling diminished each time. The setting sun cut slant through the windows, lanced the smoke with light and heat.

Vince finally said, Shit dude, that old boy didnt know what the hell he was talking about. You were saying for weeks that the damn thing was a firetrap.

Naw. That took some sac, Sully said.

Shit.

And everybody had a good laugh. You tell it real funny.

Sully spat and leaned against the back bar.

It's just a story, Sul. I didnt mean to—

Show me up?

Hell no.

Dont matter. I always come out lookin like chickenshit, dont I?

Then Sully began to drink like he'd seen his father drink. Little glass of brown water, big glass of yellow foamy water. Vince was already bloodshot and reeling. Footing the peanut shells. They were quiet.

Would it have helped if there had been girls at Charlie B's that night, with Sully drinking so much and Vince keeping up and joining him for hits of crystal in the Subaru parked on the street, right there out in the open like they just wanted to spend the night in jail?

Perhaps. Maybe not. The crystal was wrong, cooked or cut funny, thick with jitters and shy on euphoria. Though it burned in their lungs, jolted them from beer and whiskey bleariness, they hardly spoke, and when Vince tried to fault himself, to apologize, Sully would shake him off, say, We cool, and turn up the hardcore in the tape deck, and take another hit.

Could it really be called a fight what they had when the tape ended and Sully lurched out and Vince followed him and called him back and Sully strode off into the alley where Vince chased him and tried to grab and hold him and Sully shoved him and like brothers they had it out grappling and headlocking and even a little crying, like brothers turning in that alley in the dark who would have appeared to passersby as groping lovers or clutching cowards but were in fact fierce and bruising and abrading, uncoupling and panting and coupling again in muffled violence that sounded in grunts and would not escalate but seemingly could not abate?

No. For there was an inarticulate but no less binding pact that fists would not enter into it. There would be no hitting. This was bad enough, for dumbshit hillbillies fought with fists, fought at all. Not them. They were free. Fatherless. There were no disciplining men or gods except what each of them was to himself alone.

But Vince at last submitted to Sully's main strength and burnt and sweaty reek and fell backward onto the ragged alley pavement and broken glass. Sully straddled him and even this was like Vince had thrown the contest, the fight they were not in fact having. Sully's face glistened from sweat and where his blistered face wept, as if the tears came from his whole face and not his eyes.

What did Sully whisper in Vince's ear as they sat on the back bumper of his Subaru, which Vince did not listen to, having heard it a hundred times, and because it embarrassed him to hear it even once, and because he was swollen, dizzy, and grateful at least that Sully was beside him partly because they were friends bosom and true, and partly because Sully beside him meant that there was one less of them out there, and he was grateful that the world was not swollen with people such as he and Sully, who were broken and stupid and every bit as bad as hicks, and deserved everyday to be lashed by fire gods and who would have made a fire to burn themselves if the world did not see fit to provide one? What was it Sully whispered?

It was me and Daddy in there. In the camper. I didnt want to go. But Mom made me. For my tenth birthday we was going hunting. Big deal, I thought. I was a shit about it. Pouted the whole way up. We got settled in somewhere around Deerwater, and he has a ton of beers that I fetch for him. He lets me beat him at cribbage and we go to bed.

I woke and I was choking. I dont know. I could breathe, but the air was like it wouldnt, you know, take. And all down my hands, all down my arms, it was so cold it burned. But bearable, not like real fire, and I knew it was killing me.

I musta hit every corner and cabinet trying to just get out of that motherfucking camper. It was cold outside, boy. And not just the air. Well the air is what I'm talkin about, but the air that got into my lungs. I gagged on it at first, that clean air. I walked about twelve feet from the camper. Clear cold night like tonight. I was seeing extra stars. Oh I was sick. Headache like you never had and my ears ringing and throwing up.

What does Sully always say at this point?

There wasnt any going back in there for him. I just knew it. It was all matter a fact like that. I'm ten years old. He weighs two-fifty, easy. The camper is filled with propane. I'm sick. I aint gonna save him. No one is.

What does he say this time instead?

I closed the door, Vince. I went right by him, his big still body. And I closed the door behind me.

If not to make Sully look like chickenshit, why did Vince jump on the paver and turn closed the tank?

In the winter the bus came in the dark and dawn came after class had begun, when their chilblains had quit itching. Sully hunched behind an angled desktop, his forearm in his mouth as if to eat it. With a smack he popped the arm free and inspected his efforts in the new sun and was pleased. He showed Vince where blood died in pools just under his skin, where he had splotched and flattered his arms with purple blooms, the possibilities if you were not afraid.

Jason DeYoung

The Funeral Bill

At one time, the landlord Jeffers had been a busy person, but not anymore. Now he had time to think, and he had recently decided that he was going to die. His stomach was no longer the taut paunch it had been. Food passed his tongue joylessly. He no longer lusted. His feet and legs often went numb, and he'd taken to massaging isopropyl alcohol on them to regain some feeling. The smoke from his pipe remained one of the only things that seemed right—perhaps the craving for vice was the last thing to leave a person. Just before his mother passed away she would only eat soft candies. Jeffers' death wouldn't be immediate: he wouldn't pass away today or tomorrow. It just landed upon him, pressed upon him, that his own passing was imminent, and he had no idea what to expect in the afterward.

Alone on the front porch in a frayed and stretched lawn chair, eyes closed, he imagined funerals. His tenant's wife had died a few days ago. He pictured her supine like all bodies he'd seen in a coffin—clenched eyes, somewhat enlarged nostrils, mouth gently closed as if asleep. Peaceful rest. He remembered the summer evening years before when he'd had a body removed from Ashcross. The renter's daughter draped across her father's swollen body, weeping "daddy... daddy." Her little fists sinking into her father's stomach, her fingers groping at his shirt. The mortician's assistant, grinding his teeth, pulled the little girl off the body, rending the moist stitching around the shirt's collar. The renter didn't appear as if he slept. In the near-subterraneous light, gape-jawed with eyes half-closed and unfocused, his waxy face was constricted into a rictus articulating the ineffable of the beyond. Or perhaps the lack thereof. He didn't look heaven-bound. If Jeffers had not gone when the rent stopped coming in, he wondered how long the kid would have stayed there, caring for her father's corpse.

Jeffers envied those who had seen a person die. He believed they understood what he didn't—what death brought. He asked the renter's little girl what had happened when her father passed. Without a tear in her eye, she said she didn't know. She hadn't seen it.

This envy had taken root when his son, James, witnessed his mother pass away while Jeffers was out making a deal with a man named White who was ignorant enough to believe a handshake was still as good as a notarized contract. For James, watching his mother's passing had been such a powerful thing he'd gone into the seminary. He now ran a church out of the storefront of an old third-rate grocery in the lower part of the state; its sanctuary still smelled of hoopcheese and day laborers. (Jeffers thought his son would have been better off re-opening the grocery.) But James had witnessed many of his parishioners die, some of old age, others from disease. Each time his son told him of another death, Jeffers' resentment grew. He never asked his son what it was like, afraid he'd get an earful of capricious religious nonsense, a tangle of words that would make him feel stupid.

He opened his eyes to stop the images and looked at the clear plastic freezer bags filled with water and four pennies hanging from the upper porch railings. Craziest thing he'd ever heard—a suggestion from James, an article he'd sent Jeffers on how to ward off flies. It said to hang plastic freezer bags with pennies and water outside to keep flies away. It worked. But as the sunlight shot through them casting a liquid-copper glow, he thought of the coins once used to cover the eyes of the decease. He spat over the porch railing. He put his unlighted pipe in his mouth.

He tried to recover his mind, replacing contemplating death with what to do about the Ashcross property, in which—he'd been told—a set of kids were now squatting. He'd let the place go to seed since the renter died in it nearly three years ago. Its roof and plumbing leaked, its walls drilled out by all manner of nest-builders, but he couldn't abide the squatting. But apathy or something like it had gotten hold of him; it had embraced him at the same time the numbness started creeping into his legs. In quiet times such as these, something in the boredom and the numbness and the nature of age drew back like a bow and twanged when he tried to move, and a misdirected laugh or, on occasion, a hiccup-like cry sprang from his mouth. He didn't understand it. But it locked him in his chair, kept him from getting anything done.

He tapped a wooden, bald-headed match on the arm of the chair while trying not to look at the pennies. But images of edemas, time at work, wasting disease, null and vacant and quicklime-covered faces impinged upon his concentration. His pipe hung limply from his lips. He sucked on the raw tobacco packed inside it to get a hint of sweetness mixed with a burned residue.

Jeffers saw the tenant who lived across the street walking up the driveway. As he walked, he smacked at the ash-brown leaves of the spent okra that framed one side of the property.

Jeffers dropped the unlighted match in his palm.

The tenant stopped at the porch steps. A scrawny man with brow-darkened eyes and a fresh crookedness barbing his face as if he'd been howling or banging his head against the wall.

"RD, what's ailing you?"

"We buried LaRae this morning," RD said, closing his eyes.

"I was sorry to hear about LaRae," he said. He looked down at RD, who shifted his weight between his feet like a child needing to pee. He patted the porch railing, causing it to wobble. "It's a hard thing to lose a wife," Jeffers continued to fill in the silence. He pictured his two wives in his mind, pondered which one might meet him in heaven, if there was a heaven. Age had made him hopeful again that there was such a place. Experience made him doubtful. "I've lost two myself."

RD nodded thoughtfully at the bottom of the porch steps. He shifted his weight and squinted at the pennies and water bags.

Jeffers studied RD. He knew little about him. Looked mid-thirties, but Jeffers had stopped believing he could guess a person's age a long time ago. A quiet tenant—paid his rent. But RD had a bottom-of-the-litter look, runt-ish, forgotten. He looked given to schemes. He might have been the skinniest grown man Jeffers had ever seen—his shoulders angled like those on a starved child. He'd known scrounging for sure. RD and LaRae had come from Tennessee.

"She saw haints, you know," RD said.

"Haints?"

"Ghosts."

"Ghosts?"

RD nodded and splashed a brown vein of spit into the grass. A wind buffeted his face, and he looked a slight better to Jeffers, who supposed the little man had come over just to talk out his sadness. Jeffers struck the match, sheltered its flame, and pressed it to the tobacco while making gentle, moist pops to pull the fire into the pipe.

"In that house of yourn," RD said.

"What's that?" Jeffers said.

"Haints in your house."

"This house?"

"No, ourn. The one you lettin us have."

Jeffers lowered the pipe and shook out the match. "Rent."

"Yep. Haints in that house you lettin us rent."

Jeffers leaned forward and looked across the porch where he could see through a stand of weather-broken pines the squat gables of the house RD rented. Below the boundary of trees, a graying neighborhood dog was working over road-kill flattened on the unlined blacktop that split the properties.

"I'll be damn." Jeffers looked back at RD, who had climbed the first step and was leaning toward the porch as if he wanted to come up. He was almost panting.

"Them haints killed LaRae."

Jeffers leaned back in his chair and drew on his pipe. The spirit of the tobacco warmed his mouth as he considered his next words. RD climbed another step. He shuddered and proffered a what-are-you-going-to-do-about-it glare. Behind the spindly man, the sun was low and the sky bloodied in a balsam light.

Jeffers took the pipe down: "I am sorry about LaRae. But what do you want me to do about a ghost? I cain't charge it rent."

"You could pay for LaRae's buryin expense that's what, since it was your haints that killed her."

"How you figure they're mine?"

"It was in your house."

"Well, they could have come with you from Tennessee. I've had untold number of folks live in that house. Not one of them complained of 'haints.'"

RD squinted, catching the sarcasm in Jeffers' voice. He quivered.

"If there are haints in that house, as you say, RD, they must've come to roost the same time you did. And that house is only supposed to be occupied by two people. The way I see it, you might owe me money, housing your haints, when your lease says only two shall live there." Jeffers drew on his pipe, satisfied with himself. He felt a pleasant jolt of blood and adrenaline shock his body.

"That house killed her."

"House or haints?"

RD chewed the inside of his cheek. The broad outlines of his skull were visible. He reminded Jeffers of the half-fed prisoners who worked chain gang years ago.

"RD, how do you make money? You work?"

RD, leering, backed down a step.

Jeffers held his gaze wide-eyed until he squinted from the falling sun breaking from the clouds. If this was a scheme, Jeffers thought, it's awfully weak.

"Before LaRae passed, she told me that you would take care of her funeral bill. She said it was your wives who told her that you'd cover it."

Jeffers peered unblinkingly through white smoke.

"You going to pay?"

"What do you think?" Jeffers said.

"I think you will."

For a brief moment he considered giving in before a surge of meanness rose up: "Get the hell off my porch 'fore I throw you off."

RD stood up straight and a haughty tic ran through his shoulders. He turned and headed back in the direction he'd come from.

Jeffers called to RD when the little man was equidistant between the porch and the road: "If you see them haints, send them my way."

RD didn't respond. As he passed the old dog in the road, he stopped to stare at it, and then for no reason scared it off its tire-mangled dinner.

Jeffers spat a long slivery streak into his boxwoods. He relaxed and puffed, satisfied. But the reminder of LaRae's passing made him think again about his own shortening time, of what was to come. He lowered the pipe and leaned once more to see the house across the road, looking for the little, dissatisfied man, angry with him for his audacity and privation and for his existence, which Jeffers suddenly considered unearned.

The little spat with his tenant left Jeffers wanting some more excitement and so he went to the Ashcross property to run the squatters out. He found no one there. They had trounced the weeds around the house creating a cowpath to a five-gallon bucket simmering with turds and urine. In the long-untended shade tree hung wispy catfish skins. Several catfish heads had been hammered into the tree's trunk and their husky mouths and eyes gawked in bewilderment. Redneck trophies, Jeffers thought.

Standing on the Ashcross porch Jeffers recalled the last time he'd been inside the house, holding the little girl by the shoulder, quizzing her on his father's death, and her dry-eyed answers. Her little fingernails had been chewed to the quick.

His remembrance was broken when he glimpsed a young pregnant woman walking down the road, her hair a freak of colors—yellow, red— her stomach full and hanging low. Jeffers thought for a moment she was the squatter, but she passed the weed-lined driveway as if she were headed elsewhere. And then Jeffers felt a twinge of lust, something he hadn't felt in a while. He stifled a half-laugh. If asked what he thought of the young woman, he would have ranted over her hairstyle and clothes—he knew a slut when he saw one! But in truth she was lovely, and her pregnancy made her all the more so. What if she had been his squatter? Could he have thrown her out? He'd never felt sorry for squatters. One winter he had thrown a whole family out, and learned later that one of their children died of pneumonia. Still he thought he'd made the right decision. He was well off and thought it was because he'd made good decisions. These people had to earn their place; they couldn't just take. Wanting something for nothing, that was the problem.

He still liked to brag that he once held over a million dollars in his hands. It had come from the sale of the White property, which he considered bad luck, seeing as how he got it the same day his first wife died. His second wife came with property but she died within a year of when they married. Her kids had taken her away from Jeffers, back to her home state, to care for her. He'd given all of her property to her children. It seemed the right thing to do. And after she passed, he sold off several large sections of his holdings. But he wished he had it all back now. It worried him how easily he'd accepted age, how he'd told himself he was getting old and selling off his properties was a good idea. At one time he'd owned twenty-one rental properties, most of them run-down farmhouses in which he installed young couples and hard-working hillbillies. Grief-pierced, he yearned to have it all back. Now he just had the house next his own to give him his pocket money, and the Ashcross place.

James wanted Ashcross to put a church on, and he wanted Jeffers to donate it. But there was promise still in the property and money to be made. He needed to get the squatters out, and install fresh tenants. It was also that his son wanted the plot so bad that Jeffers couldn't let it go; he couldn't let his son take the last of his holdings, leaving him with just the squat-gable home. In his imagination, Jeffers saw his son holding the hands of a dying parishioner, whispering that the man who had owned the property had donated it, just gave it up. The face of the imagined parishioner looked up with a wink and smirked. And Jeffers saw that this was where his son would bury him, too—under a light-grey headstone carved with his birth and death and ASHCROSS UNITED METHODIST CHURCH BENEFACTOR.

The young woman passed behind some trees. His lust abated, the numbness in his feet stretched out as if originating from inside the bones. The numbness, the age. There would be a time soon when he wouldn't be able to care for himself. He wouldn't be able to rise from a chair, wouldn't be able to put himself to bed, wouldn't be able to cook or attend to his own needs. Perhaps giving the land to his son would a good thing, and then James would have no choice but to make it his duty to devote himself to Jeffers. But what he really wanted was someone who would care for him without demand. He would pay for that.

That night Jeffers dreamed of LaRae. He dreamed of going over to the little house with pockets full of cash. He found her there with a baby up to her breast while she smiled brightly at him. He looked down at the baby, its jaw fluttering, gnawing. Unhealthy, pallid, the child unmistakably RD's: they shared the same sunken cheeks. LaRae draped a frayed copper-colored shawl over her chest and tugged the baby from her nipple as if to show Jeffers the infant, and the child gave out an insufferable squall, bile resembling doused ash dribbled from its mouth. Its cry wasn't like any infant's he'd heard before, and Jeffers woke to hear that the sound wasn't the child's at all but was coming from something else nearby. He sat up in bed, switched on the bedside lamp.

The painful howl went up again.

His feet and shins were numb as they often were when he woke. He slipped on his yard shoes and tried to stand. He sat down on the bed and then stood up again. It felt as though he was walking on peg legs. He stumbled across the room. Another wail went out. He forwent his pants. He went to the closet, held to the doorjamb, his legs muscles smarting and stinging. He pulled out his pistol. He tromped down the hall in his boxer shorts and undershirt; he said a prayer that his varicose legs wouldn't give out and that he'd have sense enough to protect himself. He looked out the living room window and saw nothing. He eased his front door open, his pistol pointed in the direction he imagined the sound was coming from, his lips parted, ready to receive a breathe of cool air.

The outdoor lamp washed everything in a plaintive white or buried it in shadow. At the far end of his yard, a quaking silhouette crouched under a pecan tree. He walked slowly over to it—his face jutted trying to see what it was. His pistol lowered.

The old dog moaned as Jeffers approached. Its gut had been slit open. Blood adorned its fur in black blotches.

He heard rustling in the pine trees that flanked his property. He kept the pistol lowered and listened. He called for the cutthroat to come out. He called again. The base of the pine trees were bleached white from the lamp's light and between their trunks Jeffers could see only darkness.

He looked down at the dog. One visible eye glinted in the sparse light. Jeffers looked back at the stand of pine trees before gripping the barrel of the pistol. He brought its handle down swiftly on the dog's skull to avoid firing a bullet in the middle of the night, which would bring the curiosity and ire of neighbors. And there was the cost of the bullet to consider.

He hit it again—and then a third time. After each strike, he glanced back at the trees and saw only rib-white pine trunks and night. Jeffers peered down at the extinguished dog before limping back to the house, knowing the man in the pines was watching.

His sleep was chancy these days. Many nights he sat up, the vapors from the isopropyl alcohol rising from his feet, a subsuming numbness creeping further up his legs. He often mapped its assent, trying to sense the true direction of the numbness, what area would it covet next, whether it had or would enter his spine or some other territory. When would it be too late to ask for help? When would the numbness settle in his stomach and make it impossible to eat? Or would it skip his stomach and spine and ground itself with fresh purchase in his heart? And then what? Death.

But this night Jeffers sat at his kitchen table, puffing on his pipe, replaying the events. He figured it was RD who had gutted the dog. He imagined the two, both lean and dirty animals—RD with the upper hand only because he had sense to bait the scrawny thing and could wield a knife.

Just before light, he went out with a shovel to remove the dog from the yard. Taped to the door was a list of LaRae's burial expenses written in an untrained hand. At the bottom, beneath the tally, was the message, "You O me that much RD".

It was unlike Jeffers to befoul one of his properties and he wished he hadn't. He knew he might suffer for the considerable effort it took to carry the animal up a ladder, but he was angry and dropping the dog's gut-slung body down RD's chimney made him feel young as if he were playing some outlandish prank. He knew the dog would get stuck in the flue and create an unbearable stink. But it had felt good, his legs felt strong.

Seated on his porch, a warm breeze eased him. Numbness slowly budded in his toes. Soon it would blossom up his legs, and then like vines it would gather around his waist and approach his back. Unrelieved numbness: faintly its tendrils would furl the base of his spine. He knew paralysis would take soon. He looked up at the bags of pennies and water. Such a simple measure, and a small cost to keep the flies at bay. With lips folded between teeth, he squelched a whimper.

As the numbness grew, he pondered over the list of expenses RD had tacked to his door. He thought of his own wives. One was buried in the city's cemetery and the other was buried in North Carolina. Even though it had been almost a decade, he knew by the tally tacked to his door that he'd spent more, given more respect, to his wives than RD had to LaRae.

He saw RD coming up the driveway, gripping something nearly hidden in his hand.

"Ain't you got business?" Jeffers blurted.

"I'm here on business. I've been to the funeral home."

He gazed down at RD, who was dressed in a shirt Jeffers wouldn't have used for a rag—threadbare in the chest as if it belonged to a man who itched a lot. He noticed that RD was petting a rabbit's foot in his left hand, part of a keychain: "You bring that for luck?"

"Hell, I don't need no luck."

"You need something. You've eaten or buried the best part."

"You get my note."

"Yeah, I got your duns."

"I told them at the Home you'll pay for it."

"You kill that dog?"

"LaRae said it was your wives that haunted her. Said you beat 'em."

"I never struck them."

"That's not what they said."

"You kill that dog?" Jeffers asked again.

"Said you should have to pay."

"You kill that dog?" Jeffers leaned forward, puffed smoke.

RD gnawed at the inside of his cheek: "Why don't you give me a smoke and I'll knock off a few dollars on that bill."

"You kill that dog?"

"I know who did. I'll tell you for ten dollars."

"So you know it's dead."

"I know you been asking about a dead one, and that one's been lately put out of its misery."

Jeffers shot a gleaming stream of spit at the little man without hitting him: "I didn't cause its misery."

"But you killed it."

"I put it down."

"Then why are you ragging on me about killing a dog?"

"Cause you're the one who gutted it to start with."

"I don't know about that," RD said.

"You don't know you gutted a dog?"

"I didn't."

Jeffers was silent.

Looking at the spit webbed across the parched-green leaves of the boxwoods, RD said: "What's that dog mean to you?"

"Nothing. Having it slaughtered on my property does mean something."

"Well I'll help you look for your dog-gutter if you pay for LaRae."

Jeffers felt the slight palpation of his heart: "I'm not paying you for a goddamn thing."

"You will."

"Why do you think I'll pay?"

"You want peace, don't you?"

Jeffers legs were numb, up to his stomach. At that moment, he wanted more than anything to chase RD down and beat him senseless.

Slightly hunched, RD eased up onto the porch as if he sensed weakness. He stood up and reached for one of the Ziploc bags of pennies and plucked it down from its nail. Jeffers' head twitched and he ground his teeth. There was no feeling whatsoever in his legs, as if he were dead from the waist down.

RD turned and walked down the steps.

"Hey," Jeffers called. "Come get this." Jeffers held up the funeral bill.

RD stood in the yard, with a big smile on his face, danced a burlesque and mocked masturbation and then spat a reddish-brown streak. He wiped his chin: "You can knock four cents off that bill," he said. He turned and walked out of the yard, disappearing behind the trees.

His Sunday evening phone calls with James were little more than reminders—for James it reminded him that his father was still alive, and for Jeffers that his son was little more than a beggar, begging for a donation. Tonight James called asking about some article he'd sent Jeffers regarding blood circulation. Poor circulation: that was what was wrong with Jeffers' according to James.

They sat in silence, Jeffers listening to his son's breath and the hum of foreign ambience at the other end of the line. He yawned. He flicked off the lamp beside the chair and sat in the dark so he could see through the window to the little, unlighted house across the road. He opened his shirt and put a hand to his chest, his heart. His feet were cold in his bedroom shoes.

"Any more thought given to what you're going to do with the Ashcross place?"

"Some," Jeffers said.

"I spoke to the United Methodist Ministries. They said if I could get the land, they'd help me with the church."

"That so?"

"Yes."

James called it a perfect little hill to build a church upon. For Jeffers property had to be earned. He had earned it, bought with monies he got paid from other lands, which he bought with monies he earned originally from labor in a dust-filthy mill. Everything he owned he'd earned. He wanted his son to earn it. James prated on about church, but Jeffers couldn't listen to him. He was angry with RD, angry with himself. He was going to have to get rid of the little man, evict him.

"Anything else going on up there?" James asked.

"Nothing."

"Did you get the squatters out the house?"

"Not yet."

"You can't do anything with the place until you get them out."

Jeffers let out a meek huh, which his son didn't respond to. He flicked the light back on and saw himself in the blacken window with a hand across his chest as if he were taking a pledge. His face was sullen. He smiled at himself, mirthless, false. When he stopped smiling the leaden expression returned. His son wasn't speaking. Who was his confidant, Jeffers wondered.

"Don't make any decision about that place before talking to me," James said.

Jeffers didn't respond.

James sighed on the other end and told his father goodnight.

Jeffers got up the next morning surprised he'd had a good night's sleep. His feet were warm and when he stood he could feel them—he could feel the coolness of the floor. He was still angry, but he felt good and up to running off squatters. He would have to deal with RD soon and getting Ashcross taken care of would be one less thing to worry about. He'd foregone calling the police. In years past, just telling the squatters to leave did the trick. Sometimes he'd flash his pistol.

When he got to Ashcross he knocked on the front door and a young woman with a gaudy bloom of red- and yellow-dyed hair answered. She was very pregnant, and she smiled so brightly that Jeffers couldn't help thinking of a flower he wished he could pick. The young woman said her name was Lucinda, but that everyone called her Panky.

He didn't mention that he'd seen her before. He began by telling her that she was a squatter and that the property belonged to him. If she didn't clear out immediately, he would have her arrested for trespassing and demand back-rent by garnering future earnings.

The young woman stood quietly as Jeffers finished speaking. After a few moments she spoke: "Someone told me and Toby it was empty and we could just stay a while until Toby got a job."

"I am the landlord. I charge rent on the people who live here."

"But it's been empty for a long time."

"That doesn't mean anything."

"But we have nowheres to go."

He'd never felt sorry for squatters or tenants, but Panky's festival hair, spray of freckles across her nose—her belly—released an unexpected shock of tenderness in his chest. He looked away, toward the trees and the catfish heads, as she continued to talk about their plucky intentions to stay briefly, have the baby, find a job for herself, find a better place. She just needed a little more time.

He hustled his pants around his haunchless hips. The weight of the pistol tugged on his trousers. His feet were going numb.

She was silent for a moment, and he looked back to see why she'd stopped talking. Then she said: "We could do some repairs on the house. Toby's good with that. Let us stay here and we'll fix it."

He hustled his pants again. He felt squirmy. His legs were being subsumed. His mind snarled with untethered thoughts. The woman before him, unpleasantly steady, continued to plead for more time. Her words became senseless in his ears.

He needed her. Or someone like her. This sudden upstroke of clarity frightened him. He needed someone to relieve him of the unrelenting loneliness of the last few years, someone to care for him. He was going to need care. He was dying and she was about to give life. She couldn't help it. Panky carried it inside her freely. He saw that.

Jeffers' mouth palsied inward before he stammered: "Do I look sick to you?"

Panky took a step back: "Maybe a little."

Jeffers stumbled forward: "How little?"

"Your face."

"What about my face?" He took another, cautious step forward.

She parried his gaze and reached back for the doorknob.

Something uncoiled itself within his body. For a moment, he believed he might have pissed himself, and he patted his crotch, checking for dampness. He took another step toward Panky. He murmured—he wasn't sure what he had intended to say. He reached for his crotch, still not convinced that he hadn't soiled his trousers. He felt his mouth gape inexplicably. Panky blurted: "Mister, I don't know what you want." He stumbled forward and clasped his hand on her shoulder. She smacked at his hand. His thumb bit into the meat between her collarbone and ribcage. Panky grimaced and threw Jeffers' hand away.

He lurched forward: "I want you to tell me what I look like."

"You look sick. Like an old man," she said, swatting his hand as it reached out again.

"I am sick."

"Do you need me to get help?"

"Yes. Yes." He then turned and left the porch—Panky already behind the door. Jeffers heard scraping as if heavy furnishings were being drawn to block entry.

He cranked the truck and drove out of the pea-gravel drive. He wanted to howl or squall. He sensed he was running out of something. He gripped the steering wheel so tightly he felt the rubber give loose of the wheel inside the tubing.

He clenched his jaw until his partial denture bit into his gums and he could taste blood. He belched a laugh, or maybe it was a cry. He was stunned by how empty he felt. His crotch wasn't wet, but the numbness swarmed his legs and was advancing upward, a gripping numbness combined with a pressure that seemed to gnaw at the bone. He could no longer sense how deeply he pressed the accelerator or the brake. He let out a yowl and then wondered for a half second if there was someone else in the pickup with him. And then he did it again.

When he got home, RD was on his porch steps, smoking a pipe.

Jeffers hissed.

He pulled his truck into the yard, coming as close to the porch as he could, got out, with the pistol in his hand, and walked slowly, purposefully, painfully the few steps to where RD sat, puffing, his lips drawn into a mirthful grin. All the bags of pennies were gone.

"That yours?" Jeffers asked, snatching the pipe out of RD's mouth.

"Just smoking a little. There's a God awful smell over there and just wanted to smell something sweet for a little bit." RD cocked his head at the pistol. "That's a nice one."

"Maybe it's that haint of yours stinking up the place. Is it house trained?"

"Where you been, landlord? You do some shooting?"

"What do you want, RD?"

"Money."

"Charity?"

"Call it what you like. It's all the same to me."

Jeffers collapsed in his porch chair, put the pistol across his lap, and cleaned RD's spit off the mouthpiece of the pipe with a handkerchief.

"Smells like something died over there, Jeffers."

"Well, she did." Jeffers swatted at a fly that had landed on his arm.

RD looked at him darkly. "Something new."

"Maybe you ought to clear out then, RD. Maybe it's that haint. Or it might be my wives wanting the house for themselves. Maybe they're tired of your laying about."

"Maybe." RD turned to leave. He spat a brown streak of spit in the yard. "When you're ready to settle up, you know where I live."

When RD was behind the pines, Jeffers exhaled a short strangled laugh, and then another, but it was more like a gasp. He placed the pistol on the little table beside him. His right leg twitched, his left crackled as if its very veins and capillaries were bursting. He rapped the pipe on the porch railing to clean out the tobacco RD had been smoking. He took out his pocketknife and scrapped the chamber clean; he lighted a match and burned the mouthpiece a little. He sighed and let his body rest for a few moments.

He reached under the chair where he kept a pack of tobacco. Its weight was wrong—too light. Jeffers spread the bag open. Dust, ash, dirt? He wasn't sure. He leaned over and poured out the contents. Teeth fell out. Fragments of bone. The dog's? LaRea's? Another copy of the funeral bill lined the bottom of the tobacco bag. A small deduction had been made for the tobacco RD had smoked and the pennies.

A fly landed on his hand.

By the time he walked to the squat-gable house, he was sweating and quaking with a chill. The numbness in his legs scoured him bone to flesh. He didn't know why he hadn't driven the short distance. Impatient with RD's games, he'd gotten out the lawn chair and shoved his pistol in his right front pocket and descended the porch steps half blind with anger

He entered the front door with his own key and limped into the tiny living room, bare except for a tattered recliner and an empty TV stand with a midden of chicken bones and stale French fries littered across it. The smell of the dog was monstrous.

In the kitchen, empty bean cans lined the counter and most of the cabinet doors hung open. A spoon, crusted and unpolished, reclined in the sink. Jeffers could hear RD moving around in the back of the house. He listened for a few moments before continuing down the hall. He passed a slender closet, empty except for a lone, bent coathanger. He passed the bathroom, darkened and faintly urinous.

When he reached the bedroom, he was surprised by the vision of RD seized in a blade of dust-speckled sunlight—shirtless, his bones seemingly lifted to just under his skin. It was as if Famine itself stood before Jeffers in a swirl of ash and red-brown light. RD smiled at him.

As if heat lightning passed through the little house, he glimpsed a future and past. He re-imagined the death-rictus of his Ashcross renter long ago. His first wife's closed coffin. He saw his own death—the paralysis, the absolute loss of modesty. His son, robed, offering up thanks to heaven for his Father and for land. Jeffers removed the pistol from his pocket, pointed it at RD and pulled the trigger. The little man snapped up in the dusty air and landed on his back.

He looked down upon the little man gasping, observed his twitching, witnessed a tiny spring of blood bubble up and then flow. RD grasped at his chest, his breath already shortening.

"What do you see?" Jeffers demanded

"What?" RD spat.

Jeffers crouched over RD and moved in close enough to feel the other's moist breath: "What do you see?"

A half-smile, half-grimace palsied RD's face, "I see you." He rolled over and tried to stand.

Jeffers shoved RD back to the floor. He stepped to the window and drew the copper-colored curtains.

"You goin to get me some help?"

Jeffers turned from the window and in the cheap light raised the pistol and shot RD again. A shallow splatter of blood leapt from RD's chest, a near-inaudible grunt left his mouth. Jeffers resumed his position over RD's face.

"And now, do you see anything?"

RD squinted. "You got to help me."

"What do you see?" Jeffers roared.

"You don't have to pay that bill."

Jeffers stepped away from the spread of blood. He pointed the pistol at RD again, but then didn't shoot. He thought he saw some change in the little man: "What do you see?"

"You," RD gasped. "I see you. Help me."

Jeffers asked him again and again what he was seeing, but it didn't change. Jeffers was in disbelief that he was awaiting a man so given to lies as RD to tell him the truth. RD tried to crawl. Jeffers struck him, and then again, thrashing like a man at labor. The little man curled tighter and clutched his head after each blow.

Finally both men were still. Jeffers leaned in. He turned RD's head and held his crumpled cheek tenderly as a nurse might do. "What's there? What do you see?"

There was no answer. RD was dead.

Jeffers sat for a spell in the recliner. With his index finger he pushed at the pile of dry chicken bones and withered fries. He could no longer smell the stench of the dog rotting in the chimney. He could feel his legs and feet, but knew it wouldn't last long. He could sense the numbness creeping in again and he removed his shoes and socks so he could rub his toes. We are perched atop nothingness, Jeffers thought, we make up heavens, but we are atop nothing. He didn't want to go home. He called his son.

They took his pistol, his belt, and the laces of his shoes, and put him in the back of the patrol car. His son was running his mouth to the police. He couldn't hear what was being said. He wanted his pipe, which still rested on the porch railing where he'd left it.

He was numb up to his waist.

As Jeffers began to close his eyes, the glimpse of a specter stopped him. In the distance, crouched between pine trees he saw something beautiful. She was unmistakable with an ornate flourish of hair, her round pregnant belly. She had come to his house, had come to see him, to help him. Jeffers stared at her, hoping that she would turn and look his way, see him behind the glass, give some forgiveness. He needed that gift. But she looked past him, watching James and the police. He wept dryly, knowing that he had earned nothing today. She turned to walk back into the pines. Jeffers watched the disappearing carnival of hair and the bubble of a cry burst from his lips.

Geoff Wyss

Exit Strategy

Every time she used a kitchen knife, she imagined cutting her finger off. You know how your brain gets stuck, looping its junk on cue? Freaking itself out, filling time as it falls apart? Except that lately she'd been seeing it so vividly that she'd started to think it wasn't dementia, her mind misfiring, but a premonition: the knife slipping off a tomato and diving into the first knuckle of her finger, shushing through the bone, clean and for a moment painless, the exposed rings of her finger glowing like a lit cigarette. She had never cut herself in the kitchen. Didn't that make it more likely every time?

"Well, I think you're safe with that."

That was the plastic knife they had given her with her bagel, and the voice telling her this was the guy from the gym with the legs.

"Unless I frustrate myself to death with it."

"They make those all wrong," he commiserated, lacing his hands over one knee and watching her skim and re-skim the too-thin tip of the knife through the little cup of cream cheese, each time coming away with almost nothing. It was the kind of annoyance that might have nudged her into a whole day of hating contemporary life and her place in it if there hadn't been someone else there to turn it into comedy.

"How the hell do you make a knife wrong?"

"Maybe the Army Corps designed it," he said with a droll incline of his head that showed he kept this joke at the ready.

It turned out his name was Clay, which was perfect for a man who owned an autobody shop and had a gearhead mop of orange curls lapping over the collar of his polo shirt. She'd been seeing him at the Tulane gym for years, where he had earned a place on the roster of half-humans she knew by quirk and idiocy, by indiscretion and the private nicknames she'd assigned them. Always wearing the same red running shorts, the kind with panels that met in a high slit and advertised the flank of his ass, Clay would thud about the gym on his fantastically thick shaven legs, and she would glance from the TV attached to her elliptical trainer and think, I'd suck his dick or some other similarly unprotected thought before flipping to the World Series of Poker on ESPN2 because at least it wasn't Dr. Phil, and then flipping back to Dr. Phil because her hate for him was so familiar and bracing. Most men at the gym worked only their arms and chests, the parts of themselves they imagined winning fights with, but Clay's upper body was undistinguished, a little slushy, and he paraded his legs among the apparatuses with a self-mocking joviality that seemed to say, It's what I've got, let's enjoy it together! Which was mostly what he did there, socialize, gabbing from victim to victim while Shannon scrupulously avoided eye contact.

He was wearing those same red shorts this morning in the coffee shop where, seeing all the tables taken, he had asked to share hers with an inquisitive finger-pistol and a pow of his thumb when she nodded. And then, because he had offered up his name and occupation and how many people he employed and his belief that small business would bring the city back and how nothing could ever make him leave New Orleans in a million years—and because she had to back him off with something—she had spilled across the table a gush of caffeinated blather on the theme of self-mutilation. It was 7:00 am

"It's so fucked up." She held the knife up, a pea of cream cheese at its tip.

"Turn it upside down."

"Oh. That is better." She pointed at half her bagel. "You...?"

"No, thanks. I don't eat breakfast."

"You know what they say."

"I do." He brightened at this first tip of the conversation in his direction. "About a lot of things."

The wry nod she gave, and which she was still dorkishly giving thirty seconds later, might have looked to an observer like nervousness. But at thirty-six she was post-nervous about men, just as she was post-voting, post-screaming in traffic, post-really bothering with her hair, and post-believing that her education had improved her in any important way. But making room for Clay in the three dimensions of her mind was doing a temporary violence to the disposition of all the other items there, and her words felt pushed to the side, looking back at where they used to be.

"So what do you think about Iraq?" He pointed at her Times-Picayune, where there was a photo of something bombed and sandy.

"You must be joking."

"My son's there."

"Your son? How old are you?"

"Forty-three. The math works out."

"Sheesh."

"I think we need an exit strategy."

"I think we need a we-shouldn't-have-fucking-gone-there-in-the-first-place strategy."

He backed his chair out.

"You want anything?"

"You drank that already?"

"I need like three or four of these to get going."

I'd say you're going already, she murmured as he powered off through the noise. In this new context his legs weren't so daunting, less forged showpieces than everyday tools that would soon take him, like her, to work. She pictured him squinting through goggles at the sparking wheel of a disc sander, wielding multifarious forms of the word fuck in an atmosphere of clangs and hisses. His slicked legs and hard-rock hair were the parts of him he kept polished against the machine world whose cuts and scrapes owned his hands and whose junk lunches had colonized his midsection. So, strangely, just when he was farthest away—up handing his refill cup over the glass counter—he seemed to be standing too close, his details leaning into her personal space, and she slipped the rest of her bagel into the trash so she could dart when he returned. She had a hand on her purse and was standing when he swipped a business card to the table where her plate had been.

"There's a thing this weekend at my camp." His last name was DeLille, its letters in computer-cursive beneath a cartoon hot rod with swollen tires. "Barbecuey-type stuff, hanging out by the water. Just low key? If you're not busy?"

His mouth and eyes didn't seem to be doing any of the things she remembered men's mouths and eyes doing when they wanted to fuck you. And the card wasn't saying: it just lay there exerting its mute social weight, its doom of entanglements or evasions. But it would have been even more awkward for her not to take it than it had been for him to offer it, so she doffed the card at him and said she'd check her calendar.

"I didn't catch your name?" he said as she turned.

"Oh. Right. Shannon. Sorry."

Stuck, she crossed her arms in a narrow self-hug that didn't hide her six-foot frame any better than it had in tenth grade.

"You're Braid Girl," he offered.

"No shit," she said, equal parts pleased by the epithet and distressed at the intimacy of declaring and disarming their nicknames. "You're Leggy Joe."

Clay pursed his lips, admitting that he'd been pegged and that he loved it.

"Should we get capes?" He sparred the air. "Fight crime?"

"There's no crime in New Orleans. Just black-on-black whatever."

He shook his head, missing her irony. He wore an unfocused frown. "I don't know why we can't solve that. It's so sad."

Did conversations play and replay in other people's heads the way they did in hers? Echoing and recombining as she stood by the copy machine or took an extra minute in the restroom, just sitting in peace? Did other people find the insignificant so significant and the significant so meaningless? Did her employer have any idea how little of her active mind was required to do her job?

The braids she wore at the gym were purely utilitarian, keeping the long hair that serious women her age had long ago cut out of the sweat and stick. Except not really, because then why wear two? She made the braids quickly, without a mirror, and she wanted credit for their haphazardness. But she also wanted whatever credit might accrue to the braids as a conscious choice, stating something about her difference and inscrutability, the personal angle she took, and she spent a psychologically suspicious amount of time at the gym enjoying her ownership of the mystery she must represent to others as a grown woman with the braids of a child doing sit-ups on a resist-a-ball. Because the thing about the gym was, you carried yourself on a split screen to keep track of what everyone else was seeing as they assessed you in your every detail.

But work kept her late, and she skipped the gym. Her job involved performing the tasks of the 21st century with a job title that interfaced with other job titles all starting with the word Assistant and which was therefore difficult to define, a job that left the afternoon feeling about the same whether she got home at four or six. No one surveilled her emails.

She fired one off to her friend Jill, who sat in front of her own computer across town, advancing the fiction that Clay, not a spreadsheet, had nixed her workout.

How could he hold her gym-life hostage like that? That's what it amounted to, because if she didn't go to his party, which she had no intention of doing, she would either have to banish herself to the pool to avoid him or lie to him in the weight room, and she always squinted when she lied, people saw it immediately, and the tic got worse the longer she rehearsed for the moment. And if she did go to his party, there would be that trapped feeling you always get when food is prepared over fire? All those hours while the fucking meat got brushed? Multiplied by twenty people she didn't know and didn't want to, the product of which would inevitably be drinking too much? You wave flies off the potato salad and listen to some guy in a tanktop talk about landing bull reds. You longsuffer those silences when everyone just sits back and pretends to enjoy nature. You know how every office has that freak who's always asking about your weekend and telling you you look nice, and you have to say fake stuff in return? That was Clay. That relentless niceness: what was the pathology of that?

But in the end the word itself, camp, convinced her to go, because if she didn't, she would end up watching "Saturday Night Live" with its noisy syllable bumping through her head, reprimanding her about the kind of fun people were supposed to have.

"Oh, it's like a party house," Jill chirruped. Jill had moved to New Orleans only six months ago and was still stunned and cowed by the city, by its words and weather, its advanced orders of beauty and terror. She had apparently been expecting a tent and picnic table, men on all fours blowing on tinder; instead, a dozen people lounged on cast-off couches under the stilts of a raised house, a big-screen TV flashing in one open corner.

Shannon pointed along the graying gravel road. "Check it out. The next four or five were completely washed away. I bet he built this brand new since the storm." The lit windows above them were in fact still decaled by manufacturers' stickers. "What do people spend their extra money on in Kansas City?"

"Just like. An extra car."

They weren't the sort of women who usually got attention at parties—Jill was drawn with a straightedge and vagued in with watercolors and wore glasses that looked twenty years out of date even though she'd just gotten them last month—but Clay's friends didn't seem too concerned with the usual. In a way that wouldn't have been acceptable in a world that took itself seriously, a tiny, nervous man named Noah made straight for Shannon and smoked at her in a manner so fiendish, his eyes birding to all points of the compass, that his cigarette was revealed as merely a stopgap between joints. Speaking to Jill directly made her splotch and cringe, and this irresistible effect was soon being tweaked by Scott, a thickly furred and deeply bellied man who could barely get his cigarette smoke jetted from the corner of his mouth before Jill's latest one-word answer toed the ball back into his conversational court.

"So you want to get high?" Noah asked.

They walked over among the sheared pilings of the next camp and performed the rituals that, after a certain age, were performed in silence, without ceremony or fanfare.

After the joint, Shannon considered getting back to protect Jill from some of the torment the world was always causing her, but after all it wouldn't hurt her to play grown-up for a while, and Shannon couldn't really abandon Noah, who was rushing a cigarette alight and winding himself up to speak.

"So are you and Clay...?"

"No, we just met. Anyway, no. He's just a guy I know from the gym."

Noah had heard the one word that was important.

"Maybe we could go out sometime."

"I'm big enough to bounce you on my knee."

"I don't mind."

His voice was full of squeezed bravado, like a kid talking tough before he cries.

"You like getting spanked and all that? Are you one of those guys?"

He shrugged, his throat making a noise of possibility, ready to consider whatever shelter she was building against the world. Jesus, to wear your need so nakedly!

"You like feet? Sucking on toes?"

"Nnnn," he grimaced, then laughed a catch-up laugh when he realized she was goofing with him. "I don't think so."

"You've seen those websites?"

"Surfing. But I'm always like, why am I wasting my time on this when there are sites completely devoted to great big titties?"

"I'm at work this time, right. I forget how I got there, but suddenly I'm looking at this guy with footprints all over his face. That was the whole thing, they would walk through garbage or whatever and then step on guys' faces."

"That's OK," he said, waiving his right to know about this particular byway in the labyrinth of human conduct. She realized that he was not so much squinting as marshaling all his energy to keep his eyes from falling the rest of the way shut. "Ever feel like you've seen too much?"

"Yeah, that."

"Yeah, that! Exactly!" Years of smoking had clipped a playing card across the spokes of his laugh.

"What do you do, Noah?"

"I'm a substance abuse counselor."

"Of course."

"Of course!"

So they were all partial people, people-fragments tumbling through the evening, until Clay, finished grilling, swept in to give them gravity and a centered system. The way babies enjoy the undisputed right to stun and occupy a roomful of people? How the phenomenon of a baby, its excellent oneness and how it hasn't fucked anything up yet, makes everyone forget the holding pattern of their own lives?

That's what it was like when Clay bustled in, wiping his brow with a towel, and yanked a beer from the cooler, those smiles of dumb reverence all around. Scott whispered some bit of hagiography to Jill as Clay mussed the hair of a passing toddler. Three women who'd been sitting by the TV (one of them, Noah whispered, Clay's ex-wife) groupied up to ask about the best way to Hattiesburg and nodded as Clay sent a finger out from the neck of his beer to trace I-10 to 59 in the air.

And then Clay was zipping in to land a peck on Shannon's cheek. "Look at you, you look great!" He followed this patent lie by drying his beer-hand on the bottom of his Saints t-shirt and snatching up Jill's skelly mitt, speaking his name into the daze of her face. "Don't let this guy feed you a bunch of lies," he warned, backhanding Scott's gut. "He's moving to Houston next week. Oh, hey, Shannon, Scott's a swimmer too!" pointing back and forth between them.

In another age Scott would have been a pirate gnarling out tales of whiskered mischief, but in 2008 he was a male nurse, and his most swashbuckling exploit was a third place in the 200 I.M. at the 1985 State tournament. Clay grinned at details he'd been hearing since high school and then somehow got Jill calmed down and talking about herself; and when Scott learned that Jill administered the intranet at Touro Hospital, he revealed the normal voice beneath the growl he'd been baying her with.

Even when Shannon said one of those things she didn't know she was going to say and didn't really mean—Fuck the Saints!—Clay rolled his eyes left and right in jocular horror, unruffled and savoring life, the way you might at a child who blurts I'm bored during Mass. He was a freak of ease and charisma, a man fitted so perfectly to the shapes of the world that they felt like his own skin and voice. But did he know any one person, really? Wasn't unremitting charm just a way to keep everyone at the same distance? He seemed terribly genuine, but what was he—genuinely what?

She went upstairs to pee, moving herself beyond the party in mind and body, and sat considering the superior rightness of the shape of her own toilet seat. But between the bathroom and the steps back down, there was a blue couch that really wanted her to try it and whose cool suede spoke with all the persuasiveness it had gathered from the air conditioner about the idea of slipping off her shoes and putting her legs up, and then she was being awakened by a gray cat smelling her eyelid.

"That's Reggie," Clay said from somewhere behind her. Reggie arched against the hand she offered and then cantered off to his next appointment with a businesslike air. "He showed up after the storm."

"Who feeds him?"

She sat up to see Clay running water over a begrimed platter in the sink. Her head felt shrunken and set on a shelf, all its moisture leached.

"I'm out here every two or three days. Which, if you ever want to just get away, let me know, I'll give you the key."

"Wow. Okay."

"Oh," ineffectually snapping his wet fingers, "this Saturday? We're doing a fishing-tubing-drinking thing, a going-away for Scott. Jill's coming."

"She said that because she doesn't know how to say no."

It was excruciating! She stood up to better defend herself against his next solicitude, squinting to concentrate.

"That's my son," he said, thinking she was looking at a picture on the counter that she was in fact staring through. Inside the tilted plastic a kid willed himself faceless under a wedge of cap. "I probably need more pictures in here, don't I? I mean on the walls?"

"I'm so tired I can't really think about what you're saying." She managed two steps toward the door. "I was talking to Noah, and I somehow got stoned."

"He has that effect. You okay to drive?"

"Jill drove."

"Because I'm going that way, I could run you home and then bring you back out to the car tomorrow."

Whatever it was you called the stuff that went on beneath a conversation, Clay simply didn't have much sense of it. But something in him had felt the dismal lean inside her and was trying to prop it back up with a double dose of cheer.

"She's a great kid, by the way. I'm glad you brought her."

"She's twenty-six, so there's that whole thing."

"But super sweet."

"Whatever that means."

Done at the sink, he crossed his arms and pretended to think about the nothing thing she had just said. Shannon was exactly torn between seeing what else he would agree with and getting the fuck out of there, except that getting the fuck out of there sounded infinitely better. Three quick steps would do it, but he would not stop nuzzling the bone of his idea.

"Anyway, I really like her."

That was one of those words, like, that if you said it a few times, didn't seem to mean anything. It sounded ugly, basically a turned-around version of kill.

"But who don't you like?" His eyes flinched in incomprehension. "I mean, you'd make friends with Osama bin Laden."

"I guess I never thought about it," finally beaten back. She said Saturday was iffy and got out before he could round the counter and give her another kiss.

She was a more generous person in the pool. Removing her contacts fuzzed all the handholds for her hate, and her senses swam to the center of their own soft ether. If Clay said he had never thought about it, maybe he hadn't, maybe for him there were only people he liked and people he hadn't met yet. Maybe that wasn't a mental illness. Maybe it took the Clays of the world to move people past their nicknames and make them human. She was human and should appreciate his efforts, respond to them. Because if you were a person whose habit it was to run from people, that was life-denying, wasn't it? What do you think, you're better than life? Above life? You think you won't die at the end if you don't take part?

For five laps, she mummed along to Blondie's "Rapture" tinning from the poolside radio, her thoughts watering forth pictures—Noah blowing smoke at her tits, Jill's timorous shoulders, Reggie's face in convex—that floated dumb amidst the blue.

This was the only place she achieved grace. On land she hunched and clomped. She bumped into way more things than the average person. But in the water there was no hard or sharp, and the body could live its wish that the rest of the world were so, and the mind leaked into the body, wearing its buoyancy. Water diffused what land compacted.

Had she really asked Noah if he liked to be spanked? That was inappropriate, embarrassing. It was a way of talking scavenged from the trash of modern culture, and in this way it was typical of all her speech, which rooted through garbage while her better self averted its eyes. What her language knew best was its own dirt, so when a man asked her earnestly for a date, she mocked and titillated him with references to a perversion which itself she mocked without right or authority. This was the speech of a coward. The great crime of the digital age was that it frightened people into banter. If she could speak always from the pool's undistracted blue, its underwater world-muffle, she would never need recourse to a word like spank.

How much did that undergraduate lifeguard weigh, one fifty? And what did she weigh, one eighty-five? Was there any way he could swim her up from the bottom if she sank there inert and lungless, her skin going dull?

People who prayed reported going forth into the day refreshed and fortified and certain of some center in the self. Swimming was the closest thing she had to that. But she couldn't make the peace she found there work outside the building, as if the god of Tulane's pool were a purely local deity, resident only in its trapped waters.

"He bumped my boob."

"And then asked you out. After feeling you up."

"I mean, not my boob. We had on life jackets. But kind of. We both reached for a volleyball."

"Cute. Do you not realize that he is high ALL THE TIME?"

Because Jill was equally shaken by every tremor of existence, she had no sense of what was truly shocking, and she answered Shannon's question with the same apologetic but undeterred No she would have used to answer whether she knew who had won the last Super Bowl. She was wearing some kind of perfume for teenagers that Shannon could smell even over the three kinds of salsa the waiter had brought.

"Well, so, what. Besides Noah punching your tit and then beating off underwater, you just floated around in the lake and drank beer?"

"Scott almost drowned."

"He competed for a fucking state championship in swimming."

Jill's throat choked off one of its pained giggles, her eyes dropping with embarrassed affection for the memory.

"He jumped off the boat into an inner tube. It flipped upside down, and his feet got stuck in the air. Clay had to jump in and save him."

"Of course he did. Because he's Captain Ameri-Jesus. He's going to save us all." The image of Clay bounding from a pontoon boat made Shannon wonder what his legs looked like in swimming trunks, but not very much.

"He asked why you didn't come."

"And you said."

"That…you're a private person. Or something."

"'Cause, yeah. This looks really private, me and you in a public restaurant." It wasn't so much that Shannon had a history of estranging her friends as that her friends had a history of proving they were strange. "I mean, that's awesome. I don't come dumbass around with Moe, Larry, and Curly, so I'm a private person."

"Why don't you like him?" Jill rounded her hair tightly over one ear. "What's wrong with him?"

"If you don't know, I'm not going to tell you."

"Well, I don't know."

Jill made conversation like a bird, her head considering and reconsidering and never quite looking at the person she was talking to, her expression always some variation on worry, and it occurred to Shannon that maybe Jill's fluttery mien was less assigned by nature than assumed for personal advantage, even if that advantage was as pitiable as pretending to be dumber than she was.

"All right. You mean besides being boring?" Shannon saw the blossoming of Jill's delicate surprise and crushed it. "Because he's deeply fucking boring."

"Boring?"

"He's like one of those stuffed animals, you pull a string and it's all, Let's be friends. Hey, I like you. I don't see the appeal."

Jill shrugged again, this time defeatedly, as if a toy had been bullied from her hands.

"He's nice. He's really nice to me."

"For all you know. But three guys we just met, and you're out there alone with them on a boat? You're lucky you weren't gang-raped and thrown in the lake."

Jill's eyes aimed their distress in three or four directions, the last one Shannon's.

"Why would you say that?"

"Just—forget it," because the answers were too obvious to state. But as many times as she replayed Jill's question later, she couldn't get any answer to sound quite right, not to this or to any of the other questions crowding into the echo box of her mind.

On Saturday she followed Clay home from the gym to either tell him his friendship was smothering and unwelcome, or to sleep with him and tell him his friendship was smothering and unwelcome.

He had made her half hour on the Stairmaster a crawling torture, glomming over every few minutes and having to repeat everything he said because she had her earphones in the first time. Worse, he made her captive to the woman on the next machine, Crazy Jane, whom Shannon had long detested for the way she heaved herself retardedly against the stairs' resistance and grunted aloud to her iPod. Bad enough that he introduced them—Jane's sweaty, freckled hand shot out inescapably, her eyes leprechauning madly—but then he left Shannon alone to withstand a fifteen-minute nutmercial for Dennis Kucinich, the only benefit of which was that it made her feel better about not having bothered to learn anything about Dennis Kucinich. So when Clay said there was this thing he needed her help with at home, she shut down the machine in mid-stride and left Jane quacking happily to no one about a national reinvigoration of hope.

She left her braids in because if they were going to screw, Clay would probably want to think of her the way he saw her at the gym; but when they got to his house, he led her into a half-renovated bathroom and asked her to hold a faucet on center while he tightened some sort of nut from below. Rolling up and swiping dust bunnies off his ass, he appraised the finished work.

"Nice!"

"That's what you asked me over for?"

Clay's whole face yearned to tell the truth and say yes. She watched it search for other philosophies of asking people over.

"I also need some help with this other thing."

"Faucet does look good," she said as he clashed his wrenches up off the floor.

"Yeah!" he brightened. "I got it from this guy."

"You're keeping the tub?"

"It needs new feet, but yeah."

"It's supposed to be good for resale."

How remarkable that life could still bring people to a moment when they had no idea what would happen next! The bathroom held itself with that particular afternoon stillness.

"So the grand tour," thumbing them into the hallway. "I just finished the room where the roof came off."

Now that she was only waiting for the right moment to make her final escape, feeling her freedom in advance, she was able to enjoy Clay's cloying geniality as he gave her the name of his crown-molding guy, explained how sponge-painting worked and offered to come do it for her, and then handed her a knife and onion in the kitchen, pretending he needed her help to make enchiladas. They sang "Mother-in-Law" with the radio, and Clay told her about the time he saw K-Doe in a fur coat piloting a rusty VW Beetle up Oak Street. Shannon had gone to K-Doe's wake at Gallier Hall, and Clay lapped up the details wide-eyed. But soon enough he was asking questions about her family and her future in the city that felt more intimate than any part of his body could have, so when he said, "What is this, Saturday? This could be enchilada night for us," she laid the knife down in mid-onion and said, "Okay, so listen, Clay."

But her declaration was interrupted by the doorbell and three firm knocks that rattled the pane.

"Hold that thought," he said and rode his earthmoving legs around the breakfast bar and across the living room. She returned to the onion, brushing a flutter of skin from the blade. But before she could make another cut, the knife was shivered from her hand by a wail so low and close, so comprehensive, that it seemed to come from inside her, hollowing her stomach and filling her lungs as it cycled up her neck and scalp. The knife clattered to a stop. Her arms were flinched and frozen. That the wail had been human she recognized only when she looked up to see Clay's silhouette struck and kneeling in the doorway. On the steps outside, two men in full-dress military uniforms blinked grimly in the sun. The first man had his cap lodged under his arm. The second held a thin, dark box and a folded flag.

This time Clay managed to find words.

"Oh, no! Oh, Jesus!"

If he had cried her name, she would have disappeared—out a back door, if necessary, finding a way to blame him for the awkwardness, the presumption. It was that he had nobody to call to, that he was alone in the waste the world had made around him, that broke her forth and sent her running to him.

Contributors

WILLIAM BORDEN's novel, *Superstoe*, first published in the U. S. by Harper & Rowand in England by Victor Gollancz, was reissued recently by Orloff Press. His short stories have won the PEN Syndicated Fiction Prize and The Writers Voice Fiction Competition and have been published in over forty magazines and anthologies. The film adaptation of his play, *The Last Prostitute*, starring Sonia Braga, was shown on Lifetime Television and in Europe and is on video. [31.1]

C. W. CANNON writes fiction and nonfiction. His work has appeared in *Other Voices, Third Coast, Exquisite Corpse, American Book Review, Constance, Louisiana Cultural Vistas, The Rumpus,* and *The Times-Picayune.* His work has been anthologized in *In Our Own Words: a Generation Defining Itself, Do You Know What It Means to Miss New Orleans?, Louisiana in Words,* and *New Orleans by New Orleans.* He is the author of a novel, *Soul Resin* (FC2 Press, 2002). He is a frequent contributor to *The Lens* (thelensnola.org), where he writes on New Orleans culture, the south, and race. His work in *The Lens* earned him the 2013 New Orleans Press Club Award for best columnist of the year. [31.2]

BILL COTTER was born in Dallas in 1964. His short fiction has appeared in *McSweeney's Quarterly Concern, The Paris Review,* and elsewhere, and an essay, "The Gentleman's Library," was awarded a Pushcart Prize. His third book, *Saint Philomene's Infirmary*, a middle-grade adventure novel, is forthcoming from Henry Holt in 2016. [35.2]

JASON DEYOUNG lives in Atlanta, Georgia. His work has appeared or is forthcoming in numerous publications, including *Booth, Corium, The Austin Review, The Los Angeles Review, Monkeybicycle, Music & Literature,* and Houghton Mifflin Harcourt's *Best American Mystery Stories* 2012. He is a Senior Editor at *Numéro Cinq Magazine.* [37.1]

SCOTT GARSON is the author of *Is That You, John Wayne?*—a collection of stories—and *American Gymnopédies,* a book of microfictions. His fiction has won awards from *Playboy,* the Mary Roberts Rinehart Foundation and Dzanc Books, and has appeared in many journals. He edits *Wigleaf,* a Pushcart-Prize-winning journal of very short fiction. [29.1]

KAREN GENTRY's fiction and nonfiction have appeared in *Bayou, American Short Fiction, PANK, The Southeast Review* and elsewhere. Her flash fiction has won the World's Best Short-Short Story contest and was selected for The Wigleaf Top 50 Very Short Fictions of 2010. She lives in Georgia and teaches creative writing at Agnes Scott College. [34.1]

CHRIS HAVEN's fiction has appeared in *Threepenny Review, Massachusetts Review, Arts & Letters, Washington Square, Hunger Mountain* and elsewhere. He recently completed a novel set in Oklahoma in 1955. He teaches creative writing at Grand Valley State University in Michigan. [34.1]

SMITH HENDERSON was born and raised in western Montana. He worked with traumatized children for a few years, and briefly as prison guard experiences which informed his first novel *Fourth of July Creek*, (Ecco, 2014), set in his native Montana. It was shortlisted for The Flaherty-Dunnan First Novel Prize and was on the Folio Prize longlist. It won of the 2014 Montana Book Award and was shortlisted for the "Reading the West Book Award 2014." [33.1]

DYLAN LANDIS is the author of a novel, *Rainey Royal*, a *New York Times* Editors' Choice, and a linked story collection, Normal People Don't Live Like. Her work has appeared in *Tin House, Bomb*, and *The O. Henry Prize Stories*. She received a National Endowment for the Arts fellowship in fiction in 2010, and in a past life wrote six books on interior design. She lives in New York City. [32.2]

SAMUEL LIGON is the author of a book of stories, *Drift and Swerve*, and two novels, *Among the Dead and Dreaming* and *Safe in Heaven Dead*. His stories have appeared in *New England Review, Prairie Schooner, The Quarterly, Post Road, Gulf Coast, Alaska Quarterly Review*, and elsewhere. He teaches at Eastern Washington University in Spokane and is the editor of *Willow Springs*. [32.2]

JILL MARQUIS lives in Portland, Oregon. [28.2]

RICHARD MCNALLY was born in Miami in 1947 and is currently rewriting a novel typed on a Royal office-model in the late-1980s. He spent this morning (April 3, 2015) reading in *The Genealogy of Morals*, finding it earthshaking. He lives on worn boot heels and boiled slippers. [26.3-4]

KATE MILLIKEN's debut collection of stories, *If I'd Known You Were Coming* (University of Iowa Press), won the 2013 John Simmons Award for Short Fiction. She has received fellowships from the Vermont Studio Center, Tin House, and Yaddo, and has written for television and commercial advertising. She lives with her family in Northern California. [36.2]

ANDER MONSON is the author of six books, most recently *Letter to a Future Lover* (Graywolf, 2015). [28.1]

GLEN POURCIAU's collection of stories, *Invite,* won the 2008 Iowa Short Fiction Award. His second story collection is forthcoming from Four Way Books. His stories have been published by *AGNI Online, Antioch Review, Epoch, New England Review, New Ohio Review, Paris Review,* and others. [33.1]

DANIEL TERENCE SMITH was formerly the Director of Creative Writing at the University of Louisiana, Lafayette. His fiction, poetry, essays, and reviews have appeared in *The Southern Review, The Laurel Review, The Cincinnati Review,* among others. [28.1]

EVA TALMADGE is at work on a novel and a collection of stories. Visit her at evatalmadge.net. [33.2]

ANDREW R. TOUHY, a recipient of the San Francisco Browning Society's Dramatic Monologue Award and *Fourteen Hills'* Bambi Holmes Fiction Prize, is also a nominee for inclusion in *Best New American Voices.* His stories appear in *New England Review, Conjunctions, New American Writing, The Collagist, Colorado Review, Eleven Eleven,* and elsewhere. He teaches at The Writing Salon in San Francisco and Berkeley, and lives in Oakland with his wife and child. [27.2]

PALO TUNG lives, works, surfs and occasionally plays a little jiu jitsu in Santa Cruz, California. His story "One for Ma" was honorably mentioned in the O. Henry Prioze Stories 2002. He's currently at work on a novel after a long hiatus from writing fiction. [26.3-4]

ROB TRUCKS is the author of a book on Fleetwood Mac's Tusk album, part of the 33 ⅓ series. He lives in Long Island City, New York. [26.3-4]

MATT VADNAIS is the author of *All I Can Truly Deliver* (Del Sol Press, 2005), a collection of stories including "The Treesitter" that explore the musical notion of the cover in a variety of literary contexts. He wrote extensively and autobiographically about music in a social media project, The Best 200 Songs in My iTunes Library. He hosts "The Liminal Space," a cover-heavy weekly radio show on WBCR, the campus radio station for Beloit College where he is an assistant professor of renaissance literature and creative writing. [30.1]

VALERIE VOGRIN is the author of the novel *Shebang*. Her short stories have appeared in print in journals such as *Ploughshares, AGNI,* and *The Los Angeles Review,* and online at *Wigleaf* and *Bluestem*. In 2010 she was awarded a Pushcart Prize. She teaches at Southern Illinois University Edwardsville. [28.2]

M. O. WALSH is from Baton Rouge, Louisiana. He is the author of the short story collection *The Prospect of Magic* and the novel *My Sunshine Away.* His stories and essays have appeared in the *New York Times, The Southern Review, Oxford American* and *Epoch* and have been anthologized in *Best New American Voices* and *Louisiana in Words* among others. He is currently the director of the Creative Writing Workshop at the University of New Orleans. "Sardine" was one of his very first published stories. [29.2]

WIL WEITZEL's fiction has appeared in *Southwest Review, Conjunctions, The Kenyon Review, Prairie Schooner* and elsewhere. He has been nominated for a Pushcart Prize, was a finalist for the 2014 David Nathan Meyerson Prize for Fiction, and won the 2014 *Washington Square* Flash Fiction Award. He is currently a NYC Emerging Writers Fellow at the Center for Fiction in Manhattan and is at work on a novel. [38.1]

AURELIA WILLS' stories have been published in *The Kenyon Review, Salt Hill, Hayden's Ferry Review,* and other journals, and in the anthology *American Fiction Volume XII: Best Unpublished Stories by Emerging Writers.* Two of her stories were nominated for the Pushcart Prize. She teaches creative writing through The Loft and has led workshops for teenagers through Saint Paul Public Libraries. She teaches ESL to immigrants in Minneapolis. Her debut novel, *The Last Truest Name of Leah Lobermier* will be published by Candlewick Press in 2016. [34.1]

KEVIN WILSON is the author of a story collection, *Tunneling to the Center of the Earth* (Harper Perennial, 2009), which won the Shirley Jackson Award, and a novel, *The Family Fang* (Ecco, 2011), which was adapted into film in 2016. He lives in Sewanee, Tennessee, with his wife, the poet Leigh Anne Couch, and his two sons. He teaches in the English Department at Sewanee: The University of the South. [27.2]

GEOFF WYSS's book of stories, *How*, won the Ohio State University Prize in Short Fiction and was published in 2012. His novel *Tiny Clubs* was published in 2007. His fiction has appeared in *Glimmer Train, Image, Ecotone, Tin House*, and others and has been reprinted in *New Stories from the South* and the *Bedford Introduction to Literature*. He teaches and lives in New Orleans. [35.2]

Editors

PEYTON BURGESS is the author of the short story collection *The Fry Pans Aren't Sufficing*. His work has appeared in *The Paris Review, Tin House online, Joyland Magazine, AUTRE, The Catamaran Literary Reader, McSweeney's Internet Tendency, New Orleans Review, and Chicago Quarterly Review*. He received his MFA in Creative Writing from New York University and is pursuing his PhD in Education at Virginia Commonwealth University, where he works as an instructional designer and creative writing instructor. He also teaches fiction workshops for Catapult.

CHRISTOPHER CHAMBERS is the author of two short story collections, *Delta 88* (2013) and *Kind of Blue* (forthcoming in 2022). He received a National Endowment for the Arts Fellowship and his work has been published in magazines and anthologies including *The Southern Review* and *Best American Mystery Stories*, and has been cited in *Best American Essays*. He is the founding and current editor of *Midwest Review* and is past editor of *Black Warrior Review* and *New Orleans Review*.

Acknowledgements

Grateful thanks to editorial assistants Rose Dicks and Nelle Edge for all their work on this anthology, and to the editors and readers who helped with the original selection of these stories for *New Orleans Review:* especially Sophia Stone, Jeff Chan, Mark Lane, Robert Bell, Kelly Wilson, Amanda Regan, Dale Hrebik, Nancy Rowe, Kevin Rabelais, and Michael Jeffrey Lee. Special thanks to Mary A. McCay for her tireless support of the magazine and of good writing in New Orleans and to Ralph Adamo, Marcus Smith, Miller Williams, and Walker Percy for paving the way.

www.ingramcontent.com/pod-product-compliance
Lightning Source LLC
Chambersburg PA
CBHW030529030726
47495CB00004B/917